Here Comes the
GROOM

Wedding Party Collection

D0530816

Don't tell the
BRIDE

Wedding Party Collection

Kelly **HUNTER** · Tessa **RADLEY** · Cindy **KIRK**

April 2017

Marrying the
PRINCE

Wedding Party Collection

Kate **HEWITT** · Sandra **HYATT**

May 2017

Always the
BACHELOR

Wedding Party Collection

Michelle **CELMER** · Amanda **BERRY** · Barbara **HANNAY**

June 2017

...e a
BRIDESMAID

Wedding Party Collection

Avril **TREMAYNE** · Sophie **PEMBROKE** · Gina **WILKINS**

July 2017

Here Comes the
GROOM

Wedding Party Collection

Rebecca **WINTERS** · Emma **DARCY** · Sophie **PEMBROKE**

August 2017

Proposing to the
PLANNER

Wedding Party Collection

Susan **STEPHENS** · Aimee **CARSON** · Teresa **CARPENTER**

September 2017

Here Comes the
GROOM

Wedding Party Collection

Rebecca
WINTERS

Emma
DARCY

Sophie
PEMBROKE

MILLS&BOON

Published in Great Britain 2017
By Mills & Boon, an imprint of HarperCollins*Publishers*
1 London Bridge Street, London, SE1 9GF

WEDDING PARTY COLLECTION: HERE COMES THE GROOM
© 2017 Harlequin Books S.A.

The Bridegroom's Vow © 2001 Rebecca Winters
The Billionaire Bridegroom © 2003 Emma Darcy
A Groom Worth Waiting For © 2014 Sophie Pembroke

ISBN: 9780263931105

09-0817

Our policy is to use papers that are natural, renewable and recyclable products and made from wood grown in sustainable forests.
The logging and manufacturing processes conform to the legal environmental regulations of the country of origin.

Printed and bound in Spain
by CPI, Barcelona

THE BRIDEGROOM'S VOW

REBECCA WINTERS

*My story takes place in Greece, a country
of incredible history and beauty,
My favorite living artist, Thomas McKnight,
fell in love with Greece, too.*

*He has created one masterpiece after another
of Mykonos, Chora, Kalafati, the Aegean and
much, much more. It is to him and his wife,
Renate, that I dedicate this book.*

Rebecca Winters lives in Salt Lake City, Utah.
With canyons and high alpine meadows full of
wildflowers, she never runs out of places to explore.
They, plus her favourite holiday spots in Europe,
often end up as backgrounds for her romance
novels, because writing is her passion, along with
her family and church. Rebecca loves to hear from
readers. If you wish to email her, please visit her
website at www.cleanromances.com.

CHAPTER ONE

DIMITRIOS heard footsteps in the passage outside his door. It was the middle of the night. Curious to know what was going on, he flung his covers aside and hurried out into the hall.

"Leon?" he whispered when he saw his adored elder brother carrying a suitcase. "What's happening?"

Leon spun around. "Go back to bed, Dimi."

Ignoring the command, he rushed up to Leon. "Where are you going?"

"Lower your voice. You'll find out soon enough."

"But you can't just leave!" He worshipped Leon who'd been father, brother and protector all rolled into one this last year. "Wherever you have to go, I'll come with you. I can be ready in two minutes."

"No, Dimi. You have to stay here with Uncle Spiros and our cousins. I should be back in a week."

Tears filled his eyes. "The cousins aren't fun like you, and Uncle Spiros is too strict."

"Since our parents died, he's been good to us in his own way, Dimi. It won't be so bad."

Panic-stricken, Dimitrios threw his arms around Leon, trying to prevent him from leaving. "Please let me come with you."

"You can't. You see, I'm getting married before the night's out. It's all been arranged."

Married?

Dimitrios felt like his world had come to an end. "Which one of your girlfriends is it?"

"Ananke Paulos."

"I've never heard of her. Will you bring her here?"

"No," he said on a heavy sigh. "We'll be living in our parents' villa."

"Then I'll come and live with you. I can sleep in my old room like always."

He shook his head. "I'm sorry, Dimi. A woman likes her own house."

"But that means you and I'll never live together again!"

"Hey—we'll always be brothers. I'll visit you every day, and you'll come to visit us."

The pain kept getting worse. "Do you love her more than me?" His voice wobbled.

Leon stared down at him with eyes full of anguish. Dimitrios didn't know his brother could look like that. It terrified him.

"Not at all. In fact I would give anything in the world if I didn't have to marry her. But she's pregnant with my child."

Dimitrios blinked in astonishment.

"She's going to have your baby?"

"Yes."

"You made a baby with a woman you don't love?" He couldn't comprehend such a thing.

"Oh, Dimi—listen to me. You're only twelve, not quite old enough for a man's feelings to have taken over inside you yet. When that day comes, your body will react when you see a beautiful woman. You'll want to hold her, make love to her. The pleasure a woman can bring you is to die for.''

Dimitrios frowned through the tears. "To die for?"

A sound of frustration came out of Leon. "I only mean that when a man and a woman make love, it's wonderful beyond your imagination."

"Was it that way with Ananke?"

"Yes."

"But if you don't love her?"

"You can feel great desire for a woman without loving her. I would never have married her but for the baby. Now I have to do my duty as a Pandakis."

"No, you don't!" Dimitrios cried from the depths of his soul. "What kind of a woman would want to live with you if she knew you didn't love her?"

A groan escaped Leon's throat. "Dimi? There are other reasons she wants to marry me."

"What reasons?"

"Money, status."

"I don't understand."

"You know our family has run a successful financial empire in Greece for generations. Our reputation is known throughout the corporate world. Uncle Spiros meets with important, influential people, just like our father did before he died.

"That's the reason Ananke tricked me. She was hoping to have my baby so she could belong to our family. Now she's going to get her wish, but it won't be the wedding she imagined. We're going to be married at the church by the priest with no one there but her grandmother to watch."

"I hate her!" Dimitrios blurted in fresh pain.

"Don't say that, Dimi. After tonight she'll be part of our family."

"I *will* say it!" With tears streaming down his face, Dimitrios backed away from his brother. "Do you think our mother married our father because of his money?"

Dimitrios had to wait a long time to hear a response. "Probably."

Leon was always brutally honest. His answer crushed Dimitrios. Sick with grief over what his brother had just told him, he said, "Can't a rich man find a woman who will love him for himself?"

"I don't know the answer to that question. The point is, I don't want you to make the same mistake I did. Unfortunately that's where you've got a problem."

"What do you mean?"

"One day you'll be the head of the Pandakis Corporation because Uncle Spiros says you've got the smartest head on your shoulders of anyone in the family. You're also better looking than all the Pandakis men put together.

"You'll be able to have your pick of any woman in the world. They'll throw themselves at you. You, little brother, will have to be more careful than most men to make certain no woman gets pregnant with your baby and tricks you into marriage."

Dimitrios ground his teeth. "That will never happen to me."

Leon gave him a sad smile. "How do you know that?"

"I won't ever make love to a woman. Then I won't have to worry."

"Of course you will." He tousled Dimitrios's curly

black hair. "We'll continue this conversation next week when I take us hiking."

Dimitrios watched his brother disappear around the corner of their uncle's villa. It was just like the night a year ago when they learned that their parents had been killed. Dimitrios had wanted to die then, too.

Alexandra Hamilton didn't trust anyone to dye her hair except Michael at the Z-Attitude hair salon in her home town of Paterson, New Jersey.

He was a genius at his craft. That went without saying. But more to the point, she trusted him with secrets the way she would a father confessor.

Today he was wearing his hair in blue spikes. Michael wasn't a mere coiffeur par excellence. He entertained everyone who flocked to his busy salon. Women adored him, young and old.

Her green eyes met his in the huge mirror with its border of stage lights.

"When are you going to emerge from this boring brown chrysalis and reveal your natural blond mane to *his* wondrous gaze?"

"Not until *he* falls in love with me as I am."

He meaning Dimitrios Pandakis, of course. Alex loved him with every fiber of her being.

"I hate to tell you this, but you've been saying that ever since you went to work for his company. Four years now, isn't it?"

Alex stuck her tongue out at him.

"Sorry," he said in the most unrepentant voice she'd ever heard.

Her softly rounded chin lifted a good inch. "I'm making progress."

"You mean since you slipped a little poison into his private secretary's coffee six months ago?"

"*Michael!* That's not funny. She was a wonderful woman. I still miss her and know he does, too."

"Just kidding. I thought the trip to China went without a hitch."

"It did. He gave me another bonus."

"That makes quite a few. He'd better be careful or he might just find himself on the losing end of a very clever takeover orchestrated by none other than his own Ms. Hamilton." A devilish expression broke out on Michael's face. "Are you still making him call you that?"

She tried to hide her smile. "Yes."

"It gives you great pleasure, doesn't it."

"*Extreme.* I must be the only woman on seven continents who doesn't fall all over him trying to get his attention."

"Yes, and it shows."

"What it *does* is make me different from all the other women," she defended. "One day he's going to take notice."

"Let's hope it happens before he marries one of his own kind to produce an heir who'll inherit his fortune. He's not getting any younger, you know."

A familiar pain pierced her heart. "Thank you for playing on my greatest fear."

"But you love me anyway for telling you the truth."

She bit her lip. "He has a nephew he loves like a son. Mrs. Landau once told me Dimitrios's brother died, so he took over the guardianship of his nephew. There's this look he gets on his face whenever Leon calls him from Greece.''

''Well, then—'' He fastened her hair in a secure twist. ''I guess you have no worries he's anxious to start a family of his own.''

''Oh, stop!''

He grinned, eyeing her from the darkened roots of her head to the matronly black shoes she wore on her feet.

''Only your hairdresser knows for sure. I must say I did a good job when I transformed you.''

''It doesn't suit you to be modest, Michael. Why not admit you created a masterpiece.''

Thanks to his expertise in doing hair and makeup for a lot of his friends in the theater, he'd come up with a disguise that made her look like a nondescript secretary much older than her twenty-five years.

''Possibly,'' he quipped. ''However, I may have gone too far when I suggested those steel-rimmed glasses you wear. You could walk on the set of a World War Two film being produced as we speak and fit right in.''

''That's been the idea all along. You know I'm indebted to you.'' She handed him a hundred-dollar bill, which he refused.

''We worked out a deal, remember? In return for some free hair appointments, my friends and I get to stay free at your hotel suite in Thessalonica during the fair.''

She shook her head. ''I've been thinking about it and have decided I'm getting the better end of that deal.''

He wiggled his eyebrows. ''Do you even know how much a suite in that place costs for *one* night?''

''No.''

"I guess you don't have to know when you're the private secretary of Dimitrios Pandakis. Oh, if the rest of the world had any idea how you really live these days," he said dramatically.

"You know I don't care about that."

His expression grew serious for a moment. "Is it really worth it to be the bridesmaid, but never the bride?"

He'd touched a painful nerve and knew it. "I can't imagine not seeing him every day."

"You're hopeless, darling."

"Tell me about it." She got out of the chair and gave him a kiss on the cheek. "See you in Greece next week."

"We're coming as Mysian troubadours. Are you sure I can't bring you a costume along with his? There's this marvelous gold affair—Italian renaissance. I can borrow it from the opera company."

She shook her head. "Ms. Hamilton doesn't do costumes. It's not in her character."

"Pity."

Alex chuckled. "Have a safe trip over, Michael."

"You mean with three hundred of us on our charter flight squashed like Vienna sausages in the can? Lucky you, riding in the Pandakis private jet."

"I'll admit that part's nice. Bye for now."

She left the salon, grateful that the disguise Michael had created for her had worked perfectly during the four years she'd been in Dimitrios's employ. She'd won the man's confidence. But the thought that it was all she might ever win from him wasn't to be considered.

As for her other fear, it was foolish to worry that when she arrived in Greece, Giorgio Pandakis might recognize her from the past. Not when Dimitrios had never shown any signs of remembering.

Nine years was too long a time for a man who'd been drunk to recall accosting an unsuspecting sixteen-year-old girl. Thankfully someone had been outside the silk museum in Paterson that night looking for him and had heard her screams.

Alex could still see her protector's face as it had appeared in the shadowy moonlight. Like a dark, avenging prince, Dimitrios Pandakis himself had pulled his cousin off her before knocking him to the ground, unconscious.

Assisting her to her feet, he'd told her he would help her press charges if she wanted him to. Alex, who stood there on trembling legs thankful for deliverance, had been shocked that he would defend an anonymous teen-age girl over his cousin.

Dimitrios didn't accuse her of encouraging the situation. He didn't try to pay her off. He showed no fear of the scandal that would naturally ensue once her father heard about it. With a name as famous as Pandakis, that kind of news would make headlines. Yet he'd been willing to put his family through embarrassment for her sake.

In that moment, she loved him.

Once her sobs began to subside, she assured him it wouldn't be necessary to call in the police. He'd come to her rescue before things had gone too far. All she wanted was to forget it had ever happened.

After thanking him again for saving her, she ran off across the garden to her house, clutching the torn pieces of the silk blouse to her chest.

Just before she disappeared around the corner, she

watched him throw his loathsome cousin over his shoulder with the ease only a tall, powerful man possessed.

Her green eyes stayed fastened on him until she couldn't see the outline of his silhouette any longer. But even if he'd gone, the man was unforgettable.

By the time she climbed into bed that night she determined that one day, when she was older, they would meet again. It would be under vastly different circumstances, of course. And no matter what it took, she'd make certain he found her unforgettable, too.

As Dimitrios buttoned his shirt, he heard a rap on his bedroom door. Assuming it was Serilda, the housekeeper who'd been like a favorite aunt since he was a little boy, he told her to come in.

The door opened, but the usual burst of information about the weather and the state of the world wasn't forthcoming.

Unless she'd sent a maid to him with coffee and rolls, it wouldn't be anyone else but his nephew.

Dimitrios felt great love for the twenty-two-year old whose build and mannerisms were a constant reminder of Leonides Pandakis, Dimitrios's deceased elder brother.

By some miracle, his pregnant bride survived the car crash that took Leonides's life on their honeymoon. Their unborn child, christened Leon at birth, had also been spared.

Like his father, he was a happy boy with a friendly, outgoing nature. A typical teen with his share of problems, he'd survived those years and had grown into a fine young man who was halfway through his university studies and showed a healthy enthusiasm for life. Or so Dimitrios had thought.

But since Dimitrios's return from China yesterday, he'd seen a big change in his nephew. Normally Leon sought his company at the slightest opportunity, giving him chapter and verse of anything and everything happening in his world.

This time he'd only greeted his uncle with a hug, then disappeared from the villa without a word of explanation. It was totally unlike him. Dimitrios had glimpsed shadows in the brown eyes he'd inherited from his mother.

Something was wrong, of course. He hoped it wasn't serious. Maybe now he'd find out.

"You're up early, Leon," he called to him. "That's good because I was about to come and find you. I've missed you and have been looking forward to one of our talks."

After shrugging into his suit jacket, he emerged from his walk-in closet, hoping his nephew would reveal whatever had been troubling him. But when he discovered it was Ananke still in her nightgown and robe who'd crossed his threshold uninvited, revulsion rose like bile in his throat.

He'd always felt a natural antipathy toward the woman who'd tricked his brother into marriage, and never more than at this moment. Yet love for his brother's son had tempered that destructive emotion enough for him to tolerate her presence in the villa while acting as guardian to young Leon.

Plastic surgery had removed all traces of the scars on her forehead left by the accident. Would that it could as easily erase the scars in Dimitrios's heart. But nothing

could take away the memory of a mercenary female
who'd lured Leon to her bed for the express purpose of
begetting a Pandakis. Because of her, his brother was
dead.

Back then Ananke had been a precocious eighteen-
year-old, aware of her assets and how to use them. Now
she was a forty-one-year-old female, only six years older
than Dimitrios. A woman most men found attractive, yet
she showed no interest in them.

Not for the first time had he wondered if she was hoping to become *his* bride. Though she'd let it be known
to family and friends that she refused to consider marriage until she saw her son settled down with a wife of
his own, Dimitrios knew it was an excuse to stay on at
the villa. No other man could offer her the Pandakis lifestyle.

At a recent family birthday party, his cousin Vaso had
speculated with similar thoughts to him. Dimitrios's eyes
must have reflected his abhorrence of the subject because
the eldest of Spiros Pandakis's sons didn't broach it
again.

Unfortunately nothing seemed to slake Ananke's ambition. Her temerity in seeking him out in a place as
private as his own bedroom at seven in the morning gave
him proof that she had few scruples left.

Out of love for his brother and nephew, he'd treated
her with civility all these years. Regrettably this morning
she'd stepped over a forbidden line and would know his
wrath.

"You have no right to be in this part of the villa,
Ananke."

"Please don't be angry with me. I have to talk to you

before Leon finds you." She looked like she'd been crying. "This is important."

"Important enough to put false ideas in the minds of the staff, let alone my nephew?" he demanded in a quiet rage. "From here on out, if you have something to say to me in private, call me at my office."

"Wait," she cried as he swept past her and strode down the corridor toward the entrance to the villa, impervious to her pleading.

"Dimi!" She half-sobbed his nickname in an effort to detain him.

The use of the endearment only his parents and brother had ever called him had the effect of corrosive acid being poured into a wound that would never heal.

Compared to the sound of his ever-lengthening footsteps, the rapid patter of her sandals while she tried to catch up with him made the odd cadence on the marble tiles. To his relief, the patter finally faded.

He'd just shut the front door and had headed for the parking area around the side of the villa when Leon called to him.

Dimitrios wheeled around, surprised to discover his nephew following him.

"Uncle." He ran up. "I need to talk to you. *Alone*," he added in a confiding voice. "Would you let me drive you to the office?"

For a fleeting moment Dimitrios felt guilty for dismissing Ananke. She had obviously been trying to alert him to something. But when he considered her reckless actions, which would be misconstrued by his staff no matter how loyal they were to him, he wasn't sorry he'd cut her off.

Years ago Leonides had married Ananke to do the honorable thing and give his child the Pandakis name. After his brother died, Dimitrios determined no breath of scandal would ever touch his nephew if he could help it.

Of course Leon was a free agent, capable of getting into trouble on his own—*if* that were the case. Under the circumstances, Dimitrios knew he wouldn't be able to concentrate on business until he'd learned what was plaguing his nephew.

"Work can wait. Why don't we take a drive and stop somewhere for lunch. I'll call Stavros and tell him I won't be in until afternoon."

"You're sure you wouldn't rather spend time with one of your women friends now that you're back from China?"

"No woman is more important than you, Leon."

"Are you sure? When I was at Elektra the other night, Ionna went out of her way to ask me when you were coming home. She said it was urgent that she talk to you. She even asked me for your cell phone number, but I told her I didn't remember it."

Dimitrios shook his head. "If she was that forward with you, then she has written her own death sentence."

His nephew eyed him steadily. "She's very beautiful."

"I agree, but you know my rule, Leon. When a woman starts to take the initiative, I move on."

"I think it's a good rule. I've been using it, too, and I must say it works."

For some strange reason, the admission didn't sit well with Dimitrios. It sounded too cynical for Leon.

"To be frank, I'm glad you'd rather be with me this morning," came the emotional response.

Dimitrios gave his nephew a hug. Minutes later their car was headed into the hills of Thessalonica overlooking the bay. While Leon drove, Dimitrios checked in with his assistant. 10 7 5, 103 ALF

"Stavros? Can you spare me for a few hours longer?"

"The truth?"

His question surprised Dimitrios.

"Always."

"Ms. Hamilton and I may work an ocean apart, but since she became your private secretary, I've begun to feel superfluous."

"You're indispensable to the company, Stavros. You know that," he rushed to assure him. The sixty-six-year-old man had kept the Greek end of the Pandakis Corporation running smoothly for decades.

Ms. Hamilton, the understudy of his former private secretary in New York until Mrs. Landau's unexpected passing, was a six-month-old enigma, still in her infancy. Yet Dimitrios could understand why Stavros made the remark.

In a word, she was a renaissance woman. Brilliant. Creative. A combination of a workaholic and efficiency expert who, though she was no great beauty, happened to be blessed with a pleasant nature. She was many things—too many, in fact, to put a label on her. Mrs. Landau had known what she was doing when she'd hired her.

Before their trip to China, Dimitrios had wondered how he'd ever gotten along without her. During their week's stay in Beijing while he'd watched her weave her magic before their inscrutable colleagues with the finesse of a statesman, he finally figured it out.

She had a woman's mind for detail, but she thought like a man. Best of all for Dimitrios, she had no interest in him.

"Ms. Hamilton brings her own genius to the company, just as you brought yours many years ago and tutored me, Stavros. I'm looking forward to next week when the two of you meet for the first time. She holds you in great reverence, you know."

"I, too, shall enjoy making the acquaintance of this American paragon. Spring greets Winter."

"Since she's in her late thirties, it would be more accurate to say summer, and you're sounding uncharacteristically maudlin, Stavros."

"You have to allow me the vicissitudes of my age."

Dimitrios chuckled, but beneath the banter he could sense his assistant's vulnerability. Perhaps a word in Ms. Hamilton's ear that she leave something important for Stavros to handle for the fair would help.

"Just so we understand each other, I won't allow you to retire until I do. See you later this afternoon."

"What's wrong with Stavros?" his nephew asked as he clicked off the phone.

Putting his head back to relax, Dimitrios murmured, "He's suddenly aware of growing older."

"I know how he feels."

Dimitrios would have laughed if Leon hadn't sounded so serious. "You said you wanted to talk. Since you brought up Ionna, I have to wonder if you're not about to tell me you've fallen for a girl your mother doesn't like."

Leon shook his head. "That's not why we argued. I told her I dislike my business classes and want to drop out of the university. It's only September. I can still withdraw without penalty before the fall semester starts in three weeks."

Dimitrios schooled himself not to react. "To feel that strongly, you must have a very good reason."

"My heart isn't in it!" he cried. "I don't think it ever was. Mother's always had this vision of me taking my place in the family corporation. She says I owe it to my father's memory. But business doesn't appeal to me. Do you think that makes me some sort of traitor?" he asked in an anxious voice.

"Of course not," Dimitrios scoffed.

At this point he could have told his nephew a few home truths. Like the fact that Leon's father hadn't been interested in the family business, either.

There was information Leon didn't know about his mother that would shed more light on her determination to make certain he held onto his birthright.

But Dimitrios's hands were tied, because telling his nephew the truth about the past would hurt him more than it would help.

"What do you want to do with your life, or do you even know yet?"

His nephew heaved a sigh. "It's just an idea, but it's grown stronger with every visit to Mount Athos."

Mount Athos.

"You took me there the first time. Remember? We did a walking tour, and ate and slept at the various monasteries."

Yes. He remembered. Especially his nephew's fascination with the monks...

Dimitrios straightened in the seat.

Like a revelation he knew what Leon was going to say before he said it.

"Uncle? Last night I told mother I'm thinking of entering an order. That's when she ran out of my bedroom in hysterics. I've never seen her react like that to anything. Would you talk to her about it? You're the only person she'll listen to."

Lord.

Was it possible that Leon's hero-worship of him had caused his nephew to dismiss a woman's love as unimportant?

Ananke's unprecedented visit to his bedroom this morning was beginning to make sense in a brand-new way.

Since the death of Leonides she'd lived on sufferance under Uncle Spiros's roof until his passing, then under the protection of Dimitrios.

If her son renounced all his worldly goods and went to live on a mountain, Ananke wouldn't only have lost a son to the church, she would have no choice but to move into a house Dimitrios would provide for her. A comfortable enough pied-à-terre befitting the widow of Leonides. All her dreams smashed.

"Before I say anything to your mother, I'd like to hear more about how *you* feel."

"As I said, I'm only thinking about it."

"Our trip to Mount Athos took place ten years ago. That's a long time to give a young man to think."

Leon blushed. The reaction tugged at Dimitrios's

heart. Perhaps his brother's son truly did have a vocation for the religious life. If it was the path he was meant to travel, far be it from Dimitrios to try to dissuade him.

Then again, like greener pastures, the monastic life might sound good to him because he was still young and lost.

Dimitrios had never questioned what direction his own life would go. He couldn't relate to Leon in that regard, but he *was* his guardian. As such, he felt it incumbent to listen as his nephew poured out his heart.

Afterward he would point out the ramifications of a decision that a twenty-two-year-old mind wasn't capable of envisioning yet. For one thing, it would break his mother's heart. Ananke might be many things, but she loved her son.

For another, it would destroy something inside Dimitrios if he thought his own tormented past had anything to do with the drastic step his nephew was contemplating.

Suddenly Dimitrios felt older than Stavros.

CHAPTER TWO

ALEX'S family always complained that she didn't stay long enough when she came to Paterson for visits. Her parents had never approved of her intentionally making herself look older in order to get hired by the Pandakis company. It was a sore point Alex argued with her mother every time they got together.

"Surely after four years you could start easing back to your normal self by lightening your hair in increments, wearing clothes that suit your age. I haven't seen my own daughter for so long, I don't remember what you look like."

"Mom…" Alex took a deep breath. "I wanted to be hired so badly, I would have done anything to gain Mrs. Landau's approval. I thought if I looked like a solid, more mature, dependable type, I'd have a better chance with her. Mr. Pandakis may have the reputation of being a womanizer, but he's totally professional with the staff at the office.

"But Mrs. Landau's not there anymore, darling. Now that you've taken over her duties, it seems to me you can start being our daughter again."

"You don't understand, Mom."

"Oh, but I do. You're not willing to risk anything that would prevent you from being around him. He's a man to turn any woman's head, and he has, especially yours."

"Yes," she admitted. "He's—"

"Bigger than life?" her mother preempted her. "I

know. He's the reason you've stopped dating and no longer have a social life.''

"I can't right now. But when the trade fair is over, he's taking a three week vacation. I've been ordered to do the same.''

"Which means all you'll do is mope around here waiting until you can be back with him.''

Her mother knew her too well.

"Alexandra? I've tried not to interfere in your life too much. But it's obvious to me you're in love with the man. Because of that you're blind to certain truths.''

Alex didn't want to hear them.

"Darling— Can't you see he's not normal?''

"You mean because he's not married with three or four children by now?'' she cried.

"Yes. He's a person who's been blessed with so many gifts, I think he got lost somewhere along the way.''

Alex shook her head emphatically. "If you knew him, you'd never say such a thing.''

"I'm not talking about his business prowess. There's something in his makeup that isn't right. My guess is he was marred in childhood and it stunted his emotional growth.

"How else do you explain his inability to settle down with one woman? Or for that matter, why Mrs. Landau seemed to choose only plain women to work for him. He's simply not an ordinary sort. Don't you agree? Honestly?''

Tears prickled Alex's eyes. "Yes,'' she whispered.

"Darling.'' Her mother put an arm around her. "All I want is your happiness, but I'm afraid if you continue to work for him, he'll go on taking advantage of your generous nature and you'll never find joy in being a wife, or a mother.''

Alex broke down for a minute, then wiped her eyes. ''Mom? There's something I have to tell you. Maybe then you'll understand why I can't seem to let him go. I—I didn't apply for a job at the Pandakis Corporation by chance,'' she stammered.

''I suspected as much. When their people came to Paterson for the international silk seminar your grandfather hosted ten years ago, I remember the huge impact so many wealthy, dark-haired men made on everyone. Not a bad place to start a career for a girl right out of college.''

''Actually it was nine years ago.''

Her mother sent her a shrewd regard. ''What went on that night? Did Dimitrios Pandakis's wandering eye light on you? Did he tell you to come and see him when you were all grown up?''

''No!'' Alex cried out. ''If only it had happened like that, I wouldn't have been forced to resort to subterfuge. It was Giorgio Pandakis—''

In a torrent of words she explained what had gone on nine years earlier when Dimitrios had saved her from his cousin. After confiding everything she said, ''He was willing to stand by me, Mom. He offered to help me because that's the kind of man he is.''

''No wonder you fell in love with him,'' her mother murmured in a saddened voice. ''I've tried to imagine what hold he's had over you all this time. Everything you'd done since than has been with him in mind.''

''I've never been able to look at another man. I couldn't!''

''But what has it really gotten you except heartache?

This has to stop, darling. A teenage fantasy is one thing. But he's become your obsession. Surely if it was meant to be, he would have returned your feelings by now.''

She knew her mother was right. Everyone was right. Michael. Her friend Yanni.

But the pain was killing her.

"I'm afraid for you to go to Greece with him. It can only put you on a more intimate footing with him without getting anything back in return.''

"I know, but I *have* to go. I'm in charge of the trade fair.''

"I realize that. Oh, Alexandra, you've gotten yourself in way too deep. I particularly don't like the idea of your being anywhere near his cousin. Obviously he'd caused trouble in their family long before he set eyes on you, otherwise your boss wouldn't have been so straightforward in dealing with the situation.''

It had taken Alex a few years before she'd figured that out.

"Don't worry, Mom. Giorgio's been married a long time and has a family. Besides, I'm not a teenager anymore, and he wouldn't give me a second glance now.''

Her mother stared at her with anxious eyes. "I'm not so sure of that. You may look older now, but you'll always be a beautiful girl. Even so, lies have a way of surfacing. How do you think Mr. Pandakis will react if he finds out you intentionally disguised yourself to get hired?''

"Literally speaking it was Mrs. Landau who gave me the job.''

"You know what I mean.''

Alex sucked in her breath. "I have no idea how he'd feel.''

"Yes, you do. You've just told me he's an honorable man when it comes to business. Men like that expect honor in return. Mark my words, Alexandra. Every minute you're in his employ, you're playing with fire."

"Don't you think I know that?" she blurted in agony. "I—I've been giving it a lot of thought. Between you and Michael, I'm convinced that the only thing to do is resign."

"If you really mean that, then go to Greece. Do your job. Don't go near his family, then come straight home on the first available commercial flight and hand in your resignation. He'll have three weeks to find another secretary within the company to replace you."

"You're right," she whispered brokenly. "My assistant Charlene would give anything to have my job. As soon as I get back, I'll look for something around here."

"Promise?"

"Yes." She gave her mother another hug. "Kiss Daddy for me. I have to run."

"Call me as often as you can."

"Okay. I love you, Mom. Thanks for the advice."

"It's more than advice, darling. It's a warning."

Tears swamped Alex's cheeks as she left the house and drove off with those words ringing in her ears. All the way to New York she relived the conversation with her mother. The fissure had cracked open wide, wide, wide.

What a fool Alex had been. Four years had come and gone. She was still forgettable to Dimitrios.

But if he never gave her another thought after she left his employ, she was determined he'd remember the fruit of her labors.

For the last eight months she'd given the international

textile fair her all. She hoped it would make Greece the forerunner in establishing business relations on a global scale.

Before Mrs. Landau had passed away, she'd told Alex that Dimitrios had been asked to host the trade fair at the behest of the Greek government. They needed a name guaranteed to bring success.

It was a project dear to Alex's heart in more ways than one. She immediately went to work on it and received glowing praise from Mrs. Landau. But before the older woman could present the complete project to Dimitrios for his approval, she suffered a fatal heart attack at her home.

Her death affected everyone in the company, especially Dimitrios, who'd considered her his right hand away from Greece. Suddenly he was trying to do Mrs. Landau's work plus his own.

When he'd asked Alex to take over as best she could, she'd sensed he felt she was a lightweight who couldn't handle the enormous trade fair project along with her normal duties.

Fearing she'd miss the one big opportunity to make her mark, Alex rushed to assure him that she'd already worked out most of the details with Mrs. Landau. Whenever he gave the word, she would start implementing the plans.

She remembered that evening so clearly. Her mind's eye could see the way he lounged back in his swivel chair and unfastened his tie. Fatigue lines had darkened his attractive face whose shadowed jaw gave evidence that he'd been going too hard, traveling too much without proper rest.

He stared at her with incurious eyes, causing her heart

to plummet. Although he hadn't told her no, she realized he had little faith in her abilities to take on something of such vital importance.

"Have you ever been to Greece, Ms. Hamilton?"

"No, but I have a history degree."

In the uneasy silence that followed her response, she watched him rub his forehead as if he had a headache. No doubt he did and was barely holding on to his patience.

"Do you have something written up you can show me now, or do you need more time?"

She took a deep breath. "I'll get the portfolio out of my office and be right back."

Upon her return she asked if she could spread the materials out on his desk. He nodded.

The second she positioned the first twenty-by-twenty-four inch drawing in front of him, the complacency left his face. As he sat forward, his well-shaped black brows drew together.

"This isn't Athens." His voice trailed off.

"Was your heart set on it for the trade fair?"

Instead of answering her, he continued his perusal.

Swallowing hard she said, "That's a rendition of medieval Thessalonica during the great Byzantine fair held in the twelfth century. Everyone came—from Constantinople, Egypt, Phoenicia, the Peloponnese."

His head finally lifted. This time his eyes reminded her of twin black fires. "*You* drew this?"

"It's only a sketch. I thought because Thessalonica is your home, it would be exciting and fitting to recreate that same fair with colorful merchant booths and flags from every country participating. The whole city can get involved by providing local foods and drinks, everyone in native costume. Troubadours, music, dancing.

"Since it was the great cultural center then and still is today, I can't think of another place in Greece more appropriate to host a trade fair, certainly not one of this magnitude."

She placed a sketch of a closeup of the bay in front of him. "We could invite the countries around the Mediterranean and as far away as Scandinavia to bring their restored ships and anchor them here like they once did. Everyone can go aboard to see their wares.

"It will be like stepping back in time, but the products will be the latest in materials and textiles from around the world.

"We'll launch a massive ad campaign on the Internet with each country having its own Web page to list their products. I've already procured Web addresses. People who aren't able to attend can place orders.

"Think what it would mean economically to the Greek Island cottage industries for example, not to mention new world markets. Of course the pièce de résistance will be *this*." He hadn't interrupted her yet, so she whipped out her next drawing.

"Follow the silk road from Thessalonica to Soufli. At various points along the route, the delegations will set up their silk exhibits. Visits to the mulberry tree farm and the silk mansion in Soufli will be the highlight of the tour.

"The weather will be warm and perfect in September. Imagine the streets of Soufli lined with booths showing every stage from the secretions of the silkworm, to the silk thread ending up as a cravate or a gown.

"We'll woo the media ahead of time so there'll be a blitz that hits airwaves around the wor—"

"Ms. Hamilton." He cut in on her.

Her body broke out in a cold sweat. *He didn't like it.* Afraid to look at him, she said, "Yes?"

"What you've put together here is nothing short of sheer genius. In fact I'm having difficulty assimilating everything all at once."

Alex had been ready to pass out from disappointment. She still felt light-headed, except that now it was for an entirely different reason.

"Unfortunately none of this can happen without hotel space," he muttered. "Every place of lodging in Macedonia and Thrace should have been notified months ago in order to carry out such a fantastic plan."

"They were."

His dark head reared back in stunned surprise.

"In Athens and the surrounding regions, too. I also notified the head of all the businesses involved, the restaurants, the universities, the musicians' network, the transport services, port authorities, police, so they would set aside the time and plan ahead how to accommodate the huge crowds.

"I assume this is what it's like mobilizing for war, except that in this case everyone will enjoy the spoils of victory."

"Lord," she heard him whisper.

"It's a good thing we're talking about this tonight," she informed him. "The day after tomorrow is the final date for me to confirm or cancel everything without penalty.

"I've been waiting to discuss the fair with you until you'd recovered from Mrs. Landau's passing. She was extremely fond of you, too. It should please you to know that every contact person has assured me they wouldn't have held on this long for anyone but Dimitrios Pandakis. It's an honor to work for you.'' She had a struggle at the last to keep the emotion out of her voice.

In an unconscious gesture he raked his hands through the luxuriant black hair she longed to touch. ''Here I was beginning to think you were perfect, Ms. Hamilton. Now I can see you're not above bribery to get what you want. For that flaw, you've won yourself a full evening of work that could take us well into the night.''

With those words he'd just given her the first taste of her heart's desire.

''While you arrange to have our dinner sent up, I'll cancel my plans to attend the symphony and we'll start again. I want to hear this from the beginning.

''Slowly this time. Detail by detail until I've picked that brilliant brain of yours. I can see I've also under-estimated the value of your American university educa-tion. Did you study any languages?''

''My degree specialized in classical European history, so there were several classes I had to take in Latin and Greek.''

''You speak and understand Greek?'' He sounded in-credulous.

''No. But since I came to work for your company I've been trying to do both with the help of a tutor.''

''Who?''

''A graduate student from Athens who lives in my apartment building. He trades me lessons for meals.''

''You cook, too?''

''Yanni's not particular.''

Alex couldn't remember Dimitrios ever smiling at her before now. *What a gorgeous man he was.*

"When you call downstairs, tell the kitchen to send a gallon of coffee with the food."

"Which brand of decaffeinated do you prefer?"

He lifted a sardonic brow. "Forget everything you learned from Mrs. Landau."

"You don't really mean that. I happen to know she had your very best interest at heart."

Once more his black eyes flashed fire. "You happen to know a lot more than I thought possible."

I sincerely hope so. Otherwise how will I ever become unforgettable to you?

More tears dripped down Alex's face as she remembered that evening with him. He'd loved her idea and had let her run with it. But nothing else had changed in the intervening months. Nothing personal.

Her mother was right about him not being normal. Even Alex knew it was time to give up. The trade fair would have to be her swan song.

Unless she died of pain first...

Dimitrios left his New York office with the morning newspaper under his arm and rode the elevator to the parking garage level of the building.

"Ms. Hamilton hasn't arrived yet?" he asked his driver who was waiting for them with the limo.

"I haven't seen her, Mr. Pandakis."

He checked his watch. No crime had been committed because it was a only few minutes past eight. It surprised him because she was the most punctual person he'd ever met.

At the end of work yesterday he'd told her he would

drop by her apartment on the way to the airport to pick her up. To his surprise she'd said it wouldn't be necessary because she'd be coming by the office early to take care of some last-minute business.

"Mr. Pandakis?"

Dimitrios turned in time to see one of the parking attendants approach him.

"Your secretary just called. She said she was running late and her friend would drive her straight to the airport."

He blinked. No doubt Ms. Hamilton had many friends, but the only one he'd ever heard about was Yanni. A compatriot.

Besides cooking him meals in exchange for language lessons, was she his pillow friend? It might explain why she'd chosen not to call Dimitrios on her cell phone to tell him about the change in plans. Particularly not if her tutor were lying next to her having a hard time saying goodbye.

The idea that Ms. Hamilton might have a love life made her more of an enigma than ever because she'd never let it interfere with her work. For quite some time he'd been aware that she wasn't like most women. That's why she'd become so valuable to him.

He climbed in the back of the limo. "Let's go to the airport."

"Yes, sir."

Dimitrios unfolded the paper. The first thing he noticed on the front page of the *Times* was a fantastic shot of three ships. At closer inspection they turned out to be a Viking longboat plus a Greek and a Roman galley moored in the bay of Thessalonica awaiting the fair. A nice-size article accompanied the photo.

He saw Ms. Hamilton's hand in the write-up. Except to give her the okay on the project, Dimitrios really hadn't been—

His thoughts were interrupted by the ring of his cell phone. He pulled it from his pocket and checked the caller ID. It was someone from the villa.

"*Yassou?*"

"*Kalimera,* Uncle. You *are* coming home today aren't you?"

His nephew sounded anxious. "I'm on my way to the airport now."

"Good. There's a lot I have to talk to you about."

"I take it things are still at an impasse with your mother."

"Yes. She refuses to discuss anything with me when she doesn't even know what I'm going to say."

"You and I have been over this before. She's afraid of losing you, Leon."

"How do I convince her that couldn't possibly happen?"

I'm not sure you can. He rubbed his eyes. "Tell you what. Tomorrow morning the three of us will sit down together and talk this out."

"Thank you. Mother's much better with you there. Can I pick you up at the airport?"

Dimitrios wasn't immune to the pleading in his nephew's voice. "It will be late. I'll have my secretary with me."

"Where's she staying?"

"I've booked her at the Mediterranean Palace."

"No problem. We'll run her by there on our way home, but it may take us a while. The traffic's horrendous. You're going to be surprised at what you see when you get here. The city's been transformed while you've been in New York.''

"I'm looking forward to viewing the finished product.''

"Besides all the booths that have gone up, the buildings and churches, even the White Tower is festooned with pennants and medieval banners. The city's been invaded with people, and there are six ships in port now.

"Wait till you get a look at the Egyptian barge from Cleopatra's time on loan for the event! Five days aren't going to be enough for people to see everything.''

"I think five days is about all our fair city will be able to handle.''

"That's what Vaso said. We had lunch with some government officials from the prime minister's office who were looking around yesterday. They said they'd never seen anything like this in their lifetime. The praise for you is pouring in already and the fair hasn't even started yet.''

"My secretary will be gratified to hear it. She's the mastermind behind the entire concept.''

"You're just saying that because you never like to take credit for anything.''

"No. If you don't believe me, I'll have Ms. Hamilton show you the contents of her portfolio after we get there.''

"I'm glad you're coming home, Uncle.''

"Me, too. See you soon.''

Dimitrios clicked off.

One look at her artwork and Leon wouldn't believe his eyes. The drawings were remarkable. When everything was over he intended to have the first sketch framed for his office.

As his private jet came into view, his cell phone went off again. "Leon? Obviously you forgot something important."

"It's Ananke."

Dimitrios should have known better than to answer that way, but his mind had been on Ms. Hamilton.

"*Yassou,* Ananke."

"It doesn't surprise me my son reached you before I did," she began without preamble. "I have to know— Is he willing to stay in school one more semester? Please tell me yes," she cried.

Her desperation found a vulnerable spot inside Dimitrios. He wasn't exactly enchanted by the bombshell his nephew had dropped on them.

"I'm still working on it."

"How soon are you coming home?"

"Late tonight. I told Leon we'd all sit down and discuss this in the morning."

"Thank you." Her voice trembled.

"Ananke? Just remember, there's only so much I can do."

"You can stop him!"

Dimitrios heaved a sigh. "If this is his destiny, then no earthly power will make a difference."

The sobbing on her end meant the conversation was over, for the time being, anyway.

He undid his seat belt. "I'll see you tomorrow," he murmured before ringing off.

As the vehicle pulled to a stop, Dimitrios levered himself from the back of the limo and hurried up the steps of the plane.

"*Kalimera, Kyrie Pandakis.*"

Instead of his pilots or his steward speaking to him in

Greek, it was Ms. Hamilton who greeted him in his native tongue as he entered the plane. It was a first for her. She never failed to surprise him.

"Kalimera," he said back to her, relieved she was here.

"Hero poli."

"It's nice to see you, too." He responded in Greek once more, impressed by this latest display of her many talents. She'd spoken with barely a trace of accent. Continuing in the same language he said, "Shall we carry on this fascinating conversation after we've fastened ourselves in?"

"I'm sorry." She reverted to English. "I didn't understand anything else you said after you told me it was nice to see me, too."

Her honesty was so refreshing, he burst out laughing. For a moment it dispelled the cloud that had enveloped him since his nephew had confided in him.

The rest of his crew welcomed him aboard, but he was barely aware of them as he gave the nod to prepare for takeoff.

"What I just said to you, Ms. Hamilton, was that I was looking forward to a lengthy discussion in Greek, but thought it would be wise to strap ourselves in first so the pilot can do his job."

"Oh." She took the seat opposite him and fastened her seat belt. "I'm afraid you've heard my full repertoire until we reach Greece. Then I'll impress you by asking where the post office is, how much does a stamp cost, that sort of thing."

His chuckle got lost in the scream of the jet engines.

After a smooth liftoff it didn't take long until the plane

had attained cruising speed and they could unstrap them-selves.

Out of the periphery he saw that she already had her nose in the notebook she called her bible. He noticed it went everywhere with her.

"Your friend didn't mind bringing you to the airport so early?"

She lifted her head. "Yanni's on his way to Athens, so it worked out fine."

"To be with family?"

"That, and to attend the fair."

The steward chose that moment to serve them tea. Dimitrios thanked him, then sat back in his seat, won-dering why her answer mattered. It was none of his busi-ness if she planned to be with her lover in Thessalonica.

As soon as the brew had cooled, he took a long swal-low. It was so delicious he drank the rest without pause, then requested more.

Speaking in Greek, he complimented his steward who murmured in the same language, "She brought it on board. Insisted on steeping it herself."

Intrigued, Dimitrios flicked his gaze to his secretary. For once she had irritated him by being too absorbed with her work. "My compliments, Ms. Hamilton. This tea tastes like the proverbial nectar of the gods."

She raised her head in his direction. "According to Yanni who won't drink anything else, that's the name of it in Greek. He says it comes from the sage that grows wild on the mountains of the Peloponnese. I told him you have a sweet tooth, so he said to add honey instead of sugar. I'm glad you like it."

Dimitrios should have been appreciative of her desire to please him with a special treat. He *was* pleased. But for some reason it irritated him that Yanni had any part in her thoughtful gesture.

She opened her laptop computer. "Shall we go over the timetable of events now? I've made a hard copy for you. If there's anything you want to change, I'll enter it and print it out when we reach Greece."

In an oddly rebellious mood Dimitrios adjusted the seat so he could fully relax and close his eyes.

"Why don't you read it out loud instead. I'll interrupt if I think of something you haven't."

He sounded tired, bordering grumpy.

Alex had thought the tea might sweeten him up. Normally he was very even-tempered for a man who shouldered so much responsibility.

But she'd worked closely with him over the last six months and had started to notice a pattern to his change in mood. It only came on when he was getting ready to fly home to Greece.

If her mother was right about his past, he probably had hidden demons still to be conquered.

It happened to a lot of people. Alex's only unmarried sister chose to feel like a victim. Except for the occasional visit, she preferred to remain in California rather than come home and deal with family on a more frequent basis.

Deciding it would be best to humor her boss, Alex began reading the countdown of the first page out loud. Halfway through, she detected a change in his breathing. He was asleep.

Zeus at rest.

That's how she thought of him.

This was only the second time she'd flown in the

Pandakis jet with its eagle emblem. As on her first flight with him to San Francisco, she had the feeling she was being spirited away by the legendary Olympian god to his private kingdom in the sky.

Through her lashes, she studied his long, powerfully built body stretched out in his seat opposite her, his piercing black eyes closed for the time being.

She wished she were a painter so she could capture him on canvas. He had the bold facial structure of his Macedonian ancestors, and that beautiful olive skin born from the kiss of a hot Mediterranean sun. Yet there was something childlike in the quiet way he slept.

More handsome than the young god Adonis. The paparazzi claimed he was the lover of many women, yet faithful to none. Alex could vouch for a goodly number of females who called the office anxious to talk to him.

However, she really had no idea what he did after she left for her apartment at the end of the day. Presumably there was a certain amount of truth to the gossip in the tabloids.

But Alex regarded him in a different light. To her, raven-haired Dimitrios Pandakis could well be the supreme ruler of the gods who shaped the corporate world below. One word of displeasure from his sensuous lips was like the proverbial thunderbolt hurled at those who lied or broke oaths.

The experience nine years ago had already provided her with firsthand knowledge that he was the god of justice and mercy and a protector of the weak.

After saving her from the unwanted attentions of his cousin, he'd shown her kindness before removing the other man from her sight. But he'd taken away a lot more than that. He'd gone off with her young girl's heart.

Quite simply, his intervention changed the course of her life.

As her eyes took their fill of him, the ache to touch him intensified. More than ever she realized it would never be enough to be *just* his private secretary. Reason declared that the end of the fair would have to be the end of the road for her. The cessation of all fantasy.

Exhausted from too little sleep and her emotional struggle, she put her things away and lay back, willing oblivion to come if only for a little while.

It was a shock to finally wake up to her surroundings and discover that the interior lights had come on. Outside the plane they were cloaked in darkness.

She checked her watch. Heavens. How could she have been asleep seven hours?

Though alone for the moment, she was conscious of the sound of male voices coming from the cockpit area. Judging by their chuckles, someone was telling an amusing tale.

Probably she'd snored, or her stomach had growled so loudly they'd all heard it. Either possibility was so humiliating, Alex shot out of her seat and used the time to freshen up in the bathroom.

While she was repinning her hair to secure it better after her long sleep, she noted that the plane had started to encounter some turbulence. She didn't pay much attention to it until the Fasten Seat Belts sign flashed overhead.

Alex put in the last pin, then left the bathroom and hurried to her seat. As she strapped herself in, she saw Dimitrios emerge from the cockpit, his expression sober.

"I was about to do that for—"

But she wasn't destined to hear him say anything else

because the plane hit an air pocket, sending him flying. He crashed against the wall. By the position of his body, he'd been knocked unconscious. She saw blood.

"Dimitrios!"

They were dropping out of the sky as if being pulled toward a giant lodestone.

Please, God. Don't let anything happen to him.

CHAPTER THREE

"HE'S coming around."

"Don't let him move his head."

"No. I've got him."

"An AirMed helicopter will meet us when we land."

"The bleeding's stopped."

"That's good. Keep that compress over the wound."

"Do you think his arm is broken?"

"No. Nothing's broken that I see, but he's going to have an ugly bruise on his shoulder for a while."

Dimitrios had been hearing voices for the last few minutes. Now he was aware of stinging at the crown of his head. Slowly his body was coming back to life.

Mingled with the smell of alcohol was a delicious scent, like pears, that permeated his nostrils. It came from a smooth, cool hand cupping his jaw along the side of his face. He seemed to be resting on something soft and warm. His eyelids fluttered open.

Waves of dizziness assailed him. He blinked several times until his gaze focused on a pair of soulful green eyes staring down at him. They seemed to take up her whole face.

Good Lord. What were they both doing on the floor of the plane with his head in her lap?

"Ms. Hamilton?"

"Thank heaven you know me," she whispered emotionally.

"Welcome back," came the voice of his copilot. Both

he and the steward had to be standing somewhere near his feet.

Dimitrios blinked again. Maybe it was the angle of the recessed lighting that made him think moisture clung to his secretary's long, silky lashes. He'd never seen her without her steel-rimmed glasses. She had flawless skin and a beautifully shaped mouth.

"What happened?"

"We hit an air pocket before you could make it to your seat," she explained.

"I remember now," he muttered on a groan. "How soon before we land?"

His copilot hunkered at his side. "We're approaching Macedonia International now."

Dimitrios started to get up, but all three of them held him down. "Don't move," his steward ordered. "You have a lump on the top of your head and must be seen by a doctor."

"I heard you say nothing was broken. Let me up," he ordered.

Still they restrained him. *Damnation.*

He felt the tightening of his secretary's diaphragm before she asked, "How many stones are there in my ring?"

What?

She held the top of her hand in front of his eyes so he couldn't possibly miss it.

"Five."

"Good. There's nothing wrong with his vision, gentlemen. I think Kyrie Pandakis is recovered enough to get to his seat."

His steward shook his head. "I don't know—"

"Well I *do!* Don't worry. I'll take full responsibility

if anything should happen to him. Now if you'll both assist me and we're all very careful, we can get him strapped in before we begin our descent.

"Don't you dare pass out on me now," her lips whispered against his ear before she told the two men to support his elbows so he could stand up.

Dimitrios could count on the fingers of one hand the times in his life when he'd been filled with wonder. To see his steward and copilot cowed into submission without further remonstration qualified as one of them. Once helped into his seat and buckled in, he gripped the arm rests, fighting not to succumb to his dizziness and fall over again.

His head felt like it weighed a thousand pounds. In fact it hurt like hell except for that moment when her lips brushed his ear. Then all he could feel was a little explosion of electricity shooting through his system.

"You see?" He heard her speak to his staff from her seat. "He's fine. Tell the pilot to cancel the helicopter. If Kyrie Pandakis isn't well after he gets home, his family will send for his doctor."

After more hesitation, his copilot went to the cockpit to do her bidding. The steward remained nearby, still looking unsure about things. It had to be a first for him.

"Is this your wish?" he demanded

"As my secretary said, I'm all right. Thank you for your help and concern. Tell the pilot everyone is grateful he was able to stabilize the plane in time."

The other man gave a reluctant nod before disappearing.

"When the world stops spinning, Ms. Hamilton, remind me to give you a bonus for keeping a cool head. It must have been a terrifying experience for you."

"Only when I saw you go flying."

The Fasten Seat Belts sign went on. They were beginning their descent. His head swam.

"It won't be long now." Her voice seemed to come from a long way off.

The next thing he was aware of was his secretary bending over him to undo his seat belt. He could smell the pear scent once more.

"We're home, Mr. Pandakis."

"What happened to Kyrie?"

She ignored his question. "Stand up and lean against me while we exit the plane."

His dizziness was as bad on the ground as in the air. He put his arm around her shoulders and they started for the door. A few steps from the entrance he had to cling to her.

Who would have guessed at the warm, full curves and flare of womanly hips hidden beneath the folds of the shapeless, loose-fitting outfit she wore.

Why in heaven's name did she dress in clothes that masked such a voluptuous figure? For that matter, why didn't she wear contacts? Her steel-rimmed glasses hid one of her best assets. It didn't make any sense.

"Come on," she urged. "We're almost there."

"Give me another minute." The world was still whirling. So were his senses. This sharp awareness of her as a flesh-and-blood woman had caught him completely by surprise.

The steward opened the door.

Dimitrios heard footsteps on the stairs leading up to the plane's entrance. "Uncle?"

When a dark-haired man close to Alex's age suddenly appeared in the opening, she didn't know who looked more surprised. Somehow she'd thought his nephew would be younger.

He halted mid-stride when he saw his uncle clinging to her. Dimitrios had closed his eyes for a moment. Given his pallor, she could understand why his nephew had concern written all over his face.

"Kyrie Pandakis has had a slight accident. He's a little dizzy from a bump on the head, but it's nothing serious," she assured him. "If you'd like to help your uncle out to the car, I'll gather my things and be right with you."

"Of course." He rushed forward and put his arm around his uncle. "Do you think you can make it now, Uncle?" The deep affection in his voice touched Alex.

"As soon as I introduce the two of you," came the dry response. "Leon? This is my secretary, the legendary Ms. Hamilton." He was weaving on his feet as he said it.

She eyed his nephew, hoping he received her silent message. "We'll have time for that later. Right now what's important is to get you home."

Between Leon and the two pilots, Dimitrios was helped to the car with little problem. Alex followed with her purse and briefcase. The steward stowed it in the trunk with her suitcase, then helped her into the front passenger seat.

Dimitrios had been put in back so he could spread out. She winced at the shadows beneath his eyes. He would never admit to the horrendous pain he was in.

She thanked the staff, then told Leon to step on it. He obviously didn't need any urging because the car accelerated at a faster speed than she imagined was allowed.

"How long will it take to reach the Mediterranean

Palace?'' She asked this in a low tone as they drove away from the plane.

''Normally fifteen minutes,'' he whispered, ''but because of the tourists in town for the fair, the traffic is heavy at all hours now. It could take longer.''

''Ms. Hamilton won't be staying at the hotel, Leon. Drive us straight to the villa.''

Alex caught the surprised glance Leon flashed his uncle over his shoulder. But she understood. Dimitrios felt too ill to put up with any detours tonight.

She leaned closer to his nephew. Mouthing the words, she said, ''As soon as we get him home, I'll take a taxi to the hotel.''

He nodded.

With that understood, she moved next to the door so she could rest her head against the glass.

It was hard to believe she was in Greece.

She should be thrilled, exhilarated. It was a lovely warm night. They were driving through one of the oldest cities in Europe. Some sites dated back to 2300 B.C. She was passing over ground of saints and scholars.

There was so much history to absorb. But after the shock she'd lived through, she was too enervated to do anything more than close her eyes.

Only one thing mattered. Dimitrios was alive and seemingly in one piece. His injuries could have been so much worse. She still hadn't recovered from seeing his big body hurtled to the floor of the plane, lifeless.

If Alex needed proof of what he meant to her, that experience would stand out for all time as the defining moment.

At one point she'd seen Leon pull out his cell phone and make several calls. Therefore it didn't surprise her that the guard at the gate of the estate let them through without Leon having to brake.

A sizable group of people were assembled in the courtyard by the time they wound around the tree-lined drive to the front of the ochre-toned villa. Large and square-shaped in design, it looked fairly impregnable and quite unlike what Alex had imagined.

That was probably because she was used to seeing travel brochures with pictures of the white, cube-style villas nestled close together on the Greek Islands.

Two women rushed forward. One old, with a face that looked a trifle wizened from being in the sun too long. The other fortyish and attractive, with big brown eyes that reminded Alex of Leon.

"Dimitrios!" they both cried at once as his nephew got out of the car and opened the back door for him. A spate of Greek Alex couldn't understand poured out of both women. One of the male staff members somebody called Kristofor worked with Leon to help his uncle from the car.

The rest of the staff stood by with anxious expressions. It was evident that everyone held Kyrie Pandakis in great affection and were upset to see him incapacitated in any way.

Alex knew just how they felt.

Relieved he was home in the comfort of his family, she climbed out of the front seat to get her things from the trunk. To her surprise she caught the full brunt of headlights from a taxi that had pulled up behind the car. It had gotten here quickly.

More conversation in Greek ensued. This time it was Dimitrios's voice overriding everyone else's. A subdued, confused-looking Leon walked to the taxi. Alex saw him pull some money from his wallet and pay the driver, who backed around and took off.

"Everyone speak English, please," Dimitrios declared. For a man who was barely hanging on, his voice sounded amazingly strong and authoritative.

"My secretary, Ms. Hamilton, will be our houseguest for a while. Serilda? If you will be kind enough to prepare the guest room down the hall from mine for her. Nicholas? Please bring her things from the back of the car."

The staff seemed to take everything as a matter of course, but Alex didn't dare make a scene right then. Not in front of the woman who had to be Leon's mother, Ananke. She stared at Alex like she was a visitor from another planet.

When they entered the palatial villa, it felt like Alex had just stepped into another time period. The flavor of old Byzantium called out to her. Under other circumstances she would love to explore every inch of it, learn the story behind every exquisite artifact.

But Alex could hear her mother's warning. *Go to Greece, do your job, don't go near his family, then come straight home.*

The front door clicked shut behind her. She had no choice but to follow Dimitrios who, with help, managed to make it down two hallways to his own suite of rooms.

Though the lump on his head was hidden, Alex could see that some of his black hair was still matted with blood, a potent reminder of an experience that could have taken his life.

At the thought, she felt sickness sweep over her. Her steps slowed until the moment of sudden weakness passed.

Leon's mother stayed right with him, talking in Greek to her son even though Dimitrios had requested otherwise.

"Ms. Hamilton?" he called over his shoulder without looking at her. "When you've freshened up, please come to my bedroom. There's some business we have to discuss."

"I'll come now if you'd like." The sooner he said what he had to say, the sooner she'd be able to phone for another taxi and slip away. Thanks to Yanni, she could do that much for herself in Greek without anyone's help.

"I'd like," she heard him mutter.

His suite came as a complete surprise. It was modern and unquestionably masculine down to the tan and black striped bedspread. Alex sank down on one of two chairs arranged around a coffee table while Leon and Kristofor helped Dimitrios stretch out on top of the bed.

His eyes were closed. He looked wan and exhausted. There was blood on his rumpled shirt, which was partway unbuttoned, revealing a dusting of black hair on his chest. Alex closed her eyes to shut out the sight before her.

She'd never loved him more. All she wanted to do was crawl onto the king-size bed and take care of him. Hold him like she'd done on the plane. Her arms ached from the loss.

While she'd steadied his head, she'd been able to study the tiny lines that radiated from around his eyes, the set of his jaw, the sensuality of his male mouth she yearned to cover with her own.

"Serilda has called for the doctor. Until he has examined you, you're not to discuss business or anything else.''

''Mother's right, Uncle. Let me help you get ready for bed.''

''As you can both see, I'm fine, just dizzy. It will pass. I appreciate your concern, but right now Ms. Hamilton and I have matters to discuss that won't wait.''

''I'm sure she's exhausted, too,'' Ananke persisted.

Sensing Dimitrios's impatience simmering beneath the surface Alex said, ''Actually I slept seven hours on the plane and feel very well rested. I promise I won't work your brother-in-law too long.''

''Leon? Will you bring Ms. Hamilton's briefcase to her?''

His nephew nodded before hurrying out of the room.

Alex watched the other woman's hands curl into fists at her side. ''I'll bring you some tea and pain killers.''

''I—I don't think he should have anything yet.''

At Alex's interjection, Ananke flashed her a hostile glance.

''I only mentioned it, Mrs. Pandakis, because I'm sure he has suffered a concussion.''

Despite his injury Dimitrios seemed to be alert enough to address his sister-in-law. ''Ask the cook to make tea and sandwiches, Ananke. My secretary slept through lunch and dinner and must be starving by now.''

Her brown eyes glittered angrily before she left the room.

''Here's your briefcase, Ms. Hamilton.''

''Thank you.''

''Leon— I'm glad you came to the plane. I couldn't have gotten along without your help. In the morning, we'll have that talk. All right?''

"Only if you're feeling much better, Uncle."

"I'm sure I will. Would you mind closing the door on your way out?"

"No. Of course not." His brown gaze darted to Alex. "Good night, Ms. Hamilton."

"Good night. It was very nice to meet you."

A strange silence filled the room after he'd gone.

Alex was relieved to see Dimitrios's eyes had closed. Finally he could rest. That's why it came as a surprise when he spoke to her.

"After today's experience, I realize that along with your many attributes, you were born with an ability to read minds, too."

"You mean about my canceling the helicopter."

"Among other things."

"I did it for self-preservation."

"How so?"

"You're Thessalonica's favorite son. The media would've had a field day if word had leaked out that you were being transported to the hospital from the plane. I'd have been forced to ward them off. To be honest, I didn't particularly relish the thought after—"

"After you thought it was the end, and your life flashed before your eyes?"

She bowed her head. "Something like that, yes." Except that was a lie. There'd only been one thought on her mind. *One* man.

"I was concerned about the publicity. It would probably have given your government officials a heart attack to know you were hurt this close to the trade fair. As it is, your name's going to be all over the news by morning."

"You think?" came the deep voice.

It amazed her he had the energy to tease in his condition.

"I'm sure your loyal pilot was shaken by the incident. No doubt he issued some strict orders to the hospital to stand by because they were going to be receiving some very precious cargo.

"Right now the phones are probably ringing off the hook to every journalist that you're back in Greece and something terrible happened to you in flight."

"Something did."

His comment sounded faintly cryptic. She kneaded her hands together.

"We don't have any business to discuss tonight. Why did you ask me to come in here?"

"You're the mind reader, Ms. Hamilton. You tell me."

She took a steadying breath. "I think your sister-in-law was right. You need rest, and I need to call the hotel."

"Don't worry about canceling the reservation. I'll take care of it."

"That's the problem. You *mustn't* do that."

His eyes opened. He seemed very alert all of a sudden.

"Why not? If I'm to be confined over the next few days, it makes the most sense."

"The hotel is simply a place to sleep." She tried reasoning with him. "I'll be available to you at all hours otherwise."

The tension was mounting. "What aren't you telling me?"

She'd seen him in this mood before. He wouldn't give up until he had the answer he wanted. She'd learned from past experience it was pointless to try to thwart him.

"Someone else is staying with me."

His black eyes penetrated the distance between them. "Yanni?" he asked in a deceptively silken voice.

"No. His name is Michael. I don't think I've mentioned him before."

"No, I don't believe you have. Does this Michael appreciate the fact that you're here on business?"

"Yes. Of course. Please don't think that I was attempting to take advantage of your generosity. I'm willing to pay for the room personally." She didn't believe it was necessary to mention Michael's friends.

"Do you suppose he'll live if I ask you to stay here at the villa until I'm back to normal?"

Unless his pain was much worse, she couldn't understand why he sounded so surly. Under normal circumstances he never allowed any weakness to show.

Obviously the trade fair was even more important to him than he'd let on. It was only natural he didn't want anything to go wrong this close to the opening. The thing to do was placate him until he started feeling better and could walk around without too much discomfort.

When she thought about it, she realized he was used to having her in calling distance at the office. Oftentimes they sat across from each other at his desk to do business until late. She could see it would frustrate him to have to phone back and forth to the hotel.

"Apparently my request is causing you grief."

At the sarcastic comment, heat filled her cheeks. "Not at all!" she rushed to assure him. "I was just thinking that I have to get something from him."

"Leon can run by the hotel in the morning and pick up whatever it is you need, unless you require it tonight."

"Oh, no. I— It's a costume."

A half-smile broke the corner of his mouth. For some reason her comment had pleased him.

"Let me guess. For your television interview you're going to appear as Thessalonica, wife of the King of Macedonia."

She chuckled softly. "It's not for me. In any case I won't be going anywhere near the media."

"Who then?"

"The man in charge."

"If you're referring to me, I haven't been in charge of anything since you took over Mrs. Landau's job."

Not to be put off, she said, "You'll need to try it on first to make certain it fits properly before you appear on camera."

He stirred as if he were trying to get up, but then he slumped back. It revealed so much.

"You actually went to the trouble to find a costume for me?"

She swallowed hard. "I had it made."

After a pregnant silence, "Give me a clue."

"Well—you were a military commander of Thessalonica in the early fourth century."

"There were dozens of those." His voice grated.

"This one was appointed by the Emperor Maximian to take his place."

"As I recall, Maximian persecuted Christians."

"That's right, but this commander was a defender of Christ. For defying the emperor he was cast into prison. Then an angel of God came to him and told him to be brave. A few days later he was martyred and became a saint."

Another silence ensued. Much longer this time. He'd guessed who it was.

Before she could hear him say it, there was a rap on the door. Then the housekeeper appeared with a tray. Behind her came Ananke and Leon, followed by a bearded, middle-aged man carrying a doctor's bag.

"So, Dimitrios. I hear you received a big bump on your head. Let me take a look at it."

Alex stood up to leave.

"Sit down and eat, Ms. Hamilton," Dimitrios ordered her.

The doctor winked at her. "Dimitrios never did make a good patient. Since he has spoken, you'd better obey."

The housekeeper set the tray down on the table, then left while the other two stood waiting to hear what the doctor had to say. Alex had little choice but to abide by her boss's wishes.

After checking Dimitrios's vital signs, the doctor asked Leon to bring him some warm water from the bathroom. He explained he was going to clean the wound.

As he examined it he said, "Tell me how this happened."

"Ms. Hamilton knows more about it than I do," came the wry response.

Everyone looked at Alex, who had to finish swallowing her bite of sandwich before she could say anything.

"As he was coming back to his seat, the plane hit an air pocket. His body flew, and his head hit the wall of the plane knocking him unconscious." It was still distressing to recall the incident, let alone talk about it.

"Hmm. Considering what you've been through, Dimitrios, you seem in amazingly good shape. But I don't doubt you've got a concussion.

"I'm not going to give you anything for the pain yet. Someone will have to watch you for the next twelve hours. If you become ill or sleep too long, then you'll have to be brought to my office for an X ray.

"However, if all goes well, and I think it will, by noon tomorrow you can start to eat and drink what sounds good to you. You'll be dizzy for a time. Don't try to overdo when you first get up. Call me if you have any questions."

He closed his doctor bag and started to leave. Ananke accompanied him to the door. "I'll stay with him."

"I'll trade off with you, Mother."

"I appreciate both your offers, but Ms. Hamilton has already agreed to sit up with me."

His declaration shocked everyone, especially Alex, who almost fell off the chair at the lie.

"She slept most of the way over on the plane," he continued. "Now that she's awake and I'm too dizzy to go sleep, we'll be able to get our work done without interruption."

"But you can't expect your secretary—"

"My secretary has the entire responsibility of the trade fair on her shoulders, Ananke," he cut in. "She needs tonight to go over the details with me. If I should suddenly lose consciousness, she's perfectly capable of letting you know. Isn't that true, Ms. Hamilton?"

The tension in the room was unbearable. There were strange undercurrents Alex couldn't begin to understand. His nephew looked confused and hurt. Along with an angry look at Alex, his sister-in-law reflected her son's feelings. Unfortunately Dimitrios was waiting for an answer.

"Yes, of course."

CHAPTER FOUR

ALEX felt tremendous guilt to hear the bedroom door close behind Leon and Ananke.

"Don't worry, they're going to be fine," Dimitrios murmured. "There are things I know that you don't. Tonight I'm not up to anything but a little peace and quiet. With you here to be my own guardian angel, I'll be assured of the rest I crave."

One glance at the lines of strain around his nose and mouth and she could tell his energy was spent. No doubt at this point he was starting to feel other aches and pains.

She slid out of the chair and turned off all the lights, hoping it would help. The sigh that escaped his throat told her she'd done the right thing. Taking advantage of the dark, she removed her glasses and put them on the table.

"This is almost as cozy as the plane. I don't suppose you'd come over here and hold my head again."

Alex was surprised by his banter, but she knew how awful it was to be dizzy. Combined with unrelieved pain, he had to be in a terrible state. She wished she could do what her mother did when her father suffered from a severe migraine.

If Alex had the temerity, she would sit next to him and use the tips of her fingers to tickle his face until he fell asleep. First his forehead, then across his brows and eyelids, down his straight nose to his mouth.

Though it was dark, it wasn't pitch black by any

means. Alex was able to use her eyes for fingers. She imagined tracing a line over every masculine feature and plane of a face that was so beautiful to her.

An hour must have passed before she saw the drawn look around his mouth relax. He was finally asleep. She found a light blanket and put it over him.

For the rest of the night she kept a constant vigil. Every so often she checked his pulse and felt to see if he was running a temperature.

Fearful he might go into too deep a sleep, she listened carefully for any change of sound in his breathing. At one point the urge to touch him was so strong, she smoothed the black curls off his forehead before sitting in the chair she'd pulled next to him. The joy of taking care of him was inexplicable.

At five to ten, the sun spread spokes of light across the bed through the shutters. As she leaned over once more to check his pulse, his eyelids opened.

He caught her hand with surprising strength before she could remove it. Though she hadn't escaped in time for him to realize what she'd been doing, it proved he'd passed through the period of crisis without problem.

His black eyes glanced at the chair, then seemed to look straight into her soul. "You sat next to me all night?"

"Yes." Fearful he'd get the wrong idea she said, "I told you before you went to sleep, you're the most important person in Thessalonica. If anything had gone wrong during the night, I wanted to be prepared to handle it in case your doctor needed to be phoned. We couldn't afford for the media to know anything."

As an afterthought she blurted, "Fortunately this

morning your pupils don't look dilated, so I'm assuming you're feeling better.''

"I'm still a little dizzy, but I only see one pair of green eyes this morning instead of three.''

Alex trembled that he'd even noticed her eyes, but she didn't dare take it personally.

"That's a very good sign you're on your way to a full recovery.'' Hard as it was to separate herself from him, she moved the chair to the table. "Your family's going to be delighted with the news.''

"Unfortunately I'm not delighted to see how exhausted you are,'' came the less than flattering remark, underlining her belief that his comment about her eyes held no significance whatsoever.

"I catnapped here and there. Do you feel ready for something to eat or drink?''

"Like you, I'm ravenous, and could swallow a gallon of that sage tea with honey.'' He sounded like he meant it.

"Let me find your housekee—''

"You're going to bed!'' he interrupted her. "I'll ring the kitchen and ask them to send us trays. They'll deliver one to your room. Then I want you to sleep for as long as you need to. We'll talk business later in the day when you're up and feeling refreshed.''

She was his secretary and had been banished to the guest bedroom. It was the surest sign that he was once more in command.

Without further words passing between them, she left his room and shut the door. At the click, she felt a death knell in her heart because those precious moments of intimacy while he'd been at his most vulnerable would never come her way again.

A few minutes later she stood beneath a hot shower, attempting to shut out her mother's warning. But it was too late.

I'm afraid for you to go to Greece. It can only put you on a more intimate footing with him without getting anything back in return.

Dimitrios moved slowly to reach for the phone. His housekeeper sounded relieved he was well enough to eat. He told her to send one breakfast tray to the guest room and another to his bedroom.

After he hung up, he realized Ms. Hamilton must have covered him with a blanket during the night.

She'd done more than that. He'd felt her fingers like little angel wings brushing his forehead. Though it was hours since the experience, he could still feel her touch. So soft…yet it had electrified him. He'd actually wanted to pull her down on the bed next to him and…

Lord. The accident on the plane must have done something more serious to him than he'd thought. Never in all these years had he been tempted to break his vow and take a woman to bed.

Frustrated and shocked by feelings of desire for his secretary, of all women, he made another vow that he wouldn't allow her to disturb him again.

Carefully pushing the blanket aside, he got off the bed. The action reminded him he'd hurt his shoulder. He winced while he clung to the nightstand, waiting for his equilibrium to return.

Every muscle in his body ached, but at least he was standing on his own. It didn't surprise him to hear a knock on the door. Everyone else would have been up for several hours.

"Uncle? Serilda said you called for breakfast. Can I come in?"

"Of course."

His nephew rushed over the threshold. He looked worried to see Dimitrios standing by the bed. "Should you be up yet?"

"I'm all right."

"That's a great relief. Let me help you into the shower."

"Tell you what. Stay close by while I try to make it on my own."

It was a struggle, but he managed without having to rely on his nephew for support.

"Be careful, Uncle. The doctor said not to get your head wet for another day."

"Thank you for the reminder."

The hot spray felt good on his sore shoulder. Deciding to forgo a shave, he dressed in a clean robe. By the time he'd joined his nephew for breakfast, he was feeling reasonably normal except for certain memory flashes. He could still remember being held in her arms on the plane, of being touched when she'd thought him asleep.

"I hope Ms. Hamilton didn't allow you to stay up too late."

Dimitrios finished off his orange juice in one swallow. When he put the empty glass down he said, "You don't have to worry. She's that rare secretary who anticipates my every need." It would be too much to hope she would repeat last night's experience tonight.

Once again it dawned on Dimitrios he was entertaining thoughts that had no place being there. He groaned at his lack of mental discipline. Damn if the room didn't spin when he moved his head too fast.

"I'm glad you're so much better, Uncle."

That was debatable. But a few minutes later, after he'd consumed a cheese omelette and butter biscuits, he felt ready to take care of a little personal business.

"I might have an errand for you to run. Afterward, we'll go out on the terrace with your mother and talk. Would you mind handing me my cell phone? It's in my suit jacket hanging on the chair. I'll also need the phone directory."

"Don't move. I'll get everything."

Once his nephew gave him both items, he looked up the number of the hotel and called reception.

"Mediterranean Palace. *Kalimera.*"

"*Kalimera.* This is Dimitrios Pandakis. Put me through to Ms. Hamilton's suite, please. It's booked in my name."

"Mr. Pandakis! We heard you'd had an accident."

"A small one, but I'm fine."

"I'm pleased to hear it. Just a moment and I'll put you through."

"Thank you."

On the third ring, a man speaking English answered the phone. "Better late than never, Alexandra, darling. What happened? I was beginning to wonder if Zeus had whisked you off to parts unknown in that private jet of his, never to be seen again."

Dimitrios felt a negative rush of adrenaline. "This is Dimitrios Pandakis. Sorry to disappoint you. Ms. Hamilton is staying at my villa for the moment. This *is* Michael, I presume."

"That's right."

"My secretary's asleep, but I'm sure she'll be in touch

with you as soon as she wakens. She mentioned a costume. Do you have it with you?''

''Yes.''

''I'll be sending my nephew for it within the half hour. His name is Leon Pandakis.''

''If you'll tell your nephew to meet me at the front desk, I'll wait there for him.''

''How will he know you?''

''I'll be carrying a golden scepter in one hand.''

He clutched his phone tighter. *She'd really had a costume of Saint Dimitrios made for him?*

''Thank you, Michael.''

''You're welcome, Mr. Pandakis.''

After the line went dead he felt the childish urge to knock the man's block off. What the heck was wrong with him?

''Uncle? Are you all right? Are you nauseous?''

He eyed Leon, unable to explain to himself, let alone his nephew, the unsettling mixture of emotions running through him.

''No. Do me a favor and run by the Mediterranean Palace. There'll be a man who's a friend of Ms. Hamilton's waiting in the lobby. He'll be carrying a costume. You'll recognize him because he'll be holding a gold scepter.''

''That sounds interesting. I'll go right away.''

''Thank you, Leon. On your way out will you ask one of the maids to bring me the morning paper?''

He nodded. ''Promise me you won't move while I'm gone.''

''You have my word.''

As soon as his nephew left, he phoned Stavros, who sounded touchingly emotional to hear that Dimitrios was on the mend after his accident. Apparently the whole family had heard about the plane mishap over the morning news and were worried about him.

Dimitrios rushed to assure him he was fine. During the course of their conversation, Serilda brought him the newspaper, then slipped out of the bedroom with his empty tray.

It was just as his secretary had predicted. The pilot's call to the hospital had made front-page headlines. Damn the media.

He tossed the paper aside in disgust. In a foul mood, he told Stavros he'd call him later. After they hung up, he knew he ought to ring Vaso, at least, but he couldn't bring himself to do it.

The way the man named Michael had answered the phone—"Alexandra, darling"—not even waiting to find out if she was the person calling had set his teeth on edge.

Dimitrios couldn't help but wonder how soon Yanni would show up in Thessalonica. Where and when was Ms. Hamilton planning to meet *him*?

His secretary was going to be stretched pretty thin to accommodate both men and do her job at the same time.

Though she'd never done anything to disappoint him or make him angry, it pleased him to know she was in the guest bedroom sleeping alone for a change. He wagered neither man would be happy to learn she'd spent last night with him.

Would she tell either of them the exact nature of her ministrations, and why? Or was she a tease? He supposed it was possible his perfect secretary was as deceitful as the next woman when it came to a man. It would be well to keep that in mind.

"I'm back!"

His nephew entered the room for the second time that morning carrying a garment bag over one arm and a golden scepter in the other. He laid everything on the unmade bed.

"I see you found Michael."

"He was impossible to miss. I think he was a little worried because this was supposed to be a surprise for you."

"My secretary already told me about it."

"I don't think he realized that. He was nice. So American, you know? But really funny."

Dimitrios could have done without Leon's favorable observations. On the other hand, he had no right to criticize anything. After all, he'd sent his nephew on that errand for the specific purpose of learning more about the man Ms. Hamilton would be sharing a room with while she was in Greece.

If his curiosity over his secretary didn't stop, Dimitrios was going to be in deep trouble.

"Do you know what it is, Uncle?"

The question brought him back from plaguing thoughts. "I have a fairly good idea."

"Shall I unzip the bag for you?"

"Under the circumstances, I think I'll let my secretary do the honors when she wakes up."

"Is it for you?"

"I'm afraid so."

His nephew grinned. "She certainly doesn't know you very well if she thinks she can get you to wear a costume to the fair."

You'd be shocked if you knew how well she reads my

*mind, Leon. That's the problem. That's why she's man-
aged to get under my skin without my realizing it.*

"It's the thought that counts," Dimitrios muttered. "I
presume your mother is up."

"Hours ago."

"Then let's find her. On our way out, would you mind
hanging the costume in my closet?"

"I'll do it right now."

It couldn't be six in the evening! But it was.

Anxious to find out how her host was feeling, Alex
sprang from the bed, incredulous that she'd slept so long
again. Her body clock was completely off kilter.

Luckily she'd had a shower before going to bed. Once
she was dressed in one of her matronly suits, it was her
hair that took time to fix. While she stood in front of the
bathroom mirror, she remembered leaving her glasses in
his bedroom.

Alarmed because anyone looking through the lenses
would know they were clear glass, she realized how vital
it was to get them back as soon as possible. It would
provide her with a good excuse to check up on Dimitrios
at the same time. But before she did anything else, she
needed to make a couple of important phone calls.

To her chagrin, Michael and his friends weren't in the
hotel room. She left a message welcoming them to
Thessalonica. After explaining that she'd have to stay at
the villa another night because her boss had met with a
minor accident, she assured Michael she'd be in touch
tomorrow morning.

With that done, she phoned her parents, who were
greatly relieved to know she was all right. Word of the

plane mishap that had injured Mr. Pandakis had even made the news in Paterson.

She didn't let on that she hadn't spent the first night at her hotel. Though she knew her mom would understand if told about the unusual circumstances, it would still worry her. It was better to say nothing until she could leave the villa.

She hung up with the promise that she'd phone them sometime tomorrow. She hoped by then she'd be at the hotel.

With the calls out of the way, she left the guest room and went down the hall to his suite. She knocked, wondering if he was inside.

"The door's open."

Hearing his deep voice made her heart leap. She pushed on it and entered.

He was sitting on top of his bed with his back against the headboard, listening to the news coming from the television. Her gaze traveled from his sandaled feet to the white sailor pants and royal blue knit shirt. The kind with the short sleeves and ribbing that looked good only on a man with some muscle.

She swallowed hard because Dimitrios's arms were darkly tanned and as powerful looking as his legs. If she could paint him like this she'd entitle it, Zeus Reflecting.

Embarrassed to be caught staring, she reached for her glasses, which were still sitting on the coffee table.

He'd improved a great deal since morning. His color had returned. She was pleased to see that the bruised look beneath his eyes had almost disappeared. It made her wonder at her temerity in touching him as she'd done last night.

With a flick of the remote, he turned off the television

and studied her. "You look rested, Ms. Hamilton. Come all the way in. Dinner will be here before long. In the meantime, we have work to do."

She reached for her briefcase and walked over to the coffee table. "You must be feeling better."

"I'm getting there. You said you'd made a copy for me of the countdown of events."

"Yes. But should you use your eyes yet? Reading might be bad for your headache."

"I've read the morning and evening papers from cover to cover and feel none the worse for it."

He sounded out of sorts. Some people didn't have as hard a time as others staying down while they were convalescing. Dimitrios was one of those others. Her boss was about as happy as a restless panther trapped inside a cage, going around and around the bars looking for a way to escape.

She dove into her briefcase and found the wanted item. "Here you are." After putting it on the bed next to him, she pulled out her laptop.

Once she'd set the computer on her thighs and turned it on, she brought up the file in question. "If you want to start, I'm ready to make any changes."

"Bring your chair closer so we don't have to shout at each other."

Alex wasn't aware they'd been shouting. In fact he'd just spoken to her in a low voice, and she'd been able to hear him perfectly. But she did as he suggested.

Lifting her head in anticipation of what he would ask to be added or deleted, her attention was caught by the sight of a gold scepter lying across the quilt next to the footboard of the bed. She hadn't noticed it when she'd entered his bedroom.

Her questioning gaze darted to her boss. He, in turn, eyed her with a complacent expression that didn't fool her.

"I found I wanted to see it," he confessed, "so I sent Leon to the hotel this morning. Michael met him in the lobby with it."

Uh, oh.

Had Dimitrios learned there were two actors staying there, as well? Not that he would have cared. It was just that she hadn't mentioned the others, and she didn't want any unnecessary talk to go on.

"Your doctor wasn't kidding when he said you made a terrible patient. If I'd known you were going to be so bored today, I would have asked Stavros to come over and keep you company."

Still worked, up she added, "Something tells me you were the kind of little boy who sneaked a look at your Christmas presents long before it was time to open them."

"Guilty on all counts."

Alex took a deep breath, willing herself to calm down. "What do you think of it?"

"I haven't seen it yet. Leon hung the garment bag in my closet. I thought I'd wait until you unveiled it before my eyes."

"Considering you went to such lengths to get it, I'm puzzled you would show that much forbearance."

"Some surprises are worth savoring."

She was stunned that he would have bothered with any of it.

"To be honest, I haven't seen it myself. I gave the seamstress a sketch months ago. It wasn't ready until the last second, so Michael picked it up for me."

"Why don't we have a sneak preview before dinner."

"I thought you wanted to work."

"Indirectly, I would say a costume to promote publicity for the fair falls under that particular umbrella."

Her hands tightened on her laptop before she got up and put it on the coffee table.

Certain things in life were private. If she were his fiancée or his wife, she couldn't imagine anything more wonderful than having the right to be in his bedroom, rummaging around in his walk-in closet, handling his clothes.

This was the danger her mother had talked about. To share all this with him—*except the most important thing*.

"What color is the bag?" she called to him.

"Dark blue."

He had a good size wardrobe, and she saw several bags matching that description. Before looking inside each one, she decided to open the floor-length cupboard. Maybe Leon had hung it in there so it would be easier to find again.

What she discovered caused her to forget why she was in there. Both sections contained boxes full of trophies, plaques and cups lying in haphazard fashion, some large, some small. Dozens of them.

One thing was clear from some of the trophies depicting a man in climbing gear with a pickax. He was an expert mountaineer.

Most of the engravings were in foreign languages, including Greek, but a few were in English. He'd climbed all over the world. There were dates going back fifteen years, yet there was one as recent as this year.

She remembered a trip he'd taken in June. He said he'd be out of the office a week and she wouldn't be able to reach him unless he phoned her. If there was a problem, she should consult Stavros.

He'd returned with a deep tan. Alex had assumed he'd gone sailing on the Aegean or some such thing. She had no idea the mountains were his great love.

"You haven't lost your way in there, have you, Ms. Hamilton?"

She shut the cupboard abruptly. "I'll be right out."

Without wasting any more time, she felt the bags until she found one that she could tell didn't contain a man's suit jacket.

Emerging from the closet, she walked over to her chair and unzipped it. A soft gasp escaped her throat when she held it up and saw what a fabulous job the seamstress had done.

Faithful to the colored sketch Alex had made from the well-known Greek icon depicting Saint Dimitrios on his horse, the short-sleeved, hip-length vest was authentic in every detail.

She found a pair of dark gold braided boot covers in the bottom of the bag. They were meant to hide his shoes and hug the trousers to his legs at a point above the calves.

Along with the boots, Cossack-style rust trousers and a great flowing ruby cape completed the outfit.

"Bring everything closer."

She did his bidding. "You have to visualize yourself on horseback wearing all this and carrying your scepter, of course." He would look magnificent.

One black eyebrow lifted. "Did you arrange for a mount, too? Am I to be interviewed on the back of it?"

No amount of self-control could hide the blush that swept up her neck and face.

On cue a knock sounded at the door causing Alex's head to swerve around.

"Uncle? I've brought your dinner." The next thing she knew Leon came into the room wheeling a tea cart laden with food. "I hope you're hungry because the cook outdid—"

He paused mid-sentence when he saw her standing next to the bed holding up the costume.

"I'm sorry. I didn't mean to interrupt."

"It's all right, Leon. My secretary was just showing me what she had made for me to wear for the initial television interview to open the trade fair. What do you think?"

Leaving the cart, his nephew stepped closer to examine everything. His brown eyes moved in fascination from one item to the other, then he looked at her with a dumbfounded expression.

"This is fabulous," he whispered. "You picked his namesake."

"I told you she was clever, Leon."

"But Uncle, this is really fantastic!" He kept looking at it, then at her.

"Do me another favor and try it on so I can see what I'll look like in it."

"That's a wonderful idea," Alex encouraged him. "You're almost the same height as your uncle. If something's wrong, I'll be able to get the alterations done in time."

He took the costume from her. "How did you know about Saint Dimitrios?"

"I love European art history."

"So do I! It's too bad you can't see some of the icons

and stained glass windows in the monasteries on Mount Athos.''

''That's the holy mountain where women aren't allowed.''

''You know that, too?''

She smiled. ''I would suppose every woman who has studied Greece has heard of it. I think it's sad only men get to see its beauties. If it weren't for women, those monks would never have been given life in the first place.

''In fact I think it's sad they can't marry and worship at the same time. They miss out on so much. Can you imagine never watching the birth of your own baby?''

She'd said the last without thinking. Between the way Dimitrios's face darkened, combined with the hostile glance Leon suddenly flashed his uncle, she knew her words had been offensive to both men.

Leon's eyes slid away from hers. ''If you'll both excuse me, I've just remembered something I have to do.'' He handed the things back to her and strode out of the room.

Alex felt sick.

Leon was always so polite and deferential in front of his uncle. For him to leave like that meant she'd really affronted him.

''I'm so sorry.''

''For what, Ms. Hamilton? Speaking your mind?''

She shook her head. ''I'm the one who drove him away with my remarks. I meant no irreverence, but I'm sure that's how they sounded to him.'' *And you.*

''If you must know, he's at a crossroads in his life and feeling it. His hasty departure from the room had nothing to do with you. Personally I find your opinions refreshing. Now I think we'd better eat dinner before it grows cold. Perhaps by the time we've finished, Leon will come back to say good-night and we can prevail on him to model that fabulous costume for us.''

Dimitrios was doing his best to shield her because that was his nature, but it was clear her comments had upset both him and his nephew. What Alex would give if there'd been no accident. She'd be at the hotel right now where she belonged.

After laying the things on the end of the bed, she pushed the cart next to Dimitrios. All he had to do was put his feet on the floor. But her heart was heavy because she knew Leon wouldn't make another appearance to-night, at least not in front of her.

Even if it meant defying her boss, she would leave tomorrow morning to inspect the silk exhibits in Soufli. Being so close to Dimitrios had caused her to lose all perspective.

With the opening of the trade fair only two days away, she needed to focus on that and make sure everything was ready. Afterward, she would return to Thessalonica and check into the hotel.

She needed other people. Michael and his friends would provide laughter and camaraderie. As soon as Yanni arrived, he could join in. With their help she'd make it through this bittersweet experience. *She had no choice.*

CHAPTER FIVE

DIMITRIOS awoke the next morning feeling much more his old self. Although he was still sore here and there, the dizziness had pretty well disappeared.

He realized he hadn't been in his right mind for the last few days where his secretary had been concerned. Determined to reestablish professional distance with her, he started out the day by asking Serilda to send breakfast trays to their separate rooms.

Now that he'd showered and dressed, he was anxious to get to the office. He hoped Ms. Hamilton was ready to go.

When he entered the dining room looking for Leon, he found Ananke eating breakfast alone. He greeted her before asking why his nephew hadn't joined her. She looked at him with wounded eyes.

"Did you think he would stay around after the way you hurt him yesterday?"

He poured himself a cup of coffee from the buffet, then stood staring at her while he drank. "What exactly did he tell you?"

"That you had discussed his personal life with your secretary, and she'd had the nerve to offer her opinion as if it were her right!" Her voice shook. "You know how he adores you. How could you betray him like that?" she cried.

"Aside from the fact that I've never discussed Leon

79

with Ms. Hamilton, it might interest you to know she's on your side without realizing it.''

Ananke's eyes rounded. "What do you mean?"

In a few words he told her what had happened. "Her opinion obviously hit a nerve, otherwise he wouldn't have left the room so fast." As far as Dimitrios was concerned, it was exactly the kind of thing his nephew needed to hear before he made a final decision about his future.

"Nevertheless you can see why Leon's so upset," Ananke persisted. "Since you came from New York, you've been virtually inaccessible."

Even Ananke had picked up on his preoccupation with Ms. Hamilton. *Damn.* Well, that was over now.

He finished his coffee. "I recall spending part of yesterday afternoon with you and my nephew."

"But nothing was resolved!"

"We have to give him time to talk this out, Ananke. Maybe that's all he needs to realize this is a phase that will pass."

The irony of those words weren't wasted on Dimitrios when he considered his own alarming state of mind since he'd left New York. His interest in Ms. Hamilton better be a phase.

Ananke jumped up from the chair. "There's something different about you since your return."

No one knows that better than I do.

"If I'm different, it's because I'm feeling the weight of a father's responsibility without being a father. Perhaps it's time you knew that my brother never wanted to be a part of the family business, either."

She shook her head. "That's not true!"

"I wouldn't lie to you. Leon always preferred to be out-of-doors."

"Surely you're not saying he would rather have had a career in forestry than work for the Pandakis Corporation!" Her angry laugh resounded in the room.

"I have no idea how his life would have turned out had he lived." His voice grated. *Thanks to you, we'll never know.* "The point is, my nephew shows the same lack of interest in business as his father."

A stricken look crossed her face. "You're so cold, Dimitrios. Don't you care that he might leave us for good?"

"You already know the answer to that question. But forcing something that goes against his nature will only push him in the opposite direction that much faster."

"You wouldn't say that if he were *our* son."

"If Leon were my son and I'd been the one who'd died—" he spoke without acknowledging her attempt to personalize the situation "—I'd like to believe my brother would have listened to him, guided him as much as possible, then let him come to his own conclusions. Fortunately he hasn't made a definite decision yet."

He checked his watch. "We'll have to continue this conversation another time. My secretary and I need to get to the office."

"She already left."

His head reared back. The sudden movement reminded him of his recent head injury. "When?"

"I saw her leave in a taxi half an hour ago."

If he didn't miss his guess, Michael had asked her to come to the hotel room before her workday began. Dimitrios felt like he'd just been kicked in the gut.

"If Leon wants to talk, tell him to call me on my cell phone. I'll see you later."

He left the dining room and rang Kristofor to bring the car around. While he waited, he phoned his secretary on her cell phone. If the call came at an inopportune moment for her, he didn't particularly care.

To his surprise she answered on the second ring. "Hello?"

"Good morning, Ms. Hamilton."

"Mr. Pandakis. How are you feeling?" She sounded bright.

He gritted his teeth, trying to shut out certain pictures in his mind. "Well enough to be headed for my office. Shall I swing by the hotel and pick you up?"

"I—I didn't realize you meant to go into work today," she stammered.

Obviously not.

Attempting to tamp down his anger, he said, "Does that present a problem for you?"

"Actually it does."

Dimitrios inhaled sharply. "When can I expect you?"

"Tomorrow morning? You see, I was under the impression you needed to convalesce one more day, so I thought this would be the perfect time to visit Soufli and check out preparations. My flight's just been called."

"You're at the airport?" he demanded incredulously.

"Yes. It's one of those commuter planes we've advertised for the trade fair. After it lands in Alexandroupolis, I'll rent a car to drive the rest of the way. So far everything's working perfectly. If the car is at the airport waiting for me as I requested, then I don't foresee any problems for the fair attendees.

"I'll check each silk exhibition en route. In case there

are any glitches, we'll have time to sort them out tomorrow. I'll return on the first flight back to Thessalonica in the morning and report straight to your office.''

No boss could ask for more than that from his secretary. She gave a thousand percent all of the time. He had no right to be upset with her. No right at all.

''That's fine,'' he muttered, still trying to recover from the shock of realizing she wasn't anywhere in the villa. ''Keep in touch with me.''

''Yes, of course. I'm sorry, Mr. Pandakis, but I have to board now or they're going to close the gate. Goodbye.'' She clicked off.

Goodbye? Her cheery tone irritated the hell out of him.

If his secretary thought she'd seen the last of him until tomorrow, she had another think coming.

Using his phone once more, he canceled the car, then sent for the helicopter. While it was coming, he made one more call, to a lodge in Dadia requesting two rooms for the night. After that was accomplished, he returned to his bedroom for some additional clothes and his backpack.

One thing he knew about Ms. Hamilton. She would never lie to him, but that didn't mean she'd gone to Soufli alone. If joining her meant he interrupted something private, then so be it.

Alex walked through the Alexandroupolis terminal to the car rental counter where she'd arranged for transportation.

Everywhere she looked, whether in or outside the terminal, she saw flags and banners advertising the trade fair. It had been the same at the airport in Thessalonica.

There was a sense of festivity in the air that seemed to have affected everyone except her.

Two nights of living in close proximity to Dimitrios had created a physical ache for him that wasn't about to go away. For her own good, she'd wrenched herself from the villa early this morning in order not to see him.

She thought she'd escaped him until she'd heard his deep, familiar voice on the phone at the airport. Now she was in more pain than before. It was absolutely vital she leave her job the second the trade fair was over.

While waiting to board her flight, she'd phoned her mother to let her know she was all right. She'd kept their conversation brief. As for Michael, she'd finally been able to connect with him.

It sounded like he and the guys were having a terrific time. But when he wanted to talk about the costume and Dimitrios, she told him she had to go and would debrief after her return from Soufli.

"*Kalimera.* My name is Alex Hamilton. I requested a car?" She displayed her passport.

The employee was all smiles. "It's the black four-door right outside the building at the curb," he said in beautiful English. "You can't miss it because it has our company logo on the back window."

"Thank you." When nothing else was forthcoming she said, "May I have the key?"

"We have provided you with an English speaking driver."

"Oh. I had no idea."

She shouldn't have been surprised. The Pandakis name insured outstanding service. Dimitrios was a very special man, and no one knew that more than Alex.

There were women he dated who would have fought

to be first at his side had they known about the accident, yet he'd insisted on Alex's attentions. Looking after him all night had bonded her to him in a brand-new way.

But she had to face the fact that if he'd preferred her company for the last two nights, even over that of his own sister-in-law, it was because he'd known he didn't have to pretend in front of his secretary.

Dimitrios paid her a fantastic salary to do whatever was needed and place no demands on him. She might as well be another man for all the interest he took in her as a woman.

"Enjoy your trip to Soufli."

The man's parting comment brought her back from her torturous thoughts. "I'm sure I will."

With her suitcase in one hand, her briefcase in the other, she made her way out of the busy terminal.

As she approached the lane where a string of cars were idling, she noticed there were quite a few black ones mixed in with the others. Not certain which of them was hers, she started down the queue searching for the rental agency's logo.

"Alexandra?" came a vibrant male voice from behind her.

She spun around in surprise to hear her name, then almost fainted to discover who it was.

"Dimitrios—"

Alex had been thinking so hard about him, the word slipped out before she realized she'd said it. He was wearing sunglasses, a rare sight, but after his accident she assumed his eyes were still sensitive to the light.

"It's nice to hear you say my name," he drawled.

Suddenly she was out of breath. "I—I don't know what you mean."

His white smile dazzled her. "It's one thing to be formal in front of other people, but it's long past the time we functioned on a first name basis in private. Don't you agree?"

He took the cases from her hands and put them in the back seat of the car. While she watched, it dawned on her he was really here. To make things even more difficult for her, he was such an attractive Greek male, she couldn't look anywhere else.

The sage-colored summer suit with a white, open-necked silk shirt brought out the blackness of his hair and olive-toned skin. She had the overwhelming urge to hold him as she'd done on the plane when she'd cradled his head and shoulders in her lap.

"Why didn't you tell me you were coming while we were on the phone?" This wasn't the way this day was supposed to go, yet she was so thrilled to see him, she could hardly stand it.

"It was a last-minute decision. Rather than work at my office alone, I thought it might be more fun to join you while we both test the system for flaws." He opened the passenger door for her.

Fun?

Alex didn't know what to think. He'd teased her before, but never to this extent.

Averting her eyes, she climbed in the front seat. After he'd shut the door and had gone around to the driver's seat she asked, "Should you have flown anywhere this soon after your accident?"

He turned the key in the ignition, revving the engine. "Do I detect a note of pique in my secretary? I promise I won't bother you while we make our inspection."

"That isn't why I asked the question," she said in a

quiet voice. "I realize that without a command of your language, you were probably concerned I couldn't do this by myself. I just hope you won't suffer a relapse."

They pulled away from the curb and followed the exit signs. "If you're worried you'll have to nurse me halfway through the day, I promise I'm feeling fine."

"That's reassuring, especially when it's so close to the opening of the fair."

He didn't respond to her comment. Instead, he drove the car with the same expertise he did everything else. Before long they'd left the airport and were headed for Soufli, which according to her map was sixty-five kilometers away.

She sent him a furtive glance. It was still hard to believe he'd come all this distance when there were other things that needed his attention at his office.

He caught her looking at him. Her heart did a little kick. "Why did you bother to bring your suitcase, Alexandra?"

To hear him say her name with that slight trace of accent sent a ripple of forbidden excitement through her body.

"I didn't think I'd have enough time to visit all the exhibits and make it back to Thessalonica in one day, so I booked a room in Soufli for the night."

"Which hotel?"

"The Ilias."

"Considering the influx of tourists for the big event, I'm amazed they had anything available."

"I don't think they did. But as soon as I said your name, there was no problem."

At that remark he pulled his cell phone out of his suit jacket pocket and made a call. Except for words like hello and goodbye, it was impossible to follow his Greek. Curious to know who he was phoning, she waited for an explanation after he clicked off, but it never came.

Finally she couldn't stand it any longer. "Is everything all right?"

"It is now," came the mysterious reply.

She hated it when he refused to explain his actions, particularly in this case because she was afraid they had something to do with her. In order to get her mind off him, she studied her map. It was printed on the brochure the man at the car rental desk had given her when he'd handed back her passport.

"You see that little area outside Soufli?" He touched the spot with his index finger.

At his close proximity, she drew in an unsteady breath. "Yes."

"That's called Dadia. We'll be sleeping there tonight."

She bit the inside of her lip. "Have you forgotten the government dinner at the Dodona Palace this evening? I accepted for you a month ago."

"On my way here I told them I needed another twenty-four hours to convalesce from my accident. My cousin Vaso is going to attend in my place."

Alex turned her head to look out the side window. No matter which member of the illustrious Pandakis family was sent, the officials would be disappointed because it was Dimitrios they wanted. Instead, he was going to be with *her*.

If he didn't have worries about her being able to get around the country without his help, then the only other reason she could imagine him showing up like this was that he needed a legitimate excuse to put space between him and his nephew.

Maybe there'd been another unpleasant episode with Leon this morning, and Dimitrios hadn't recovered enough to deal with it yet. Ananke Pandakis hadn't said more than two words to her at breakfast.

Alex had wanted to ask the other woman to tell Leon how sorry she was for having offended him with her insensitive remarks. But the negative tension radiating from his mother had made conversation impossible. As soon as the taxi arrived, Alex had been only too glad to slip away from the villa.

"What should we do about the Ilias?"

"Don't worry. I canceled your reservation."

"Some desperate tourist is going to be very happy."

"But not you?"

He was playing the relentless inquisitor again. When he was like this, there was no stopping him.

"I'm perfectly content to spend the night anywhere, you know that. Is there something special about Dadia?"

"It's the forest that's famous. As a boy, I explored every centimeter of it with my brother."

"Your favorite place?" She couldn't help asking. His love of mountaineering must have been born there.

He nodded. "I've been back several times, but I haven't climbed to the top of Gibrena Peak since my brother Leonides died."

He'd spoken of his brother's death to Mrs. Landau, but this was the first time he'd mentioned it to Alex. Moved by his tone, her hands clutched together. "You'll see it through different eyes this time."

"That's true. You can't return and expect things to be the same. But knowing you and your passion for life, I shall enjoy watching your reaction. Tell me now if you didn't bring suitable clothing. There's a store in the village we're coming to where we can buy what you need.''

Panic gripped Alex in its vise.

"I—I didn't bring any walking clothes to Greece.''

"No problem.''

Perspiration broke out on her hairline. "Why don't you drop me off in Soufli to do my work? It will leave you free to visit your old haunt unencumbered. We can meet at the silk mansion in the morning for the trip back.''

"Have you forgotten your hotel room is gone?''

She shifted in the seat. "I'll find something else.''

"It's already noon. Too late in the day to make other arrangements.''

"Is it very steep in the forest?''

"I suppose that all depends on your definition of the word steep.''

"Can I explore it in this outfit and my sneakers, or are you talking about scaling walls?''

Deep-throated laughter rumbled out of him. "I'm not asking you to climb a mountain.''

"That's good.'' She could have wept in relief. "A picture of all those plaques and trophies in your closet flashed before my eyes. It almost gave me a heart attack.''

"So that explains why you took so long to find the garment bag.'' He was still chuckling.

Heat filled her cheeks. "I admit I'm a bit of a snoop.''

"I prefer to call it an inquiring mind. It's what makes you an irreplaceable secretary. If I haven't said it before, you've redefined the word for me, and I'm indebted to you, Alexandra.''

Whenever he said her name, he made it sound so beautiful.

"Thank you," she whispered in agony. A nagging voice cried, *Is it worth it to be the bridesmaid, but never the bride?*

"Tomorrow will be soon enough to inspect the exhibits. Today I'd like to reward you for all your hard work by showing you a national treasure. How does that appeal to you?"

Oh, Dimitrios. If you only knew. "That sounds lovely."

Convinced she'd arranged to spend the night with her American boyfriend, Dimitrios should have felt guilty for thwarting her plans. But heaven help him, all he could feel was a sense of elation that they were going to be alone together far from the horde.

Since they'd been driving, he hadn't heard her cell phone ring. For that matter, she hadn't tried to use it. He was surprised she didn't want to stop at a local shop, if only to excuse herself long enough to make contact with Michael.

Of course she could have planned to get in touch with him later in the day. Then again, maybe she was meeting her Greek boyfriend, and Michael didn't have a clue.

Dimitrios grimaced at the thoughts assailing him.

Was it possible Yanni had flown up from Athens? Why not enjoy a private interlude with her before she had to return to Thessalonica where her other lover was waiting for her at the hotel.

Did both men resent the time Dimitrios demanded of

her? The late nights at his office? The early-morning con-
ferences?

He wondered how Michael felt about having to pick
up the costume she'd had made for him, let alone be
asked to bring it all the way to Greece on the plane.

Had it upset him to learn she'd be staying at the villa
instead of the hotel? Or was he so sure of her, it would
never occur to him to worry what she was doing with
her employer.

If Dimitrios were in either man's shoes, the thought
of her making love to anyone but him caused a blackness
to sweep over him. The feeling was so staggering, so
powerful, it took him a minute to recognize it for what
it was.

"Shouldn't we have taken that turnoff for Dadia?"
Her voice seemed to come from far away.

"There'll be another one in a minute," he muttered,
still gripped by the sheer force of emotion too painfully
raw for him to shake off. Jealousy had never touched his
life until now.

*"Oh, Dimi—listen to me. You're barely twelve. Not
quite old enough for a man's feelings to have taken over
inside you yet. When that day comes, your body will react
when you see a beautiful woman. You'll want to hold
her, make love to her. The pleasure a woman can bring
you is to die for."*

Dimitrios struggled to control his rapid breathing.

The night she'd brushed those magic fingers of hers
across his forehead had brought him pleasure to die for.
The thought of those same fingers on his body tonight…

Lord. He was already so far out of control where she
was concerned, he didn't know what in the hell he was

going to do about the situation. He'd made reservations for two rooms, but the way he was feeling right now, one of them would be going to waste. Dimitrios couldn't believe he'd reached this point.

"Your cell phone's ringing," she reminded him.

There was no way he could talk to anyone right now. He handed it to her. "When you answer it, tell whoever it is I'll get back to them."

"It's coming from the villa. What if it's your nephew?"

She knew him too well. But the question drew his attention to the generous curve of her lips with their flare of passion.

When he'd awakened the morning after the accident to find her face mere inches from his, he remembered thinking she had a mouth nature had made without flaw.

"Shall I let it ring?"

He rubbed the back of his neck. "If it's Leon, I'll talk to him."

Except that as he listened, it became clear someone else had called. The conversation was over so fast, he realized it had to have been Ananke. These days she was so upset over Leon, she'd forgotten her manners.

After his secretary had clicked off she said, "That was your sister-in-law. She told me to tell you her son is no longer a student at the university. He just left the villa with his backpack and indicated he wouldn't be around for the family dinner tomorrow night."

That didn't surprise him. It was a knee-jerk reaction to punish Dimitrios for taking Alexandra into his confidence, or so Leon had thought. "What else did she say?"

"That was all, but she sounded…desolate." Her head

swerved in his direction. "I got the distinct impression she blames me that he's gone away so upset."

He changed into a lower gear so the car could begin its gradual ascent to the lodge. "My sister-in-law's one dream has been to see her son rise to the head of the Pandakis Corporation. What she forgot to remember is that Leon is capable of dreaming his own dreams.

"Whether they have substance or not, he thinks he wants to be a monk on Mount Athos. She's terrified of losing him."

"Oh, dear God— I'm so sorry—" The voice of the woman next to him shook with pain.

"Don't fall apart on me now, Alexandra. For him to run away because you happened to express an innocent opinion in his presence means he's more childish and immature than I thought."

She shook her head. "That's not it. He must have believed you'd confided his dream to me, a mere secretary. He couldn't help but think I was trying to influence him on your behalf. If I'd been in his shoes, I would have felt a trust had been broken, too."

Dimitrios had to clear his throat, not only because of her understanding and sensitivity of the problem, but because of her earnestness in trying to make him understand how badly she felt.

"He worships you!" she cried. "I saw it in his eyes and expression the moment he boarded the plane and found you suffering. And later at the villa, until I ruined everything, he was so excited to try on the costume for you."

"I love him very much, and appreciate what you're

saying, but I'm not blind to the fact that he's still very young for his age.''

''Age doesn't matter when you're not used to sharing the person you love with a stranger,'' she came back. ''I don't blame Ananke for being beside herself. If I could just tell Leon you bear no fault in this.''

''I appreciate your defense of me, Alexandra, but if my nephew can't see how petty he's being, then he's not ready to make life-changing decisions.''

''I think it's more a case of his being afraid he could never measure up to you. Perhaps he sees the monastery as a place where he won't have to try.''

He marveled at her ability to see through to the heart of a situation. Her mind was as exciting as everything else about her.

''My uncle Spiros used coercion on everyone in the family in order to have his will obeyed. Even my own father gave in to him out of fear. When I became Leon's guardian, I determined that was the one thing I would never do.''

''Perhaps you succeeded so well, it has led him to believe you don't think he's capable of following in your footsteps. Maybe it's your approval he's been waiting for to give him that final push in the right direction, but he never received it. If that's the case, then my comments to him would have come as a double blow.''

''What do you mean?'' Her understanding was rather astounding. He found himself anxious to hear what else she had to say.

''Have you told him straight out you don't want him to be a monk?''

''No.''

"Why not?"

"Because it's possible he has a true vocation."

"But don't you see—" She broke off talking.

He turned his head toward her. "Go on."

"I—I'm much too outspoken. It's none of my business."

"After what happened in my bedroom, I'd say you're very much involved. Finish what you were going to tell me."

She was making more sense than anyone he'd ever known. With every word that came from her mouth, he found himself more enamored of her.

"Maybe he took my remarks to mean that you don't think he'd make a very good monk, either. Coming from me, it must have been humiliating for him."

Good heavens. Was it possible she had hit on the truth?

He couldn't count the number of times Ananke had begged him to take Leon in hand. But all these years he'd shut his mind and heart to her entreaties because *she'd* been the one doing the pleading.

From the moment Leonides had told him he'd been trapped into a loveless marriage, Ananke had been emotionally dead to Dimitrios.

If Alexandra was even partially correct, then he'd done a terrible disservice to his nephew, who could be floundering. It made sense he'd gone off to lick his wounds.

Dimitrios struggled to contain emotions erupting inside him. To think Alexandra had applied for a job with him four years ago, yet only now was he beginning to understand what a true prize she was.

Without wasting any more time, he reached for the

phone to call Leon, but his nephew had turned off his cell phone. The only thing to do was leave a message.

"Leon?" he spoke in Greek. "Wherever you are, I hope you hear this in time. I thought I was recovered enough from my accident to take part in the opening ceremony of the trade fair. But I flew in the helicopter to inspect the silk exhibits and found out I'm still too dizzy to contemplate anything that vigorous.

"I need you home, preferably by tomorrow afternoon. Thank goodness for all the polo you played. You ride like you were born in the saddle. We can also be grateful you inherited your father's height and build. Besides me, you're the only other man in the family who could wear that costume Ms. Hamilton went to so much trouble to have made.

"You'll be leading the parade with a regiment of mounted soldiers. That means giving a speech on horseback while you're in front of the dignitaries' stand. You're the only Pandakis I'd trust to face the media with their cameras.

"After the many talks we've had, you know how important this trade fair is. I have every confidence you'll make all of Greece proud, especially your mother who has raised such a fine son."

Dimitrios could admit that much about Ananke. She'd been devoted to Leon.

"If you hear this message before I get home tomorrow afternoon, phone me and we'll talk."

He clicked off, anxious to find out what kind of response he would get from his nephew, if any. At least he'd taken the first step to rectify a situation he may have unwittingly created years ago. Unfortunately it might be too late if Leon had already shut down. Only time would tell.

Thanks to the wisdom of the woman seated next to him, Dimitrios had been given a fighting chance to make amends.

Right now he felt an urgency to get her strictly alone with him. What better spot than the pristine forest that lay ahead of them.

CHAPTER SIX

ALEX didn't know what Dimitrios had said to his nephew. But the expression on his face revealed a world of love and concern.

After he put the phone back in his pocket he said, "If Leon hears my message, he'll be under the impression I'm still too dizzy to ride in the parade. I told him he was the only Pandakis I trusted to stand in for me at the opening ceremony. We'll find out if he takes the bait."

She looked out the side window so he couldn't see her blinking back the tears. There were many ways to love a man. At sixteen, he'd been her handsome knight in shining armor who'd come to rescue her.

After she'd gone to work for his company, she'd learned to love him for his generosity to the staff. When she became his private secretary, she fell in love with his little foibles along with his most endearing traits. Above all, she admired that selfless quality about him which was rare in a man so influential.

Right now her heart was swollen with emotion because he hadn't been too proud to find a way to reach out to his troubled nephew.

The man had no vanity.

Alex loved him with a searing intensity that needed to find expression soon or she'd go mad trying to hold back her feelings.

She continued to stare out the window as the car wound through a small village on its climb to a more forested area. They passed a tiny white church sheltered by dark pines. There were cars all around it and a few people outside the doors in native dress. It had to be some kind of religious celebration.

She was on the verge of asking Dimitrios about it when he announced they'd come to the lodge.

Alex turned her head to the other side of the road in time to see a cluster of white buildings nestled in the trees. It looked deserted.

"After we've freshened up and changed, we'll walk to the top of the peak. From there you'll be able to see over the entire forest."

In such a remote place, this was going to be even more intimate than her stay at the villa.

"How long will it take?"

"The rest of the day." He drove up to the front of one of the buildings, which appeared to house a dining room. After he'd shut off the motor he said, "Is there a reason you're in such a hurry?"

A wry tone had entered his voice. Whenever he sounded like that, she knew he was probing for something. *But what?*

"Not at all. I just wondered if it might be too soon for you to exert yourself to that extent."

Her explanation was part lie, of course. Any time spent alone with him was too long because she kept falling deeper and deeper in love. On the other hand, she *was* worried that he hadn't fully recovered yet.

"Nothing relaxes me more than to get out in nature." He pulled off his sunglasses, revealing those penetrating black eyes to her gaze for the first time that day. "We both need a break from the stress before the fair begins."

So saying, he levered himself from the car and came

around to help her. When they went inside the reception area, the lodge keeper rushed to greet Dimitrios in Greek. He obviously knew him well.

While they conversed at some length, the man's wife brought them tea and biscuits. The repast tasted good. After they'd finished, she bid Alex to follow her from the office to one of the nearby cottages.

It turned out to be a pleasant room with an ensuite bathroom and three twin beds. Dimitrios came inside with her suitcase. He tipped the woman, then shut the door behind her.

Turning to Alex, he pinned her with his dark, level gaze. "I arranged for two rooms before I left Thessalonica this morning. However, the concierge just informed me that a problem has arisen and now there's only this one available. Apparently the granddaughter of the concierge and his wife is being married today, and they're expecting more family."

"In that little church we just passed?" she cried in delight.

He nodded. "The wedding party is staying here for the night, so the lodge is closed to the public."

She smiled to herself. "But there's always a room for you."

"Because I serve on the eco council for special preserves like this throughout Greece, an accommodation is usually made available if a member is in the area."

He served on many boards, but being his New York assistant, she hadn't heard of this one. It seemed that every day in his presence meant she learned something new about him.

"*How* special?"

His eyes gleamed. "If we're lucky, you're going to

find out. Don't worry about tonight. I brought my bed-roll. After we have dinner, I plan to sleep in the forest. Excuse me for a moment and I'll bring in my things.''

Once he left the room, Alex stood there immobilized with fresh pain.

Given the unexpected circumstances, any other man might have tried to take advantage of the situation. Not Dimitrios. The night of the accident he'd wanted her to stay with him to help run interference. But now that he was recovered, it didn't occur to him to ask her to share the room with him.

She had to admit it wasn't anyone's fault but hers. Michael had created this persona for her. One that made her blend into the woodwork.

Alex blended all right. So well, in fact, that Dimitrios saw her as one of the guys. She could be Stavros for all he cared.

Of course he cared a great deal for his Greek secretary. She knew Dimitrios cared a lot for her, too. Wanting to show her a favorite place of his meant they'd become friends. *But never lovers.*

Back in high school and college she'd dated quite a bit, but because she'd lost her heart to a certain Greek, no other man had ever meant enough to her to become intimate with him.

Tonight that was what she wanted. To lie in his arms and get so intimate with him, he would never let her go.

But if she dared shed her disguise right now in order to make him see her in a different light, it would end their friendship. He would despise her for misrepresenting herself to get a job with his corporation. Everything would blow up in her face. It was going to blow up anyway after she resigned.

The mere thought of never seeing him again was anathema to her. She couldn't imagine getting through the rest of her life without him, yet the day of parting was almost here. There was nothing she could do now but play this out to the bitter end.

Stifling a tiny sob, she hurried into the bathroom with her suitcase. After freshening up, she pulled out the plastic bag holding her sneakers. Once she'd slipped off her matron pumps, she put on her navy and white tennis shoes.

They didn't match her three-piece, oversize suit with the high square neck. It was an unattractive jacquard design of intricately woven salmon pink, gray and brown. During the hike she imagined she'd get hot wearing it, but that would have to be her punishment.

When she finally went into the room, the sight of his powerful body in cutoffs and a white T-shirt revealing the well-defined chest beneath caused her to suck in her breath.

On the same note, his eyes passed over her with less interest than if he'd glimpsed a plate of fried eggs left out on the table for the better part of a week.

How awful she looked. It killed her to go on wearing such unattractive clothes in front of him, never being able to let down her hair and be herself. Just once she'd like to see those black orbs ignite when she walked into a room....

He hung his suit in the closet, then reached for his backpack. It was sheer poetry watching his bronzed, hard-muscled arms slip into the straps.

"What have you got inside?" she inquired. "It looks heavy."

"This is nothing. Some food and water plus a few

other items. Shall we go?'' He locked the door behind them.

For the next twenty minutes she followed him along a path, which started to wind into foothills studded with black pine and oak. ''Are we on sacred ground yet?''

Dimitrios paused to look back at her with an amused smile that tripled her pulse rate. ''We'll be coming to the strictly protected area before too long. When you see something move, I'll give you the binoculars.''

Startled, she said, ''I'd settle for a clue about now.''

His lips twitched. ''That would spoil all the fun.''

Uh-oh. This outing seemed to have brought out the boy in him. She had an idea she was in for it.

He handed her a bottle of water from his pack. ''Don't drink too much all at once,'' he cautioned.

After a moment she returned it and they resumed their trek. He continued along the path, pacing himself so Alex could keep up. Though the scenery was beautiful, she found herself watching the backs of his legs. They were perfectly molded machines of whipcord strength.

Content to feast her eyes on Dimitrios, she almost bumped into him when he stopped ten minutes later to point out a family of badgers partially hidden by the underbrush. Alex took a step off the path to get a closer peek at them. They were burrowing for all their worth.

''Oh—look how hard they're working!''

''They remind me of you.''

The mocking comparison to the grizzle-coated mammals was hardly flattering, but she'd come to recognize his mockery as a compliment of sorts.

''Thank you very much.''

She thought she heard a chuckle as they continued up the path. The higher they rose, the more she became aware of a forest alive with the sounds of rustlings and whirrings. No doubt foxes and other creatures abounded in the wooded setting.

They stopped to drink more water. When he'd put the bottle away, he took out the binoculars. Before she knew how it happened, he'd hung them around her neck.

In the process, his hands brushed her hair and shoulders, setting her on fire wherever there was contact. She quickly averted her eyes, afraid to look at him.

"We're getting closer to the peak. Keep your gaze skyward."

She nodded, unable to talk with his body practically touching hers, radiating his male warmth. Once he'd turned and started up the trail again, she was able to expel the breath she'd been holding.

They hadn't been hiking more than five minutes before she saw several dark specks in the sky. With each leisurely circle, they came closer.

She took off her glasses and lifted the binoculars to her eyes. Unprepared for the powerful magnification of the lenses, she gasped in shock at the incredible sight.

"I don't believe it! They look like gargoyles come to life! I've never seen anything like them."

"You're viewing a pair of Griffon vultures," sounded her companion's deep voice. "They would be extinct by now if there weren't forest preserves like this to provide needed habitat. Along with the Black and Egyptian vultures, they're one of the most endangered species of raptors in the world."

"No wonder you love to come here! I feel like I've gone back in time. I wish I had my sketch pad with me."

"Wait till you see the Imperial eagle."

"Is that the one you have emblazoned on your plane?"
She was still looking through the field glasses.

"So you noticed." He sounded pleased.

I notice everything about you.

"Well, it didn't look like an American bald eagle, so
I figured it had special significance."

"You don't miss much."

Not when it comes to you.

"Once when Leonides brought me here, we found an
Imperial eaglet that had been poisoned. We notified the
authorities and they took it to the bird hospital. After it
recovered, we were allowed to watch it from the observatory when it was returned."

She swallowed hard. "That must have pleased you
both."

"We were very happy. My brother felt it was important to fight for their preservation."

"So you took up the cause. What a perfect way to
honor his memory." She handed him back the binoculars
and put her glasses on. "Does your nephew know about
that story?"

He stared at her with brooding eyes. "No. In the beginning, I found it too painful a subject to talk about. I
realize it's another oversight I intend to rectify if it isn't
already too late."

"I don't imagine it's ever too late for a son to hear
something truly wonderful about his father."

She saw his throat move before they continued the last
of their climb side by side.

"You had a happy childhood, didn't you, Alexandra."

"My parents are loving people who gave me and my
sisters a wonderful life."

"Is that the reason why you don't talk about it around

me? Because you've learned enough to know mine was less than idyllic?''

No. It was the fear of loving him too much when she knew it was one-sided that kept her silent, but she couldn't let him know that. With his all-seeing gaze focused on her, she started to feel nervous.

"I guess I've been too busy being your secretary to realize much of anything else. Where did you say that observatory was?'' Their conversation was getting too personal.

"Along another path. It'll be closed today, but we have our own binoculars and can stop there on our way down to watch the raptors feed."

The next three hours were sheer delight for Alex. They ate by the ruins of a Byzantine castle on top of the peak, then made their descent. Dimitrios identified fifteen endangered species for her, including the Imperial eagle.

Almost at the bottom, she thought she heard music and stopped along the trail to listen.

"It's the wedding party. See that little meadow through the trees? They must have arrived from the village church."

Her breath caught in her throat to witness the joy of a radiant bride in her wedding dress with a crown of flowers in her hair, dancing with her dark-haired groom.

In the background their friends and relatives clapped and cheered to the music while the little children played.

Tears sprang to Alex's eyes. "I've never seen anything so beautiful."

The scene before her was too painful to watch because she wanted to be that bride smiling into her husband's eyes. She wanted that wedding to be her wedding. She wanted Dimitrios for her husband. To have and to hold. Forever.

"I agree that village weddings tend to have a certain charm," he murmured. "Come stand over here where we can see better."

Needing to touch her, he grasped her shoulders from behind and moved her off the path where they could remain hidden behind the undergrowth to watch. But it was a mistake.

There was no way he could focus on the bridal party when the intoxicating scent of pear from her shampoo made him want to take down her hair and bury his face in it.

Like before, on the plane, Dimitrios was aware of the superb mold of her body. Considering the eighty-degree heat, it came as a shock to discover she was trembling. He knew she wasn't afraid of him. Was it desire she felt for him?

If that were the case, then her struggle to conceal it made her different from all the other females who'd come on to him since his teens. She was that rare woman he never expected to meet.

Earlier that morning he'd awakened full of determination to keep her at a professional distance. Yet here he was, held in the grip of sexual desire, wanting to turn her around so he could kiss her senseless.

He knew he should be feeling guilty for spending time with her in activities that had nothing to do with business. For that matter, he should never have insisted she stay at the villa. But it was too late for that now, too late to remember the vow that no woman would entice him to bed before marriage.

He wanted, needed Alexandra in all the ways a man could want a woman. He'd fallen in love with her....

"I—I hope you don't mind if we hurry back to the lodge now. All of a sudden I'm fading fast." She eased away from him and started down the path.

Dimitrios followed at a more leisurely pace, wondering if guilt over betraying Michael or Yanni had caused her to put distance between them. Determined to find out, he closed the gap.

"You're reading my mind again. An early night is exactly what I need, too."

She slowed down before darting him a backward glance. "Are you feeling dizzy?"

"No. Only pleasantly tired."

"Somehow I don't quite believe you. Thank goodness the lodge isn't very far now. That backpack must feel heavy."

He waited for her to say he could lean on her, but the offer didn't come.

Because she didn't trust herself to get that close to him again?

Desperate to know the answer to that vital question, an idea came to him how he could discover the truth.

Filled with a sense of anticipation for the evening ahead, Dimitrios walked her toward the lodge. The pines cast their long shadows across the path. His heart thudded to realize evening had crept up on them without him realizing it. He would have her all to himself.

It didn't matter that there were cars in every parking space. The wedding guests would stay occupied for hours, leaving him and Alexandra strictly alone.

"Do you mind if I stretch out for a few minutes?" he asked as soon as he let them inside the room.

She looked at him in alarm. "Are you feeling sick? Sometimes a cola helps. I could ask for one at the lodge."

He loved it that she showed this kind of concern for him. It staggered him how much he loved her.

Shaking his head, he said, "I'm sleepy. That's all. If you want to shower, go ahead. The concierge said they'd bring dinner to our room. I'll call the office now."

After putting his backpack on one of the chairs, he laid down on one of the twin beds and picked up the receiver to order their meal. Through veiled eyes he watched her reach for her suitcase.

"I'll hurry," she murmured before disappearing.

The second he heard the shower, he called Stavros for a short chat on his cell phone, then listened for any messages. So far there was no response from Leon. He hoped by morning he'd hear from his nephew.

His eyes flicked to the radio on the table between the beds. He turned it to a popular music station, curious to know Alexandra's taste. With the curtains drawn and the lights turned low, there was nothing else to do but wait for her. He couldn't think of anything else more important.

The shower had felt wonderful, but Alex stood before the mirror in a panic.

It had grown dark. Before long it would be time for bed. She couldn't go out there in front of him wearing another three-piece suit. But to suddenly appear in jeans and a T-shirt would be disastrous.

When she'd packed for this trip, it never occurred to her she might need a granny gown. All she'd thought to bring with her were some shortie nighties. Her robe was a simple yellow brushed nylon that fell to the knee and looked too youthful compared to the other things she'd been wearing to work.

Of course if she didn't use the belt, and wore one of her heavy white blouses and a half slip beneath it, she'd be able to conceal her figure. Alex hadn't brought slippers, but she'd packed a clean pair of white socks. In a moment she'd pulled them on.

Once her glasses were in place, she left the bathroom with her suitcase.

"I'm sorry if I took too—"

But she didn't finish what she was going to say because everything had changed since she'd been in the shower.

Her gaze shot to the square table, which had been set with candles and flowers. Dimitrios stood next to it filling two tall stemmed glasses with wine. She could smell something delicious. Greek music played in the background.

When he'd ordered dinner, she hadn't expected all this! Her heart couldn't take anymore.

Dimitrios turned toward her. In the flickering candlelight, his eyes gleamed like polished jet. He looked amazingly refreshed. "Leave your bag there and join me."

Once she'd done his bidding, she crossed the expanse on legs that had turned to jelly. He held the chair while she sat down. What was going on?

He took his place across the table from her and lifted his wineglass. "Shall we drink a toast to the fair?"

Trying not to look at him for fear he'd see the love in her eyes, she raised her glass. "May it be the success you envisioned."

"Amen."

They clinked glasses before he drank from his.

Alex rarely touched alcohol, but she needed something to steady her nerves, and the wine was very sweet to the taste. Unfortunately she swallowed too much, too fast. Grabbing the napkin, she coughed into it. "I'm sorry," came her muffled apology.

As he removed the covers off their dinner plates, a faint smile curved the corners of his mouth. "Perhaps this wedding fare will go down more easily."

She took a bite of the roast lamb and found it as delicious as everything else. But her awareness of the man seated opposite her had taken away her appetite.

Something was different. *He* was different. By his behavior, she could almost believe he was attracted to her, too. *Dear God.* Was it possible? Or had her desire for him grown to such a degree she saw only what she wanted to see?

"If the food isn't to your taste, I can go to the village for fruit and a sandwich." By now he'd practically devoured everything on his plate.

"Oh, no— I mean, that isn't the problem, but thank you anyway."

His gaze scrutinized her. "If you'd shed your jacket during the climb, you wouldn't have overheated."

"I'm fine. It's simply a case of my being more sleepy than hungry."

"Alexandra, you needn't pretend with me."

Her head reared back. "What do you mean?"

"I realize you were planning to spend your free evenings with Michael. So far I've claimed all your time."

She blinked. It hadn't occurred to her he would think she was romantically involved with Michael. Yet what else would he assume considering she'd offered to let Michael stay in her hotel room.

That put a different complexion on things. She hated the idea of deceiving Dimitrios any more than she already had.

"Michael knows my work for you comes first."

He finished off the rest of his wine. "Is that what you're going to tell him? That it was all work?"

"If he should ask, naturally I'll be honest with him."

"And he won't be jealous?"

"Heavens, no! You're my boss."

He sat back in his chair eyeing her narrowly. "If you were my girlfriend, I wouldn't allow you to spend a whole day with your employer in the woods."

Alex couldn't help smiling despite the pain she was feeling inside.

"My remark amused you?" He sounded anything but pleased.

"Today's woman doesn't consider herself a man's property. But the truth is, if I were Michael's girlfriend, I wouldn't have chosen to spend my free time with you, even if you do pay my salary."

There! She'd told him the truth.

"Does Michael know you're not his girlfriend?" He persisted in the same vein.

"Did he say something to Leon when he went for the costume that led him to believe we're more than good friends?"

"Not that I'm aware of," came the silky response.

Dimitrios was after a certain answer. She wished she knew was it was. Unless—

"It was probably one of Michael's friends playing a joke."

Her host's dark brows furrowed. "I don't follow."

"Michael's an old friend of mine who brought two of his buddies to Greece with him. One of them is divorced. Michael and the other one are between girlfriends at the moment.

"They work in the day and act in the theater at night. When they heard about the fair and the idea of wearing costumes, they were so excited to come, I told them they could stay in my suite. There weren't any more rooms to be had, and I knew I wouldn't be using it except to sleep."

She hoped that was the end of the questions. Alex reached for her wine and drank most of the contents.

"What about Yanni?"

She almost choked again. "I don't understand."

"Is he planning to stay in your suite, too?"

Alex put the glass on the table, wondering when the interrogation was going to stop.

"Yes. He went to Athens first to be with his family. From what I understand, he's bringing a girl along I've never met. As far as I know, they haven't arrived in Thessalonica yet."

"It all sounds very cozy," he murmured. "I wonder what would be your response if I asked to sleep over, too."

It was a teasing comment, but at the mere thought, her heart leaped. "Everyone would love it."

"Even you?"

Dimitrios. He sounded very much like a man who cared. If by some miracle that were true...

"Naturally it would be worth it to see the look on their faces. They wouldn't believe the legendary Kyrie Pandakis came down from Olympus to—"

Oh, no!

"Go on."

"I—I don't remember what I was going to say," she dissembled. The wine had made her careless.

"Maybe it will come to you while I'm in the shower."

CHAPTER SEVEN

AFTER Dimitrios had left the room, she decided the best thing she could do to get rid of the light-headed feeling was eat her dinner. Without him torturing her with questions, she found her appetite had returned.

Now that everything was out in the open concerning the friends staying at the hotel with her, she felt a lot better.

Once she'd finished her meal, she put the covers on the plates. As she blew out the candles, Dimitrios emerged from the bathroom wearing a pair of gray sweats and another T-shirt in pale blue. He brought the tang of soap into the room with him.

She noticed that his black hair was still damp from the shower, but he hadn't taken the time to shave. The shadow of a beard made him look so dark and handsome, she could only stare at him.

His gaze swept over her, igniting her senses all over again. "I don't know about you, but watching that bridal couple has put me in the mood to dance. Would you honor me with one before I leave you in peace?"

Dance? With her? When she'd never looked worse in her life?

Her boss probably knew she was in love with him. Maybe he'd known it all along and had decided to give his old-maid secretary a few thrills while she was in Greece. Let her have a memory to take back to New York.

"Something you have to learn about the Greek male. He loves to dance." Dimitrios put out his hands. "Indulge me."

Delicious waves of excitement raced through her body. Maybe her dream to become unforgettable to him was starting to come true. Her legs almost buckled as she dared to imagine he might really want to hold her close. "I don't think—"

"This is one time when I don't want you to think, Alexandra. Just go with the music. The bouzouki is too compelling to ignore."

"I don't know any Greek dances," she grumbled.

But her declaration had no effect on him as he drew her resisting body into his arms.

"All you have to do is relax," he whispered near her ear. After he'd removed her glasses and put them on the bed, he held her close enough that she could follow his lead.

Earlier she'd practically melted to feel his broad chest against her back. Now that her curves were melded to his rock-hard physique, her bones turned to liquid every time their legs brushed against each other.

Zeus in her arms.

She didn't dare let this go on any longer.

"I think we'd better stop. You've had enough activity for one day."

"I'll live to see another."

As if to make his point, he pulled her closer and moved her around the room with practised ease.

"Dimitrios," she begged.

"I like it when you say my name. I like being with you. Admit you enjoy my company, too." She felt his deep voice resonate to every cell in her sensitized body.

"If that weren't true, I wouldn't have worked for you all these years."

"A man likes to hear the words once in a while, even from his secretary."

"Well, now that you've been given your wish, I really must insist we stop. We have a big day ahead of us tomorrow."

"So we do."

He stopped moving his legs, but continued to rock her in place. "Thank you for the dance, Alexandra. It was exactly what the doctor ordered."

His hands seemed to slide away reluctantly, leaving her bereft. "I'll see you in the morning. Be sure to lock the door after me." He reached for his backpack.

"Wait," she cried.

"Yes?" He paused at the entrance.

"Where's your sleeping bag?"

"In the trunk of the car."

"What if you should become ill during the night?"

He shot her an enigmatic glance. "It isn't going to happen."

"But it could!" After their hike, she was fearful he might have overdone things. "I don't think I'll get any sleep tonight knowing you're out there somewhere in the forest where you might suffer a dizzy spell and no one would be there to help you."

He rubbed his jaw absently. "If you're that concerned, then I'll sleep in the car outside the cottage door."

"No!" she cried. "You're too big and you need a good night's rest," she stammered. "Stay in here. It isn't as if we haven't spent all night in the same bedroom before. That way if you're sick, I'll be here to help you."

She could read nothing from his expression. "That's very generous of you. If you're sure—"

"Of course." Once again she disappeared into the bathroom.

With pounding heart, he turned off the lamp and slid under the covers. When his adorable secretary finally emerged, his hungry gaze followed her silhouette as she got in her bed and purposely rolled away from him.

One dance with her and a fire had been lit that wasn't about to go out. He could still feel her delectable body pressed against him. In fact he was dangerously close to joining her in her bed.

The cell phone rang. Smothering a groan of frustration, he reached for it and clicked on.

"*Yassou.*" He spoke in Greek.

"Uncle?"

Relief swept over Dimitrios. "Leon, thank goodness. Where are you right now?"

"With Nikos."

"He's a good friend."

After a brief silence, "You shouldn't have left the villa until you were better," he blurted in a voice of chastisement, which was very touching.

"I found that out earlier today. Fortunately I'm in bed now."

"Where?"

"At the lodge on the edge of the Dadia forest."

"With Ms. Hamilton?"

He sucked in his breath. "Yes."

"Mother told me I jumped to conclusions about your confiding in her. I'm sorry. It was rude of me to walk out on you like that."

"There's no need for apologies. It was a misunderstanding all the way around."

"What are you doing in Dadia?"

"Reliving a memory I have of your father. I should have shared it with you years ago, but when he died, I was in so much pain, I shut off emotionally."

"Uncle Vaso told me you two were really close."

"Very. When your grandparents were killed, Leonides became mother, father and brother to me. After his death, I suffered. Then you were born, and it was like having my brother back. Only you were my little brother, and I could boss *you* around for a change."

His nephew laughed. Dimitrios felt the dark clouds begin to disperse.

"I'd like to climb the peak with you, Leon."

"I'd love it," his nephew responded emotionally.

"Good. Then we'll plan it after I get back from my honeymoon."

"Honeymoon?"

"Yes." Dimitrios realized that nothing less than marriage would satisfy him. "I'm going to take a long one, and I'll need someone to run things in New York while I'm away."

"Are you serious?"

"Of course. Who else would I ask to fill in for me? Maybe by the time I return home, you'll know better if you want to finish college and go into business with me, or live the religious life.

"Personally, I'd like my nephew with me. Any sons or daughters I have won't be able to help me until I'm a much older man."

"Uncle, you're going too fast for me."

That's the point, Leon. I want to fill your head with enough ideas to confuse you.

"I feel breathless these days."

"You're in love with Ms. Hamilton, aren't you."

Dimitrios's eyes closed tightly. "Yes."

"I knew it the moment you told me to take her to the villa with us."

"You have all the right instincts, Leon. That's why you'll make it in business if that's what you choose."

Another long period of quiet followed before his nephew spoke again. "Have you asked her to marry you?"

"As soon as the fair is over."

"I don't pretend to know her, but she must be wonderful because I've never seen you this happy in my life."

"She's a gift, but you're the only person I've told. I'd like to keep it a secret until we're ready to announce our plans."

"I won't say anything, not even to Mother."

"I've always been able to trust you. Thanks again for being willing to stand in for me at the parade. We'll meet at the villa tomorrow before the family dinner. I want to see you in that costume."

"She had it made for you."

"True, but we're blood, so it's the same thing."

"You're sure you're going to be all right?" The concern in his voice spoke volumes.

"Alexandra is better than any nurse. She won't let anything happen to me."

"That's good. Just be careful. I love you, Uncle."

"I love you, too, Leon. More than you know."

He rang off, then sank back against the pillow.

Seeds had been sown. Only time would tell if they'd fallen on fertile ground.

As for the woman lying within touching distance, her days of being known as Ms. Hamilton were almost over.

If it weren't for the fair, he'd snatch her away this very night to somewhere they could lose themselves in each other for days and nights on end. It was going to be a long night.

The next morning after breakfast at the lodge dining room and a quick inspection of the impeccable silk exhibits in Soufli, the flight back to Thessalonica in the helicopter provided its own set of thrills for Alex.

Under Dimitrios's guidance, the pilot flew low over castles and churches dotting the ancient landscape, giving her a history lesson she would always cherish. But when it came in for a landing on top of the Pandakis building, Alex was the one who suddenly felt strange.

Dimitrios got out of his seat, ready to assist her. She undid her seat belt and started to stand up, then weaved in place.

His powerful arms immediately went around her. "What's wrong?" he demanded anxiously.

"Would you believe I'm the one feeling dizzy?"

"You're having a bout of vertigo. It sometimes happens when you're not used to landing above ground. I'll carry you inside."

"No, please!" she cried in a hushed tone. Last night she'd tasted a little bit of heaven. But it was morning now, and everything had gone back to reality. "Just let me hold onto your arm and I'll be fine in a minute."

"Would you prefer to wait here until it subsides?"

"No— I think maybe that's what's wrong. Knowing we're up so high and—"

"Come on. Let's get you inside the building."

She clung to him while he half pulled her along. Part of the time she kept her eyes closed. He helped her down the stairs from the roof to his suite of offices on the top floor.

Being inside helped a lot.

"Better?" he whispered close to her cheek.

"Much." *Just don't touch me anymore.*

"Drink this."

He'd stopped at the water dispenser and put a cup of it to her lips. It tasted good. She drank the whole thing. As she handed it back, their eyes met. His searching gaze revealed a depth of concern that shook her to the foundations.

"Thank you." Her voice trembled.

She felt him take a deep breath. "You're welcome. Your color's come back. Are you ready to go the rest of the way? It's only a few steps further."

"I think I can do it without your help now."

He ignored her comment and assisted her inside his office where his staff waited to be introduced to her.

"This is probably the most embarrassing moment of my life."

He ushered her to the couch where she could sit down. "But think what it's doing for Stavros, who has been under the impression you're superhuman."

Alex chuckled in spite of the situation. Within minutes everyone had taken turns greeting her so cordially, she felt right at home. Stavros showed up last of all with a glass of lemonade for her.

He sat down next to her. "I have a confession to make,

my dear,'' he said in excellent English. ''I've never liked flying in the damn thing.''

''Now he tells me!'' Dimitrios pretended to be upset, but his eyes were smiling. When they did that, he was virtually irresistible to Alex.

She drank half the lemonade before she said, ''I think if I just don't have to land on a roof again, I'll be all right.''

''Good for you,'' Stavros murmured. He looked at Dimitrios. ''You're hovering.''

''He does that on occasion,'' Alex couldn't help adding. Already she liked the older man who'd been with the Pandakis firm for so many years.

Now it was Stavros whose eyes were smiling. ''There's a lot of work waiting for you, Dimitrios. If you want to get busy, I'll show Ms. Hamilton into her office.''

She'd never known anyone who spoke to Dimitrios that way. It showed the measure of affection, even love between the two men who treated each other as equals.

Dimitrios muttered something about his secretaries being partners in crime before he wheeled away and strode toward his private office, taking her heart with him.

After finishing her lemonade, she felt restored and was able to get up and follow Stavros without problem. The fabulous office that would be her headquarters during the fair was obviously someone else's inner sanctum. He didn't tell her which of the Pandakis cousins had been asked to make the sacrifice.

For the next hour they got down to business. Toward the end of their meeting, she acted on a suggestion Dimitrios had made in regard to Stavros.

''Before I leave, can I be frank with you?''

"Of course."

"I'm not much of a people person. I would prefer to work behind the scenes from here to make sure every event goes off as planned. You're the mainstay of the corporation, and the only one who can handle the VIPs flying in for the fair. Would you take over in that department? Please?"

He looked surprised. "If that's what you wish."

"It is. To be honest, if I thought I had to entertain foreign dignitaries, I'd probably have a nervous breakdown."

"Dimitrios told me you're not the type to fall apart on him."

"I have to retain a few secrets to stay in with the boss."

The older man's hearty laugh delighted her.

"If I'd known this was going to be a party, I wouldn't have left."

At the sound of Dimitrios's vibrant voice, Alex got up from the desk. Stavros remained in his swivel chair, eyeing her employer in amusement.

"Ms. Hamilton and I have been sorting things out. She's afraid for me to tamper with her work agenda, so it looks like I'm going to be the fair's goodwill ambassador."

"Whatever makes the two of you happy. Now I'm afraid it's getting late. We have to go, Alexandra."

She turned to Stavros. "I'll see you later then. Thank you for everything."

"It's been my pleasure."

Dimitrios cupped her elbow and ushered her out to the elevator. On their ride down to the lobby he seemed to be staring into her soul.

"Did you know that Stavros rarely laughs like that? You made him a happy man. For that, you're going to get a reward."

She shook her head. "Please. No more bonuses."

"Actually I had something else in mind," he said in a quiet voice. "When the fair is over, you'll find out what it is."

Alex didn't want gifts from Dimitrios. What she did want was still out of reach. Last night had to have been an aberration. Right now she had to keep reminding herself that the only reason he kept a hold was because she'd been dizzy earlier.

He didn't let go until he'd helped her climb in the back of the limousine waiting for them.

"Oh—my suitcase!"

"It's in the trunk with my backpack."

Dimitrios went around to his side of the car. After he issued instructions to the driver, they were off.

"Isn't the hotel the other way?" Alexandra cried as the limo made an unexpected right turn.

He nodded. "Yes. However, we still have work to do after dinner. There's no time to ferry you back and forth. Now that I know Michael and his friends can entertain themselves, it only makes sense you stay at the villa. As for your friend Yanni, he and his girlfriend might as well use the other bedroom in your suite, which is going to waste."

After a pregnant pause, "How long do you expect the party to last?"

"I have no idea. Does it matter? You're my guest. Naturally you'll be attending the dinner with me."

"But I'm not family."

Dimitrios cursed beneath his breath. "You must have

a poor opinion of me if you think I would leave you on your own! Everyone in the family is anxious to meet the woman who has managed to bring back the splendor of Thessalonica to a world that is looking on in fascination.''

She bowed her head. ''Thank you for the compliment, but as usual, you exaggerate my part in things.'' He heard a deep sigh. ''Should I dress up for dinner, or will one of my suits be all right?''

''Whatever makes you the most comfortable.''

''Maybe I should ask your sister-in-law. She'll have definite ideas.''

''It's not up to Ananke to decide.''

''Isn't she the hostess?''

''No. We'll be eating at Uncle Spiros's villa.''

''I thought he'd passed away.'' Her voice trailed.

''He did. After his death, his son Pantelis moved in with his family. You'll like his wife, Estelle. She doesn't fuss about things that aren't important.''

Another long silence ensued. He glanced at her. ''What's going on in that mind of yours to put such a fierce expression on your face?''

''It may surprise you to know that even nondescript secretaries want to look their best when the occasion demands.''

''In *my* employ you've never presented a less than perfect picture,'' he bit out in frustration. ''If you thought I implied otherwise, you'd be wrong.''

He could feel her pulling away from him. Nothing was the same since they'd left Dadia.

When Nicholas appeared, Dimitrios asked him to bring in their luggage, then he grasped Alex's elbow to escort her through the villa. She seemed in a great hurry to reach the guest bedroom. After what had transpired in the last twenty-four hours, he rebelled at the idea of their being separated for any reason.

"Be ready to leave in an hour."

She nodded, then started to shut the door.

"Alexandra—"

"Yes?" she said, sounding as breathless as he felt. "Is there something you forgot to tell me? Something you want me to do?"

There was so much he wanted from her, he wasn't able to think with any coherence. "It can wait."

With that oblique comment, he turned and strode toward his suite. Alex shut the door, then leaned upon it. She couldn't understand what had come over him. Maybe it had to do with this house that once upon a time contained the family he'd lost. He always seemed happier away from it.

Last night when he'd held out his hands for her to dance, he'd been a totally different person. Alex had never known such ecstasy as those moments in his powerful arms with the wine and the music feeding the flame of her desire.

Again she was struck by the fact that he'd always accepted her just the way she was. She loved him for it. But right now he sounded so upset. What had she said?

A shiver passed through her body. There'd only been a few times at the office when she'd seen him truly angry. The last thing she'd ever want was to be his target, even if it were deserved.

Once again Alex found herself wishing she dared to be her real self for tonight. If it weren't for the likelihood of Giorgio being at the party, Alex was tempted to end the charade for good.

A knock on the door made her jump. She thought it was Dimitrios, that he'd changed his mind and had come back to ask a favor of her. When she opened it, she discovered Nicholas standing there with her suitcase. He placed it inside the room.

Though she needed it to get ready, she felt a bitter disappointment that it wasn't Dimitrios. She quickly thanked the other man, then shut the door after him.

Almost to the bathroom, tears streamed down her face. Too much had transpired in the last twenty-four hours to contain her emotions any longer. She needed a release.

Half an hour later, she padded over to the suitcase with a towel wrapped around her and pulled out the only dressy outfit she'd brought from New York.

When Michael had planned her wardrobe, they'd laughed over the choices he'd come up with. But Alex wasn't laughing now. She lifted the boxy, drab, gray three-piece suit to her gaze. The wrinkle-proof affair felt like stiff taffeta. Her eyes studied the beading on the collar and cuffs.

It was hideous. She could hardly bare to put it on, but she had no choice.

One glance in the mirror and she was equally repulsed by her dyed brown hair, which she wore in an eternal twist pulled back from an unimaginative center part. Alex's mother wasn't the only person who didn't know what she looked like these days.

It astounded her that Dimitrios didn't appear to mind being seen with her.

"Alexandra?" His peremptory voice was followed by a rap on the door.

"I'm ready."

She slipped into her black matron shoes once more,

then reached for the door handle. If he said one word about how nice she looked…

But at her first glimpse of the tall, virile male dressed in a long-sleeved black silk shirt teamed with black trousers, she forgot all about the ghastly picture she presented.

"Leon and his mother are waiting for us in the car. They're both under the impression that I'm still too unsteady to mount a horse, so play along with me while I hang onto you for support. Shall we go?"

Once again he ushered her down the hall with his arm around her shoulders. The familiar smell of the soap he'd used in the shower assailed her again. He was clean-shaven tonight. Dimitrios had to be the most gorgeous man alive. How comical she must look standing next to him!

The strange glance Ananke flashed her when they got in the back of the limousine verified Alex's opinion of herself. But Leon's eyes were kind as they rested on her.

"Good evening, Ms. Hamilton."

"I'm so glad to see you again, Leon. Since the other day I've wanted to apologize to you for anything I said that upset you."

He shook his head. "No, no. I was the idiot. We don't need to talk about it again." Just then he sounded and acted very much like Dimitrios.

His mother chose that moment to say something to her brother-in-law.

"Speak English, Ananke."

"It's my opinion you should stay home from the party, Dimitrios. You should never have left your bed yesterday."

"I agree with you, Mrs. Pandakis," Alex inserted.

"Considering the fact that we still have work to do this evening after dinner, I don't think he should stay long. Not when he's still feeling light-headed."

"Then it's settled," his nephew declared with surprising finality. "We will eat quickly and leave."

"Thank you all for deciding for me."

Dimitrios's wry comment prompted Alex to mutter, "Someone has to."

"I'll make it a short night on one condition."

"What's that?" Ananke asked the question foremost on Alex's mind.

"After Ms. Hamilton went to all the trouble of having a costume made for me, I want the family to see Leon model it before he wears it in the parade tomorrow."

"I'd be happy to do that, Uncle, but it's too late now. We'll be at the villa in a moment."

Alex darted her host a sideward glance and caught a gleam in his eye. "As it happens, I asked Nicholas to put it in the trunk."

Leon wouldn't be able to wiggle out of it now.

Pleased to see Dimitrios's tactics working where his nephew was concerned, Alex turned her head and looked out the window.

They'd been passing through another beautiful residential area of the city. As they turned into a private drive lined with cars, she caught sight of a pastel villa built along neoclassical lines. It looked even larger and more imposing than the one they'd just come from.

Mrs. Landau had once confided to Alex that even if Spiros headed the Pandakis family and had four sons to help run the company, his brother's son, Dimitrios, was the driving force.

True to her prediction, after Spiros's death there really

wasn't a transfer of power because Dimitrios was already the natural leader to whom the entire family and business magnates deferred.

It would be interesting to see if, after all Dimitrios had done to let Leon make his own decisions about life, his nephew ended up showing the same spark of business genius as his illustrious uncle. Stranger things had happened.

For Ananke's sake, Alex hoped her son would marry and have children. The other woman was suffering. Her husband had been dead too many years for her to be actively grieving. Alex surmised that her pain stemmed from another source. She also had the impression Leon wasn't the sole cause of it.

"We've arrived," Dimitrios whispered against her ear. She knew it was accidental, but his lips grazed her lobe. His touch sent tiny ripples of delight through her system.

"Leon?" he called to his nephew. "I'll help your mother inside while you take the garment bag and get ready."

"Yes, Uncle."

Alex struggled not to smile. Leon wasn't used to Dimitrios making demands, but as far as she was concerned, it was exactly what he needed.

Within minutes both Alex and Ananke flanked Dimitrios as they made their way around the side of the villa to a terrace where a large crowd was gathered. Alex counted at least thirty beautifully dressed family members.

Spiros's sons were all married with children, some of whom looked to be in their teens. Coupled with staff loading food on the tables placed around the ornate gardens, it made an impressive sight.

"Dimitrios!" someone cried in delight.

"Don't move from my side," he cautioned her.

CHAPTER EIGHT

ALEX was only too happy to oblige her host. Before he'd spoken, she'd spotted Giorgio Pandakis among the crowd. He was shorter than his brothers and had put on weight since the frightening experience trying to fend him off outside the silk museum.

Back then she'd found him the least attractive of the Pandakis men. The same held true tonight. She shuddered.

Dimitrios eyed her curiously. "Are you cold?" He noticed everything.

"No. I thought I saw a bug coming for me," she lied.

His quick smile made her breath catch. "If you did, it was a moth. We get them this time of year. It won't hurt you."

She looked away as everyone came rushing toward them speaking Greek so fast and furiously Alex could only catch certain words or phrases. Her host was the obvious favorite, especially with the little children who grabbed hold of his legs wanting him to pick them up.

But Ananke put a halt to that and led him to a chair at one of the tables where she sat down next to him. Alex followed and took her place at his other side.

Besieged by questions she knew concerned his accident, Dimitrios patiently answered each one while they ate. After being introduced to his cousins Pantelis and Takis, she was glad they spoke to him and Ananke. Alex was able to stay in the background.

She was halfway through her meal when she heard someone cry out. This time the attention turned away from Dimitrios because Leon had walked out on the terrace.

Alex let out a quiet gasp because the costume fit him perfectly. With the flowing ruby cape and scepter, he looked like the saint on the icon come to life. All the noise quieted down as the family stared at him in fascination.

Alex saw Dimitrios smile at his nephew. Whatever he said to him in Greek caused Leon to smile back with real affection.

"Attention everyone," her host switched to English. "Tomorrow Leon will be taking my place in the parade. Thanks to the genius of my secretary, Ms. Hamilton, who planned the entire trade fair and had this costume made, I can see that Leon will do the Pandakis clan proud."

Everyone clapped and begged him to walk around so they could get a good look. Alex had the distinct impression his nephew was loving all the attention. He really did look wonderful and stayed in costume throughout the duration of the dinner.

Little by little, different family members came over to the table to make her acquaintance. One of the wives said in excellent English, "How did you ever think of such a clever costume?"

Guilt made the heat rush to Alex's cheeks. "Actually it was very simple. Saint Dimitrios is a well-known figure in history, and my employer happened to bear his name."

Dimitrios cocked his head. "So if my name had been Hades, you would have immediately produced a costume for me?"

His comment was so unexpected, Alex burst into laughter, forgetting where she was. "Except for the god of the underworld, I've never heard of anyone being named Hades."

"I've never heard you laugh like that before," he said in a husky aside. "You should do it more often."

Her heart ached to take his comment personally, but she knew he was only trying to help her feel comfortable among a crowd of strangers.

By now another of his dark-haired cousins had approached their table, obviously interested in the byplay that made her and Dimitrios the center of attention instead of Leon.

"Ms. Hamilton? Meet Vaso, my cousin and good friend."

Vaso smiled and shook her hand. "It's a pleasure to be introduced to you at last. You and Dimitrios should have been at the dinner I attended last night. The prime minister expressed disappointment that he wasn't able to compliment the American woman who put this spectacular trade fair together. Those were his exact words."

"Thank you," she murmured.

Vaso gave Dimitrios a playful punch on the shoulder. "He says he might steal her away from you to work on his trade council in the future. Watch out, cousin."

Dimitrios smiled at her with his eyes. It would have been one of the most exciting moments of her life if she hadn't seen Giorgio moving toward them at the same time Vaso walked away.

Since her arrival in Greece she'd been afraid of the time when she would have to come face to face with him. Now that time was here, and there was no place to run.

"Good evening, Dimitrios. Sorry to hear you're still not completely recovered from your mishap."

"Thank you, Giorgio. May I present my secretary who has made me the envy of the prime minister himself. Ms. Hamilton, allow me to present my cousin Giorgio."

"How do you do," she said without meeting his gaze.

He kissed the back of her hand, but didn't immediately relinquish it. She couldn't stand for a man to do that and was reminded of the time he'd grabbed hold of her, not letting go until Dimitrios had pulled him off her. It brought back the terror of that night with a clarity that made her break out in a cold sweat.

She removed her hand, uncaring if it offended him.

Undaunted, his cousin remained in place. "That is a famous American name."

"You're right, Giorgio. As it happens, Alexandra was named after her great-great-great-grandfather Alexander Hamilton, the renowned American politician who started the national bank and became the first United States Secretary of the Treasury."

"Ah. That explains your phenomenal rise in the Pandakis Corporation. With the trade fair to your credit, you've made yourself indispensable to my cousin. Congratulations."

Alex didn't miss the flash of hostility in Dimitrios's eyes before Giorgio excused himself.

Her heart hammered in her ears. "How did you know about my ancestry?"

"If you recall, Mrs. Landau was a genealogy buff. One day she happened to mention it to me."

"She was a regular treasure trove of knowledge," Alex muttered in a sarcastic tone to cover her relief at the explanation.

For a minute she thought he had made the connection to her grandfather who'd hosted the silk seminar nine years ago. That would have meant telling Dimitrios the whole truth tonight. Thank heaven she could wait until she wrote her letter of resignation before unburdening herself.

"Mrs. Landau had great faith in you. Her praise of your work was the only reason you became my private secretary after her passing."

She ought to have been pleased Mrs. Landau had championed her, but somehow she wasn't. Sometimes it was better not to know the truth.

"Forget what Giorgio said." The light had gone from Dimitrios's eyes as if it had never been. "Unfortunately he has a propensity for making mischief. Since I can see he's put you off your dessert, we'll leave now."

Alex needed no urging to get as far away from Giorgio as possible. Together they stood up from the table.

Ananke followed suit. "I'll find Leon and meet you both at the car."

As she hurried away, Dimitrios slanted his gaze toward Alex. "For my nephew's sake, be prepared to steady me, even after we get home. I don't want him to think he can squeeze out of this now."

"I don't think he wants to," she whispered. "From where I was sitting, your mantle appeared to feel good on his shoulders."

"I hope you're right."

Within a few minutes they were ensconced in the limo. Alex sat back to watch the scenery while the three of them conversed in Greek. Leon chatted nonstop with a continual smile on his attractive face. It was a very good sign. Even Ananke's spirits seemed to have picked up a little.

Almost to the villa, Alex's cell phone rang. As she pulled it out of her purse and clicked on, a grimace suddenly marred Dimitrios's features.

"Hello?"

"You're a difficult one to get hold of these days."

"Michael! Are you all having a good time?"

"Of course, but we haven't seen you yet. Your friend Yanni and his girlfriend arrived a few minutes ago."

"Yanni's there now?"

"Yes. Why don't you come over to the hotel for a while and prove to us you're not a figment of our imagination. I want to hear the lowdown. That is, if your lord and master will let you go."

She bit her lip. "I—I don't think I can tonight," she murmured, not able to explain while Dimitrios was aware of every breath she took. Giorgio had changed the tenor of the evening for both of them.

"It's obvious you can't talk right now so call us later, darling."

The line went dead.

She put the phone back in her purse, pretending that she had no idea Dimitrios had been listening.

When the limo pulled up in front of the villa, Leon helped his mother out, then opened the door for his uncle before he took Ananke inside.

Alex got out and hurried around to offer Dimitrios her support, but he didn't make a move to enter the foyer. Instead he leveled his black gaze on her.

"I'm sorry if you wanted to be with your friends tonight, but your presence here will convince my nephew I'm still not back to normal."

"I realize that."

He checked his watch. "It's only ten to ten. Why don't you invite them over here for a swim."

"Tonight?" she cried in shock.

"Yes. The evening is warm. Perhaps it will prove I'm not quite the ogre they've imagined."

She blushed, recalling Michael's last comment. "They don't think any such thing!"

One corner of his mouth lifted, making him overwhelmingly attractive. "That's nice to hear. In that case I'll tell Kristofor to pick them up while you make the call."

"It's very kind of you. You have no idea how thrilled they'll be to meet you in person. To be a guest in your villa will make the whole trip for them."

"Good. I'm glad we have that settled. Leon liked your friend Michael. He'll probably want to join us."

She hesitated. "I—I don't swim." She hated telling lies. She hoped this would be the last one.

"No problem. My nephew will find it suspect if he discovers me doing laps in the pool when I'm supposed to be recuperating. You and I can lounge in the deck chairs and do some last-minute business while we watch them."

In the next breath she could hear him giving directions to Kristofor. So in love with Dimitrios she didn't know where to go with her feelings, Alex did the only thing she could do and pulled out her cell phone to call the hotel. Michael was about to get the surprise of his life!

"I've never seen you looking lovelier, Alexandra. With that shade of brown hair, gray is definitely *your* color," Michael quipped sotto voce forty-five minutes later. How he could keep a straight face was beyond Alex, who gave him a hug.

"You're wicked, you know that?"

"Of course." He winked. "Where's the great Kyrie?"

"By the pool."

"This place is a living museum. How would it be…"

"Heavenly," she answered in a tremulous voice.

"I can see that. You'd better be careful or he's going to see it, too, if he hasn't already."

"I know," she murmured, suitably chastened.

They followed Leon, who offered to give them a tour of the ground floor of the villa before their swim.

It pleased Alex that her friends got along so well with Dimitrios's nephew. The three of them had performed in many Greek plays and shared his love of the theater.

Yanni loved contemporary theater. He took in every New York play possible. Between the six of them, they kept up a lively discussion until Leon led them to the rectangular pool at the back of the villa. There the Grecian garden setting took everyone's breath.

But Alex had eyes only for Dimitrios who got to his feet when he saw them. Still in his black shirt and trousers, he was so devastatingly handsome it hurt to look at him.

He couldn't have been more gracious. His arresting personality made an impact on everyone, but especially on Michael, who during a stolen moment arched an eyebrow as if to say, *Your obsession is no longer a mystery.*

Leon showed them where to change. In a few minutes he'd jumped in the deep end of the pool with them. Before long he had them competing in a frantic game of water polo.

Dimitrios's nephew possessed the same kind of athletic ability as his uncle and could outplay the lot of them. As the night wore on, Alex realized she wasn't the only person who noticed what a fine specimen Leon was.

The longer the others played, the more obvious it became that Yanni's redheaded Greek girlfriend found Leon attractive. To Alex's chagrin, it appeared Leon returned the compliment. Unfortunately that wasn't supposed to have happened. Yanni was no longer smiling.

Alarmed by the unexpected situation, Alex put down the notes she'd been going over with Dimitrios. Her troubled eyes met the speculation in his. Nothing escaped his notice.

"Are Yanni and Merlina engaged?" He'd asked the question in a low voice that no one else could have heard.

She took a deep breath. "No. He has another girlfriend in New York."

"Do you want me to do something about it?"

Alex knew what he meant. It was a loaded question.

She liked Yanni and didn't want to see him hurt. It would be hard to compete with all this and Leon, a good-looking man who was showing all the charm and promise of the breathtaking male sitting next to her.

On the other hand...

"It might not hurt for Leon to realize he's the object of female admiration right now. Merlina's a beautiful girl. If her interest in him can add to his confusion about where he wants to go with his life, it could be a good thing."

"You're reading my mind again. So what about your friend Yanni?"

She hunched her shoulders. "He says he isn't looking for anything permanent yet. Maybe a little healthy competition is what he needs. Someday he'll have to make an honest woman out of one of his girlfriends.''

He studied her briefly. ''Until I met you, I didn't think there was such a thing as an honest woman.''

His cynical comment, delivered without a trace of levity, swept the foundation out from under her. She could hear her mother's warning.

You've just told me he's an honorable man when it comes to business. Men like that expect honor in return. Mark my words, Alexandra. Every minute you're in his employ, you're playing with fire.

Groaning inwardly, she got up from the lounger with her notes. ''I can't thank you enough for opening up your beautiful home and making my friends feel welcome. But it's getting late, and I have to be down by the grandstand early in the morning to help coordinate everything for the parade. I'll tell Michael they have to leave.''

To her surprise, he rose to his feet. ''They're having a good time. Let's not interrupt them. Leon will take care of everything.''

He grasped her upper arm as if he really needed help. They left the pool area without anyone noticing. On their way through the villa she asked him where he planned to be during the parade.

''I'll drop Ananke off at the grandstand, then go to my office and watch the proceedings on television. As soon as Leon has given his speech, I'll meet you at the launch where we'll be taken out to the Cleopatra barge for lunch with Stavros and some visiting dignitaries.''

Outside her room she finally dared to look up at him. ''I hope the fair is going to be a success. I want things to be perfect for you.''

"They already are. Good night, Alexandra. Sleep well."

"You, too," she said before closing the door.

But the moment she found herself alone in the room, she realized she'd reached a point of no return with Dimitrios. Tonight he'd told her she was the only honest woman he knew. Alex loved him too much to let him go on believing something that wasn't true. She had to go to him right now and make a full confession, otherwise she wouldn't be able to live with herself another second. If he fired her on the spot, then it was only what she deserved.

Without wasting any time, she left her room. Hoping no one would see her, she hurried to his door. Silence followed her knock. Maybe he was in the shower. She didn't know what to think.

"Dimitrios?" she called urgently and knocked again.

Suddenly the door opened.

He'd answered it with his shirt partially unbuttoned. One look at the rapid rise and fall of his well-defined chest with its dusting of dark hair and her mouth went dry.

She lifted her eyes to his, but that was a mistake. They were veiled, making it impossible to tell if he was annoyed at the interruption.

He leaned one hand against the doorjamb. "Was there some last-minute decision concerning the parade you needed to talk to me about?"

His deep male voice played havoc with her senses. She could smell alcohol on his breath. Alex had never caught him drinking alone. There had to be a reason for such uncharacteristic behavior.

She rubbed her damp palms nervously against her taffeta-covered hips. "No— What I wanted to talk about doesn't have anything to do with the fair. But obviously I waited too long to disturb you. Forgive me."

He must have sensed her intentions because he grasped her forearm before she could walk away. "There's nothing to forgive. Come in, Alexandra. I was just having a nightcap to help me sleep."

"You must be more worried about your nephew than you've been letting on."

His eyes narrowed on her mouth, making her insides quiver. "That and other things," came the vague explanation. He pushed the door closed behind her. Her gaze flitted to the table where she saw a small half-empty glass.

"I'd offer you a drink, but something tells me you wouldn't like the flavor of retsina. If this is going to take a while, come all the way in and sit down."

She couldn't back down and followed him to the table where she did his bidding. "Dimitrios—"

"That's a good beginning. For some reason I haven't figured out yet, you seem to have trouble saying it."

"B-because first names blur the lines between a worker and an employer."

"Surely by now I mean a little more to you than that."

"Yes. We've become good friends." Her heart was pounding so outrageously, she squirmed on the chair. "I feel I could tell you anything."

"Is that why you're here?"

"Yes." She moistened her dry lips nervously. "Tonight you made a statement about my being the only honest woman you'd ever met."

"I never say anything I don't mean."

"Then you need to know I haven't been completely honest with you about something very important."

His eyes held a strange glitter. "It must be, for you to come knocking at my door. Go on. I'm listening."

"T-this has to do with an experience that happened to me a long time ago."

"With a man?" he demanded quietly.

"Yes."

She felt his stillness before hearing his sharp intake of breath. "Were you raped?"

"Almost," she answered shakily. "But another man came along in time to save me."

"Thank God," sounded the emotional response. "How old were you when it happened?"

"Sixteen."

"*Now* I understand why you wear clothes that intentionally hide your body."

Her eyes closed tightly for a moment. He was so close, yet so far from the mark.

"I hope the man who saved you beat him to a bloody pulp before turning him in to the police."

"H-he knocked him unconscious, and I loved him for it," she said on a half-sob. "In fact I've loved him ever since. Dimitrios, that man—"

But Alex was prevented from finishing her confession because the door suddenly flew open.

She turned in the chair as Leon swept into the room. He slowed to a stop when he saw her.

"Ms. Hamilton—I didn't realize you were in here. I knocked." His gaze darted to Dimitrios. "Are you feeling worse?"

"That's what I came in to ask him," she interjected

before Dimitrios could say anything. "But he insists he's fine and felt like having a drink before going to bed."

"You really shouldn't, Uncle. Not until you're completely out of the woods."

"Perhaps you're right," Dimitrios muttered. "What can I do for you, Leon?"

"I was hoping if you weren't too tired, I could go over my speech with you. Tomorrow morning will be too late. I don't want to shame you in front of the whole world."

Alex shook her head. "You couldn't possibly do that, Leon."

Alex got up from the chair and raised herself on tiptoe to whisper in his ear. "At least a half year ago Mrs. Landau confided that your uncle wanted you to open the trade fair. He should have acted on those feelings sooner, but he's never wanted to force you into doing things. His uncle Spiros did enough strong-arming to last a lifetime."

Leon's eyes grew suspiciously bright. "Thanks for telling me," he whispered back.

"You're welcome."

"I resent being treated as if I'm not in the room," Dimitrios bellowed.

"You're supposed to be resting," she teased with more daring than usual.

Her confession would have to wait a little while longer.

She'd go to her room and leave the door ajar. As soon as Leon passed by, she'd return to Dimitrios and finish what she'd started.

"Before I say good-night, I'd like to thank you for being so nice to my friends, Leon. They loved the tour of the villa. I've known them for years and could tell they had the time of their lives tonight.''

He grinned. ''I had a good time, too. In fact they asked me to go back to the hotel to party with them. But this speech has made it impossible. I asked Kristofor to drive them home. Tomorrow we're all going to meet after the parade and enjoy the fair together. I'm going to bring some girls I know to come with us.''

''The guys will love it. Greek women are as gorgeous as the men.''

''Did you hear that, Uncle?'' Leon threw his head back and laughed exactly as she'd seen Dimitrios do on their trip.

Alex smiled. ''Go ahead and mock me all you want, but it's true. By the way, you looked pretty terrific in that costume. Merlina's eyes are going to pop right out when she sees you in the parade tomorrow.''

A ruddy color stained his cheeks. ''You think?''

''I *know*. All's fair in love and war,'' she teased. ''Good luck tomorrow, but your uncle told me you won't need it.'' She kissed his jaw.

''Good night, Kyrie Pandakis.''

''Don't I get one of those too?''

She ignored Dimitrios's comment and slipped out of the room.

Under the circumstances, she was thankful that as long as Leon had been determined to see his uncle tonight, he'd come in before she'd had the chance to blurt everything out.

There was no miracle gauge to calculate how angry Dimitrios was going to be when he learned the truth. Since Leon had needed his uncle tonight, it was best that she'd left Dimitrios in a somewhat mellow mood.

Upon reaching her room, she left the door open a few inches, then turned out the lights. She hoped Leon wouldn't stay too long.

Alex lay down on her side across the bed so she could keep an eye on the hallway. She decided not to change. It would require all the confidence she could summon to face Dimitrios.

Whatever the consequences, her mother would be overjoyed when Alex phoned to report that the truth was out at last. In Alex's heart of hearts, she would be relieved, too. But it meant never seeing Dimitrios again.

Zeus would have to return to his immortal state as the mythological god in her art history book. A book she would never open again.

She rested her head on her arm as hot tears trickled out of the corners of her eyes.

CHAPTER NINE

"So what do you think, Uncle?"

Dimitrios got up off the bed to face his nephew. "Would you believe me if I told you?"

Leon answered yes.

He eyed his brother's boy who'd become a man over the last year. Dimitrios didn't know the exact moment the transformation had occurred, but he liked what he saw very much.

"It's a masterpiece of fresh ideas, optimism and surprising faith in mankind. Many people feel the world has already seen its golden days. You have a vision that sees golden days to come." He put a hand on his shoulder. "I'm proud to be related to you."

Leon had to clear his throat. "I feel the same way about you. Thank you," he muttered before hugging Dimitrios hard.

"I'm sorry to have walked in on you and Alexandra like that. I had no idea."

Dimitrios patted him one more time, then stepped back. "She and I have the rest of the night."

"Then I'm going to get out of here now. When I wave from my horse tomorrow, I'll be waving to you and Mother."

"She'll be in tears the entire time she's in the grandstand. I'm going to have it taped at the office so she can watch her son's triumphant entry into Thessalonica whenever she gets lonely for you."

Leon's eyes slid away.

Dimitrios didn't know whether to take that as a sign that his nephew had definitely made up his mind. But now wasn't the time to solve all the riddles.

The woman next door had been on the verge of telling him something vital when they'd been interrupted. He had the awful premonition she was planning to leave his employ to marry the man who'd saved her from being violated.

Dimitrios couldn't accept that.

Whatever she felt for her rescuer was hero-worship, gratitude. It had nothing to do with the kind of intimacy Dimitrios had enjoyed with her these past few days. Theirs was that rare bonding of flesh and spirit. A trust that couldn't be broken. *A love to die for.*

Leonides hadn't been allowed to live long enough to find what Dimitrios had found.

Aching to express his feelings, he left the room after Leon disappeared and walked next door to Alexandra's room.

To his surprise, her door was ajar. He pushed it open a little more. There was enough light from the hall to see her lying on the bed, still dressed in what she'd been wearing earlier. She had to have been exhausted to do that.

He listened to her breathing. She was in a deep sleep.

After everything she'd done to make the trade fair run to perfection, it would be criminal of him to waken her now.

Afraid to stand there for fear he'd join her on that bed, he went to his room for a cold shower. As he turned on the spray, he vowed that this was the last night he was going to lie in his bed alone writhing with unassuaged longings.

Eight hours later, a beaming Stavros tossed half a dozen newspapers on the table in front of Dimitrios while he sat in front of the television waiting for the parade coverage to start.

"In Japanese, English or Greek, it's the same story on the front page of every major journal." He shook his head. "Ms. Hamilton is a veritable genius. Trust her to give the newspapers a quote from the chronicler of the twelfth-century fair to begin the article."

It pleased him that Stavros held the future Mrs. Pandakis in such high regard. He reached for the Athenian News and began reading.

The Demetria is a festival, the most important fair held in Macedonia. Not only do the natives flock together to it in great numbers, but they come from all lands and every race.

Dimitrios put the paper down and cleared his throat. "You're right, Stavros. She's recreated something people aren't going to forget."

"She has the attention of the prime minister."

"So Vaso told me."

"Do you think she would leave you to take another position?"

"I hope not. As soon as the fair is over I'm asking her to marry me."

When Stavros didn't say anything, Dimitrios turned his head to glance at his mentor, who'd just pulled a handkerchief out of his pocket.

He frowned. "Are you all right?"

"Yes, yes. Of course."

"Then why aren't you saying anything?"

"I think I'm overcome."

Dimitrios smiled to himself. "I didn't know that was possible."

"Congratulations, my boy."

"Keep it under your hat."

"Since when have we ever announced a deal until it was all sewn up?"

"All sewn up is the operative phrase, Stavros. Last night I found out she thinks she's in love with someone else."

"Knowing you as I do, you'll get around that little problem. Oh—the coverage is beginning." Stavros sat down on the couch next to him to watch.

Dimitrios felt gooseflesh as trumpets sounded and he saw his nephew lead a contingent of soldiers on horseback through the throng of people lining the packed streets under a sunny sky. They shouted and waved to him in celebration.

Leon sat tall in the saddle, his red cape flowing, the gold scepter held high in his right hand. Dimitrios's eyes blurred.

But inevitably his thoughts wandered to Alexandra, who'd slipped away from the villa earlier in the morning before he could catch her.

If she'd never come to work for him, there would be no trade fair in Thessalonica. Without her there'd be no costume made expressly for him. He'd find no joy in getting up to meet the day because she wouldn't be a part of it. The thought of life without her was too unfathomable to contemplate.

Stavros pulled out his handkerchief again. "If Leon decides for the ministry, he definitely looks the part."

"Yes."

"I can only hope that wherever your brother is, he's looking on to see what a fine son he has. Ananke will be the proudest mother in all Thessalonica today."

For the next two hours they stayed glued to the set watching the tumbling acts, banners, dancers and floats from every province in Greece. Enchanted, Dimitrios was bursting with pride by the time his nephew delivered his speech to the crowd.

When he'd finished, the prime minister stepped forward. He bid Leon kneel so he could place a garland of laurel leaves on his head. The throng roared their approval.

Stavros's voice sounded gruff when he said, "I don't think that was in the original script."

"A very nice gesture from the prime minister."

"He asked you to get the job done. Your bride-to-be answered him a hundredfold."

"I'm going to find her, Stavros. We'll meet you on board the barge in an hour."

Except that plans had a way of changing.

After Dimitrios had been pacing in front of the launch at the pier for half an hour, Alexandra phoned to say something had come up to do with a group of translators for the fair. Their bus from the university had broken down en route to a designated location. She needed to go back to the office arrange other transportation for them and wouldn't be able to join him for lunch.

Dimitrios's degree of disappointment was so severe, he realized he couldn't go on this way any longer. With his emotions in utter chaos, he made his own excuses regarding the lunch, then called for his driver to take him to the office. He'd reached the point that if he couldn't be with Alexandra, nothing else interested him.

Alex spotted Dimitrios's well-honed frame as he swept through the reception area of the suite. The place resembled a florist's shop at the moment. Several hundred offerings of flowers sat on desks, lined corridors and decorated file cabinets.

The outpouring from business associates and government officials was a touching tribute to Dimitrios, but he seemed oblivious as he headed straight for her office.

Her heart leaped at the sight of him. He was dressed in a dove-gray silk suit and dazzling white shirt, but lines had darkened his handsome face, making him appear remote.

"What's wrong?" she asked the second he stepped over the threshold.

"Remind me to tell you when we're alone. Now that Leon's part in the fair is over, we won't have to worry about being interrupted again."

If she didn't have a confession to make tonight, his words would have brought her the greatest joy imaginable.

"Your nephew was magnificent today."

"I thought so, too," he murmured.

"It's been very exciting to hear all the favorable compliments about the parade and the part he played."

He captured her gaze. "The moment you presented me the drawing of Thessalonica during the twelfth-century fair, there was never any doubt in my mind it would be a success."

This had been her hope and dream for Dimitrios. She could be thankful for that much.

"The prime minister sent that huge spray of flowers over in the corner."

Dimitrios stood behind her while she opened the card

to show him. When his body brushed against hers, she almost fainted from the sensation.

"How do I thank him?"

"Would you like to accept a position on his trade commission? That's what he's angling for."

And remain in Greece so close to you, knowing I can never be with you again?

"I'm very honored, but no."

"In that case you could pen him a personal note. I'll see that it's attached to an acknowledgment from the corporation. We'll be sending one to every donor. He'll enjoy that."

"I'll write it before I leave the office today. Shall we send the flowers to the hospitals?"

He nodded. "The staff will take care of it."

"Then I'd better get busy answering e-mails."

"Uncle?"

Alex was getting used to the sound of Leon's voice.

She looked over her shoulder in time see Dimitrios hug his nephew. Then it was her turn to congratulate him.

To her surprise, he wasn't alone. Michael and his friends had trailed in after him, but there was no sign of Yanni or Merlina.

"We've had a change in plans," Leon began without preamble. "If it's all right with you, I'm taking the guys to Mount Athos. We'll be back tomorrow evening to take in a play. They're putting on *Phaedra*."

To Dimitrios's credit, he didn't reveal his emotions. It was Alex who had to bite her tongue not to say anything. Her disappointment in his nephew's decision caused her spirits to plunge to new depths.

"I'm fine with that," Dimitrios said with enviable calm. "Mount Athos is a unique place."

Michael eyed Alex. "When Leon was telling us about it last night, we asked if we could visit it with him."

"There's just one problem," Leon murmured. "Yanni wants to join us, but Merlina shouldn't be left alone."

Before Leon said anything more, Alex knew what she had to do. It meant her confession would have to be put off a little longer, but it didn't seem she had a choice.

"I'll stay at the hotel with her tonight, Leon. I hear it's a fabulous place and I haven't even stepped inside it yet. Besides, it's the least I can do to repay you for looking after my friends."

"Thank you, Ms. Hamilton."

"I tell you what. I'll phone Yanni right now and tell him to bring Merlina here. She can hang around with me."

Without glancing at Dimitrios, she went over to the desk to make the call. Michael followed.

"Your sacrifice has been noted, but don't look now, darling. Your lord and master is anything but pleased."

"You don't understand, Michael, and there's no time to explain."

"What's going on between you two?" For once Michael had dropped the banter.

"Nothing."

"Then how come you look like your heart is breaking? Why did you let things get this far?"

She blinked hard to fight back the tears. "Because I'm a fool."

"I'm sorry you're in so much pain, Alex. I wish there was something I could do."

"You've been warning me. So has Mom. As soon as I can, I'm telling him the truth. I tried last night, but

Leon interrupted us. I should tell him tonight, but under the circumstances, I'll have to wait a little longer.''

"This is a hell of a time for me to be leaving. When I get back tomorrow we're going to have one of our talks, so plan on it!''

But Michael didn't get back. The other guys were steeped in the arts and wanted to see all of Mount Athos. That meant they had to spend two nights away. Being responsible for Merlina meant Alex was forced to put off her talk with Dimitrios another twenty-four hours.

After months of being with him constantly, the few days without seeing him were the longest, loneliest hours she'd ever known. While he was out covering their VIP lunches and dinners with Stavros, she and Merlina walked all over the city visiting the stalls.

Late Friday afternoon, after the guys had finally returned, Alex took a taxi to the villa. She was going to use her guest room to get ready for a special dinner with some high-ranking Greek dignitaries, which signaled the last night of the fair. On Saturday it would be over.

With one terse message from Dimitrios earlier in the day making it clear she was to attend with him, he clicked off just as abruptly. There was no escaping the fact that tonight he intended getting her alone so they could finish their talk.

Alex dreaded the outcome. But if she could be thankful for just one thing, it was that she'd been given the opportunity to fulfill her professional obligations before everything in her world fell apart.

According to Serilda, who greeted her warmly and brought a cup of tea to her bedroom, no one was home yet, not even Ananke. But she expected Dimitrios home within the hour.

After drinking the hot, sweet liquid, she stepped in the shower to wash her hair. It felt good, but she didn't dare stay in too long. Dimitrios expected her to be ready by six-thirty, which didn't leave her much time to blow dry it and arrange it in a twist. Afterward she'd dress in the ghastly gray suit once more.

Draped in a fluffy towel with her damp hair falling over her shoulders, she padded to the bedroom for fresh underwear. Halfway across the room she froze.

A dark, overweight man dressed in a blue business suit stood against the closed door watching her.

Giorgio.

As his eyes crawled over her body drinking their fill, she tugged the edge of the towel closer around her.

"I was right. You're the sexy little Hamilton girl all grown up."

Terrified because her worst nightmare had become reality, Alex fled to the bathroom. But he'd already lunged for her, preventing her from locking the door against him. He stood over the threshold blocking the exit.

Though he wasn't as tall or powerfully built as Dimitrios, he was still a man. He could best her without problem.

"And you're still the sick little man who'll never measure up to your cousin. Not in an eternity!"

The smile vanished from his face. "You're very clever. I give you credit for that. For the first time in his life, Dimitrios appears to be smitten. That's a major coup considering it's my inscrutable cousin we're talking about."

"Get out!" she raged.

"I don't think so."

"What are you going to do? Finish what you tried the first time before he knocked you unconscious?"

He hunched his shoulders. "If I were drunk, I might be tempted. But I was forced to give up that habit a long time ago. I think what we're going to do is wait for Dimitrios to arrive."

She gritted her teeth. "What is it you want?"

"To see the expression on his face when he realizes the sweet little innocent he once protected so gallantly is none other than the calculating whore who wiggled her ripe body at me one summer night. You were asking for it then.

"Dimitrios didn't believe me, of course. But he will now. Believe me, he will. And then the joke will be on him because he'll realize that even he, the *infallible* one as my father loved to call him, allowed you to slip past his radar."

Dear God. Was everyone in the Pandakis family in pain? The blame for Giorgio's jealousy of Dimitrios could be laid at Spiros's feet. But the damage had been done so long ago, Alex couldn't imagine how any of them would ever heal. It probably wasn't possible.

"You may not believe this, Giorgio, but I had every intention of telling Dimitrios the truth tonight. Why don't you let me get dressed? When he comes, the three of us will sit down and talk this out. No one else will ever have to know."

His bark of angry laughter reverberated against the bathroom walls. "No wonder he was deceived! You have a brain as well as a velvet tongue. You almost got to me just now. No. We'll wait right here where he can see what you've been hiding under those clothes. It was the work of a master."

Tears filled her eyes. "It was the work of a friend who knew how much I loved your cousin and wanted to be close to him."

His head shot forward. "You were a teenager back then. What could you know of love?" he mocked.

Her body shook with pain. "He saved me from you. And he was kind to me. That was the beginning of love." By now the moisture was dripping off her cheeks.

In the silence that followed she heard Dimitrios's rap on the bedroom door. "Alexandra?"

Her heart thudded in her chest.

"Go ahead," Giorgio prodded. "Tell him to come in."

Dimitrios called out a second time.

"Listen to him. So eager for you."

She shook her head. "Don't do this," she begged. "You'll live to regret it."

"My life's been one regret for being born. What's another one? Go on. Tell your beloved he can come in. Or do you want me to invite him in for you?"

Either way she was damned.

Oh, Dimitrios. Forgive me.

"C-come in," she cried in a halting voice.

The door opened and closed. "I hope you're ready. We'll make an appearance at the dinner, then I've planned a surprise for you."

Giorgio's mouth broke into a slow smile. She knew what he was going to do before he clamped a hand on her arm and forced her to walk out of the bathroom in front of him.

"Great minds must think alike, cousin. Ms. Hamilton has a little surprise of her own for you, too."

Dimitrios, dressed in a formal black tux, stood in the

center of the room, his legs slightly apart. When Alex made eye contact with him, he didn't move. There wasn't the slightest flicker of an eyelid or twitch of a muscle.

But as surely as she watched a whiteness creep around his chiseled mouth, as surely as she saw the light extinguished, turning his eyes to black holes, Alex knew everything had changed between them.

She felt her heart die.

Giorgio lifted his palms. "Before you make the mistake of telling me to get out and never darken your doorstep again, you'd better listen to someone who's been lured by Ms. Hamilton's siren song before.

"What I'm attempting to do now, cousin, is save you from yourself. The way you once saved me.

"Of course she was nine years younger then, but well enough aware of her potential to make a play for the youngest Pandakis cousin who couldn't hold his liquor or take his eyes off her during the fashion show. How could I resist her offer of a tour of the silk museum?"

"My grandfather told me to do it as a favor to *your* father!" Alex defended. "That was my job. I received a salary for it. If he'd known you were drunk, he would never have allowed me near you! I didn't know it until you forced me out to the garden." Her voice shook in remembered pain.

"So you say," Giorgio murmured. "Nevertheless we all know how that ended. But what we didn't know at the time was that she would decide to go after her savior. That was you, Dimitrios.

"Only her plan had to be much more cunning because this time she wanted to capture the favorite son."

Alex's eyes closed tightly.

"No more blond hair. A whole new identity. Everything a fait accompli. In the end we were both duped.

"Because you're a man of honor who didn't expose my embarrassing lapse to the family, Dimitrios, I've decided to return the favor. When I leave this room, no one will ever know she almost made a fool of you, too.

"Let us pray that in future, you'll set your sights somewhere other than the Pandakis family, Ms. Hamilton. My brother Vaso tells me the prime minister was very taken with you, even in your altered state. If he could see what I'm looking at right now, you would end up his pillow friend."

Blind with fury, Alex slapped him hard across the face. It was something she'd been wanting to do for nine years. He put his hand to the place where she could already see red.

"Cousin." He nodded to both of them before leaving the bedroom.

A stunning silence filled the room.

Dimitrios's wintry regard froze the blood in her veins.

"Please— If you'll just give me a chance, I can explain everything."

"No explanation is needed. I'll be waiting for you in the car. Don't take too long."

She was shaking so hard, she felt faint. Her body broke out in a cold sweat. Then a salty taste filled her mouth. "I—I couldn't go anywhere right now."

Alex reached the bathroom in time to lose her lunch.

She felt his presence in the doorway. After everything else, this was a humiliation beyond enduring.

"I'll send Serilda to you. Have your desk cleaned out by the time I get back to New York on Wednesday.

Charlene will give you an envelope containing your bonus and severance pay.''

"Uncle? What are you doing up here on this peak with me?"

They were both sitting against one of the ruins of the castle, looking out over the forest.

Dimitrios bit down on a blade of sweet grass. ''I thought it was obvious.''

"It might be, except for the fact that you're in love with Alexandra. She should be the one here with you. For that matter, the trade fair's still going on.''

"Today was the last day. Vaso's in charge. Stavros can handle any unforeseen problems.''

"You mean Alexandra, don't you?''

His eyes closed tightly. *Lord,* the pain.

"No," he finally murmured. "I've relieved her of all responsibilities.''

As the words sank in, Leon's head turned sharply in his direction. His brows formed a black bar. ''She couldn't have turned down your marriage proposal!''

"She didn't get one," he ground out.

Leon leaped to his feet. His hands went to his hips. He stared at his uncle. ''Good grief, you didn't fire her—''

"As a matter of fact I did. By now I presume she's on her way back to New York.''

His nephew shook his head. ''I only have one question. Why?''

"I don't want to talk about it.''

"Then why did you drag me up here?'' His nephew sounded angry. It surprised him.

"I wanted you to understand why this place was so important to your father and me."

"But you could have done that anytime!" Leon declared. His mild-mannered nephew seemed to have disappeared. "Why don't you just admit that for once in your life you need someone to confide in?"

Now it was Dimitrios who got to his feet, anxious to change the subject. They'd been up here long enough. It was time to get back to the lodge for the night.

His nephew faced him without blinking. "It's funny, you know? All my life you've been there to listen to my problems, yet you never tell me yours."

"Leon—"

"It's true!" he defended. Color filled his cheeks. "You say you want me around, that you'd like me to go into business with you. But if you can't open up to me about the woman you love, then there's not much point to anything, is there?"

He walked off with the binoculars to study some raptors circling overhead. As Dimitrios watched his long legs eat up the distance, it began to dawn on him that his nephew might just have told him something he'd been longing to hear.

"Alexandra lied to me."

Leon remained where he was. "If she did, she must have had a damn good reason."

Dimitrios followed him, puzzled by Leon's fierce defense of her. "When she applied for a job with the company in New York four years ago, she presented herself as a dowdy, thirty-year-old woman who had brown hair. In reality…"

Images of her curvaceous body and long slender legs barely covered by the towel flashed before his eyes. She was so gorgeous he could hardly breathe when he pictured her in his mind.

"Yes? In reality, what?"

Dimitrios rubbed his chest absently. "She's a green-eyed twenty-five-year-old with long blond hair."

After a moment Leon looked over his shoulder. There was a trace of a smile on his lips. "Really. Since when is that a sin?"

"It's not. But to live with the lie this long *is*."

"Alexandra's a smart woman. No doubt she wanted to look efficient enough to get hired. I doubt she would have gotten past Mrs. Landau if she'd been a knockout." Leon cocked his head. "Is she?"

He knew what his nephew was asking. "She's incredible."

"So what's really wrong? You don't fire the woman who's become your right hand because she's younger than you thought, *and* beautiful."

His nephew's shrewd analysis jolted him.

"You do when you find out she had a plan to trick me into marriage as far back as nine years ago."

"Now we're getting somewhere. You two met nine years ago? How?"

Dimitrios only hesitated a moment, then he recounted the details of that night in New Jersey.

Leon's face lit up. "Forget Giorgio and anything he had to say. She's been in love with *you* all this time. If a woman ever loved me that much, I'd be the happiest man alive."

Maybe they were talking at cross purposes. "Isn't that a bit ironic coming from you?"

"What do you mean?"

"You're planning to enter a monastery."

"I've changed my mind about that, Uncle. This last trip with the guys made me realize I'm more into religious art than religion. That business you talked about? I was thinking that if I finished my studies, we could start a company that manufactured religious artifacts.

"I was talking with some vendors at the fair. They claim there's a huge international market out there for them if they could find the right distributor."

By tacit agreement they started down the peak. Dimitrios let his nephew chat away. It was like hearing beautiful music after a cacophony of sounds.

Talking with Leon about Alexandra had at least brought him out of his near comatose state. Unfortunately there were things his nephew still didn't know. Things Dimitrios could never tell him without painting Ananke in a bad light.

"Have you told your mother the news?"

"As soon as we get home tomorrow."

A groan came out of Dimitrios. Without Alexandra, he had no idea how he was going to get through the night, let alone tomorrow. He didn't even want to think about the rest of his life.

CHAPTER TEN

IT WAS after ten p.m. when Alex drove the rental car into the parking area of the Dadia lodge. With Michael's help they'd found a hairdresser who could speak English. He followed Michael's directions to put her hair back to its normal blond color.

The appointment had taken hours. Then she'd bought some new clothes, including the khaki shorts and white knit top she was wearing. That barely left enough time to make the last flight to Alexandropoulos.

Dimitrios had ordered her back to New York, but she couldn't leave Greece until she'd spent a day in the forest where she'd known joy with him. It was her own way of saying goodbye to her dreams.

She didn't have a reservation, but she'd decided to use Dimitrios's name just one more time. If that didn't work, then she'd stay in the parking lot and sleep in the car all night.

Tomorrow morning she'd hike the trail to the observatory. She could be up and down the mountain in time to get a flight back to Thessalonica. Once at the airport, she'd switch terminals for her overseas flight to New York.

When she went inside the office, there was no one at the counter. She tapped the bell with the palm of her hand. In a minute the concierge who'd waited on them before came out from the dining room area.

He nodded to her, but there was no sign of recognition.

It was like being reborn in a different skin. Before she could ask, he waved his hand back and forth. "No rooms. All is full for the fair."

"I'm Alexandra Hamilton, Kyrie Dimitrios Pandakis's secretary? I came with him a few days ago?"

That perked him up. "Yes? One moment, please." He reached for the phone receiver to talk to someone in Greek.

Thank heaven her plan had worked. She desperately needed a bed. After sobbing all night, then going hard all day, Alex was so exhausted she was ready to drop.

He put the receiver back on the hook. "If you will wait five minutes, your room will be ready."

"Thank you very much. Let me pay you now."

"That is all right. It is already taken care of."

"But I insist on paying." She signed two one-hundred-dollar traveler's checks and left them on the counter.

He nodded again. "Here is your key. The room is number twenty on the far end."

"I'll find it."

She got back in the car and drove past the other cottages until she came to the last one. Relieved there was a light on inside the room, she climbed out of the car and removed her suitcase from the back seat.

Lugging it to the door, she inserted the key and let herself inside, dragging the suitcase behind her. She nudged the door shut with her hip.

That's when she saw the man who'd haunted her dreams for so many years emerge from the bathroom wearing nothing but a pair of low-slung navy sweats.

"I don't believe it," she whispered in shock.

Their gazes fused as if a sizzling bolt of electricity connected them.

He'd thought he'd seen the last of her!

Zeus had banished her to the nethermost regions of the universe, yet here she was back again at the foot of Olympus, his favorite place, using his name to gain entrance, no less.

"Some coincidences defy every known law," she began in an unsteady voice. "I wouldn't blame you if you thought I'd charged the room to your account. If you'll call the concierge, he'll tell you I left money for the room on the counter. Forgive me for intruding."

Alex had to get out of there. But when she turned to go, Dimitrios had reached the door ahead of her, preventing her from leaving. She had no idea anyone could move that fast.

After locking the door, he picked up her suitcase like it was full of air and put it on the extra bed. When he turned out the light, only the soft glow from the bedside lamp remained.

She backed away to one of the other twin beds and sat down on the end of it. In truth, her legs would no longer support her.

He came closer, his fists on his hips. Since she'd been in Greece she'd seen several statues of Zeus standing in that exact position, his magnificent body nude except for a drape.

That's how she thought of Dimitrios. A man who was more than a man. Bigger than life.

"How long did you plan to continue being someone you're not? No more lies, Alexandra." His voice seemed to come from a dark, deep cavern.

"You would have known everything if Leon hadn't come in your bedroom the other night."

His intake of breath sounded like ripping silk. Distracted by the stunning virility of his body, she lowered her eyes. *To think a mortal man could look like that!*

"Leon's not here now. Let's have it all, then be done with it."

Her head was still averted. "Everything your cousin accused me of was true except for one thing. I was a pretty naïve sixteen-year-old who wouldn't have known how to attract an older man if I'd tried.

"But there is one thing I do remember about that night. It was the deep disappointment I felt when my grandfather asked me to escort Giorgio around the museum instead of you. Your cousin probably sensed it. Maybe that's what set him off."

To Alex's wonderment he said, "It wouldn't have taken much. You were the most beautiful of your sisters, even back then. With your long golden hair, you were exceptionally appealing to a family of dark-haired men. All my cousins commented on you during the fashion show.

"In fairness to Giorgio, one could forgive him for being enchanted. But everything else that happened that night was criminal. I saw him go off with you and sensed there could be trouble. When too much time lapsed without your reappearance, I went to look for you."

Alex's body shook convulsively. "What if you hadn't come?"

A sound of exasperation escaped his throat, permeating the room. She didn't know if it poured from pure anger or frustration, or both. Suddenly Dimitrios was sitting next to her, his hand sliding beneath her hair to the nape of her neck.

"I blame myself for that night," he murmured, stroking her skin to gentle her. "I'd known for a while he was an alcoholic. He had no business being around you in that condition.

"When I got him back to the hotel, I waited until he'd sobered up, then I threatened to expose him to his father.

"Giorgio knew what that would mean. Uncle Spiros put the fear in everyone. He would have disowned Giorgio had he known the truth. We made a pact that night. If he never went near alcohol again, I'd never tell my uncle. To my cousin's credit, he got help and left it alone."

"But he's so jealous of you it's painful to hear him talk."

His fingers tangled in her hair. "I know. It's been a burden I wouldn't wish on my worst enemy."

Moisture stung her eyes. "It's because you're so wonderful. There's no one to match you, Dimitrios. I love you so much," she blurted. "But I was wrong to deceive you."

"Why did you?" He got up from the bed, leaving her desolate. "If you wanted a job with me so badly, why weren't you straightforward? You could have passed on your grandfather's name through Mrs. Landau. I would have remembered and given you a personal interview."

She clasped her hands. "I know that now. But at the time I thought I'd have a better chance if I toned down my apparearance so Mrs. Landau would consider me for a job. Michael helped me, and I was hired. Mrs. Landau was so good to me, I couldn't admit to her what I'd done. After she had that heart attack, I wanted to tell you everything. I swear it. But you were so upset about her passing, I thought I'd wait a while. Unfortunately no time ever seemed right.

"Dimitrios?" she whispered in anguish. "The thing I feel worst about is destroying the trust you had in me. Without it, there's nothing!"

"Exactly."

What did he mean? She wiped her eyes. "Are you going to let what I've done prevent you from having faith in a woman's love?"

"Does it matter?" He lay down on the other bed.

"What happened to hurt you so deeply?" Without conscious thought she moved to the other bed and sat down next to him.

"Please, Dimitrios—" Her voice throbbed. As if it had a life of its own, her hand reached out to touch him where she could feel his heart pounding. "Tell me who did this to you."

His great body shook. "One night when I was twelve, I heard my brother in the hall of Uncle Spiros's villa. He was stealing away to get married to Ananke because she was pregnant with his child. At that moment, I *hated* her."

Alex was listening, trying with all her heart to understand. "Of course you did, darling. He was your whole world and she was taking him away from you." Poor Ananke had borne a burden she knew nothing about.

Dimitrios grasped her hand so hard it hurt, but he wasn't aware of the pressure. His thoughts were somewhere else.

"It was more than that. He said she didn't love him. He said she'd gotten pregnant on purpose so she could become a member of the Pandakis family. I begged him

not to marry Ananke if she didn't love him, but he said
he had to. It was a matter of honor.'' His body went taut.

They were close to the truth now, but she sensed there
was still more to come. "What else did he say?"

"He said our mother probably married our father for
the same reason."

Groaning with sorrow for the heartbroken boy inside
the man, she waited for the rest.

"Leonides warned me that one day many women
would come after me for my money. They would try to
trick me into marriage by getting pregnant with my
child."

How cruel his brother had been to disillusion a vulnerable boy.

"And what did you say?"

"I told him that would never happen to me because I
would never make love to a woman before I married
her."

Alex's thoughts reeled as she considered all the
women Dimitrios had ever known or been with.

Her heart caught in her throat. "Did you keep your
vow?" *Was it possible?*

His chest rose and fell. "Yes. It was easy. No woman
ever tempted me beyond my power to resist. I was so
pleased with myself, I didn't realize my secretary had
stolen my heart."

At last Alex expelled the breath she'd been holding.

"Oh, darling—" She buried her face in his luxuriant
hair. "I can't believe that out of all the beautiful women
you've known, you would be tempted by a non descript
little nobody like me."

"Brown haired or blond, there's nothing non descript
about you, Alexandra." He pulled her to him. His hands

started to roam over her body, finding every line and curve. "When you nursed me through the night and stroked the hair off my forehead, that vow was the last thing on my mind. If Leon hadn't interrupted us, you could be pregnant with my child right now. You don't know how hard it was trying not to drag you into my bed."

She kissed the corner of his mouth, delirious with longing for her first taste of him. "Then I might have been tempted to break my vow, too."

His hands stilled, then suddenly their positions were reversed. Dimitrios gazed down into her eyes. "You made the same vow?" His voice sounded husky.

"When you saved me at sixteen, you won everything I have to give, what I'm dying to give. I'm so in love with you," she cried. "Nine years has been too long to wait. Kiss me, Kyrie Pandakis. Love me," she begged.

"*Agape mou.*"

The Greek endearment was smothered as his mouth descended on hers with primitive hunger. On fire after such long-suppressed passion, they sought to absorb the very essence of each other.

This was ecstasy. She couldn't stop moaning from the pleasure pain of being in his arms like this at last.

Their legs tangled until Alex was trapped right where she'd always wanted to be. Her heart streamed into his until it felt like they'd always been connected.

She'd dreamed about loving him like this, but to finally be the participant in a love match with her real-life Zeus was wonderful beyond bearing.

"I'm ready to eat you alive," he confessed on a ragged breath after they'd been devouring each other over and over again. Their passion knew no bounds.

"I've been ready for that much much longer than you can imagine. You're my addiction. If I had my way, we would never leave this room again."

"It's your choice whether we wear white at our wedding tomorrow morning."

Alex groaned. "That wasn't fair to propose marriage and abstinence in the same breath." She covered his neck and powerful shoulders with feverish kisses. "Now I understand why the opposition runs when they see you coming. No one drives a harder bargain."

Laughter rumbled out of him as he buried his face in her golden hair splayed across the pillow.

"Are we really getting married tomorrow?"

He smoothed some gleaming strands of hair off her forehead. "I must have said something to please you. I can see your gorgeous green eyes shimmering."

"I wish we were man and wife already."

"You think I don't?" he came back on an almost savage note. "I've arranged for a special permit. If the priest were willing, we'd be in that little church down the road saying our vows this very minute. As it is, Leon is in Dadia right now making all the arrangements."

"Leon's here?"

Dimitrios cupped the back of her head and kissed her long and hard before finally letting her go again. He sounded out of breath.

"After I left your bedroom, my state of mind was so black, I had to get out of the villa. I dragged him with me. We flew here. Today I forced him up to the top of the peak with me.

"It was an illuminating experience for our roles to be reversed. After he informed me that being with Michael

and his friends convinced him he doesn't want the life
of a religious after all—''

''Dimitrios—''

He smiled at her joyous outburst. ''He demanded that
I tell him what was wrong with me. One thing led to
another, and it all came out.''

''I love that nephew of yours more every day.''

Dimitrios kissed every feature of her upturned face.
''He's crazy about you, too. While I was showering earlier, the phone rang in our room. Leon answered it. The
concierge told him my secretary had arrived and was
asking for a room. My nephew took it upon himself to
tell the man to give you a key.

''When I came out of the bathroom, Leon was on his
way out the front door with the rental car keys. I asked
him what was going on. A smile lit up his face. He said
he was sleeping in Dadia for the night because my future
bride would be entering the room any second now.

''Before he shut the door, he added that he would call
on the local priest to arrange a wedding. He'll return
tomorrow complete with the clothes we'll be married
in.''

Overjoyed, Alex threw her arms around his neck.
''When the priest finds out he's been given the honor of
marrying the most revered man in all Greece, he won't
let anything stand in the way. Now I know it's really
going to happen! I'm so excited. Dance with me, Kyrie.''

''Now?''

''Yes. Like we did the other night.''

''I prefer you right where you are.''

''So do I, but dancing's safer.''

''Really,'' he said in a devilish voice.

She rolled off the bed to turn on the lamp. After she'd

flipped on the radio to a music station, she looked back at him.

Her eyes widened as he levered himself off the bed. All six foot three inches of him were hard-packed muscle. With his black hair tousled and those black eyes glowing like hot coals, she really couldn't catch her breath.

"Have I ever told you what a sensational looking man you are? It's a shame you can't go around in your sweats all the time."

His white smile robbed her of breath.

"That's the difference between a man and a woman. I'm looking forward to watching you run around in nothing at all. But right now I'll settle for what the gods have dropped in my lap tonight.

"Come here to me, you beautiful creature. I need to hold you," he said in an aching voice. He began dancing and held out his arms. Alex ran into them.

"I'm so happy, I'm afraid I might have a heart attack before morning and then I'll never know what it's like to—"

Dimitrios stopped moving because his body was riddled with laughter. He rocked her back and forth.

"Oh, Alexandra. Life with you is one continual gift."

"I hope so. The thing is, what if I don't know how— I mean—"

He chuckled harder. "We'll learn together." He pivoted her around the room. "We'll have children together. We'll do it all, my love."

Her eyes closed tightly. "I love the sound of that. But do you suppose there's a lot more to it than we realize?"

"If there is, we have the rest of our lives to find out."

She threw her head back as he spun her around. "Morning, noon and night."

His lips twitched. "I hear that's a rather exhausting schedule for the husband on a regular basis."

"Why not the wife?"

"I don't know." He pulled her close. Growling into her neck he said, "I guess that's something else we're going to find out."

She stared up at him with stars in her eyes. "It's thrilling, isn't it. Tomorrow we're going to go where neither of us has gone before."

He whirled them to a stop. "With you, everything is thrilling." Then his handsome face sobered.

"I would never have wished the experience with Giorgio on you, but—"

"I know." She kissed his lips quiet. "I'd like to think it was all meant to be. He stopped drinking and turned his life around."

Dimitrios nodded.

"You and I are so lucky, we can afford to be kind to him."

He crushed her in his arms. "I tremble to imagine my life without you."

"I don't even want to think about it." She clung to him. "Darling? Ananke has suffered, too. Did it ever occur to you that she might have loved your brother the way I loved you in the beginning? Especially if Leonides was as handsome as my husband-to-be," she whispered in his ear before biting his lobe gently. "You Pandakis men make an enormous impact on the female population, you know."

He sculpted the back of her head with his hand. "I

hadn't thought about it before, but I'm thinking hard now. Leonides slept with her because he wanted to.''

''That's right, and they got caught. It happens to lovers every day. At that point he was down on all women. Maybe even your mother?''

''You're reading my mind again.'' He drew her over to the bed and lay down next to her. Pulling her close, his mouth roved her face, kissing every square inch. ''There's something I need to do before this night is over.''

''What?'' She'd settled against him and didn't want to move again.

''Call your parents and ask them if it's all right that I'm stealing you away. If they want to see us married, we can always fly to Paterson and say our vows again in front of all your friends and family.''

Alex just kept finding more reasons to love him. ''Mom and Dad won't believe I finally got my heart's desire. You're going to make them so happy. I've been their most worrisome child.''

The bed shook with his laughter. He'd been doing a lot of that. It was a glorious sound. Almost as glorious as hearing him call out her name after he'd fallen asleep in her arms. The longing in his voice made her heart leap. He couldn't wait for morning, either.

EPILOGUE

THERE was a rap on the cottage door. "Alexandra? It's Leon. I hope you're ready because Uncle Dimitrios is a nervous wreck. If we don't appear at the church in five minutes, he's going to charge back here to find out what's wrong."

"Just a minute!"

Alex could scarcely credit that a few days ago she'd been in pain watching another wedding celebration in a nearby meadow. With Dimitrios standing behind her, she'd wished with all her heart she'd been that ecstatic bride dancing in her new husband's arms.

Now, miraculously, this was her wedding day. Leon had come to escort her to the beautiful little forest church where she was about to be married to the man she loved more than life itself. Alex was so euphoric, she could hardly breathe.

After making an adjustment of the garland in her hair, she gave herself a final glance in the mirror. The white wedding dress Leon had purchased in the village fit her perfectly.

"Alexandra?"

"I'm coming!"

She hurried through the cottage and opened the door. To her joy, Leon had brought someone familiar with him.

"Michael!"

He took a step backward and put up his arms up as if to ward off her radiance.

181

"Oh, stop!"

He batted his eyelids like he did at the salon. "After four years, you've burst forth from your brown chrysalis. My eyes need time to adjust to your beauty."

"I'm so glad you're here!" she cried before giving him a big hug.

Leon looked on with a wide smile. "My uncle thought you would like someone from home to be here for you."

Dimitrios understood her better than she understood herself. Her love for him knew no bounds.

"Tsk, tsk. No tears today, darling," Michael admonished.

Leon opened the passenger door of his rental car for her. "I suggest we get going, otherwise I refuse to be responsible for the consequences. My uncle's never been in love before. I have a feeling my life won't be worth a drachma if we keep him in suspense any longer."

Alex didn't want to spend another second apart from Dimitrios, either. Two hours before, he'd left with Leon to make final preparations and allow her time to get ready. It had felt like three years.

Michael helped her into the car, then climbed in the back while Leon drove. The church was only a mile down the road. There was an air of unreality about the whole thing as they pulled into the parking area. Except for two cars, it looked deserted.

A hot sun shone directly overhead. Through the pines, rays fell on the exterior of the charming white church, making it glisten.

While Michael accompanied her to the entrance, Leon snapped pictures. Thankful he'd thought of a camera, she realized how important it was to preserve this day for posterity, especially photographs of her gorgeous husband.

"I guess I don't need to ask if you're ready to take this momentous step," Michael murmured.

"No," she answered in a tremulous voice.

He kissed her cheek. "Promise to come down from Olympus once in a while to pay this mortal a visit?"

"You know I will!" she cried softly.

Leon joined them on the steps. "Shall we go in and make my uncle a happy man?"

"Relax, Dimitrios," Stavros admonished. "They've arrived. Turn around and see what your nephew has brought you."

With heart thudding, Dimitrios spun on his heel in time to see Alexandra hurrying toward him with Michael holding her arm and Leon taking up the rear.

The priest broke off his conversation with Stavros's wife and Ananke in order to greet Dimitrios' bride-to-be.

She looked a vision of gold and white.

Almost suffocating with the need to love her into oblivion, he had to hold back a little longer while the priest led her forward and placed her right hand over Dimitrios's left.

Her green eyes glowed with a new light. "Darling," she whispered, out of breath, squeezing his fingers. He could feel her love like a living thing.

"You won't understand what the priest is saying," he murmured. "Just realize that when it's over, you'll be my wife."

"And you'll be my husband. It's all I've ever wanted." Her voice caught.

Dimitrios knew better than most men how much and how long he'd been loved by this woman. Humbled to be given such a gift, he was glad he'd kept his vow all these years. It was his gift to her.

After kissing the back of her hand, he nodded to the priest to start the ceremony.

The women were positioned beside Alexandra. Leon took his place next to Dimitrios, followed by Stavros, then Michael.

The priest smiled at them, then began the age-old ritual. Dimitrios couldn't help but reflect on his brother's marriage, performed by a priest in the dead of night with only Ananke's grandmother to look on.

That was an unhappy time, but it belonged to the past.

When it came time for him to slide the gold wedding band on Alexandra's ring finger, she smiled up at him with her heart in her eyes. The beautiful face lifted to his represented his present and his future, bringing him ineffable joy.

To think today was only the beginning.

THE BILLIONAIRE
BRIDEGROOM

EMMA DARCY

Initially a French/English teacher, **Emma Darcy** changed careers to computer programming before the happy demands of marriage and motherhood. Very much a people person, and always interested in relationships, she finds the world of romance fiction a thrilling one, and the challenge of creating her own cast of characters very addictive.

CHAPTER ONE

Wow! Definitely a million-dollar property! Real class, Serena Fleming decided appreciatively, driving the van past perfectly manicured lawns to the architect designed house owned by one of her sister's clients, Angelina Gifford. Michelle's Pet Grooming Salon drew quite a few wealthy people who used the mobile service provided, but Serena was more impressed with this place than any other she had visited in the course of picking up pampered dogs and cats.

Michelle had told her the land in this area had only been released for development four years ago. The Giffords had certainly bought a prime piece of real estate—three acres sited on top of a hill overlooking Terrigal Beach and a vast stretch of ocean. There were no formal gardens, just a few artistically placed palm trees—big fat pineapple-shaped palms with a mass of fronds growing out of the top. Must have cost a fortune to transport and plant them, all fully grown, but then quite clearly the whole place had to have cost a fortune.

The fabulous view was cut off as the van drew level with the house which seemed to have walled courtyards on this western side. All the windows would face north and east, Serena thought. Still, even the wall arrangement was interesting, painted in dark blue with a rich cream trim, suggesting sea and sand.

She brought the van to a halt adjacent to the front

door, cut the engine and hopped out, curious to meet the man who had designed all this. Nic Moretti was his name, a highly successful architect, also the brother of Angelina Gifford, whose husband had whisked her off for a trip overseas. The talented Nic had been left in charge of the house and Angelina's adored dog, Cleo, who was due for a clip and shampoo this morning.

No doubt it was convenient for him to stay here. According to the local newspaper, his design had just won the contract to build a people's park with various pavilions on crown land overlooking Brisbane Water. Easy for him to supervise the work from such a close vantage point, a mere half hour drive to the location of the proposed park.

Serena rang the doorbell and waited. And waited. She glanced at her watch. It was now ten minutes past the nine o'clock appointment. She rang the doorbell again, with considerably more vigour.

In her other life as a hair stylist in a very fashionable Sydney salon, it was always rich people who disregarded time, expecting to be fitted in whenever they arrived. Here she was on the Central Coast, a good hour and a half north of Sydney, but it was obviously no different, she thought on a disgruntled sigh. The wealthy expected others to wait on them. In fact, they expected the whole world to revolve around them.

Like her ex-fiancé…

Serena was scowling over the memory of what Lyall Duncan had expected of *her* when the door she faced was abruptly flung open.

'Yes?' a big brute of a man snapped.

Serena's jaw dropped. His thick black hair was rumpled. His unshaven jaw bristled with aggression. His muscular and very male physique was barely clothed by a pair of exotic—or was it erotic?—silk boxer shorts. And if she wasn't mistaken—*no, don't look there!* She wrenched her gaze up from the distracting bulge near his groin, took a deep breath and glared straight back at glowering dark eyes framed by ridiculously long thick eyelashes that were totally wasted on a man.

Italian heritage, of course. What else could it be with names like Nic and Angelina Moretti?

'I'm Serena from Michelle's Pet Grooming Salon,' she announced.

He frowned at her, the dark eyes sharper now as he scrutinised her face; blue eyes, pert nose, full-lipped mouth, slight cleft in her chin, wisps of blond hair escaping from the fat plait that gathered in the rest of it. His gaze dropped to the midriff top that outlined her somewhat perky breasts and the denim shorts that left her long shapely legs on full display, making Serena suddenly self-conscious of being almost as naked as he was, though definitely more decently dressed.

'Do I know you?' he barked.

He'd probably been a Doberman pinscher in another life, Serena was thinking, just before the shock of recognition kicked her heart.

'No!' she answered with panicky speed, not wanting *him* to make the link that had suddenly shot through her mind.

It had been a month ago. A whole rotten month of working fiercely at putting the still very raw experience in the irretrievable past; breaking off her engagement to Lyall, leaving her job, leaving Sydney, taking wound-licking refuge with her sister. To be suddenly faced with the *architect* of those decisions…

She could feel her forehead going clammy, the blood draining from her face as her mind screamed at the unfairness of it all. Her hands clenched, fighting the urge to lash out at him. A persistent thread of common sense argued it wasn't Nic Moretti's fault. He'd simply been the instrument who'd drawn out the true picture of her future if she went ahead with her fairy-tale marriage—Cinderella winning the Prince!

He was the man Lyall had been talking to *that night,* the man who'd expressed surprise at the high-flying property dealer, Lyall Duncan, for choosing to marry *down,* taking a lowly hairdresser as his wife. And Serena had overheard Lyall's reply—the reply that had ripped the rose-coloured spectacles off her face and shattered all her illusions. This man had heard it, too, and the humiliation of it forced her into a defensive pretence.

'Since I don't know you…' she half lied in desperate defence.

'Nic Moretti,' he rumbled at her.

'…I don't see how you can know me,' she concluded emphatically.

He'd seen her at Lyall's party but they hadn't been introduced, and she'd been all glammed up for the occasion, not in her *au naturel* state as she was this morning. Surely he wouldn't make the connection. The environment was completely different. Yet despite her denial of any previous encounter with him, he was still frowning, trying to place her.

'I'm here to collect Cleo,' she stated briskly, hating this nasty coincidence and wanting to get away as fast as possible.

'Cleo,' he repeated in a disconnected fashion.

'The dog,' she grated out.

The expression on his rugged handsome face underwent a quick and violent change, the brooding search for her identity clicking straight into totally fed up frustration. 'You mean the monster,' he flashed at her derisively.

The blood that had drained from her face, surged to her head again, making Serena see red. It was impossible to resist giving this snobby man a dose of the condescension he ladled out himself.

'I would hardly characterise a sweet little Australian silky terrier as a monster,' she said loftily.

'Sweet!' He thrust out a brawny forearm marked with long and rather deep scratches. 'Look what she did to me!'

'Mmm...' Serena felt no sympathy, silently applauding the terrier for doing the clawing this man very likely deserved. 'Raises the question...what did you do to her?'

'Nothing. I was simply trying to rescue the wretched creature,' he declared in exasperation.

'From what?'

He grimaced, not caring for this cross-examination. 'A friend of mine put her on the slippery dip out at the swimming pool. She skidded down it into the water, looking very panicky. I swam over to lift her out and...'

'Dogs can swim, you know.'

'I know,' he growled. 'It was a reflex action on my part.'

'And clawing you would be a reflex action on her part. Not being able to get any purchase on the slippery dip would have terrified her.'

Another grimace at being put on the spot. 'It was only meant as a bit of fun.'

Serena raised her eyebrows, not letting him off the hook. 'Some people have strange ideas of what is fun with animals.'

'I tried to save her, remember?' He glared at the implication of cruelty. 'And let me tell you *she* wasn't the one left bleeding everywhere.'

'I'm glad to hear it. Though I think you should rearrange your thoughts on just who is the monster here. Take a good long look at whom you choose to mix with and how they treat what they consider *lesser* beings.'

The advice tripped off her tongue, pure bile on her part. He didn't like it, either, but Serena didn't care. It was about time someone got under his silver-spoon-fed, beautifully tanned, privileged skin. She was still burning over the way Lyall had discussed her with this man, telling him the kind of wife he wanted, the kind of wife he expected to get by taking on a non-competitive little hairdresser who'd be so grateful to be married to him, she'd be a perfectly compliant home-maker and never question anything he did. Definitely placing her as *a lesser being*.

But perhaps she'd gone too far on the critical front. Nic Moretti did, after all, represent one of her sister's regular clients who didn't care what it cost to keep her dog beautifully groomed—a client Michelle wouldn't like to lose. Never mind that the super-duper architect made Serena bristle from head to toe. Business was business. She stretched her mouth into an appeasing smile.

'Mrs. Gifford made a booking for Cleo at the salon this morning. If you'll fetch her for me...'

'The salon,' he repeated grimly. 'Do you cut claws there or do I have to take her to the vet?'

'We do trim pets' nails.'

'Then please do it while you've got her in *your* custody,' he growled. 'Have you got a leash for her?'

Serena raised her eyebrows. 'Doesn't Cleo have her own?'

'I'm not going near that dog until its claws are clipped.'

'Fine! I'll get one from the van.'

Unbelievable that a man of his size should be cowed by a miniature dog! Serena shook her head over the absurdity as she collected a leash and a bag of crispy bacon from the van. The latter was always a useful bribe if a dog baulked at doing what she wanted it to do. The need to show some superiority over Nic Moretti, even if it was only with a small silky terrier, burned through Serena's heart.

He waited for her by the front door, still scowling over their exchange. Or maybe he had a hangover. Clearly the ringing of the doorbell had got him out of bed and he wasn't ready to face the rest of the day yet. Serena gave him a sunny smile designed to reproach his ill humour.

'Do you want to lead me to Cleo or shall I wait here until you shoo her out of the house?'

His eyes glinted savagely at the latter suggestion, conscious of retaining some semblance of dignity, even in his boxer shorts. 'You can have the fun of catching her,' he said, waving Serena into the house.

'No problem,' she tossed at him, taking secret satisfaction in the tightening of his jaw.

Though her pulse did skip a little as she passed him by. Nic Moretti had the kind of aggressive masculinity that would threaten any woman's peace of mind. Serena tried telling herself he was probably gay. Many artistic men were. In fact, he had the mean, moody and magnificent look projected by the pin-up models in the gay calendars her former employer had lusted over in his hairdressing salon.

Mentally she could hear Ty raving on, 'Great pecs, washboard stomach, thighs to die for...'

The old patter dried up as the view in front of her claimed her interest. The foyer was like the apron of a stage, polished boards underfoot, fabulous urns dressing its wings. Two steps led down to a huge open living area where practically every piece of furniture was an ultra-modern objet d'art. Mind-boggling stuff.

Beyond it all was a wall of glass which led her gaze outside to a vast patio shaded by sails, and a luxurious spa from which a water slide—the infamous slippery dip—led to a glorious swimming pool on a lower level. She didn't see a kennel anywhere, nor the dog she'd come to collect.

She threw an inquiring glance back over her shoulder to the man in charge, only to find his gaze fastened on her derrière. Her heart skipped several beats. Nic Moretti couldn't be gay. Only heterosexual men were fascinated by the jutting contours of the well-rounded backside that had frequently embarrassed Serena by drawing wolf-whistles.

It wasn't really voluptuous. Her muscle tone was good, no dimple of cellulite anywhere. She simply had a bottom that stuck out more than most, or was more emphasised by the pit in her back. Of course, wearing shorts probably did draw more attention to it, but she saw no reason to hide the shape of her body anyway. At least the denim didn't invite the pinching she had sometimes been subjected to in the streets of Sydney while waiting for a pedestrian traffic light to change to green.

It was just her bad luck that Lyall Duncan was a *bottom* man, finding that particular piece of female equipment sexier than big breasts or long legs or whatever else men fancied in a woman. More to the point, he'd told Nic Moretti so, the memory of which instantly turned up Serena's heat level. Was he recognising *this* feature of her?

'Where might I find Cleo?' she rapped out, snapping his attention back to the business in hand.

His gaze lifted but the dark frown returned, as though he was pulling his wandering mind back from a place he found particularly vexatious. 'I don't know,' he said testily. 'I've only just rolled out of bed…'

'What do we have here?' another voice inquired, a female voice lifted in a supercilious upper class drawl.

Serena's hackles rose again. Her head whipped around. The newcomer on the scene was drifting into the open living area from what had to be a bedroom wing. She was wearing a slinky thigh-length silk and lace negligee in an oyster shade, one arm up, lazily ruffling long tawny hair. An amused little smile sat on a face that could have graced the cover of a fashion magazine, as could the rest of her, the tall slender figure being of model proportions.

'Ah…Justine…' Nic Moretti said in deep relief.

Perfect name for her, Serena thought caustically.

'…have you seen Cleo? This…uh…lady…has come to collect her for some grooming.'

He'd forgotten her name. Typical! Not important enough on his social scale to remember. Which was just as well, given other memories he might be nursing.

'Grooming!' Justine rolled her eyes. Green eyes. 'Pity she hasn't come to put the monster down. You should have let the wretched little beast drown yesterday, Nic.'

'Angelina would never forgive me if I let any harm come to her pet, Justine,' he reproved in a tight tone.

'It's obviously spoiled rotten,' came the sneering response.

'Nevertheless…'

'You'll find it shut up in the laundry,' she informed with towering distaste. 'I don't know how you could have slept through all its yap-yap-yapping outside the bedroom door last night. It was driving me mad. And the little bitch was so rabid, I had to pick it up by its collar and carry it away from me.'

Half choking it to death, Serena thought venomously.

'You should have woken me. Let me deal with it,' Nic grated out, undoubtedly aware of the cruelty to animals tag which was fast gathering more momentum.

Great company he kept! Hot body, cold mean heart. Serena viewed Justine from a mountain of contempt as she carried on like a spoiled rich bitch who expected to always be the centre of attention.

'Leaving me alone while you nurse-maided a dog? No thanks.' Her eyelids lowered in flirtatious play. 'Much better to have no distractions, wasn't it, darling?'

A clearing of throat behind Serena suggested some embarrassment. 'The laundry,' Nic Moretti growled, stepping up to her side and gesturing her to follow him. 'It's this way.'

'Watch the mess!' Justine warned. 'There's bound to be some. I threw in a leftover chicken leg to stop the yapping.'

'A chicken leg!' Serena stopped and glared at the self-serving woman. 'Cooked chicken bones splinter. They could stick in the dog's throat.'

'Let's go!' Nic muttered urgently.

He was right. This was no time to be instructing anyone. Besides which, Justine would probably rejoice if Cleo was dead. At least Nic Moretti had an anxious air about him as he led the way through a space age stainless steel kitchen.

'Cleo!' he called commandingly, striding across a mud room area containing boot racks and rows of hooks for hats, coats and umbrellas. Any thought of his own injury from Cleo's claws was apparently obliterated by the fear of injury to his sister's pet.

A shrill barking instantly started up, relieving his obvious body tension before he reached the door behind which the dog was imprisoned. He flung it open and the little silky terrier charged out between his legs, flying past Serena before she could react, shooting through the kitchen like a missile, clearly intent on escaping from any form of captivity.

'Bloody hell!' Nic breathed, glancing inside the laundry.

A determined dog was capable of creating a lot of damage. Serena didn't feel the need to comment on this. It was her job to catch Cleo who was now in the living room, barking hysterically, probably at the sight of the woman who had so callously mistreated her.

'Oh, you horrible little monster!' Justine shrieked.

Serena pelted through the kitchen just in time to see a vicious kick aimed at the silky terrier who was darting away from it. 'Cleo,' she called in a singsong tone, dropping to her knees to give herself less threatening height and tossing a piece of crispy bacon onto the floor between her and the dog.

Cleo stopped the frenetic activity, sniffed, came forward cautiously and snaffled the bacon. Serena tossed out another piece closer to herself. Then another and another as the dog responded warily to the trail being laid. Finally she snatched a piece held in Serena's fingers and paused long enough to submit to a calming scratch behind the ears. The fragile little body under its long hair was trembling—evidence of the trauma it had been through.

Serena stroked and scratched, telling Cleo in a soft indulgent tone how beautiful and clever she was until the dog was happy enough to rise up on its hind legs and lick her face.

'Oh, yuk!' Justine remarked in disgust, just as Serena scooped the dog into her arms, holding it securely against her shoulder while she rose from her kneeling position.

'Shut up, Justine!' Nic shot at her.

The classically oval jaw dropped in shock.

'Just let the lady do her job,' he expounded with no less irritation at his girlfriend's total lack of any sensitivity to the situation.

Serena almost liked him at that moment. However, she headed straight for the front door without any comment. Nic Moretti followed her right out to the van.

'What door do you want opened?' he asked solicitously.

'The driver's side. I'll put her on the passenger seat beside me so I can pat her. There's a dog harness attached to the safety belt so she won't be a problem when I'm driving.'

He opened the door and watched as Serena settled Cleo into the harness. 'She seems to be okay,' he said half anxiously.

'Fighting fit,' Serena answered dryly.

'I don't think Justine is used to dogs.'

'Maybe you should growl at her more often.' This terse piece of advice took him aback. Serena was past dealing in diplomacy. She reached out and pulled her door shut, then spoke to him through the opened window. 'Normally I would deliver Cleo back at one o'clock. How does that sit with you?'

'Fine!' He was frowning again.

'Will your girlfriend still be here?'

The dark eyes suddenly took on a rivetting intensity. His mouth thinned into a grim set of determination. 'No, she won't,' he stated categorically.

The decision gave Serena a highly pleasant sense of satisfaction. 'Then I'll see you at one o'clock.'

CHAPTER TWO

Nɪᴄ Mᴏʀᴇᴛᴛɪ watched the van until it turned onto the public road, chagrined by the way the sassy little piece behind the driver's wheel had got under his skin, yet unable to dismiss the truths she had flung in his face. A pet groomer…obviously caring more about the canine breed than she did for people. Though he had to concede he hadn't cut too impressive a figure this morning. Justine even less so.

Which brought him to the sobering conclusion that the scorn in those vivid blue eyes had been justified and maybe it was time he took stock of what he was doing, shrugging off stuff he didn't like for the sake of cruising along in the social swim, doing his balancing act with people on the grounds that no one was perfect and if they were good for something, what did it matter if they fell short in other areas?

Judgment day…

He shook his head over the irony of that being delivered to him by a pet groomer who'd descended on him out of nowhere. Damned if he could even remember the name she had given! *Michelle* had been printed on the van she drove but he was sure it wasn't that.

And it still niggled him that he had seen her before somewhere. Though it seemed highly unlikely, given her job and location on the Central Coast. Sydney was his usual stamping ground. Besides, how could he forget that pert mouth and even perter bottom? Both of them were challenges he rather fancied coming to grips with.

He smiled self-mockingly at this last thought.

The hangover from last night's party was obviously affecting his brain. What could he possibly have in common with a pet groomer, except the welfare of Cleo for the duration of Angelina's overseas trip? Better get his mind geared to deal with Justine who was turning into a royal pain over his sister's beloved Cleo. Worse than that, in fact. There was a cruel streak in her treatment of the dog and Nic didn't like it. He wouldn't invite her here again.

He frowned over the memory of her laughing as she'd tossed her hapless victim onto the slippery dip yesterday. 'Here's company for you, Nic!' A great joke, laughing at the dog's frantic attempts to fight its way back up to the spa level against the inevitable skid into the pool. Unkind laughter.

He'd been annoyed by the whole episode, especially the painful scratches which had led him to transfer his annoyance to Cleo. Wrong! He could see that now. The pet groomer had straightened him out on quite a few areas that needed his attention. For one thing, dog-minding was not a breeze. It obviously required some expertise he didn't have.

Having resolved to take more positive action on that front, he went inside to face the problem he now had with Justine. She was in the kitchen, watching coffee brew in the percolator. While her attention was still engaged on getting a shot of caffeine, he viewed her with more critically assessing eyes.

Did he want their affair to continue? They'd been

reasonably compatible both sexually and socially, but the relationship had been more about superficial fun than deep and meaningful. He had the very definite feeling that *the fun* had just run out.

She turned around, probably having heard the front door shut and looking to check where he was. 'Ah! You've seen them off,' she said, rolling her eyes at the fuss of it all. 'Blissful peace for a while!'

'Cleo will be returned at one o'clock,' he informed her as he strolled into the kitchen and headed for the refrigerator. A couple of glasses of iced water should help clear the hangover.

'It is ridiculous to have our lives ruled by a dog!' Justine declared in exasperation. 'Why don't you put her in one of those boarding kennels, Nic? It would save all this aggravation and you'd be free to...'

'Out of the question,' he cut her off.

She swung on him, hands on hips. '*Why* is it out of the question?'

'I promised Angelina I'd take care of Cleo.'

'Boarding kennels are better equipped to look after that dog than you are.'

She was probably right, but that wasn't the point, Nic thought as he downed the first glass of water. Besides, he intended to learn how to handle Cleo better.

'Your sister need never know,' Justine argued.

'*I* would know. A promise is a promise.'

'What people don't know won't hurt them.'

He cocked a mocking eyebrow at her as he reached for the jug again. 'One of the principles by which you live?'

'It avoids trouble.'

'Oh, I don't know. Seems to me you get double the trouble when people find out what you've tried to hide from them.' He poured more water from the jug and drank again, wondering how many deceptions Justine had played with him.

She threw out her hands in frustrated appeal. 'You can't want to be tied to that cantankerous little bitch for the next two months.'

'I'll learn to get along with Cleo,' he answered blandly.

'Well, I won't!' she hurled at him, eyes flashing fury at his stubborn resistance to her plan. 'I'm not spending another night with that damned dog yapping its head off.'

'Then I suggest you pack up and leave, Justine, because the dog will be staying. With me.'

She looked gob-smacked.

He set the empty glass down on the kitchen bench. 'Best be gone before one o'clock,' he advised coldly. 'Please excuse me while I clean up the mess in the laundry which doesn't happen to have a doggy door for Cleo to go outside.'

He was at the doorway to the mud room before Justine caught her breath. 'You want *me* to go?' It was an incredulous squawk.

He paused to look back at her, feeling not one whit of warmth to soften his decision. 'What we have here, Justine, is an incompatible situation.'

'You'd put that miserable little dog ahead of me?'

'Perhaps the dog will be less miserable with you gone.'

'Oh!' She stamped her foot.

Nic sensed a wild tantrum teetering on the edge of

exploding from her. He didn't wait for it. If she followed him to the laundry, he'd hand her a bucket and suggest she clean up the result of her action in carelessly shutting Cleo in an inescapable place. That would undoubtedly send her packing in no time flat.

The pet groomer would have no problem with it but Justine…no way would she get down on her knees for a dog. Nor get her hands dirty. In fact, she obviously wanted to be treated like a pampered pet herself. Nic decided he didn't really care for that in a woman, certainly not in any long-term sense.

He wasn't followed.

By the time he had the laundry back in a tidy and pristine state, Justine had dressed, packed, and gone without favouring him with a farewell. The front door had been slammed shut on her way out, transmitting her pique at coming off second best to Cleo, and the engine of her SAAB convertible had roared down the driveway, punctuating her departure and displeasure.

Nic poured himself a coffee from the brew that had been left simmering and reflected that he could have appealed for understanding, maybe shifted Justine's attitude a little. Cleo wasn't just a *pet* to Angelina, more a surrogate child on whom she poured out all the frustrated love she couldn't give to a baby.

After years of trying to get pregnant, it had been a terrible grief to her when medical tests had revealed her husband's sperm count was so low it would be a miracle if she ever conceived. Poor Ward had been devastated, too, even going so far as to offer Angelina a divorce, knowing how set she was on having a family.

That wasn't an option to his sister. She and Ward

really did love each other. Their marriage seemed to have grown even stronger since the pressure to have a child had been erased. Ward had brought home the puppy for Angelina, a loveable little bundle of silky fur, and they both treated it like the queen of Egypt, nothing too good for their adored Cleo.

To put it in an impersonal boarding kennel… Nic shook his head. Angelina would never forgive him. *And* she'd know about it. Cleo was booked into the pet grooming salon every Monday morning. He'd forgotten about that earlier today but he knew it was written on Angelina's list of instructions. If the appointments weren't kept, no doubt *Michelle* would reveal that fact to his sister on her return.

Besides, as he'd told Justine, a promise was a promise. If she couldn't respect that, he was definitely better off having no further involvement with her, even if it meant being celibate for a couple of months. He couldn't overlook the cruel streak in her, either. The thought of it dampened any desire for more of Justine Knox. Good riddance, he thought, downing the last of the coffee.

A shower, a shave, a couple of hours' work in the room he'd designated as his office for the duration of his stay here, and he'd feel much more on top of everything when the pet groomer returned with Cleo at one o'clock.

'Aren't you beautiful now!' Michelle crowed indulgently as she ruffled Cleo's silver-grey silky hair with her fingers while giving it a last blast from the dryer. 'You look good, you smell good and you feel good.'

The dog's big brown eyes clung soulfully to

Michelle who invariably talked nonstop to each pet as she gave them whatever treatment was scheduled. Cleo had been given the lot this morning; nail trim, hair-clip, ears and eyes cleaned, shampoo, conditioner and blow-dry.

Serena reflected this was very little different to a hairdressing salon. Michelle even played background music, always soft romantic tracks to soothe any savage hearts, and she charged similar fees. Of course, it wasn't as upmarket, no stylish fittings or decorator items, just plain workbenches, open shelves, and a tiled floor that made cleaning easy.

The best thing about it, Serena decided, was the pets didn't talk back, dumping all their problems or complaints on the stylist who was expected to dish out unlimited sympathy even when it was obvious there were two sides to be considered. Not that that was the case with Cleo who was clearly an innocent victim, yet the darling little silky terrier hadn't even raised a bark since Serena had rescued her from the dark brute and his evil witch-woman.

'You can put on her pink ribbon, Serena,' Michelle instructed, having finished with Cleo and about to pick up another dog waiting for his turn to be pampered, a Maltese terrier who'd sat tamely in line like all the other pets in the salon, content to watch Michelle do her thing.

'I'm not sure Nic Moretti is going to appreciate the pink ribbon,' Serena dryly commented as she cut off an appropriate length from the roll Michelle kept on a shelf.

It earned the look of unshakeable authority. 'No pet leaves this salon without wearing a ribbon. It's the finishing touch. Cleo knows it and expects it. She'll be upset if you don't give it to her. You can tell Angelina's brother that from me. He has to consider the dog's sense of rightness or he's going to have a traumatised pet on his hands.'

When it came to dog handling her sister was a genius. Serena accepted her advice without question. But would Nic Moretti? Confronting him again stirred mixed feelings. The fear of being recognised as Lyall Duncan's belittling choice of wife had been somewhat allayed. It seemed unlikely that he would make the connection now, given the distraction of her current job. Besides, it would be interesting to see if he had got rid of his penthouse pet in the interests of properly safeguarding his sister's.

Smiling at Cleo as she tied the ribbon around her neck, she softly crooned, 'Pretty pink bow.'

The dog sprang up from the bench top and licked her chin. Starved for praise and affection, Serena concluded, and decided to add a bit more advice to her sister's when she spoke to Nic Moretti again. Her smile widened to a grin. Teach the brute a few lessons that would hopefully stick in his arrogant craw.

'I'm off now,' she called out to Michelle.

'Okay. Don't forget to pick up Muffy at Erina on the way back.'

'Will do.'

It was twenty minutes to one o'clock. As Serena took Cleo out to the van, she thought how good it was to be out of the city. Although Michelle's five acre property at Holgate wasn't exactly country, it was big enough to give a sense of real space and freedom while still being located close to the large populated areas of Gosford, Erina, Wamberal and Terrigal.

The salon was a large two-roomed shed behind the house and the parking area that served it took up quite a bit of room, but there was still plenty of land for Michelle's seven-year-old daughter to keep a pony which she rode every day after she came home from school. All in all, Serena thought her widowed older sister had done a fantastic job of setting up a business she could run while looking after Erin. Though she did seemed to have settled too much into the life of a single parent. Did the idea of getting involved in another relationship make her feel too vulnerable?

At thirty-two, Michelle was only four years older than herself, still very attractive with lovely glossy brown hair, big hazel eyes, a young pretty face and a whip-lean figure from all the physical work she did. Maybe her manless state was due to not having much opportunity to get out and meet people. Which could certainly be fixed now that Serena was here to mind her niece whenever her sister would like to go out.

On the other hand, not having a man in one's life was a lot less complicated. Maybe both she and her sister were better off on their own.

Serena pondered this dark thought as she settled Cleo in the van, then took off for the return trip to the Gifford house. Without a doubt she was starting to enjoy this complete change of lifestyle; not having to put on full make-up every day, not having to construct a hairstyle that fitted the out-there image of Ty's salon, not having to worry about wearing right up-to-date fashionable clothes, nor *compete* on any social scene. Lyall hadn't wanted her to compete with him but he'd certainly wanted her to shine amongst other women.

From now on, she simply wanted to be her own person. No putting on a show for anybody. And that included Nic Moretti. Wealth and success and good looks in a man were attractive attributes, but she wasn't about to let them influence her into not looking for what the man was like inside. Nor was she about to change herself to please him, just because he was attractive.

Well, not exactly attractive.

More loaded with sex appeal.

A woman would have to be dead not to notice.

But snobbery was not sexy at all, Serena strongly reminded herself, so she was not about to be softened up by Nic Moretti's sex appeal. In fact, it would be fun to get under his skin again, have those dark eyes burning intensely at her, make him see her as a person he couldn't dismiss out of hand.

Sweet revenge for how he'd spoken about her to Lyall.

Yes.

This was one man who definitely needed to be taught a few lessons.

CHAPTER THREE

IT WAS just on one o'clock when Serena rang the doorbell of the Gifford home. Perfect punctuality, she thought, and wondered if Nic Moretti would keep her waiting again. He had been told when she'd return. It was a matter of courtesy and respect to answer her call with reasonable promptness. No excuse not to.

She was constructing a few pertinent remarks about the value of *her* time when the door opened and there was the man facing her, all polished up and instantly sending a quiver through her heart. His black hair was shiny, his gorgeously fringed chocolate eyes were shiny, his jaw was shiny, even his tanned skin was shiny. The guy was a star in any woman's language.

He wore sparkling white shorts and a navy and white sports shirt and a smile that was whiter than both of them. Positively dazzling. 'Hello again,' he said pleasantly, causing Serena to swallow the bile she'd been building up against him.

'Hi!' she croaked, cravenly wishing she had put some effort into her own appearance. Too late now. Frantically regathering her scattered wits, she made the totally unbrilliant statement, 'Here's Cleo.'

He smiled down at the dog. 'And looking very…feminine.'

As opposed to her?

No, no, he was referring to the pink bow.

Get a grip, girl!

'I take it you've clipped her claws?' he asked.

'As much as they can be without making her bleed,' Serena managed to answer sensibly.

Her own blood was tingling as though it had been subjected to an electric charge. It was embarrassing to find herself so *taken* by him this time around. Hating the feeling of being at a disavantage, she seized on the action of detaching the leash from Cleo's collar. Retreat was the better part of valour in these tricky circumstances and the dog was now his responsibility, not hers.

Her fingers fumbled over the catch and the little silky terrier wriggled with impatience, anticipating the moment of freedom. Finally the deed was done, release completed, and Serena straightened up from her crouch, feeling flushed and fluttery, making the quite unnecessary declaration, 'She's all yours!'

Whereupon Cleo shot into the house, barking like a maniac.

Nic Moretti grimaced a kind of helpless appeal. 'What's got into her now?'

Here was opportunity handed to her on a plate and Serena found she couldn't resist asking, 'Is your girlfriend still here?'

'No. She left some hours ago,' he replied, frowning over the noisy racket inside the house.

'Well, I'd say Cleo is checking everywhere for her presence.'

The frown deepened. 'I think I might need some help. Would you mind coming in for a few minutes?'

He stepped back, waving her forward.

Serena hesitated, not liking the sense of having her services taken for granted just because she'd helped beyond the call of duty this morning. Being *used* by this man did not appeal to her. She wasn't his dogs-body and she certainly didn't intend to give him any cause to see her in that role.

She folded her arms in strongly negative body language. 'Mr. Moretti…'

'Nic.' A quick apologetic smile. 'I'm sorry. I didn't catch your name this morning.'

'Serena.' Which shouldn't ring any bells because Ty had decided Rene was a more fashionable name for her and Lyall had always used it, having first met her at Ty's salon where he regularly had his hair cut, styled and streaked to complement his yuppie image. 'Serena Fleming,' she added so she wasn't just a one name person. 'And I have to pick up another pet…'

'Please…' He was distracted by the shrill yapping, now in the living room behind him. It stopped abruptly, just as he glanced back at the dog. 'Oh, my God!'

He was off at a fast stride, leaving Serena standing at the door. Curiosity got the better of her earlier inclination to get out of here and away from an attraction that made her feel uncomfortable. Besides which, he had invited her in. She stepped into the foyer. On the polished floorboards of the living-room floor, precisely where the evil witch-woman had aimed a kick at Cleo this morning, was a large spreading puddle.

The dog stood back from it, wagging her tail triumphantly. Serena rolled her eyes, thinking she should have walked Cleo on the lawn before ringing the doorbell. From the kitchen came the sound of taps running full blast. Nic Moretti reappeared with a bucket and sponge.

'Why would she do that?' he demanded in exasperation. 'She knows where the doggy door is and has been trained to use it.'

'Primal instinct can be stronger than any training,' Serena dryly observed. 'Cleo has just reclaimed her territory from the enemy.'

'The enemy?' He looked totally lost.

'I'd say that's where your girlfriend's scent was the strongest. It's now been effectively killed.'

'Right!' He gritted his teeth, bent down and proceeded to sponge up the puddle.

His thighs bulged with muscular strength. His shorts tightened across a very sexy butt. From her elevated position in the stepped up foyer, Serena couldn't help smiling at the view of this magnificent male, almost on his hands and knees, performing a menial task that a woman was usually expected to do. Her feeling of inferiority evaporated.

'See what I mean?' he grumbled. 'I have a problem.'

'It is easily fixable,' Serena blithely assured him. 'You're doing a good job there.'

'This is only one thing.' He looked up, caught her amused smile and huffed his frustration at the position he was in. 'Obviously I need a dog psychologist to explain why Cleo is running amok.'

'Well, you can always contact the television show, *Harry's Practice*, and see if you can line up a visit.'

'From everything you've said, *you're* the person I want,' he declared, dropping the sponge into the bucket and straightening up to his full height to eye her with commanding intensity.

Serena couldn't deny a little thrill at his *wanting*

her, even if it was only in an advisory capacity.
Which would put her on top in this relationship. The
boss. A very tempting situation. Except she couldn't
bring herself to pretend she was something she
wasn't.

'I'm not a qualified dog psychologist.'

'But you know how dogs think. And react,' he
bored in.

'More or less,' she replied offhandedly, half turning
towards the front door as she realised he was grasping
at what he saw as the *easy* option. He didn't *want*
her. He wanted to make use of her, which placed her
as his servant, and she was not about to become his
willing slave. 'I really do have to go now,' she tossed
at him. 'Muffy's owner is expecting me to...'

'Wait! I'll pay you.'

Typical, thinking money could buy him anything.
Serena steeled herself against giving in. 'I have a
schedule to keep. If you'll excuse me...'

'When do you finish work today?' he shot at her.

That gave her pause for second thoughts. She eyed
him consideringly. 'What do you have in mind?'

'If you could give me the benefit of your expertise
for an hour or so...'

'You're asking for a consultation?'

He seized the idea of a professional appointment.
'Yes. I'll pay whatever fee you nominate.'

An edge of desperation had crept into his voice.
Serena did some swift calculation. An hour's work on
a client's hair in Ty's salon would usually cost well
over a hundred dollars. But she had been an expert
stylist with years of training behind her. As far as
canine behavioural science was concerned, she was

strictly an amateur. But Nic Moretti didn't know that and being cheap did not engender respect.

'Seventy dollars an hour,' she decided.

'Fine!' He didn't even blink at the fee. 'Can you come this evening?'

A bit of power dressing was called for in these circumstances. Not to mention a shower, shampoo and blow-dry in order to look properly professional. 'Does seven-thirty suit?'

'Great!' he said with a huge air of relief.

The guy had to be really desperate, Serena thought, feeling positively uplifted at the idea of being the font of all wisdom to him. And she'd better arm herself with a stack of practical wisdom from Michelle this afternoon so he'd think the consultation was worth every cent of that outrageous fee.

Flashing him a brilliant smile to assure him all was well between them, she raised her hand in a farewell salute. 'Must be off. I'll be back at seven-thirty.'

Deal closed.

Very much in *her* favour.

More sweet satisfaction.

Nic watched her jaunty walk to the front door, his gaze automatically fastening on the sexy roll of the delectable twin globes of her highly female bottom, pouched pertly in the tight denim shorts. He grinned in the triumphant belief he'd just won this round with the cheeky Miss Serena Fleming. Her brain was his to pick tonight and maybe—just maybe—she'd un-bend enough to let him explore the possibility of en-joying more of her than the workings of her mind.

She pulled the front door shut behind her, cutting

off the visual pleasure of her back view. Nic, however, had no problem recalling it. Her front view, as well, the firm roundness of her breasts, emphasised by her folded arms as she'd stood her ground and denied him any more of her time. No favours from Miss Fleming.

It was quite clear she disapproved of him—not the usual response he got from women—and despite his putting his best foot forward to make up for this morning's fiasco, she hadn't intended to budge from her stance. Not until he'd offered payment for her expertise. He suspected she'd done him in the eye there, too, demanding top dollar. Probably thought he wouldn't agree to it.

The money was irrelevant.

He'd picked up her challenge and forced her to come to his party. The sense of winning put Nic in such a good mood, he even grinned down at the troublesome terrier who had brought him no pleasure at all to this date. 'You might be good for something after all, Cleo,' he said whimsically.

The stumpy tail wagged eager agreement.

Then Nic remembered having to clean up the puddle and he wagged an admonishing finger at the dog. 'But you certainly don't deserve that pretty pink bow. What self-respecting female would let her bladder loose in the wrong place?'

The accusing tone instantly broke their brief understanding. A series of hostile barks reminded Nic that hostility bred hostility and he couldn't blame the dog for wanting to get rid of Justine's smell. 'Okay, okay,' he soothed, copying the soft, singsong lilt Serena had used to calm the beast. 'You probably did me a favour there, too, bringing out the worst of her character for me to see. Let's call it quits on Justine.'

Back to tail wagging.

'It's time for lunch now.' If any of his friends ever heard him talking to a dog like this, he'd never hear the end of it. However, it was definitely a winning ploy, so he continued in the same soppy vein. 'Would you like some more chicken?'

Chicken, according to Angelina, was a magic word that could winkle her darling pet out of any bad mood. It hadn't produced the desired result while Justine had been present, but right now it worked like a charm. Cleo literally bounced out to the kitchen and stood in front of the refrigerator, yipping impatiently for her treat.

Nic obliged, carefully deboning the chicken as he filled her food dish. She wolfed it all down, moved on to her water dish, took a long drink, then happily trotted off to her miniature trampoline in the living room, hopped onto it, scratched it into shape, curled herself down and closed her eyes in sleepy contentment.

Nic shook his head in bemusement. Maybe he didn't need Serena Fleming's advice after all. Maybe he'd only needed to get rid of Justine. On the other hand, one little success did not guarantee peaceful coexistence for two months. And something had to be done about the barking at night.

He knew Angelina and Ward let Cleo sleep on their bed. They actually laughed about it burrowing up between them. No way was he about to start sleeping with a dog, waking up to a lick on the face. Devotion to duty only went so far. And if he managed to get

Serena Fleming into bed with him, he certainly didn't want a jealous dog leaping into the fray.

Wondering if he could persuade the feisty little blonde into being his playmate for the next two months, Nic went back to the refrigerator to see what he could rustle up for his own lunch. His appetite for tasty morsels had been aroused. He spotted a bottle of Chardonnay and thought he might begin tonight's consultation by offering a glass of wine—a friendly, hospitable thing to do.

The idea of killing two birds with one stone had fast-growing appeal.

A desirable woman in his bed.

An expert dog-handler on tap.

Definitely a challenge worth winning.

CHAPTER FOUR

'SEVENTY dollars!' Michelle looked her disbelief.

'Well, I don't believe in undercharging,' Serena explained. 'It's a matter of psychology.'

'Psychology?'

'Yes. The more you make people pay, the more they believe they're getting something special. Ty taught me that.'

The disbelief took on a sceptical gleam. 'And what's the something special you're going to give Nic Moretti for his seventy dollars?'

'That's where you come in. I need all the tips you can give me on solving problems with dogs. And I'll go you halves on the fee.'

Michelle sighed at the offer. 'Well, I won't say no, but I think you might be putting yourself at risk, Serena.'

'How…if I'm all prepared?'

'I'm just remembering something Angelina Gifford said about her brother. She was expecting Cleo to adore him because there wasn't a female alive who didn't l…u…u…u…v Nic.'

'No way am I going to be a victim on that count,' Serena emphatically assured her sister. 'I'm simply fleecing the guy for being as arrogant as Lyall Duncan. Though I will play fair by giving him value for his money.'

'Hmm…he's got to you already. You've just been

hurt by one rich, eligible bachelor. Better watch your step with…'

'Michelle! I don't even like him!'

'He's striking sparks in you. That's more dangerous than *like*.'

'Oh, for goodness' sake! It's just a one-hour deal. And I need your help.'

'Okay. Let's see if you can keep your mind on the job.'

I am not going to let Nic Moretti close enough to hurt me, Serena silently vowed. Her sister didn't understand the score. This was simply a game of one-upmanship where she ended up the winner.

For the rest of the afternoon, her mind was trained on collecting all the advice that would make Nic Moretti's head spin with her bank of expert knowledge. Admiration, respect, gratitude…that was what she wanted from him. Balm for her wounded pride.

And, of course, it was pride behind the care she took with her appearance that evening. Not that she went all out to impress in any sexual sense. No perfume. No jewellery. No eye make-up. Only some perfectly applied pink lipstick. Her hair was newly clean and shiny and she left it long and loose, except for the side tresses which were held together at the back with a clip to maintain a neat, tidy effect.

Deciding on smart casual clothes, she teamed turquoise blue slacks with a tailored white shirt sprinkled with pink and turquoise and purple daisies. She strapped a businesslike navy Swatch watch on her wrist, pushed her feet into navy sandals and picked up a small navy shoulderbag to hold her keys and money. With this outfit, no one, not even her too perceptive older sister, could say she was man-hunting.

Michelle and Erin were settled in the lounge room, like two peas in a pod with their light brown hair cut in short bobs, their delicately featured faces recognisably mother and daughter, and both of them dressed in blue jeans and red T-shirts. Serena waved to them from the doorway. 'I'm off now.'

'You look pretty, Aunty Serena,' her niece remarked.

'Good enough to eat,' Michelle dryly added. 'Watch out for big bad wolves!'

'Oh, Mummy!' Erin chided, giggling at the reference to a fairy story. 'She's not wearing a red cape and hood.'

'Besides, I'm wolf-proof,' Serena declared.

But she wasn't quite so sure of that when Nic Moretti invited her into his lair twenty minutes later. He suddenly looked very wolfish in tight black jeans and an open-necked white shirt which played peek-a-boo with the sprinkle of black curls that had been fully displayed on the centre of his chest this morning, reminding Serena of what else had been displayed.

Fortunately, Cleo was also at the door to greet her. She bent down to scratch the little terrier behind her ears, sealing an easy bond of affection between them while sternly reminding herself that the dog had to be the focus of her attention here, regardless of how *distracting* Nic Moretti was. However, as she straightened up, the top button of her shirt popped out of its buttonhole, giving the man of the moment a tunnel vision shot of cleavage.

Which he took.

Completely destroying the sense of starting this encounter on a professional footing.

Serena sighed with frustration, inadvertently causing her breasts to lift, pushing the opening further apart. Embarrassed, she clutched the edges of the shirt and hauled them back together.

'Excuse me. This new cotton stretch fabric obviously has its perils,' she bit out, shoving the button back in its hole and fiercely hoping it would stay there.

Nic Moretti lifted a twinkling gaze that elevated the heat in her bloodstream. 'That button would have to be classified as a sexual tease,' he said, amusement curling through his voice.

'It's not meant to be,' she flashed back at him.

'Perhaps it's better left open. The temptation to watch for it to pop again might get beyond my control.'

'This is ridiculous!' Serena muttered, fighting against losing her own control of the situation. 'Why are you flirting with me?'

He laughed. 'Because it's fun. Can't you enjoy some fun, Serena?'

'This is a professional visit,' she hotly insisted.

His eyes teased her attempt at seriousness. 'Does that mean you have to keep yourself buttoned up?'

'Oh, puh-lease!' Anger at his lack of respect flared. 'If you're going to be impossible, let's call this consultation off right now!'

Cleo yapped at the sudden burst of temper from her.

'Sorry, sorry.' Nic's hand shot up in a halting gesture as he made a valiant attempt to reconstruct his expression into apologetic appeal. 'Just a touch light-headed from the relief of having you come.'

She wrenched her gaze from the lurking twinkle in his and looked down at the agitated dog. 'It's okay,' she soothed. 'As long as your keeper behaves himself.'

'She's been very good this afternoon. No trouble at all,' Nic said in a straight tone.

'Then you don't need me.'

'Yes, I do,' came the quick retort, the vehement tone drawing her gaze back to his. The dark eyes were now burning with an intensity of purpose that would not be denied. 'The nights are bad. Very bad. Come…I'll show you.'

He gestured her to fall into step with him. Relieved they were getting down to proper business, Serena moved forward, traversing the foyer to the living room with a determinedly confident walk, though feeling oddly small and all too vulnerable with her head only level to his big broad shoulders. She wasn't petite. In fact, she was above average height for a woman. It was just that he was very tall. And strong. And terribly macho looking, which was probably due to his Italian heritage.

Nevertheless, her heart was racing.

She was acutely conscious of being alone in this house with this man, not that she believed he would really come onto her but that initial bit of flirting had been deeply unsettling, making her aware that he found her attractive. Maybe even desirable.

While that was very flattering—and ironic, since he'd criticised Lyall for choosing her as his mate for marriage—Serena wished Nic Moretti wasn't quite so sexually desirable himself. He was much more of a *hunk* than Lyall, whose luxurious lifestyle and lavish romancing had seduced her into thinking herself in love with him. Which, she realised now, wasn't the same as being *hot* for him.

Every nerve in her body jangled alarm as Nic cupped her elbow to steer her towards what she had assumed this morning was the bedroom wing. 'Where are we going?' she demanded suspiciously.

'To view the damage so you'll understand what I'm dealing with,' he answered reasonably.

'Okay. Damage,' she agreed unhitching her elbow from his grasp.

He cocked an eyebrow at the somewhat graceless action. 'Do you have a thing about personal space?'

'Only when it's invaded without my giving a green light.'

'I'll remember that,' he said with a quirky little smile. 'If you're still nervous about that button...'

'I am not nervous!' she hotly denied, barely stopping herself from looking down to check that it was still fastened.

Cleo yapped again, apparently keeping a barometer on her temperature level.

'Fine!' Nic said with too much satisfaction for Serena's comfort. 'I'd much prefer you to feel relaxed.'

They were now walking down a wide curved corridor. On its south side, floor length windows gave a view of fern-filled courtyards. Closed doors along the other wall obviously led to bedrooms with their windows facing north, getting all-day sunshine and the spectacular vista of shoreline and sea.

'Where's the damage?' Serena asked, totally unable to relax her inner tension.

Nic pointed ahead to the door at the end of the corridor. 'That leads to the master bedroom suite. The first night I was here alone with Cleo, she barked continually outside that door. I showed her no one was in the suite, then took her back to her trampoline. It didn't stop her. She returned and…see for yourself…attacked the door, scratching to get in.'

'I take it Mr. and Mrs. Gifford allowed her to sleep on their bed.'

'Yes, but I thought with them gone…' He sighed. 'In the end, I let her in and left her there.'

'Problem solved?'

He grimaced. 'It only worked the first night. The second night she attacked my door. See?'

Scratches on the second door.

'She wanted to sleep with someone,' Serena interpreted.

'I am not having a dog in bed with me,' Nic growled.

'She's only little.' It was more a tease than an argument, the words popping out of Serena's mouth before she could think better of them.

The comment earned a blistering glare. 'Do you ever reach a climax?'

'I beg your pardon?'

'I can't imagine how your boyfriend manages to get you to a sufficient level of excitement if you have a dog interfering all the time.'

'I don't have a boyfriend,' she flared at him.

'Not surprising if you insist on sleeping with a third party.'

'I don't have a dog, either!'

'So why load me with one in my bed?'

'You told me your girlfriend was gone,' Serena hurled back at him, getting very hot under the collar, so hot her tongue made the unwise move of fanning the flames. 'I didn't know you had another *third party* waiting in the wings.'

His eyes sizzled back at her, lifting the heat to furnace level. 'Sometimes unexpected things happen,' he drawled. 'Have we now established that neither you nor I want a dog in bed with us?'

'There is no...*us*,' Serena hissed, completely losing her head.

'Of course there is. Here we are together...'

'In consultation!'

'Absolutely! And very interesting it is, too.'

'So let's get back to Cleo,' she shot out, desperate to get both their minds off *bed.* 'After she barked and scratched at this door, what did you do?'

'Got up, watched television, fell asleep on the chaise longue in the living room.'

'Then let's go back to the living room.'

She swung on her heel and did some fast power-walking out of the bedroom wing which was far too sensitive a place to be with a man who oozed sexual invitation.

'So, the second night you spent out here on...' Her gaze swung around and fastened on the only piece of furniture that remotely resembled a chaise longue. 'Do you mean that spiky blue thing?'

It looked like more of an instrument of torture than a place to sleep. A round stainless steel base with a central cylinder supported a curved lounger shape covered with dozens of protruding blue cones which certainly looked too sharp to lie on comfortably.

Nic grinned. 'It's a fantastic design. The cones are made of a specially developed flexible rubber foam. They wrap around your body and let you submerge into them. And they're temperature sensitive, reacting to your body heat, sinking down to cushion and support anyone's individual shape.'

Serena shook her head in amazement.

'Try it for yourself,' Nic urged, waving her forward as he moved forward himself.

Curiosity drew her to the savage looking piece of furniture. 'I've never seen anything like it,' she remarked, still with a sense of disbelief in its comfort.

'It's a prototype. Not on the market yet. It's currently being displayed in international furniture shows,' Nic explained. 'Ward, Angelina's husband, likes to showcase the latest designs. He supplies to interior decorators.'

She hadn't known what business the Giffords were in but this information certainly made sense of their space age decor. 'Well, I guess you could say the chaise longue is spectacular, but I am reminded of a porcupine.'

'Don't be put off. Sit on the concave section, then swivel onto the back rest as you swing your legs up.'

The construction was so extraordinary Serena couldn't resist testing it, though once she was fully stretched out on the cones, the experience was so incredibly sensual, it made her terribly aware of her body, especially with Nic Moretti standing over her, smiling as he watched the chaise longue adjust to her shape and length.

His gaze travelled down her legs and back again, lingering at the apex of her thighs, almost making her squirm. He made another pause at the precarious button...willing it to pop? Serena felt her nipples tightening, pushing at the flimsy fabric of her bra. Her body heat was accelerating so fast, it would probably melt the seductive cones if she didn't get off.

She jackknifed back to a sitting position, swinging her feet firmly onto the floor again. 'Okay...' He was standing too close. Her eyes stabbed at his, demanding he give her more room as she determinedly switched her mind to business. 'Where was Cleo while you slept here?'

A tantalising little smile played on his lips as he backed off and gestured to a small dog's trampoline bed, set between two weirdly curved chairs facing a huge television screen. Obviously this was Cleo's place when the Giffords watched their favourite programs.

'She's in the habit of sleeping there when it suits her,' Nic said wryly. 'Apparently it doesn't suit her at night unless I'm out here with her. I was hoping when Justine arrived on Saturday...but no.' He heaved a much put upon sigh. 'Once again I ended up on the chaise longue because Cleo was driving us mad.'

Justine would have loved that—distracted from sexual pleasure, then deserted for a dog. No doubt there'd been premeditated murder in her heart when she'd put the little terrier on the slippery dip for a fast slide into deep water. Serena smiled at Cleo, silently congratulating the dog for frustrating Justine and being the survivor. Its tail wagged in conspiratorial satisfaction. Serena decided she could become very fond of Cleo, clearly a cunning intelligence at work in that little brain.

'I had a party of friends here yesterday,' Nic went on. 'By the time they left, I fell into bed and...' He grimaced. 'Well, you know how Justine dealt with last night.'

Serena looked him straight in the eye. 'Not a kind solution.'

'No,' he agreed, then pointedly added, 'My relationship with Justine came to an abrupt end this morning.'

Exit the witch-woman...enter the dog-handler?

His eyes held a gleam that told Serena he definitely fancied her as a replacement. It was a highly purposeful and suggestive gleam, reinforcing all the suggestive stuff he'd thrown at her outside his bedroom door.

While her mind furiously resented his assumption that she would share this desire, her body had a will of its own, seriously responding with little charges of electric excitement running riot everywhere. The heat coursing through her completely dried up her mouth and throat. It rose to her brain, as well, and wiped out any sensible thought processes. The only words forming there were, *I want you, too.*

Which, of course, was mad, reckless, shocking and inadmissible. The silence stretched into a seething mass of unspeakable words...

Why shouldn't I experience him?

He's free.

He's gorgeous, sexy, and I've never felt this physically attracted to anyone in my whole life.

The voice of caution finally kicked in…
It won't lead anywhere,
Remember his snobby attitudes.
He just wants to use you while he's stuck here.
You'll get involved and end up hurt.

Her body started screaming a positively wanton protest…
Don't think pain. Think pleasure.
This could be the best you'll ever have!

Fortunately Nic broke the wild torrent inside her by speaking himself. 'I was going to offer you a drink when you arrived.' He smiled in self-reproach. 'Got sidetracked. Will you have one with me now?'

'Yes,' she croaked. Her mouth was a desert.

He led off to the kitchen. She followed slowly on legs that had gone slightly wobbly on her. By the time she reached the kitchen he had wineglasses set on a bench and was pouring from a chilled bottle of Chardonnay that he'd obviously opened and re-corked earlier. A premeditated tactic for seduction?

Serena told herself she should protest. She was driving and this was supposed to be a professional consultation. No alcohol. But her gravel throat needed an instant injection of liquid so when he handed her a glass, she took it and sipped, silently vowing not to drink much.

'Thank you.' Even with the soothing moisture of the wine her voice was still husky. She drank some more.

'You like it?' he asked.

'Nice oaky flavour,' she answered, not to be out-done on the wine-tasting front. Nic Moretti might mix with high society in Sydney, but she wasn't exactly

a backwoods girl to be patronised by him or anyone else.

He raised an amused eyebrow. 'You're an expert
on Chardonnay, too?'

'I have many talents,' she said loftily and deliberately left him guessing as she returned to the one he
was paying her for. 'Since you don't want Cleo in
your bed…'

His eyes said he infinitely preferred *her* between
his sheets.

'…and you don't want her keeping you awake all
night…'

'Please don't say I have to camp permanently on
the chaise longue,' he appealed.

Not big enough for two, putting a severe constric-
tion on his sex life, Serena thought, though a wicked
afterthought fancied it could provide some interesting
sensations. She dragged her wayward mind back to
the business in hand.

'No. But we do have to create a secure and comfortable environment for her with no access to the
bedroom wing. I presume there is a doggy door for
her to get in and out?'

'The mud room.'

'Can this room be closed off from the rest of the
house?'

'Yes,' he breathed in huge relief. 'It's just through
here.'

They moved from the kitchen to the mud room
which Serena had briefly seen this morning. She
checked out the doggy door, then viewed the rows of
hooks on the wall.

'I think they're too high to hang blankets from,' she decided.

'Blankets?'

'What I'd recommend is a kind of cage to throw blankets over at night. You put the trampoline bed inside and make it a snuggly place for Cleo so she'll feel safe.' She nodded to the corner where only an easily removable umbrella stand was in the way. 'That corner would be best.'

'The bar stools could make a cage.' Having seized the idea, he moved into action. 'I'll go and get them. Blankets, too.'

Relieved of the influence his magnetic presence had on her, Serena took a long, deep breath and tried to figure out what she should do about Nic Moretti. Before the hour was up a decision had to be made. Yes or no. Hold the line here or let it be pushed further.

She remembered her sister relating Angelina Gifford's words… *There wasn't a female alive who didn't love Nic.* So getting any woman he wanted was all too easy.

The idea of being *easy* for him did not appeal.

It smacked of being one of a queue lining up to serve his pleasure. Never mind that her pleasure might be served, too. Pride insisted that he would value her more if she played hard to get.

But then she might lose her chance.

Well, if she lost it she lost it, Serena finally reasoned. After her experience with Lyall Duncan, she wanted to be valued as the person she was, not considered just another roll in the hay, suiting Nic Moretti's convenience.

To be viewed—taken—like that would be too demeaning.

Humiliating.

The decision had to be no.

The plain truth was she was off her brain to even consider having any kind of relationship with Nic Moretti. How could she ever feel good about it, knowing what she knew about him and his attitudes?

Give it up right now.

Right now! she repeated to stamp it in her mind.

CHAPTER FIVE

Nic returned to the mud room, carrying a bar stool heaped with blankets. He grinned at her. 'If this works, I'll have a cage frame made tomorrow.'

The grin played havoc with Serena's resolution. Warm pleasure zinged from him, making her skin tingle and her toes curl. She found herself clutching her wineglass too tightly and realised she was still holding it. Nic had set his down somewhere.

He put the stool in the corner she'd indicated. 'Won't be long bringing the others,' he tossed at her and strode off through the doorway to the kitchen again, leaving Serena to catch her breath.

The guy was dynamite, especially when he was being charming. She gulped down some of the Chardonnay in the hope it would cool her down. A console table with a mirror above it stood near the entrance to the kitchen. She set her glass on it and checked her reflection in the mirror.

Her cheeks were almost as pink as her lipstick and her eyes were fever bright, vividly blue. Her hair was slightly mussed from lying on the porcupine chaise longue and she quickly smoothed it back and refastened the clip. It made her feel slightly more *together,* instead of in danger of falling apart.

While Nic brought the other three stools, Cleo trotted back and forth with him, intrigued by all this strange activity. Serena concentrated on keeping out of his way, unfolding the blankets and figuring out how best to construct the cave for the troublesome little terrier.

Once Nic had finished his task, he closed in on her again, assisting with the blanket spreading. Desperate to avoid even accidental contact, which Serena feared might lead to purposeful contact, she sent him off on another mission.

'We need a radio.'

He gave her a quizzical look. 'What do we need a radio for?'

'Company for Cleo.'

'Company?'

'She won't feel she's alone if a radio is playing. You can set it on the console table over there. I saw a power-point next to it.'

'I'm to leave a radio playing all night?' he queried.

'If you turn the volume down low, you shouldn't hear it from the bedroom wing.'

He went off, shaking his head and muttering, 'I can't believe I'm doing this for a dog.'

Serena smiled and her inner tension relaxed a little. The *pro temps* cave was as secure as she could make it by the time Nic returned with a very expensive looking radio. He looked sternly at the dog at his feet as he set it on the console table. 'I hope you appreciate I'm giving this up for you.'

Cleo yipped her appreciation.

'Best you tune it into a station now so you can just switch it on later,' Serena advised. 'Find one that plays classical music.'

Nic gave her an incredulous look. 'Are you telling

me dogs know the difference between Beethoven and
Britney Spears?'

'Which music would you prefer to go to sleep
with?'

'Now there's an interesting question.' Wicked
speculation sparkled at her. 'What turns you on...or
off...as the case may be? Violins, guitar, tom-toms...'

'I doubt Cleo will settle down to a jungle beat,'
Serena cut in with pointed emphasis on the terrier.
'Excessive drumming might well set her barking.'

'Right! Soft, soothing music.' He fiddled until he
found it, gave Serena a smugly triumphant look, then
declared, 'Now we can put Cleo to bed.'

'Absolutely not,' Serena corrected him. 'You can't
do that until you're ready to go yourself.'

His lashes lowered, barely veiling a look of searing
intent that put a host of butterflies in her stomach.
Bed was definitely on his mind, but not in the context
of sleeping. She could almost hear him thinking, *I'm
ready if you are.*

'Cleo won't settle while ever she senses anyone is
still up and around,' Serena rushed out, clutching
frantically at any defence—including the active presence of Cleo—to keep Nic Moretti at arm's length.
'Putting her in here is the last thing you do at night,'
she stated emphatically. 'And there are other things
you should do, as well.'

'Like what?' he bit out with an air of sorely tried
patience.

Three doors led out of the mud room, one to the
kitchen, one to the laundry, and the third she assumed
to a corridor that served another wing of the house.

'Mostly Cleo would come into this room via the kitchen, wouldn't she?'

'Yes.'

'I suggest you bring her in that way, with her trampoline bed which you'll set in the makeshift cave. Then turn the radio on, lay a big pillow along the bottom of the closed kitchen door...'

'A pillow?'

'To stop her from scratching at a familiar exit,' Serena explained matter-of-factly, trying to ignore the increased charge of electricity coming from him. 'You can go out the other door once you settle her into the cave.'

'Is that all?' Nic drawled, clearly wanting to move on to other scenarios which had nothing to do with canine behaviour.

Serena had to concede, 'All I can think of at the moment.'

'Good!' He picked up her wineglass which she'd emptied and set aside earlier. His grin came back in full force, barrelling into her heart and dizzying her brain. 'Let's go and raise a toast to the success of this plan. Plenty of wine left in the bottle.'

She was drawn into accompanying him back into the kitchen where he headed for the refrigerator to extract the bottle of Chardonnay. Wine was an intoxicant she certainly didn't need with Nic Moretti scrambling any straight thinking, though at least it would keep his hands occupied for a little while, Serena reasoned, and she didn't have to drink much. A quick check of her watch showed the hour was almost up. She only had to get through another ten minutes.

'You must live locally,' he said as he refilled their glasses.

'Yes.'

'Where?'

'Holgate.'

'Been there all your life?'

Alarm bells rang. Was he trying to *place* her again, a memory of her still niggling? 'It's a good place to be,' she answered evasively, then quickly returned a question which established the distance she knew was between them. 'You're usually based in Sydney, aren't you?'

'Yes. I have an apartment at Balmoral.'

North Shore million dollar territory. Serena privately bet his apartment was in a prime position overlooking Sydney Harbour. The best of everything for Nic Moretti.

He handed her the filled glass, his eyes twinkling suggestively as he added, 'But I'll be supervising a project near Gosford so I'll be commuting quite a bit until it's completed.'

He was holding out the bait that he'd be available for longer than the two months his sister and brother-in-law were away. Serena didn't believe for one moment there was a chance in hell that he'd pursue a serious relationship with her. On the social scale, a dog-handler was probably a rung down from a hairdresser. The trick was to keep him talking so he didn't zero in on her.

'I saw photos of your sketches for the park in the local newspaper. Very impressive.' She lifted her glass in a toast to his talent. 'Should be a great place to go in the future.'

'Thank you.' He looked surprised at her knowledge but the light of golden opportunity swiftly followed surprise. 'I'm pleased with the plan. Would you like to see more of it? I have it here. I've turned one of the bedrooms into a temporary office.'

No way was she going near the bedroom wing again! Her heart was galloping at the idea of sharing the intimacy of looking at his designs. The temptation to share even deeper intimacies would be hanging in the air, gathering momentum the whole time.

Stay cool, she commanded herself, forcefully overriding the strong inclination to say *yes*.

Just smile and decline.

'Perhaps another time. I must be off soon. I have family waiting for me. Do you have other problems with Cleo you'd like to discuss before I go?'

He frowned, probably at his failure to seduce her into falling in with *his* plan of action. 'The nights have been the worst. She was okay this afternoon with just having me here.'

Serena nodded wisely. 'A party of strangers would have been unsettling for her.'

'I guess so.' He grimaced at the reminder, then clinked Serena's glass with his and smiled, pouring out another dose of sexually charged charm. 'We were going to drink to the success of your advice.'

'I hope it works for you,' Serena replied, very sincerely, given the fee she'd demanded. She took a sip of the wine, battling the effect of his smile which had stirred a hornet's nest of hormones, then determinedly set the glass on the bench beside her. 'If there's nothing else…?'

With an air of reluctant resignation, he took out his wallet and handed her the seventy dollars.

'Thank you.' She tucked the money into her shoulder bag, pointedly getting her car keys out at the same time, then gave him her best smile to soften the ego blow of her departure. 'I can be contacted at Michelle's Pet Grooming Salon should you need any more help.'

'Fine!' His dark eyes suddenly glittered with the determination to take up a challenge. 'I'll see you to your car.'

Proximity was definitely dangerous. Serena seized on *the third party* to protect her from whatever Nic Moretti had in mind. 'Then I suggest you bring Cleo along. Take her for a walk on the lawn. I saw her leash hanging up in the mud room.'

The glitter turned to a sizzle. He looked down at the dog who was sitting on the kitchen floor watching both of them. More than likely it was going to follow where they went and he'd be stuck with a fuss at the front door if he tried to close her inside. Muttering something dark and dire under his breath, he went to the mud room, Cleo trailing after him, and he secured the leash on her before reappearing, the dog in tow.

'Ready!' he declared through gritted teeth.

Cleo yipped excitedly.

'Walkies for you,' Serena crooned at her, laughing inside as she went ahead of them, out of the kitchen, through the living room, up to the foyer.

She wasn't aware that her bottom was swinging in jaunty triumph at having won this round with Nic Moretti, nor that it was being viewed with a burning desire to have it clutched hard in the hands of the man who was following her. Clutched and lifted so her body fitted snugly to the rampant need she had aroused.

She paused at the front door and he quickly reached around her to open it. A whiff of tantalisingly male aftershave cologne caught in her nostrils. On top of all his other sexy attributes, he even smelled good. It put Serena on pins and needles as she stepped outside and headed for her car, a neat little Peugeot 360 which always gave her the sense of welcoming her into it. She needed that tonight. A safe refuge from the big bad wolf.

He walked beside her, emanating a tension that robbed her of any conversational train of thought. He didn't say anything for her to hit off, either. Cleo was trotting in front of them. They'd reached the driver's side of the car when the little terrier suddenly stopped, then darted back around Serena's legs, tripping her up with the leash. She stumbled in her haste to step over it and found herself scooped against a hard unyielding chest.

'I'm okay,' she gasped, her hands curling at the body heat coming through his shirt.

'You're shaking,' he said, his arm encircling her even more firmly, bringing her into such acute physical contact with him, it set off tremors that had nothing to do with almost losing her balance.

She looked up in agitated protest. The blazing intensity of his eyes so close to hers had a hypnotic force that fried her brain, turning her into a passive dummy as he slowly lowered his head towards her upturned face. Even with more intimate collision imminent, she couldn't bring herself to react. His mouth covered hers and then it was too late to think, to speak, to do anything but feel him.

His lips seemed to tug at hers, enticing them to open, though there was no blitzing invasion, more a slow, sensual exploration that had her whole mouth tingling with excitement, his tongue teasing, goading, twining. She was drawn into actively participating, compelled to respond by a need to know more, feel more.

Whether this signalled consent or surrender, Serena had no idea. Her mind was flooded with intoxicating sensation. Yet what had been enthralling suddenly exploded into wild passion and a tidal wave of chaotic need crashed through her entire body, engulfing her with such power she completely lost herself in it, craving hot and urgent union with the man who was kissing her, holding her locked to him.

Her thighs clung to the strong muscularity of his, revelling in their maleness. Her stomach exulted in the questing erection that pressed into it. Her breasts wantonly flattened themselves against the heated wall of his chest, instinctively seeking the beat of his heart. Her arms wound around his neck, as fiercely possessive as the hands curled around her bottom, lifting her into this fantastic fit with him.

She was consumed with excitement, the rampant desire coursing between them blotting out everything else until the avid kissing was broken by a muffled curse and one of the hands holding her in perfect place lost its grip on her fevered flesh. A shrill barking blasted into her ears, opening them to the outer world again, jarring her mind into sharp recognition of where she was.

And with whom!

Sheer shock thumped her feet back on the ground again, her arms flying down from their stranglehold on Nic Moretti's neck. Cleo was barking her head off and tugging hard on the leash that was looped around Nic's wrist, her claws digging at the gravel on the driveway in ferocious determination to pull the two people apart and draw attention to herself again.

Saved by the dog, Serena thought dizzily. It was paramount she pull her wits together to deal with this terribly vulnerable situation. If Cleo hadn't come to the rescue, she and Nic could have been tearing each other's clothes off and coupling on the lawn. Or against her car.

Car!

Miraculously she still had the keys clutched in her hand. She swung around, pressing the remote control button to unlock the doors. Hearing the affirmative click, she aimed a brilliant smile at Nic who was still busy persuading Cleo to calm down and come to heel.

'Got to go,' she stated firmly.

'Go?' he repeated dazedly.

'Yes.' She reached for the driver's door handle and yanked it open. 'I guess that kiss was a thank you.'

'A thank you?' He looked incredulously at her.

'Very nice it was, too.'

'Nice?' It was a derisive bark of disbelief.

'Goodnight. And good luck with Cleo.'

She jumped into the driver's seat, slammed the door shut, gunned the engine and was off before he could stop her or say anything that would deny her dismissive reading of what had actually been a cataclysmic event for her. She only just remembered to put on the headlights as she was about to turn onto the public road.

There was still enough light to see by but twilight was fast turning to night. The clock on the dashboard said eight forty-five. How long had she been in that clinch with Nic Moretti, telling him she was his for the taking? She'd lost all her bearings, as though an earthquake had hit her. In fact, she was still trembling.

Having made her escape and travelled enough distance to feel safe, Serena pulled over to the verge of the road and cut the engine. Feeling in desperate need of liberal doses of oxygen to her fevered brain, she wound down her window and took several deep breaths of fresh cool air.

The awful truth was, the big bad wolf had pounced and she'd been only too eager to be gobbled up. No hiding that. But she didn't have to put herself at risk again.

The worst of it was, in all her twenty-eight years, no man had ever drawn such an overwhelming response from her. This had to be some diabolical trick of chemistry because it was very clear in Serena's mind that she didn't fit into Nic Moretti's world and never would.

He was a high-flyer. He'd marry one of his own kind. No way would he climb down enough to consider her a suitable mate for life. The only mating he'd want with her would be strictly on the side, and she was not going to put herself in that position.

Absolutely not!

A kiss was just a kiss, she told herself, as she restarted the car and headed for home.

But what a kiss!

CHAPTER SIX

NIC let the damned dog take *him* for a walk around the lawn. He was in a total daze, his mind shot through with disbelief. Serena Fleming was a challenging cutie but he hadn't expected her to blow him away. On two counts! First, punching him out with a powerhouse of passion, then kissing him off with a dismissive goodbye.

He shook his head.

This didn't happen to him.

In all his years of dating women, never had a first kiss spun him out of a controlled awareness of how it was going for both himself and the other participant. Completely losing it was incomprehensible to him, especially over a pert little chick with whom he had nothing in common apart from a problem with a dog.

No denying she raised his sexual instincts sky-high. He had one hell of an itch to get her into bed with him. And moving right down to animal level, *she* had been on heat to mate with him. But for Cleo's untimely intervention, it could well have ended in a highly primitive *fait accompli.* Would Serena Fleming have dusted him off her then and made the same fast getaway?

Every woman he'd ever known had lingered for more of whatever he gave them. Purring for it, more times than not. Yet here was a slip of a girl, kissing him with stunning passion, then leaving him as flat as a pricked balloon.

Anger stirred. He glared at the dog who was prancing along, blithely careless of the frustration it had caused. 'She cares more about you than she does about me.'

Cleo paused and looked at him with soulful eyes.

'You needn't think I'm taking *you* to bed with me,' Nic growled. 'You go into your cave tonight.'

He was feeling distinctly cavemanlike himself. In fact, if Serena Fleming was still here, he'd throw her over his shoulder, slap her provocative backside, and haul her off to a sexual orgy that would give him intense satisfaction and reduce her to his willing slave.

Which just went to prove how far she'd got under his skin.

Nic usually prided himself on being a highly civilised man, considerate of others, obliging their needs where they didn't clash too much with his own, caring about their sensitivities, playing the diplomat with finesse. Clearly there was some strange mutant chemistry at work here with the dog-handler, changing parameters he had always controlled.

The sensible course was to simply let her go, limit their encounters to the brief dog pick-ups and deliveries every Monday. No problem with that arrangement. It was foolish to let what was really an aberrational choice of bed partner get into his head like this, disturbing the general tenor of his life.

Having decided to sideline an obviously unsuitable attraction, Nic took Cleo inside and proceeded to lock up the house. He tried watching television for a while but ended up changing from one program to another, none of them holding his interest. Taking a book to bed with him seemed a better idea. He had the latest Patrick Kennedy novel to read—good author.

Having collected a king-size pillow and Cleo's trampoline bed, he led the little terrier to the mud room. Almost forgot the water dish. He moved that from the kitchen and placed it next to the doggy door, then followed all Serena's instructions to the letter. Half of him hoped her advice wouldn't work so he could take her down a peg or two, demand his money back, but he knew that was being churlish. Better that it did work so he could get a good night's sleep.

Amazingly, after a few initial barks to protest Nic's departure, Cleo did settle. Maybe the music got to her, or she decided the cave of blankets wasn't a bad place to be. Whatever… Nic wasn't about to check as long as peace reigned. He turned off all the lights and retired to his bed.

After several episodes of his mind wandering where he'd resolved it shouldn't go, he finally had the characters in the novel sorted out and was getting the hang of the story. Then the telephone rang, wrecking his concentration again.

He checked his watch since Cleo had his clock radio. Ten-thirty. He wasn't expecting a call from anyone at this hour. Was it Serena, ostensibly ringing to check the dog situation while surreptitiously checking his response to her? Maybe *she* was thinking about that kiss, suffering some after-effects, having a change of mind about leaving him flat.

Nic was smiling to himself as he picked up the receiver. This was his opportunity to be dismissive, which would put him back on top and in control where he liked to be. If Serena Fleming was hanging out for some pillow-talk, she would come up empty tonight.

'Nic here,' he said pleasantly, projecting perfectly good humour.

'Oh, Nic darling!' *His sister's voice!* 'You weren't asleep, were you? I'm calling from New York and it's morning here. Ward said the time difference was…'

'It's okay,' Nic broke in, trying not to sound vexed and deflated. 'I wasn't asleep. How's the trip so far?'

'I haven't managed a decent sleep yet. Last night I couldn't help worrying about Cleo. Is she missing us terribly?'

'She's fine during the day but she does miss you at night.'

'Poor baby!'

'In fact, I haven't managed a decent sleep, either, with her barking non-stop.'

'Oh, dear!'

'Not to worry, Angelina. I got some expert advice from your pet grooming lady and Cleo seems to have settled down tonight.'

'Michelle is quite marvellous, the way she…'

'It wasn't Michelle. Serena came and organised…'

'Serena? Who's Serena?'

'From the salon. Serena Fleming.'

'There's no Serena at the salon. Only Michelle and Tammy.'

Nic frowned at the certainty in his sister's voice. 'Well, she drove the salon van today, picking up Cleo and bringing her back, and she impressed me as knowing a lot about dog behaviour.'

'Mmm…Michelle must have taken on a new girl then. You say she's good? She's helped with my precious baby?'

'An absolute miracle worker,' Nic assured his sister while privately notching up a host of questions to be examined later. 'Cleo is now fast asleep in her own special cave of blankets with the radio playing classical music,' he explained to soothe Angelina's concern.

'Really?'

'Truly,' he affirmed.

'I know Michelle always plays music at the salon. She says it has a calming influence.'

'Apparently it works. Anyhow, don't fret about Cleo any more. She's eating well and we're getting along just fine.'

The little terrier had a very good appetite, as long as there was cooked chicken or steak or bacon on the menu. The tinned dog food was left untouched but Nic thought it wiser not to tell his sister that her precious pet had decided it would only eat what Nic was eating. Angelina would only fuss and what was the point? He could afford to feed the dog what it wanted.

He asked about New York and they chatted briefly of non-dog things. His sister sounded happy by the time the call ended, her concern over Cleo having abated.

Nic did not go back to reading his book.

He thought about Serena Fleming…about her quick wit and air of self-confidence…her ability to take charge…her disdainful attitude towards Justine who, on the surface of it, cut a stunning image that would intimidate most ordinary women...her experienced comment on the Chardonnay...and last, but not least, her incredible *sangfroid* in dismissing their clinch as a mere *thank you* from him.

Adding all this to the fact that she was very new to Michelle's Pet Grooming Salon, Nic was strongly reminded that his first impression of Serena Fleming was that he'd seen her before somewhere, most probably at some social function in Sydney. She might well have a city background. When he'd asked if she'd always lived in Holgate, her answer had suggested but not confirmed it was so.

The suspicion grew that she wasn't what she presented herself to be, but something very different and not ordinary at all.

The picture now emerging in his mind placed her as extraordinary, which made him feel considerably better about the whole situation. She posed far more of an intriguing challenge that he had initially assumed, and Nic knew he wouldn't rest content until he got to the bottom of Serena Fleming.

He grinned to himself.

In more senses than one!

CHAPTER SEVEN

MONDAY morning…back to the Gifford house to collect Cleo for her weekly grooming. Serena wished she could ask Michelle to do it, but that would give rise to searching questions and ultimately embarrassing answers. It would also be an unfair request since her sister's time was better spent in grooming the pets to the standard of perfection which was her trademark. In short, this was Serena's job and she couldn't shirk it.

Which meant facing Nic Moretti again.

He hadn't called about any problems with the dog. Presumably Michelle's instructions had worked and the nights were now smooth sailing. A pity she couldn't say that about her own. She'd spent many sleepless hours in her bed, going over and over what had happened with the testosterone loaded architect.

It was the sheer shock of her total vulnerability to what Nic Moretti could make her feel that had sent Serena skittering into her car. Fate had played a very unkind trick on her, placing such a bombshell in her path when she was fighting to attain some level-headed wisdom after her bitter disillusionment with Lyall.

Serena told herself it was just as well Nic Moretti hadn't attempted any follow-up to that devastating kiss because temptation was a terrible thing and it would have been very very difficult to handle, not to mention maintaining the dignity her self-respect demanded.

It took true grit to put herself in the van and drive to the Gifford house. Along the way, Serena decided she'd prefer a dog's life. Much simpler.

Michelle had told her about a silky terrier who'd flatly refused to be mated with her own kind. She preferred big dogs. She'd ended up with a litter by a labrador and a litter by a Doberman pinscher before her owners gave up on getting purebreds from her and had the terrier desexed. Only people wanted purebreds, Serena thought darkly. Animals followed their instincts.

No doubt Angelina Gifford would want Cleo mated suitably with another pedigreed silky terrier. Running wild would be frowned upon in that family, especially when it came to mating. A man might sow some wild oats but when it came to marriage, it was usually to their own kind. Only men like Lyall, who wanted an underling wife, went beyond the fold. And Serena knew what Nic Moretti thought of that!

She'd worked herself up into a finely edged temper by the time she arrived at the Gifford house. One bit of condescension or snobbery from Cleo's guardian and fur might fly. At least he couldn't think she'd dressed up for him. Her work clothes were the same as last week, though she'd teamed a plain blue singlet top with her denim shorts this morning so he couldn't possibly see a bare midriff as a come-on. And her hair was stuffed back into a practical plait. Not a skerrick of make-up, either.

Serena walked to the front door with stiff-backed pride and pressed her thumb to the bell-push rather longer than necessary. She didn't want to be kept waiting. Her feet felt as though they were on hot coals.

The door opened only seconds later. Nic Moretti filled the space with such overwhelming impact, Serena found herself retreating a step in sheer defence against the male dominance of his big strong physique, once again blaring at her since he only wore surfing shorts. Her hands clenched and the nails digging into her palms helped to ground her at an arm's length away from him.

He smiled. 'You're on time.'

He had a killer smile. Serena's pulse-beat soared. Fighting the dizziness in her brain, she poured out every word she could think of. 'I'm always on time. I consider punctuality a courtesy that I like to have returned.'

'Ah!' The smile turned lopsided. 'Black mark against me last week. I promise it won't happen again.'

The warm charm had the perverse effect of chilling her nipples. She could feel them tightening into hard buds, pushing against her sports bra. Any moment now he'd see them poking at her clingy singlet and he'd know...

'I take it Cleo has settled down at night,' she gabbled, desperate to keep his attention on her face.

'Your plan worked like a charm. I picked up a wooden crate to replace the bar stools. Want to see?'

'No, no, as long as it works. I must keep moving this morning.'

She tore her gaze from the twinkling invitation in his and looked down at the dog who was waiting at his feet. The leash attached to Cleo's collar ran up to a loop around Nic Moretti's wrist. Vividly recalling how treacherous that leash could be, Serena immediately crouched and picked up the little silky terrier, cradling her against her chest, which also helped to hide the aroused state of her breasts.

'If you'll just unhand the leash, I'll be off,' she said somewhat breathlessly.

He took his time unhitching himself from the looped strap, chatting on as he did so. 'My sister called from New York, wanting to know if Cleo was fretting for her. I told her about you helping me. The odd thing was…'

He paused and Serena made the mistake of meeting his eyes again, dark probing eyes that had the searing intent to scour her mind.

'…she told me there was no Serena Fleming working at Michelle's Pet Grooming Salon.'

Her heart kicked. Was he thinking of the seventy dollars he'd paid out for *her expertise?* But the advice had worked so how could he complain? She'd simply been standing in for Michelle whose knowledge was worth every cent of that money since it had produced a week of peaceful nights.

'She mentioned a Tammy,' he went on.

'Tammy's gone. I've stepped into her place,' Serena rushed out.

He cocked a quizzical eyebrow. 'New to the job then?'

'Not exactly new,' she quickly defended. 'I'm Michelle's sister. I'm well acquainted with the business she's been running for the past five years. And I have an affinity with animals, just as she does.'

'So you're helping out your sister.'

'More a case of helping each other. I wanted to get out of Sydney.' The words tripped out before she could bite them back.

'What did you do in Sydney, Serena?'

Danger…danger…danger…

If he connected her to Lyall Duncan now she'd die a million deaths. Not only that, she needed to cover her tracks on the animal front. Leaving herself open to an accusation of false pretences would not be good. Her mind zinged into overdrive, wildly seeking an escape with honour.

'I practised a lot of psychology.'

It wasn't a lie. Dealing with Ty's clients had been like conducting a therapy session more times than not. The salon policy demanded that everyone have a smile on their face when they left. One way or another, you had to make them feel good, happy if possible, at least better than when they had arrived. Of course, listening was the big thing. And the clients lay in curved couches when they were having their hair shampooed and conditioned, same kind of relaxation as they'd get in a psychiatrist's office.

'May I have the leash, please?' she quickly asked, seeing he was digesting this information at the speed of light and deciding a fast getaway was essential. Cleo was making no objection to being cuddled so shouldn't cause any delay.

Fortunately, Nic handed the looped strap to her as he commented, 'I thought you said you weren't a qualified psychologist.'

'I'm not,' she conceded, swinging towards the van. 'That doesn't stop me from using it to get the result

I'm aiming for. 'Bye now,' she tossed over her shoulder as she got her legs moving away from him.

He didn't pursue her, though she felt his gaze burning into her body, making her acutely conscious of being watched and examined from head to toe. It was a huge relief to put the van between them.

'Back at one o'clock?' he called as she opened the driver's door and leaned in, bundling Cleo onto the passenger seat.

She popped back out to say, 'Yes. One o'clock,' then climbed into her own seat and shut the door with too much force, revealing an anxiety to depart that she hoped he wouldn't pick up. Her fingers worked very fast attaching Cleo's safety harness and her own seat belt. She didn't exactly burn rubber driving off but her inner tension only began to ease when she was well on her way to Holgate.

Escape made good.

Except she had to face Nic Moretti again at one o'clock and she knew he hadn't yet wiped her off his slate. It was possible that the smile and the welcoming charm had been employed to put their association back on a friendly footing—more comfortable all around since they would be seeing each other every Monday. Also very diplomatic if he happened to need more help with the dog.

But the curiosity about her background...her life in Sydney...that demonstrated personal interest beyond what was required to promote congenial meetings. It smacked of wanting to get close to her, and *close* was very dangerous to Serena's peace of mind. Not that she had any around him anyway. The man had a sexual magnetism that had all her nerves going haywire.

She had managed to cut him off at the pass this time, but what about the next and the next and the next? Maybe she should just say she'd been a hairdresser and have done with it. Let him link her to Lyall Duncan. It would undoubtedly cool his interest.

She'd probably fuelled it with her reference to psychology. Stupid move! Though it had seemed brilliant at the time. Brilliant and satisfying, seeing the respectful assessment of her being recalculated in his eyes. Why knock that down? She deserved respect. Everybody did. There was nothing shameful about working in a service industry. Didn't he service people, too, creating architectural designs to please them? Just because he made more *money*...

Serena sighed away the ferment in her mind.

There was nothing she could do to change the status of wealth. And if Nic Moretti was such a snob, he deserved to be misled about her status. Not that she would actually lie, but he could mislead himself as much as he liked. It should be interesting to see what he came up with next!

Nic congratulated himself on the deductions he'd made about Serena Fleming. She had been in Sydney until very recently and grooming pets was not a job she usually did. It was her sister's business. More likely than not, Serena had held some kind of consultancy position where pushing the right buttons with people would serve her very well. And charging a whopping fee came naturally to her. Definitely a smart businesswoman who was not backward in coming forward.

Though that latter attitude did not apply to sex.

Nic wondered why. Surely she was the type of woman who went after what she wanted. Why back off last Monday night? Was it because she'd suddenly found herself not on top of everything, control completely lost?

He could empathise with that shock to the system. It hit hard.

On the other hand, he certainly wasn't averse to trying another dose of it, if only to see how far it went. Nic smiled to himself, pleased with the thought that Serena had been out for the count in their clinch, every bit as much as himself. But for Cleo...

Nic's smile broke into a grin as he realised Serena had been using Cleo as a shield just now. All he had to do was think of some ruse to get her guard down so they could meet on ground they might both find highly satisfying.

One o'clock.

Having made a point about punctuality Serena arrived on the dot. It was disconcerting to find the front door wide open. Should she call out or ring the bell? Was Nic Moretti home or was the house being burgled?

Cleo pranced straight into the foyer. Naturally the dog was confident of entering its own domain. The leash Serena held was pulled tight before she could decide what to do. Then the dog yapped and Nic Moretti strolled out of the kitchen.

Shock and relief triggered a sharp rush of words. 'You gave me a fright, leaving the door open.'

He paused, threw his hands out in apologetic appeal. 'Sorry. I'm just home from a business meeting and I knew you'd be here any minute.'

He looked incredibly handsome, dressed in classic grey trousers and a grey and white striped shirt. Serena's heart pitter-pattered in helpless array. She'd geared herself up to ignore his beefcake attributes, and here she was, faced with an even more impressive side of him, the polished businessman.

He gestured to the kitchen. 'I was making a pot of coffee. Do you have time to have a cup with me?'

Temptation roared through her. He was so terribly attractive and there was nothing threatening in his expression, nothing more than a friendly inquiry. 'Yes,' tripped straight off her tongue. 'That would be nice, thank you.'

No harm in being a bit friendly, she swiftly argued, stepping into the foyer, but closing the door behind her did raise her sense of vulnerability and she wondered if she was being hopelessly foolish.

Cleo tugged at the leash, barking to be freed. She unclipped it and the little terrier raced off to Nic who crouched down, grinning as he ruffled the silky hair. 'Want to be admired, do you? All prettied up with your pink bow?' He raised an amused gaze to Serena. 'Do the male dogs get a blue bow?'

She couldn't help smiling. 'Yes, they do. And they tug like mad to get it off.'

Nic laughed and straightened up, maintaining a relaxed air as he led into the kitchen and poured the freshly brewed coffee into mugs. 'Milk, cream, sugar?'

'No. Straight black.'

'Easily pleased.'

'More practical. I've had many friends who never have milk or sugar on hand.'

'Always dieting?'

'It's the curse of modern society that skinny is more desirable than a Rubenesque shape.'

'Not too skinny. Anorexic women are a tragedy,' he commented soberly, picking up the mugs. 'Let's sit on the terrace.'

'I can't stay long.'

'I won't hold you up.'

This assurance made it easy to follow him and she was enjoying the casual banter between them. They settled at a table overlooking the spa and pool. A sea breeze wafted through the sails that shaded them. Very pleasant, Serena thought. And seductive, caution whispered.

'Have you studied art?'

The question completely threw her, coming out of the blue. Was he digging into her background again? Playing some snob card?

It spurred Serena into full frontal attack mode, eyes flashing a direct challenge. 'Why ask me that?'

He shrugged, denying the question any importance. 'I was just struck by what you said earlier about a Rubenesque figure. Most people would have contrasted skinny with overweight. It showed you were familiar with the kind of women Rubens always painted.'

He was quick to pick up anything, Serena warned herself, but there was no harm in answering this. 'I did take art at school. I guess some of what I learnt stuck.'

'Do you ever go to exhibitions at the art gallery?'

A probe into her social activities? Where was this conversation leading? Although wary now, she decided there was no danger in this particular subject.

'When there's something special on,' she replied offhandedly. 'Like the Monet one recently.'

He had seen it, as well, and they chatted on about the artist's work—a really convivial conversation which Serena was reluctant to end. However she had no excuse to stay once she had finished her coffee, and while she had actually relaxed in his company for a while, there was no guarantee that would last long. Besides which, Michelle would be expecting her back at the salon.

'Thanks for the coffee,' she said, rising to her feet. 'I have to go now.'

He returned a rueful smile. 'Needs must. I'll see you out.'

He stood to accompany her and Serena was once more swamped by how big and tall he was. She was acutely conscious of him as he walked at her side through the house. He hadn't touched her at all— didn't now—yet the memory of everything she'd felt of him last Monday night was flooding through her, stirring her own sexuality into a treacherous yearning.

'Do you happen to be free on Saturday?'

The casual question instantly set her nerve ends twitching. Was this some kind of a trap? Had she just been lulled into enjoying his company, a paving of the way for another pounce?

'If you could join me here for lunch...' he went on, rolling out temptation again, on a much bigger scale.

'No, I can't,' Serena forced herself to say. 'My

niece is riding in a gymkhana on Saturday and I promised to go and watch her.'

'Well, a promise is a promise,' he accepted without any hint of acrimony. 'Where is the gymkhana being held?'

'At Matcham Pony Club.' Lucky it was the truth so she had facts at her fingertips to back up her reply to him.

'I might go and watch for a while myself. Take Cleo out for a run. Introduce her to the world of horses.'

Serena's heart started galloping so hard, it felt as though a whole herd of horses were trapped in her chest. She barely found wits enough to effect a graceful departure at the front door. Her mind kept pounding with one highly sizzling fact.

Nic Moretti had decided to chase her.

Chase her, corner her, bed her.

That was how it would go.

Somehow she had to stop this.

But did she want to? Did she *really* want to?

CHAPTER EIGHT

CUTTING up onions was not Serena's favourite job. Her eyes were watering non-stop by the time she'd finished. Despite washing her hands and eyes at the sink in the clubhouse, the pungent smell was still getting to her as she carried the platter out to the barbecue where Michelle's friend, Gavin Emory, was in charge of the sausage sizzle.

Blurred vision was to blame for the lack of any warning. Serena didn't even look at the customer waiting at the barbecue. What focus she had was trained on handing the platter of onions over to Gavin as fast as possible.

'Here we are!' Gavin said cheerfully, tipping the lot onto the hotplate. 'Won't take long to cook.'

'No hurry,' came the good-natured reply.

Serena's head instantly jerked towards the customer. No mistaking the timbre of *that voice*. Hearing it so unexpectedly was almost enough to cause a heart seizure.

Nic Moretti grinned at her. 'Hi! Beautiful day, isn't it?'

'You came!' The words shot out before she could catch them back, revealing she'd been on the lookout for him, missed him, given up on seeing him here at the gymkhana, and now that he had come, he shouldn't have because she'd settled in her mind that he wouldn't.

'Great spot for a picnic,' he enthused, ignoring her accusatory tone. 'Wonderful trees. Plenty of shade. Lush grass. I brought a rug with me. Thought I'd relax and watch the riders go through their paces.'

'Where is…?' She looked down and there was the silky terrier under the trestle table which held the buttered rolls, bread and condiments, chomping away on a cooked sausage, oblivious to anything but food.

'She didn't want to wait for onions,' Nic said offhandedly. 'Didn't want mustard or sauce, either. Cleo likes her meat straight.'

Serena took a deep breath and moved behind the trestle table, blinking rapidly to clear the stinging moisture from her eyes. Nic Moretti had brought the dog. He couldn't *corner* her here. Not seriously. Too much public interference. So she had nothing to worry about. The only problem was in fighting his attraction.

'What have you ordered?' she asked, trying not to notice the way he filled his red and white checked sports shirt and blue jeans.

'Two rolls with the lot,' he answered, his dazzling grin sabotaging Serena's attempt to remain cool and collected. 'I've just been chatting with your sister…'

Shock slammed into her heart. *What had he wormed out of Michelle?*

'Met your niece, too. Charming girl.'

Serena gritted her teeth. Charm was undoubtedly what he'd used to get what he wanted out of her family.

'They told me Erin would be riding in an event at two o'clock.' He checked his watch. 'One-fifteen now. Will you be finished up here by then?'

'Sure she will,' Gavin chimed in. 'My daughter's riding in the same event.'

'Ah! Double interest!' Nic pounced, his eyes twinkling a challenge at Serena. 'Will you join me then and explain the finer points of the event?'

If she didn't, he'd come looking for her again, imposing his presence anyway. 'Okay,' she agreed, thinking her best defence was to get a few things out in the open with Nic Moretti. In private.

He chatted on to Gavin about the pony club until the onions were cooked and he was served with the sausage rolls he'd ordered. The moment he was gone, Gavin turned to her with a knowing grin. 'Nice guy!'

'More a master of manipulation,' Serena muttered darkly. 'I've got to go and see Michelle. Can you manage on your own?'

'No problem.'

There were problems aplenty in Serena's mind as she hot-footed it to the pony yard beyond the amenities block, hoping to find her sister and niece there. She needed to know just how much they'd blabbed to Nic Moretti before she tackled him herself. Luckily they were both there, along with Gavin's daughter, Tamsin, who was Erin's best friend.

Serena briefly reflected on how very chummy the two families were, and since Gavin was a widower, maybe there was no reason to be concerned about her sister's single state continuing for much longer. Right now, however, she was more concerned about her own entanglement with Nic Moretti who was definitely pursuing a coupling.

Michelle spotted her approach and moved to meet her, leaving the two girls to look after their ponies.

'You'll never guess who came and introduced himself to us,' she said, eyes sparkling with speculation.

'Cleo's keeper,' Serena answered dryly.

'What a nice guy! As well as gorgeous!'

'Did he happen to ask about me?' Serena pressed, ignoring both accolades since the *gorgeous* part was only too evident and it suited Nic's purpose to be *nice*.

'Only where to find you.'

'No questions about my past?'

'None at all. He did say you'd been great with Cleo. Mostly he asked about the gymkhana and chatted to Erin about how long she'd been riding. No really personal stuff.'

No reason for it if his only quest was bed. Serena was ruminating on this—her mind torn between relief and disappointment—as her sister rattled on.

'Gavin has asked me to dinner at his place tonight. And Erin will want to sleep over with Tamsin. Any chance that Nic Moretti will ask you out?'

Serena frowned at her. 'What happened to the warning about the big bad wolf?'

Michelle grinned. 'He has great teeth.'

'All the better to bite me with.'

'Come on, Serena. You're attracted. He's attracted. Might be just the man to get you over Lyall Duncan.'

'They're two of a kind,' she flashed bitterly.

Michelle shook her head. 'He wasn't patronising to either me or Erin. Not like Lyall.'

'You didn't tell me that before. I thought you liked Lyall.'

'At the time you could see no wrong in him. I just

let it pass, hoping you'd wake up to what you were getting before you married him. And you did.'

Thanks to Nic Moretti!

'Anyhow, what you choose to do is your business, Serena. I was just letting you know Erin and I won't be home tonight. Okay?'

'You *liked* Nic?'

'Yes, I did.'

It didn't prove anything. Angelina Gifford's observation just seemed more pertinent—*There wasn't a female alive who didn't love Nic.*

Michelle reached out and squeezed her arm. 'You know, I've learnt it's wrong to judge everything from a hurt that someone else has inflicted. Sometimes it's good…just to follow your instincts.'

She was referring to her own life—how the tragedy of her husband's death had cast a long shadow on her thinking, making her ultra-cautious and reluctant to let people get close.

Serena leaned over and kissed her older sister's cheek. 'I'm glad Gavin came along. Must get back to the sausage sizzle now. I've left him managing on his own.'

For the rest of the afternoon, the conversation with Michelle kept popping into Serena's mind, even though she rejected it as not applicable to her situation with Nic Moretti. She *knew* he was a snob, even though she couldn't once accuse him of being patronising in either speech or manner while they watched the riding events together. To make matters worse, being with him stirred instincts that waged a continual war with her brain, because following *them* meant abandoning all the common sense she was trying to cling to. In fact, most of the time they prompted things she had no control over.

He smiled and her facial muscles instinctively responded.

His arm brushed hers and her skin tingled with excitement.

He spoke and her heart played hopscotch to the tune of his voice.

If his gaze met hers for more than a few seconds, her body temperature heated up.

All of which brought Serena to the conclusion that she was hopelessly in lust with the man—a totally physical thing that she couldn't squash, shake off, or block. And maybe—just maybe—she should let nature take its course, especially since she'd never been affected like this before. There was something to be said for experiencing the highs in life, even if they were followed by lows.

This mental seesaw came to an abrupt crisis point when Nic casually asked, 'Doing anything in particular after the gymkhana?'

'No,' slid off her tongue, completely wiping out any ready excuses for rejecting the imminent invitation.

'I've got some great T-bone steaks and a good bottle of red. How are you at throwing a salad together? We could do a barbecue out by the pool, have a swim…'

'Sounds good,' she heard herself say, a sense of sheer recklessness buzzing through her mind. 'I have a deft hand with lettuce leaves.'

He laughed and there was no mistaking the triumphant satisfaction dancing in his eyes.

Cornered!

But not bedded yet.

Let him make one snobbish remark—just one—Serena silently and fiercely resolved, and lust would go on ice so fast, *his* head would spin.

His mouth twitched into a quizzical little smile. 'Why do I get the feeling I've just been put on trial?'

'Probably because I have the feeling you take too much for granted,' she retorted, raising a challenging eyebrow.

'With you, that would definitely be a mistake,' he declared, but there was wicked mischief in his eyes. 'Should *I* make the salad?'

She laughed at the ridiculously trivial point. 'No. I'll bring it with me.'

He frowned. 'I have the makings at home. We could just take off from here...'

'It's been a long day. I need to clean up first. I'll drive to your place with my contribution.' *And with my car on hand for an easy getaway when I choose to leave.*

'An independent lady,' he drawled.

'I like to be on top of the game.'

His eyes glittered with the promise of competition for that spot even as he answered, 'I'm happy to go along with teamwork. So when will I see you? Five-thirty?'

'Six. Gives me time to be creative with the salad.' And stops him from thinking she was only too eager to get there.

'I shall look forward to a gourmet's delight.'

A sexual feast, he meant. Every nerve end in Serena's body was twitching with the same anticipation, but no way was she going to admit it. Or go for it unless she felt it was right.

'Well, I hope I don't disappoint you,' she said, taking secret satisfaction in the double entendre. 'If you'll excuse me, I'll head off now. Have to let Michelle know what I'm doing.'

'Fine! I'll gather up my rug and dog and see you later.'

Nic smiled to himself as he watched her stroll away from him. Mission achieved. He glanced at his watch. Just on four o'clock. In fishermen's terms, he'd been playing out the line for three hours and he now had the result he wanted. More or less. Serena Fleming was a very slippery fish. He had her in his net but she wasn't leaping into his frying pan.

And she was providing herself with an escape vehicle by bringing her own car.

Nic reasoned he'd have to be fast tonight.

Very fast.

Knock her right off the top of her game before she could mount defences and retreat.

Funny…he couldn't remember relishing a date as much as he relished this one. The trick was to bring it to the end he wanted, with Serena wanting the same end, admitting it, accepting it, and wild to have it.

Wild…

Weighing up his memory of the kiss they'd shared had eventually brought Nic to the decision that *civilised* didn't hold a candle to *wild*.

CHAPTER NINE

SHE'D clicked off.

What had he said wrong?

Done wrong?

From the moment she had arrived until just a few minutes ago, Nic knew he'd carried Serena with him. The connection had been exhilarating—eye contact, mind contact, everything but body contact. Was it because the meal was now over that she was withdrawing into herself, shutting him out, getting herself geared up to evade what had been simmering between them before it came to the boil?

She'd undoubtedly felt *safe* with a table separating them, *safe* out here on the patio eating *al fresco*. Nothing too intimate about the open air. And she'd kept the conversation away from herself, peppering him with questions about his career, his recent contracts, what he felt were his greatest architectural achievements, favourite designs. Her interest had seemed genuine, yet her attention had started slipping when he'd described the town house complex he'd done for Lyall Duncan.

Her gaze had dropped to the glass of wine by her emptied dinner plate. She had the stem of it between her fingers and thumb, turning it in slow circuits. Her face was completely still, expressionless, as though the slight swirl of the claret had her mesmerised. There was no awareness that he'd fallen silent.

He'd lost her.

The need to snatch her back from wherever she'd gone in her mind was paramount. He'd been a fool to keep talking about himself, despite her encouragement. Such a one-way track could too easily become boring. He leaned forward, a tense urgency pumping through him.

'Serena…?'

Her lashes flew up, vivid blue eyes jolted into refocusing on him. But the distance was still there. He instantly felt it—an invisible barrier that was very real nonetheless. He tried a smile, adding a quick whimsical question to grab her attention.

'Where are you?'

Her responding smile was slow, a touch wry. 'I was thinking of all the connections you must have made. Friends in high places. Big property investors like Lyall Duncan…'

'Lyall is more a business associate than a friend,' he cut in, wondering if she couldn't see herself fitting into *his* world. Which was absurd. She was clever enough to fit anywhere. If she wanted to. That, he suspected was the big thing with Serena, choosing what she *wanted*.

Her eyebrows lifted quizzically. 'You don't mix socially?'

He shrugged, sensing this was a loaded question but not grasping the logic behind it. 'Business lunches. The huge party he threw to officially launch the town house complex. Lyall tends to big-note everything he does. He enjoyed parading me as *his* architect that night. We're not really connected beyond the professional level.'

He could almost see an assessment clicking through her mind. Whether it had a positive or a negative outcome he had no idea. What he did know was that this was shifting ground and fast action was required.

'Let's clear these plates.' He pushed his chair back and stood up, cheerfully announcing, 'Time for dessert. Angelina left a selection of gourmet ice-creams in the freezer—macadamia nut and honey, Bailey's Irish Cream, death by chocolate…'

She smiled. 'Okay, I'm tempted.'

Tempted by more than chocolate, Nic hoped, relieved to have her on her feet and moving with him. He quickly picked the leftover steak bone off her plate and called Cleo to give her the special treat of two good bones to chew on, which would certainly keep the troublesome little terrier occupied and out of play for quite a while. She settled under the table with her version of doggy heaven, happily gnawing away while Nic and Serena collected what they'd used and headed inside to the kitchen.

Serena walked ahead of him, carrying the cutlery and salad bowl. Her long blond hair fell like a smooth silk curtain down her back, making his fingers itch to stroke it. No confining plait or clips tonight. She wore a highly sensuous petticoat dress that slid provocatively over her feminine curves with each sway of her hips. It was white with splashes of flowers on it, some filmy kind of fabric with an underslip. No need to wear a bra with it, Nic thought, and no trouble at all sliding off those shoestring straps. Her honey-tan skin gleamed enticingly.

All evening it had taken the utmost discipline not

to touch her. The bonds of restraint were now at breaking point. Every muscle in his body was taut, all wound up to make the move he had to make. She might decide against the ice-cream, might decide to skip out on him. Her thoughts were still a challenging mystery but he hadn't missed the sexual signals. She was vulnerable to him. He had to tap that vulnerability before her mind clamped down on it.

Serena set the salad bowl on the kitchen bench and dumped the cutlery in the sink. Her mind was in total ferment. Nic wasn't a friend of Lyall's. It didn't sound as if he shared the same attitudes. There'd been a lightly mocking tone in his voice when he'd spoken about Lyall big-noting himself.

She automatically turned on the tap to rinse the cutlery while reconsidering the humiliating conversation she'd overheard between the two men. Might it not have been surprise on Nic's part that Lyall's ego would allow him to choose a hairdresser as his wife? Had he simply been stringing Lyall along while the choice was explained to him, giving understanding as a pragmatic business tactic? Taking a critical attitude would not have been the diplomatic thing to do.

'You don't have to wash up,' Nic said over her shoulder. 'They go here.'

She turned to find him lowering the door of the dishwasher which was right beside her. He proceeded to stack the plates he'd brought in, his unbuttoned shirt flapping right open as he bent down. It was a casual Hawaiian shirt with parrots and hibiscus flowers on wildly tropical foliage, worn over royal blue surfing shorts, ready for the swim he'd offered but she'd decided not to take up since it would only provoke more temptation and she hadn't been sure where she was going with Nic Moretti.

Still wasn't sure…but she found her breath caught in her throat as she was faced with a wide expanse of bare muscular chest, a line of dark hair arrowing down to the waistband of his shorts, disappearing but heading straight for the apex of his powerhouse thighs.

'Special place for cutlery,' he pointed out. 'Put them in.'

She scooped them out of the sink and bent to place them properly, only to realise too late it caused her bodice to gape and Nic was right there looking at her, impossible to miss a bird's-eye view of her breasts. Heat instantly flooded her entire skin surface, raising a sensitivity that jerked her upright in a hopelessly graceless movement.

Nic closed the dishwasher door and suddenly he was standing very close to her, and despite the high-heeled sandals she wore, he seemed overwhelmingly big and tall, making her feel frail and fragile. She shrank back against the sink, her heart thumping so hard she could feel the throb of it in her temples.

Nic frowned, raising his hands in an open gesture that promised he was harmless as he protested her reaction. 'You can't be frightened of me, Serena.'

Her mind whirled, trying to find some reasonable response. How to explain that he generated a sexual force-field that she had no power to fight?

Nice guy, Gavin had said.

Echoed by Michelle—*Nice guy.*

And he hadn't been patronising. Not at all.

So why did she have to fight?

'You...it just surprised me, finding you so close,' she babbled, feeling hopelessly confused over what she should do, knowing only too well what her body was clamouring for, but was it right? *Was it right?*

'Not fear?' he asked, wanting confirmation.

His dark eyes were burning into hers. She had the weird sense they were tunneling into all her secret places, finding the truth of *their* response to him, never mind what words she spoke. Everything within her craved to *feel* this man, and denial suddenly seemed like a denial of life, of all that made life worth living. This mutual attraction had to be dictated by nature. How could it be wrong?

A hand lifted and touched her cheek. 'Serena...?'

What question was he asking? She couldn't think. His fingertips were softly stroking down her skin, making it tingle, and her entire body yearned to be similarly caressed by him. The memory of the kiss they'd shared ignited a chaotic surge of desire, a rampant need to know if the same wild passion could be aroused again. Her chest felt too tight, holding in too much. Her breathing quickened, trying to ease the pressure. Her mouth opened to suck in more air, or was it being pushed out?

Her mind couldn't cope with all this rushing inside her. She lost track of everything but his touch, sliding past her chin, down her throat, under her hair to the nape of her neck. He loomed closer, his eyes hypnotically fastened on hers, simmering with the intent to explore the same memory that was jamming her thought processes. An arm suddenly looped around her waist and clamped her body to the heat and strength of his. Her hair was tugged, tilting her face up. Then his mouth was on hers, his hot, hungry, marvellous mouth, explosively exciting, smashing past anticipation and delivering more sensation than her memory had retained.

Her hands instinctively sought to hold him, pushing under his opened shirt, revelling in gliding over his naked skin, feeling the taut muscles of his back, clutching him hard so that her breasts swelled onto the wide expanse of his chest, imprinting them on him in a wild urge to press an intense awareness of her own sexuality, of all that made her the woman *she* was.

The hand in her hair disentangled itself and moved to her shoulder, fingers hooking under her strap, pulling it down, dragging the top of her bodice with it. One breast freed, revelling in the stripping of the fabric barrier between her flesh and his, a mega-leap in sensitivity. Better still when he freed the other and shed his shirt. Wonderful to lift her arms out of the straps and throw her hands around his neck, running her fingers through the thick texture of his hair, able to press a far more intimate contact, exultantly satisfying.

He kissed her and kissed her, a passionate onslaught of kisses that drove her wild with wanting more of him. And it was there for her to have, his erection pressing into her stomach, wanting entry, seeking entry, as urgently desperate for it as she was.

Driven by a frenzy of desire she rubbed herself against the hard erotic roll of his highly charged sex, wishing she could hoist herself up to fit where she should, needing to engulf him, possess him, draw him deep inside her to where she ached to be filled, over and over again.

Then his hands were at her waist, thrusting her dress down over her hips, dragging her panties with it. 'Step out of them,' he gruffly commanded and they were whisked away from her as she blindly obeyed—blindly, recklessly, inhibitions totally abandoned. And it seemed to her in the same instant his shorts were gone, too, discarded in a swift tumult of action that rid them of all barriers to the ultimate intimacy.

He lifted her, propped her on the edge of the bench, moved between her legs, and finally, blissfully, he was there, sliding into the slick hot depths that had been waiting for him, tilting her back so he could reach further, and all her inner muscles clenched around him in ecstatic pleasure. Her legs instinctively locked around his hips, an act of utter exultation, and he kissed her, driving the overwhelming passion for this moment of union to an incredible level of sensation, total merging, making her feel they were flowing into each other and every cell in her body was melting from the sheer power of it.

He muttered something fierce under his breath as his mouth left hers, then in a harsh rasp close to her ear, 'Please say you're on the pill, Serena.'

'Yes,' spilled from her lips on a sigh of grateful relief. She hadn't thought…didn't want to think now…only to feel.

And the feeling was fantastic as he moved inside her, a series of fast surges that left her on one pinnacle of exquisite sensation after another. Even when he climaxed it left her afloat on a sea of sweet pleasure.

She didn't want to move. Doubted that she could anyway. Her arms and legs seemed drained of strength. But for his support she would have collapsed in a limp heap.

His chest was heaving. 'Shouldn't have happened here,' he muttered, his tone raw, savage. 'Madness...'

Serena was beyond comment.

'A kitchen bench, for God's sake!' he went on, sounding shocked, horrified. He swept her off it, strong arms holding her securely against him, carrying her...swift strides being taken. 'Sorry, sorry...' The anguished apology jerked out as he seemed intent on rushing her somewhere else. 'I'll make it up to you, I swear.'

Why did it matter? Serena thought in hazy confusion. Was he worried that it hadn't been good for her? Had he somehow missed her response? Her head was resting on his wonderfully broad shoulder, her hands loosely linked behind his neck. She sighed, not knowing what to say, loving his aggressive maleness, trusting him to look after the next step to wherever they were going together. It was like being swept along in a dream she didn't want to end, and the best part was he was real. All she was feeling with him was real.

He laid her on a bed, a soft doona on its surface beneath her, a soft pillow under her head, lovely sensual comfort. He stood looking down at her, shaking his head in a kind of awed wonderment as his gaze travelled slowly from the spill of her hair on the pillow to the languorous satisfaction written on her face, the tilt of her breasts, the curved spread of her hips, the moist apex of her thighs, the relaxed sprawl of her legs.

She didn't mind being so open to his view. She could look her fill of him, too, his magnificent physique, the immense power packed into his beautifully male anatomy. *The man,* she thought with a fatuous smile, and dizzily hoped he was seeing her, thinking of her as *the woman,* because none of this would ever make sense to her unless such special terms were applied to it.

'I'm not a rough, inconsiderate lover, Serena,' he assured her anxiously. 'Let me show you.'

Rough? He hadn't done anything she hadn't wanted. As for the kitchen bench…it had helped, not hurt. He hadn't hurt her one bit. Absolutely the contrary. She hadn't needed foreplay. But she was curious now about his thoughts. He seemed appalled at himself for having lost his sense of what he considered a suitable place for sex. Or was it about loss of control?

She liked the idea of Nic losing control with her. Somehow that made it even more right, whereas a step-by-step attempt at seduction would have felt wrong. Was that what he planned to do now, or was he intent on proving something to himself? It wasn't clear to her. Nothing much was…except how he made her feel.

He moved to the end of the bed, gently picked up one of her feet and started to unbuckle the ankle strap of her high-heeled sandal. Serena was amazed she was still wearing it—both of them. They'd completely dropped out of her consciousness. He stroked the shape of her ankle, the sole of her foot as he slipped the sandal off. Her toes curled as a zing of excitement travelled up her leg, fanning the embers of sexual arousal.

He lifted her other foot, caressing it in the same way as he removed its sandal and Serena almost squirmed from the exquisite sensuality of his touch. He knelt between her legs, skimming her calves and her inner thighs with his fingertips, her flesh tingling, quivering as he parted the soft lips of her sex and bent his head to kiss her there, flooding her with such intense feeling, her whole body arched in convulsive need for him.

He moved his hand to the same place, stroking to answer her need as he lifted himself up and hovered over her. 'Cup your breasts for me, Serena. Hold them close,' he commanded huskily.

She did. His mouth closed over them, one at a time, drawing deeply on them, lashing the distended nipples with his tongue, and she found her fingers squeezing her breasts higher for him, revelling in the wild voluptuousness of the action while his fingers were stroking and circling the soft moist entry to the seething need within, preparing the way, building the anticipation to screaming point.

Which was reached.

'Come…now…now!' she shrieked, unable to hold on any longer.

And he did, surging up and plunging in, shooting her to an instant shattering climax, then taking her on a constant roll of orgasms that totally rewrote her experience of sexual pleasure. So consumed was she by what *he* could do for her, she lost all awareness of anything else. Her hands found their own paths of sensual delight, gliding over the taut muscles of his body, touching his face, his hair. Her feet slid down his thighs, savouring their incredible strength and stamina.

Sometimes he paused to kiss her and she surrendered her mouth to his with a blissful joy in the heightened intimacy. Most of the time she just closed her eyes and let the marvels of their inner world wash through her, focusing on every magic ripple of it. And the final burst of melding warmth lingered on long after Nic had moved to lie beside her, his arm clasping her so close her head rested over his heart, their bodies humming a sweet togetherness.

He stroked her hair, planted a slow, warm kiss on it, murmured, 'I hope I got it right for you this time.'

Amazing that he doubted himself in any way. 'You did the first time,' she answered truthfully.

The hand stroking her hair stilled. She could hear the frown in his voice as he queried, 'But I just…took you.'

She lifted herself up enough to smile her totally unclouded pleasure in him. 'I took you, too. Didn't you realise that, Nic?'

The V between his brows didn't clear. She reached up and gently smoothed it away, still smiling to erase any concern in his mind. 'I've loved every minute of having you.'

Taking him? Having him?

It blew Nic's mind. Serena was still on top of this game while he…he'd almost completely lost it back there in the kitchen, going for it full-on, already inside her before he'd even thought of contraception. All right for her. She'd known she was on the pill. No worries there to slow her down or give her heart a hell of a jolt. Then not saying a word when he'd brought her in here, letting him make love to her to see what that was like as opposed to the raw sex event…no wonder she looked so smugly satisfied.

She'd taken him!

While he… Nic pulled himself up on the wild flurry of thoughts. He'd got what he wanted, hadn't he? Serena was in bed with him, happy to be here. So why did he feel screwed up about it? He should be feeling great. He did. But he wasn't on top of what was going on here. It was like…she was drawing more from him than he was drawing from her. He'd never had this situation before. The need to feel secure with this woman was gnawing at him. Why it meant so much he didn't know but he had to reach into her somehow and make their connection firm.

He returned her smile. 'Well, that's good to hear, Serena. I didn't want you to feel…badly used.'

She laughed a little self-consciously. 'Not at all. It was truly a mutual thing.'

'Fine!'

A thump on the bed startled both of them. It was Cleo who proceeded to prance around them excitedly, wagging her tail, tongue hanging out, looking for a place to lick.

'Oh, no you don't!' Nic yelled, hastily disentangling himself from Serena as he silently cursed himself for leaving the bedroom door open.

The little terrier evaded his first grab. It was Serena who caught Cleo—predictably!—and lifted her down onto the floor, laughing as she patted the dog to calm the barks of protest.

'No third parties allowed in here,' she said, then turned twinkling eyes to Nic. 'I guess it's time for us to try that ice-cream.'

'Good idea!'

Giving him time to win more from the highly challenging Serena Fleming. He didn't understand how he'd got so far out of his depth with this woman...or was he already in too deep to change anything?

If he just went with the flow...

Why not?

Wasn't he winning, too?

CHAPTER TEN

NIC scooped up their clothes from the kitchen floor and laid them on the bar counter separating kitchen from living room, moving away from them to go to the freezer for the ice-cream.

'Not dressing?' Serena asked, unaccustomed to walking around completely naked in front of a man, though she liked watching him, his beautiful body in motion, the slight swagger in his carriage that denoted total confidence in himself, nude or otherwise.

He threw her a wicked grin. 'Why give ourselves the frustration of clothes getting in the way again?'

She blushed, realising he wanted her easily accessible, sexually accessible. Lust not sated yet. And in all honesty, was hers for him?

He cocked a quizzical eyebrow. 'You're shy?'

'No. Not exactly.' She wanted it to be more than lust. A total connection. Was that too unreasonable, given their different backgrounds and circumstances?

'You shouldn't be.' His gaze sparkled over her. 'You're beautiful, incredibly sexy, and I want the pleasure of looking at you.'

The compliments boosted her confidence. It was silly to feel self-conscious. She had a good figure. They had just been deeply intimate. There was no turning back from that. Nor did she want to. Wherever it led, she was going with it now, tugged by feelings she had never experienced before.

Yet as he turned away to open the freezer, her mind flashed back to their very first encounter, with Nic opening the front door in boxer shorts, obviously pulled on for a modicum of modesty—*over an erection*—then Justine strolling out from the bedroom wing in a skimpy wraparound, another modicum of modesty in front of a possible visitor. They had both been naked before the doorbell had rung. And now here *she* was...naked...with the same man...barely a fortnight later.

Had he said the same things to Justine?

Stop it! she fiercely berated herself. Jealousy was an ugly thing. Nic hadn't chased after the penthouse pet. He'd dropped Justine cold and gone all out to set up this situation. *She* was the woman he wanted to be with.

He lined up four tubs of ice-cream on the bench beside the freezer, then reached up to a cupboard for dishes. 'Spoons from the cutlery drawer, Serena,' he instructed, flashing her his dazzling smile as she brought them over. Her heart started pitter-pattering again.

'I'll give Cleo some of the chocolate,' he said, spooning ice-cream from that tub.

'Chocolate isn't good for dogs,' she automatically recited, having heard Michelle give that advice to clients.

'She loves it. And everyone deserves a treat now and then, even if it isn't good for them,' Nic blithely declared, setting the dish on the floor in front of Cleo who instantly showed approval of this particular *treat*.

'Now you...what would you like? A taste of everything?'

She laughed at the tempting twinkle in his eyes. 'Why not?'

'Why not indeed?'

He put scoops of each flavour into their two dishes and returned the tubs to the freezer. She was standing in front of the bench, about to pick up her dish and take it to wherever they were going to eat when he moved behind her and rested his hands on either side of the bench, encircling her in that space, grazing kisses across her shoulder.

Serena forgot the ice-cream, sucking in a quick breath as her heart battered her chest. The seductive heat of his mouth on her skin aroused a flood of sensitivity that paralysed any thought or action.

'What do you want to taste first?' he murmured, bringing her mind back into focus on the dishes in front of her.

'The...' She had to think hard to remember the selection. 'The macadamia and honey.'

'Uh-huh.' He was nudging her hair aside with his chin to kiss her neck. 'Go ahead. You can spoon some up to me, too.'

She did, and continued to do so at his insistence, even though she was hopelessly distracted with him moving closer, fitting himself to the cleft of her buttocks, stroking her thighs, spreading his hands across her stomach, gliding them up to cup her breasts, fanning her nipples with his thumbs. It was incredibly erotic, the cold creamy taste on her tongue, the hot excitement of his touch, spooning ice-cream up to both of their mouths while he orchestrated the intensely sensual friction of their bodies.

'Hmm...I think I like the strawberries and cream

best.' The words were softly blown into her ear, making it tingle with excitement, too.

'Not...not the chocolate?' It was wild, talking like this, pretending to ignore the slide of his erection, reaching up to the pit of her back.

'Or maybe the honey...' His hands left her breasts and moved down to the triangle of hair between her thighs. 'You're like honey, Serena. An endless store. And I want every bit of it.'

She couldn't answer. He was so good at caressing her, tantalisingly gentle yet knowing exactly what was most exciting. She wanted him, every bit of him, too. It was all she could think of.

'Lean over. Elbows on the bench.'

She didn't grasp what he meant to do. She just did as she was told on automatic pilot, unable to bear any halt to the intense waves of pleasure he was inciting. His arm encircled her hips, lifting her off her feet. The initial shock of the position he was taking was instantly obliterated by the deeper shock of penetration, fast and deep, explosively exciting.

He held her pinned to him as he pumped a fast, compulsive, almost violent possession, and somewhere in Serena rose waves of fierce, primitive satisfaction. Her feet curled around the back of his knees, giving her some purchase in the driving rhythm. He clutched her breasts, moving them to the beat within. It was wild...wild...and a wildly lustful exultation swept through her as she felt him come, spilling himself deep inside her in uncontrollable bursts, the aggression melting, shuddering to a halt, his breathing reduced to harsh gasps blowing through her hair.

'I lost it again,' he said in a tone of shell-shocked bewilderment. His hold on her shifted to bring her down onto her feet, once more standing with her back to him. 'Sexiest bottom in the whole damned world,' he added as though he needed some excuse to make sense of *losing* it. 'I think it's time we had a swim. Yes. A long, cool swim. Out to the pool.'

And Serena found herself being swept up and carried, but she didn't feel so limp and dazed this time. She felt exhilarated. Here was Nic, falling into the role of caveman on the loose, though he seemed to want to deny the more hot-headed—or hot-bodied—aspects of that role, and Serena had to admit she was revelling in not only being the object of his desire, but also the reason for his apparently much stronger than usual sexual impulses.

'Maybe we should stay out of the kitchen,' she suggested, unable to contain a smile. 'Kitchens can be very dangerous places.'

He frowned down at her happily teasing eyes. 'You're a provocative little package of dynamite, Serena Fleming.'

'So what should I call you? Nuclear fusion?' she tossed back.

'That's about right!' he said rather grimly.

'Actually it's incredibly marvellous.' She lifted her head, kissed his ear, and whispered, 'No one has ever made me feel…so much.'

It stopped him. He looked at her with burning eyes, searing away any glibness from that statement. 'Well, fair's fair,' he said with satisfaction. 'Can I take it you'll be staying the night? You're not going to hop in your car and leave me flat?'

She laughingly shook her head. 'How could I walk away from this?'

'A bit difficult when I've got your feet off the ground.'

'Do you make a habit of sweeping women up to get your own way with them?'

'No. But you're very slippery so I'm holding you fast. Only way to guarantee keeping you with me.'

'I *want* to be with you, Nic.'

'You're not going to make some excuse about having to go home to your sister and niece?'

'They're away for the night.'

'Aha! So you came here planning to seduce me.'

'I did not!'

He grinned, triumph dancing into his eyes. 'Got you then.'

It struck a bad note with Serena, bursting her bubble of joy. 'Is that what it's all about to you, Nic? Winning?'

He looked taken aback, as though she wasn't supposed to realise that. It chilled Serena into firing another arrow from the same bitter bow. 'Am I just another notch on your bedpost?'

'Another notch?' he repeated incredulously. 'There's never been a notch like you in my entire life. You can take that as gospel!'

Relief swept through her. He was so emphatic she believed him. Even more so when his eyes flashed dark resentment, as though she had totally wrecked his comfort zone by not conforming to any standard amongst the women he'd known.

Fair's fair, Serena thought elatedly.

*   *   *

He probably shouldn't have told her that, Nic thought, as he walked on across the patio. Gave her even more power over him. None of this was turning out how it was supposed to. He'd only meant to play an erotic game with the ice-cream, get her melting for him, give himself the satisfaction of knowing she was totally on heat before leading her out to the pool, wiping out any thought she might have had of dressing and going home. Instead of which…

He must be out of his mind. Still, it hadn't put her off him. Quite the contrary. And he didn't know what to think about that. Except he had achieved one end goal. She wanted to stay the night. Which meant he could put her down on her feet now. She wasn't about to run away.

On the other hand, he liked holding her like this. It gave him the sense of being in control, directing the action. He reached the edge of the pool before he thought to ask, 'You can swim?'

She laughed. 'Yes, I can. But please don't dump me in.'

'A mutual dive,' he promised, still not wanting to let her go. He wanted everything to be mutual tonight.

For Serena, it was another first. She'd never gone skinny-dipping by herself, let alone with a man. It was a fantastic sensation, feeling their naked bodies sliding together, the water engulfing them like warm silk. She kept thinking this would be a night to remember for the rest of her life.

Even when they started swimming side by side, there was a sense of intimate unison about it, the shared pleasure of watching each other, smiling, enjoying the intoxicating freedom of being together like this, no inhibitions. It was a perfect night, a cloudless sky full of stars, a full moon rising above the fronds of a palm tree, the air still warm and balmy from the hot summer day. Again Serena thought this was like a dream, too good to last, though she wanted it to…wanted it to last forever.

They kissed and played a teasing game of catch-if-you-can in the water. Nic hauled her out of the pool and wrapped her in one of the towels he'd laid out ready before she'd arrived, but they were both too aroused to dry themselves properly. The towels were dropped as desire erupted into urgent need. A nearby sun-lounger was quickly put to use, providing cushioned comfort as they merged and found more heights to climb.

It was all incredibly idyllic, lying cuddled together afterwards, looking up at the stars, Nic asking her what she wished for when they spotted a falling one.

'I'm completely content,' she answered without hesitation, feeling nothing could be better than this.

He laughed a happy laugh.

They put Cleo to bed in the mud room, leaving her with the radio playing music.

Showering with Nic was another sensual delight, leading to an even more intense exploration of their sexuality. Anything and everything seemed so perfectly right with him. Brilliantly right. So much so, Serena was tempted into thinking that they *did* suit each other. Perfectly. They *belonged* together, at least on some primal level that wasn't influenced by outside factors.

And it didn't change when she woke in the morning.

It just continued on.

They had a late breakfast on the patio—eggs, bacon, tomato and mushrooms which they'd cooked together. Nic had pulled on a pair of shorts and found a sarong for Serena to wear. The mood was happily casual, yet bubbling with an exhilarating sense of togetherness that sharpened their appetites for more and more sharing.

Serena thought fleetingly of calling Michelle to explain where she was but decided her sister wouldn't worry. Besides, she didn't want to introduce an outside note. It might jar on this very special time with Nic.

But an outside note did come.

And it jarred everything.

CHAPTER ELEVEN

SERENA and Nic were in the kitchen, cleaning up after breakfast. The Sunday newspapers had been delivered and they were about to take them down to poolside when the telephone on the bar counter rang. Nic picked up the receiver, answered 'Yes,' a couple of times, then passed the cordless instrument to Serena with a rueful little smile. 'Your sister...sounding anxious.'

She frowned as she took the phone. It wasn't like Michelle to break into what was essentially Serena's private business. Something had to be wrong at home. 'What's up?' she asked without preamble.

'Sorry to interrupt but we have a visitor here and he's not about to be turned away,' Michelle rattled out. 'Can we talk or is Nic still close by?'

He'd left her to the call, heading out to the patio, carrying the newspapers and his mug of coffee, probably expecting her sister's concern to be quickly soothed. 'We're okay,' she assured Michelle.

'It's Lyall Duncan, Serena.'

Lyall! Her night with Nic had driven her ex-fiancé completely out of her mind. It was a shock to realise that had actually happened, especially when linking them had previously affected many of her reactions and responses to Nic. Now...the memory of Lyall was like an unwelcome ghost at a feast, casting a shadow she desperately didn't want.

113

'He's driven up from Sydney this morning, arrived about ten minutes ago,' Michelle went on. 'And he's determined on seeing you. Says he'll wait all day if he has to.'

'Why?' It was more a cry of protest than a request for information.

'Perhaps it's a case of absence making the heart grow fonder.'

'Not for me it hasn't.'

'Lyall isn't about to accept that message from me, Serena. He's actually demanding to know where you are and I can't really pretend I have no idea. As it is, I've left him out on the verandah, cooling his heels while I'm on the phone, *trying* to contact you.'

Serena heaved a fretful sigh. What on earth did Lyall think he would achieve, just landing on Michelle's doorstep and throwing his weight around? Was he looking to effect a reconciliation, having given Serena six weeks to reconsider her position? Did he expect her to be grateful that he'd come to offer her a second chance?

'Serena…?'

'Sorry…I just can't believe this. What's over is over.'

'Then I suggest the sooner you tell him that, the better. And the most tactful place to do it is here, not there,' Michelle said pointedly.

Which meant leaving Nic and all they'd been sharing because Lyall's super-ego couldn't accept rejection from a woman he considered his whenever he felt like crooking his finger. After all, he was a top prize for such as Rene Fleming, and she would surely have come to her senses by now.

Anger and frustration boiled through her at being trapped into responding to a man she didn't want anymore, and being forced to part from a man she did. But this was not Michelle's problem and it was unfair to leave her with it.

'All right! I'll be home in half an hour. But please try to get Lyall to come back in an hour because I don't want him there waiting for me. Okay?'

'I'll do my best.'

'Thanks. Sorry for the hassle, Michelle.'

Even more of a hassle if Lyall saw her arriving home in last night's clothes without the make-up and grooming appropriate to them. That could instigate a very ugly scene, especially if he was expecting her to be regretting their break-up. No way would he have imagined her plunging into intimacy with someone else. And of all men, for that *someone else* to be Nic Moretti...

Serena took a long, deep, sobering breath as she returned the cordless telephone to its slot on the counter. The sense of having been on a wild roller-coaster ride with Nic hit her hard, now that it had to be brought to a halt.

She didn't know the heart of the man, yet last night...last night...the connection had been so strong, so overwhelming, surely it meant as much to him as it had to her. And this morning...it wasn't just some amazing sexual chemistry that made it feel right to be with him, was it?

Her heart fluttered with uncertainties as she moved across the living room to the door that stood open to the patio. How *did* Nic feel about her? He'd insisted she wasn't just another notch on his bedpost, but where did she fit in his thinking? Had he put her in any context at all?

He sat at the table where they'd breakfasted, looking totally relaxed, perusing the newspaper spread out in front of him. She paused in the doorway, acutely aware of the tug of attraction that made what she'd felt with Lyall seem hopelessly insignificant.

But discounting the sheer physical impact of him, was Nic so different to Lyall when it came to other aspects of his life? Did he simply want women to be there when he wanted them, while his work and how he performed in that arena remained his central focus?

She didn't know.

She didn't know nearly enough about him, nor how far her feelings could be trusted in these circumstances. In fact, the only certainty she did have in her mind was that she couldn't resume a relationship with Lyall Duncan.

Nic's concentration on a news story was broken by a prickling at the back of his neck. He turned his head quickly and caught Serena staring at him—motionless in the doorway and staring with an intensity that instantly twisted Nic's gut.

'What's wrong?' He pushed his chair back, instinctively rising to fight whatever was putting distance between them.

Her hand flew up in a halting gesture. 'Don't move. I have to go. Michelle needs me at home.'

'Why?'

She shook her head, shutting him out of her family business. 'Just a problem that has to be dealt with.'

'Can I help?'

'No.' Her mouth tilted in a wry grimace. 'Sorry about this. Can't be helped. I'll have to dress and get going.'

She was off, heading towards the bedroom wing before Nic could assimilate exactly what was happening here. One minute the flow between them had been brilliantly positive, then...total withdrawal! Not even a sharing of the problem that had caused it. With a nasty little frisson of shock, Nic realised he'd ceased to count in her mind. Serena had cut him off...point-blank.

The urge to go after her, imprint himself on her consciousness again, had him striding into the living room before he checked himself. This was not a reasonable reaction. If she had to go, she had to go. Why should she share some crisis at home with him? They weren't *close* in the sense of confiding personal problems.

Which brought him to the question of how close did he want to get?

He'd had a couple of quite serious relationships in his twenties. Both of them had eroded under the pressure of separate careers—different life-goals and values emerging as the shine of *being in love* had rubbed thin and *togetherness* had gradually ceased to exist. A few of his friends had married, but were now divorced. In fact, he could only think of his sister and Ward as an example of love holding steady, regardless of the bumps in life.

He knew he was getting more and more cynical about *love*. Those of his cousins who were married had done what he thought of as the Italian thing, making advantageous connections that added to the network of the Moretti business interests. Over the years, his parents had lined up several *choices* for him, but he'd always refused to consider a pragmatic marriage. It turned him off the whole idea of linking himself to any woman for life.

His mouth curled in distaste as he recalled Justine's attitude about sliding out of promises on the principle that what people didn't know, didn't hurt them. As far as Nic was concerned, trust and loyalty were big issues. So was family.

He frowned, realising his thoughts were drifting towards exploring a lot more with Serena than he'd originally anticipated. But what was going on in *her* mind?

It was okay for her to rush off to help her sister. He just didn't like her switching off from him, not when he was still so switched on to her, wanting more. She was one very elusive lady, had been from the start, and despite having managed to keep her with him overnight, Nic had the uneasy feeling he didn't have her locked into any future continuance.

What made her pull away from him?

She'd done it last night when he'd been talking about the people he associated with.

She'd been doing it again just now.

It didn't feel right to Nic. There shouldn't be any blocks, given the intimacy they'd shared. Whatever was causing these shifts in Serena had to be uncovered, pinned down. Having come this far with her, he was not about to lose the ground he'd won, nor give up on knowing all he wanted to know about this woman.

Footsteps coming down the corridor from the bedroom wing…

Play it cool, Nic cautioned himself. *Let her go for now and plan for tomorrow.*

Yet the moment he saw her, head down, shoulders slumped dejectedly, his heart felt as though it was being squeezed and the impulse to take on and dispose of whatever this divisive problem was, roared through his head. Her name flew off his tongue.

'Serena…'

She stopped in her tracks, shoulders squaring, head snapping up, her body stiffening in automatic rejection of any approach from him, yet the wild look in her eyes was one of intense vulnerability.

The aggression building up in Nic instantly abated. She didn't want to feel any form of entrapment with him. Force wouldn't achieve anything.

She began walking again. Faster. Making a beeline for the front door. 'Thank you for the dinner last night. And breakfast this morning,' she trotted out in a tight little voice. 'I'll pick up the salad bowl tomorrow when I come for Cleo.'

She was going.

'If there's anything I can do…' he offered again.

Heat whooshed into her cheeks. 'No. Please… I have to hurry.' She quickly averted her gaze from his, fastening it on the door as she took the steps up to the foyer. Her neck was now burning, too.

Why leave the salad bowl when it would only take a slight detour—past him—to get it? Was she remembering the two sexual connections in the kitchen? Evading any risk of tempting contact?

Her hand was on the doorknob.

'It's been a very special time with you, Serena,' he said quickly, wanting to hit some positive chord with her before she left.

She paused, looked back over her shoulder, though her lashes were at half-mast so he couldn't see what she was thinking. 'Thank you for that, Nic. I appreciate it,' she said huskily. 'It's been special for me, too.'

But it didn't stop her from going. The door was opened and a few seconds later it was closed behind her. Nic stared at it, wondering if there was something more effective he could have said or done that might have broken this unwelcome impasse.

The day ahead suddenly felt very empty.

Cleo trotted up to the door and barked at it, as though she, too, was protesting Serena's departure. 'She'll be back tomorrow,' Nic told the little terrier.

Yet he didn't feel confident about what tomorrow might bring where Serena was concerned. Which set off a strong determination to move directly into her territory and stake a claim on it.

CHAPTER TWELVE

TO SERENA'S immense relief, Lyall's yellow Porsche was not in the parking area provided for the pet salon's clients. At least she had some time to prepare for their confrontation. Having brought her own car to a quick halt, she burst into the house at a run, not knowing what leeway Michelle had managed to negotiate. Her sister met her in the front hall, hands up in a calming gesture.

'No rush. You've got an hour and a half before he gets back.'

Serena deflated on the spot. 'Where's he gone?' she gasped.

'Apparently there's some beachfront property up for auction at Wamberal and he wanted to inspect it. Said to tell you he'll take you out to lunch when he returns.'

Serena shook her head. 'I don't want this, Michelle. I don't want Lyall. I don't want to be with him, talk to him, or…or anything else.'

Tears of helpless frustration welled into her eyes and Michelle quickly wrapped her in a sisterly hug. 'I'm sorry he's putting you through this, messing up what you've got going with Nic. Did he mind your leaving?'

'I…I don't think so. He offered…to help.'

'There you are then. Nice guy. Just make it clear to Lyall your relationship with him is over and put it all behind you. I'm here to back you up if need be. Okay?'

'Yes…sorry…guess I'm too tensed up about it.'

Michelle drew back and gave her a sympathetic smile as she stroked Serena's hair away from her face. 'Chin up, love. This, too, will pass. Go and have a long hot shower and you'll feel better able to face the fray.'

Serena nodded, took a deep breath, and headed for the bathroom, grateful for her sister's understanding and support. Michelle's words, *This, too, will pass,* made her realise she was letting herself get too over-wrought with this Lyall/Nic situation. It wasn't any-where near as bad as when Michelle's husband was killed, nor the earlier shock and grief they'd had to handle when their parents had died in a car crash.

She'd only been sixteen then.

Sixteen and forced to grow up fast, tackle life as best she could because it moved on, regardless of loss. Though it was never the same as before. There were holes that couldn't be filled no matter how hard she worked or how far she travelled or how hard she played. The sense of belonging she'd craved, and had continually looked for in everything she'd done these past twelve years had always evaded her.

She'd talked herself into believing she could make it happen with Lyall. With him she could have the family she dreamed of having and they would all be secure in a wonderful home of their own. Lyall could provide everything they'd need or want and she'd love him for it. Her life wouldn't feel empty anymore.

A pipe dream.

Which had come crashing down at the realisation

that the man she'd decided to marry wouldn't stand up for her if someone put her down. How could she ever feel any sense of belonging with a man whom she couldn't trust to speak of her with love and respect? The seductive prospect of marrying money had instantly lost every vestige of appeal.

There had to be love. Real love. On both sides for a lifetime marriage to work. Never again would she compromise on that principle. Emotional security was far more important than financial security.

Lyall had been a monumental mistake.

And Nic Moretti might be one, too.

There was no ignoring the fact that he belonged to the same social arena that Lyall occupied. She could very well be jumping out of the frying pan and into the fire by plunging into intimacy with Nic. Yet she didn't want to back off. After last night and this morning…it hurt to even think of backing off. Somehow she'd already connected too deeply with him. Though maybe her feelings were being too heavily influenced by the incredibly strong sexual attraction.

Whatever the level of her involvement with Nic, Serena found herself totally untouched by Lyall Duncan when he finally turned up at one o'clock, a half hour later than the time he'd stipulated. She suspected he'd deliberately delayed this meeting so she'd be waiting on him—his time being more important than hers.

Determined not to invite him into the house, she walked up to the parking area, noting as he stepped out of the Porsche that his appearance was a perfect illustration for casual designer wear—cream jeans with tan stitching, a tan vest over a collarless cream silk shirt, sleeves rolled up his forearms to show off his Rolex watch, and, of course, his tan hair was artfully streaked with creamy strands to make it seem naturally sunbleached.

His physique was much slighter than Nic's, more wiry. He wasn't tall, either, his height only just topping Serena's when she wore high heels. Nevertheless, he could exude a charm of manner that made his amiable face quite handsome, and he always—always—looked a million dollars.

Trappings did have their impact, Serena thought, rueing her own susceptibility to them in the past. How many times had she excused Lyall's arrogance, thinking he had a right to it, considering how successful all his entrepreneurial ventures had been in the property market? But that didn't include the right to view her as someone who should be subservient to him.

He frowned as he took in her unsophisticated appearance. Her shorts and tank top did not comprise a suitable outfit for accompanying him today, certainly not to the type of restaurant Lyall favoured. She wanted to emphasise with absolute finality how very *unsuitable* she was for him.

His mouth thinned into a grimace of impatience. 'I told your sister I'd be taking you out to lunch.'

'I told you our relationship was over, Lyall,' Serena countered. 'I'm not going anywhere with you today or any other day. You're wasting your time here.'

Another deeper frown. Faced with rigid opposition, he tempered his arrogance, trying a tone of firm authority. 'I wanted to talk to you about that. You misunderstood what was going on in the conversation you overheard, Rene.'

'I don't think so.'

'That guy was my architect. No one you're likely to meet again,' he stated, as though it excused the offence. Or warranted overlooking it.

At least this statement echoed Nic's—business associates, not personal friends—but it painted her current situation with black irony. 'That's not the point,' she argued. 'It was the revelation of what you expected from me as your wife.'

'That was only what I said to him, not what I really think.' Lyall made a dismissive gesture. 'He's one of the Morettis. Huge in the construction business and they've got connections that run through everything to do with building. I mean, we are talking about money you wouldn't believe. Billions, not just millions.'

'So?' It was a defiant stance, hiding the cramp that had hit her stomach at this sickening information.

'So he brought Justine Knox to the party. Her family made a fortune out of mining gold at Kalgoorlie. Her old man is known as Fort Knox, he's sitting on so much loot.'

The penthouse pet... No doubt Justine was well accustomed to penthouses and everything else money could provide, putting her on the same elevated plane as the Morettis—an appropriate coupling of two huge fortunes.

'And since you couldn't compete with me, you put me down. Is that it, Lyall?' Serena asked coldly, feeling the chill of hopelessness running down her spine. She was way out of her league with Nic, even more than she'd been with Lyall.

Her ex-fiancé finally realised he might have to offer

some appeasement. 'I'm sorry, Rene. You weren't meant to hear those things. It just got to me...Nic Moretti being amused that I'd choose to marry a hairdresser.'

A bitter blow to his ego.

Far more important to him than anything else.

'Well, I guess you evened up the score by letting him think you'd lined up an obliging little slave-wife instead of having to pander to a gold-plated heiress.'

He grimaced at her interpretation but Serena knew in her bones it was true.

'I swear it was a one-off thing, Rene. It'll never happen again. I love the way you are. I love...'

'No!' she cut in quickly. 'Please don't go on, Lyall. I'm sorry if it's not over for you, but it is for me.'

'But we had it good. I can give you anything you want...'

'No, you can't. You kind of swept me off my feet, courting me as you did, making me feel special...'

'You *are* special!'

Serena took a deep breath and spilled out the truth. 'I don't love you, Lyall. I thought I did, but I don't. I've met someone else who's shown me that what we had wasn't real. Not for me. I'm sorry, but there it is.'

'Someone else!' he repeated as though she could not have delivered a worse insult.

No doubt it would be if she tagged Nic Moretti's name onto it, but Serena wasn't looking for more trouble. She just wanted out. Eventually she stonewalled long enough for Lyall to give up beating his head against unrelenting resistance.

It was not a pleasant parting but at least Serena was satisfied it was final this time.

This was, however, a hollow achievement, doing nothing to stop the depression that rolled in on her after Lyall had gone. He'd deepened all her doubts about getting involved with Nic Moretti, adding an edge of sharp pain to them now that she had succumbed to the temptation of following her instincts.

Trust them, Michelle had advised, but her sister didn't know what she knew. Michelle had never aspired to the high life, had no experience of how it worked. Her only contact with it had been Lyall, and Nic was different to Lyall.

One of the big differences, Serena reasoned, was that Lyall was a self-made millionaire and liked to show it off. The Moretti family wealth was clearly a given, no need for Nic to demonstrate it or flaunt it. He'd had it in his background all his life, something he took for granted, yet it had to influence his choices...life choices.

Construction...architecture...it was probably a natural path for him, an extension of the family business, and he certainly had the talent for it. He enjoyed the work, too, liked seeing his designs translated into solid reality. That had come through very strongly in their conversation over dinner last night. He was a natural achiever, and maybe that was where she came in.

Nic had wanted her in his bed.

Possibly her initial resistance had made the achievement of that goal even more desirable, striking on a need to win.

So he'd won.

What came next?

Serena inwardly fretted over this all afternoon. When the telephone rang just before six o'clock, Michelle and Erin were outside feeding the pony and filling its water-trough. Serena was in the kitchen preparing their evening meal and she took the call, expecting it to be for her sister or niece.

It stunned her when she heard Nic's voice asking, 'Everything okay there, Serena?'

'Oh…yes…' she bumbled out, dizzied by a sudden rush of blood to her head.

'Glad to hear it.'

Nice guy, nice guy, went whizzing through her mind, planting seeds of hope.

'I realised after you'd gone, I have a meeting with Gosford City Council scheduled tomorrow morning,' he went on. 'I'll bring Cleo to the salon on my way in. Save you a trip.'

She managed to get her voice working properly. 'Right! Thank you.'

'And return your salad bowl.'

She shouldn't have left it behind. She'd been in such a flutter… 'Sorry about that.'

'No problem. But I was wondering if it was possible to leave Cleo at the salon until my business with the council is done. Could be midafternoon before I can get away.'

'We can keep her here for you.'

'Great! I'll pick her up on my way home.'

'Do you know how to get here?'

'I looked up the address. Same road as the Matcham Pony Club.'

'Yes. So…we'll see you in the morning.'

'Nine o'clock sharp,' he said, and ended the call.

Serena's heart sank. It had been all business, nothing personal. Apart from the mention of the salad bowl, what had happened between them last night might not have been. Indeed, delivering the bowl back to her himself, and the arrangements he'd made for Cleo, kept her away from the Gifford house and any material reminder of the intimacy they had shared.

Was this the first step to establishing a distance which wouldn't be crossed again? Having won the jackpot, with bonus points, had Nic Moretti decided not to risk getting more deeply involved with a woman who was never going to be a suitable match for him?

A one-night stand could be brushed off.

An ongoing relationship might result in a nasty comeback further down the trail if any expectations were inadvertently raised. Men with big money could become targets of avaricious women who'd be only too happy to sell a juicy story on them.

Serena almost made herself sick with these fevered imaginings. She didn't confide them to Michelle because she knew they sounded neurotic, and probably were. If Lyall hadn't come today, stirring all those snobby issues up again, she'd probably be taking Nic's arrangements about tomorrow at face value.

By the time she went to bed, a resolution had firmed not to cross bridges until she came to them. Whatever Nic had decided about their relationship was beyond her control, and if there was still a choice for her to make about continuing their relationship, it was better made when she could assess his response to her in person.

Michelle had a valid point. There was a lot to be said for trusting one's instincts.

CHAPTER THIRTEEN

THE next morning Serena worked hard at maintaining a calm, natural manner as she went about her chores. She had just taken early delivery of a poodle at the salon and was seeing the client out of the reception lobby when a fabulous red Ferrari arrived in the parking area.

It was five minutes to nine.

Serena could hardly believe her eyes when Nic Moretti stepped out of it, followed by Cleo on her leash. He'd driven a four-wheel-drive Cherokee to the pony club on Saturday. She wasn't prepared for this in-your-face evidence of huge personal wealth, even though she knew it was in his background.

Many people could afford a Cherokee, but a Ferrari...it left a Porsche a long way in the shade, costing more than half a million Australian dollars she recollected from a motor show Lyall had taken her to. The famous Italian sports car shouted class, style and performance, and it emphatically underlined the social gap between Serena and Nic Moretti.

The fire was right in front of her now, blazing into her eyes, and it would have to be self-destructive perversity not to step back from it.

She saw Nic pluck the salad bowl from the jump-seat and forced her legs into action. She didn't want him bringing the bowl to the salon where it would be a constant reminder of her *weakness* for this man.

Better to meet him on the path and take the bowl to the house, putting it away, just as any further personal connection to Nic Moretti had to be put away. It was simply too foolish to entertain any hope at all that there could be any real place for her in his world.

He saw her coming and waited by his car, his smile and eyes radiating a warm pleasure in her that totally scattered Serena's wits again. Why did he have to be so attractive? Why, why, why? she silently railed, unable to stop her heart from racing and every nerve in her body buzzing in conflict with what common sense dictated.

'Hi!' he said, his eyes twinkling an invitation to resume the intimacy that had been so abruptly put on hold yesterday. He nodded to the departing car of the poodle owner. 'I see you're busy already.'

'Yes. What happened to the Cherokee?' she asked, wondering if he'd deliberately deceived her with it on Saturday, playing down the huge difference between them.

He shrugged. 'It belongs to Ward. He asked me to take it for a spin now and then. Stop the battery going flat.'

She gestured to the Ferrari. 'This is yours?'

'Yes.' He frowned, picking up on her guarded expression. 'I guess you haven't seen me driving it before.'

'No, I haven't.'

His gaze locked on hers with forceful purpose. 'It doesn't change anything, Serena. I'm still the same man you were with on Saturday.'

The challenge sent a quiver right through Serena

but she stood her ground, managing an ironic little smile. 'It does show I don't know you very well, Nic.'

'A situation I'll be only too happy to correct if you're free this evening.'

Her stomach cramped as his sexual magnetism came at her full-force. Her mind whirled with the knowledge that he wasn't finished with her. He wanted more. And so did she. *So did she.* Yet if she succumbed to this attraction again, got in deeper, it would be all the more painful when it did end, as it inevitably would.

'No, I can't,' she blurted out. 'Be free, I mean. I have family commitments here. Especially during the week. Michelle and Erin...' She paused for breath, shaking her head at the excuses pouring from her mouth when all she had to do was say *no* and stick to it.

'Fair enough,' Nic replied. 'Disappointing, but fair enough. Can I pass *my* family commitment to you here?' he went on, holding out Cleo's leash.

She took it, and the bowl he handed to her.

'Haven't got time to talk now,' he said with a rueful smile. 'I'll see you when I return this afternoon.'

She nodded, not trusting what might come out of her mouth if she spoke. He took off in his Ferrari— magnificent man, magnificent car—leaving Serena torn between the desire to take what she could of him and the certainty she'd be heading for miserable humiliation if she did.

A little Peugeot hatchback could never match a Ferrari. The two were worlds apart. The invitation to join him this evening had to be aimed at more sex and Serena fiercely told herself she'd done right to put him off. She hoped Nic had got the message that she was not a readily available bed partner.

The day was busy. At four o'clock, Nic still hadn't returned to collect Cleo and Serena took off in the van to return the Maltese terrier, Muffy, to her owner at Erina, an elderly lady whose arthritis made any activity difficult. Today she was in considerable pain with her hip and asked Serena to feed the dog for her as bending over hurt too much.

Serena didn't mind the delay. In fact, she made sure Muffy's owner had everything she needed within easy reach before she left. If she missed seeing Nic, so much the better. It saved her from the torment of facing him again.

Except she wasn't spared *anything*.

The red Ferrari was in the parking area when she returned home and Nic was leaning on the post and rail fence that enclosed the grazing paddock, watching Erin riding her pony around the makeshift jumps course. As Serena brought the van to a halt outside the salon, he turned to wave at her, a happy grin on his face.

She closed her eyes, wishing she was a million miles away. He hadn't given up. He wasn't letting her go. And this was all too hard. It wasn't fair, either. Couldn't he see it wasn't fair? A surge of angry rebellion against Fate and Nic Moretti's persistent pursuit of her demanded affirmative action. He had to be told in no uncertain terms they were going nowhere and he had to stop impinging on her personal life.

As this determination shot her out of the van, Nic swung around to walk towards her, a perfectly groomed Cleo on her leash trotting beside him, a pink ribbon around her neck, *and* a pink ribbon tied around a large cellophane cone which looked suspiciously like a sheaf of flowers resting in the crook of his arm.

Flowers…to lead her down his garden path!

No, no, no! She wasn't going to be bought, wasn't going to be seduced…

'Nice place you've got here,' Nic greeted her.

The comment hit very raw nerves. 'You mean this property is worth quite a bit in real estate terms,' she bit out, coming to a halt and folding her arms in belligerent self-containment.

He halted, too, cocking his head in a quizzical fashion. 'Actually I wasn't putting a dollar value on it. The grass is green, the old gum trees are marvellous, the cottage garden around this country style house is very pretty. I was simply thinking what a nice place this is.'

Which completely wrong-footed her, but Serena was not about to be moved from a full frontal attack on the wealth issue. 'Well, it's not mine. I have no equity in it at all. Nor in any other property. And it wasn't bought with family money. There is no family money. Our parents died when I was sixteen and the farm they'd owned was heavily mortgaged. We inherited nothing. What you see here was mostly bought with the compensation payout when Michelle's husband was killed in the line of duty.'

Her outburst succeeded in forcing Nic to pause for thought. He eyed her with an air of grave consideration, weighing her emotional agitation and her strongly negative body language. Whether what she'd said had shattered some pipe dream of his, Serena had no idea, but at least he couldn't argue against the truth of her situation, which meant he had to take stock of it and deal with it openly and honestly.

Finally, to her intense frustration, he said, 'I guess you're making some point here, Serena. Want to tell me what it is?'

Her arms flew out of their fold into a scissor movement of total exasperation. 'Don't tell me you can't work it out! Our backgrounds are chalk and cheese, Nic. You turn up here in a Ferrari. You have an apartment at Balmoral. You're a top of the tree architect. And the Moretti family is...'

'Always in my face,' he cut in with an ironic grimace. 'Makes me wonder sometimes if it's an absolute hindrance to what I want for myself.' His dark eyes mocked her argument. 'Being a Moretti is a two-edged sword, Serena. At least *you* know you're wanted for yourself, not for what your family can provide or the influence they can wield. You have no concept of how much that can taint.'

Somehow he'd completely shifted the ground on which she'd made her stand, turning it all around so that *he* was disadvantaged by the wealth issue, not *her*. Serena shook her head, hopelessly confused about where she should be heading with him now.

He sighed, his expression changing to one of wry appeal. 'You know, for once I'd really like it to be left out of the equation. Could you try that with me? I'll keep on driving the Cherokee if it helps.'

Serena was still desperately trying to sort herself out. She'd wound herself up, completely blinded by the negative side of his wealth for her, only to be suddenly shown there was another negative side for him. And maybe she was doing him a terrible injustice, judging from a prejudice that Lyall had fed to her.

'I'm sorry…' Her hands fretted at each other as she struggled to get her head together. 'I guess I feel a bit lost with you.'

'So why don't we take the time to find out more about each other?'

More time with him…yes, that was what she needed. All her instincts were clamouring for it. Maybe she nodded. Before she could construct some verbal agreement, he pursued the idea, offering another invitation.

'While I was at the council today I saw a poster about a new exhibition at Gosford Art Gallery. It opens Friday evening. We could take it in and go out for dinner afterwards. I hear the restaurant right on Brisbane Water, *Iguana Joe's,* is very good. I could book us a table…if you're free that night.'

A proper date, she thought, not an easy drop into bed at his sister's home. 'Yes. I'd like that,' she heard herself say, all the fight having drained out of her, leaving the still simmering desire to have what she could of this man.

He smiled and stepped forward to present her with the sheaf of flowers. 'I passed a rose farm on the way here. Thought these might say more eloquently that I want to be with you, Serena.'

The perfume flooded up from what had to be at least two dozen roses, a random selection of many varieties and colours. 'They're lovely. Thank you.' She offered him an apologetic smile. 'I'll try not to be so prickly in future.'

He laughed and wrapped an arm around her shoul-

ders as they turned to go back to the parking area.
Serena was instantly swamped with memories of how
physically intimate they'd been and she knew it
would happen again. There'd be no stopping it. But
she no longer cared where it might lead or how it
would end.

Nic Moretti had just become a part of her life she
had to live, regardless of the consequences.

'Got her back, Cleo!' Nic grinned triumphantly at the
little dog riding in the passenger seat of the Ferrari.
'A bit tricky there, but I turned it around and reeled
her in.'

He was buzzing with exhilaration and wished he
could put his foot down and feel the power of the car.
Impossible on these local roads and he didn't really
need the speed. He was riding a high, anyhow, having
broken the barrier Serena had erected between them.

He laughed and shook his head at Cleo. 'Who'd
have thought I'd ever come across a woman who was
turned off by a Ferrari?'

Clearly the dog was perfectly content to ride in one.
But then Angelina's precious darling was used to the
best of everything, as was everyone attached to the
Moretti family. Nic readily acknowledged he and
Serena had very different backgrounds, but he wasn't
about to let anything deter him from having more of
a woman who was…unique in his experience.

Tantalising.

Intriguing.

Challenging.

He didn't even mind waiting until Friday for her.
She was worth the wait. He liked the fact that she

didn't kowtow to wealth, made choices that felt right to her, spoke her mind without regard to fear or favour. No artifice. He looked forward to viewing an art exhibition with her, sure she'd give him natural, honest opinions, not the pseudo-intellectual arty stuff he usually heard at fashionable gallery gatherings.

'I really like her, Cleo,' he confided to the little terrier, who returned an appropriate look of soulful understanding. Nic took a hand off the driving wheel to ruffle the silky hair behind the pointed ears. 'You like her, too, don't you?'

There was no yap of disagreement.

Remembering Cleo's hostility to Justine, Nic felt fully justified in declaring, 'Trust a dog to know the heart of a person. We're definitely on the right track with Serena Fleming.'

CHAPTER FOURTEEN

STRANGELY enough, over the next few days Nic didn't even feel sexually frustrated by the wait. He threw himself into work with a zest that seemed to bubble through everything he did. It was as if Serena had somehow rejuvenated him, given him a new lease on life. When Friday evening finally came and he was driving the Cherokee to Holgate, he felt almost light-headed with happiness.

Serena must have been watching out for him to arrive. He'd no sooner stepped out of the Cherokee in the parking area adjacent to Michelle's salon, than he saw her stepping onto the path from the front ve-randah of the house. No waiting. She lived up to her own maxim of punctuality being a courtesy. Another first amongst the women he'd dated.

She looked beautiful, elegant, and incredibly sexy in a one shoulder cocktail dress that shimmered in shades of blue and hugged every feminine curve of her body. Her hair fell in a shiny swathe over her bare shoulder but was swept back with a silver slide on the other side. She wore strappy silver sandals and carried a small silver evening bag.

Nic just stood and watched her come to him, doing his utmost to control a rush of primitive instincts that might not serve him well in these circumstances. He sensed a tense wariness in her approach and knew he had only won more time with her. She was holding back body and soul until a deeper trust was established.

Keep it light, Nic told himself. *Make it fun.* If she was giving him the benefit of some doubt, he had to blow away the doubt. Only then would she open up to him. He smiled, relishing this further challenge, and his heart seemed to dance when she smiled back. 'You look lovely,' he said, pouring out the warmth of his pleasure in her while trying to contain the heat of his desire.

'Thank you.'

It was a slightly stilted reply and Nic moved quickly to open the passenger door, fighting the temptation to touch her. As she stepped into the Cherokee, he caught a whiff of perfume, a musky scent that instantly stirred erotic thoughts. It was just as well the driving wheel would keep his hands occupied during their trip to Gosford.

'So what are we going to see?' she asked, once they were on the road.

'The main exhibition comprises twenty years of pop posters announcing concerts featuring the band, *Mental As Anything.*'

She gave a sharp little laugh.

He cocked a questioning eyebrow at her.

A wry look flashed back at him. 'I'm feeling just a touch of insanity myself.'

'Then you're in the right mood to view such art,' he countered with an encouraging smile, aware that she was twitchy and wanting her to relax with him. 'There's also an exhibition of nudes by local artists.'

She expelled a long sigh, then dryly remarked, 'I bet the nudes are all women.'

'Would you prefer men?'

'A mix would be more interesting. Of all the art work I saw when I was backpacking around Europe, the one that sticks in my mind most is the statue of David by Michelangelo.'

'That could be because it's displayed so spectacularly in the Tribuna of the Academy Gallery.'

'You've been to Florence?'

'I've been to Italy several times.'

'Oh! Of course.'

She dried up. Heat whooshing into her cheeks. Gaze averted. Bad mistake to remind her of his family, Nic thought furiously, and focused on drawing her out about her backpacking trip.

No family wealth behind her, he reflected, as she described her travels, scrimping on lodgings everywhere, endless walking to save money, yet the walking had given her an in-depth experience of each country and its culture that transcended the usual take by well-funded tourists.

She'd only been twenty-one when she'd gone, accompanied by a girlfriend her own age, brave adventurous spirits taking on the world. He admired her resourcefulness, her determination to see and learn all she could, and realised her self-assurance came from having achieved her goals, fitting in wherever she had to, talking her way into groups that protected her, getting where she wanted to go.

He thought of other women he knew who'd done the grand tour in luxurious style. Talking to them about it was like ticking off a list of *been there, seen that*. Serena gave him a different view. It was more grounded. More real. He enjoyed listening to her. Very much.

She was more relaxed with him by the time they arrived at the art gallery, a well-designed building that faced out onto a delightful Japanese garden. They collected glasses of complimentary wine, browsed on huge platters of fruit, cheese, dips and crackers, viewed the paintings of nudes, listened to the mayor's speech opening the main exhibition, then took in all the pop posters which gave a fascinating insight of the change in street design over the years.

There was quite a crowd moving through the display rooms. It seemed natural enough for Nic to take Serena's hand, holding her beside him as people milled around them. It amazed him how pleasurable it was, this least intimate of links, the warm brushing of her skin, the acute sense of physical contact that was agreeable to her. Not once did she try to pull away. They were having fun. It was good.

By the time they left the gallery Nic felt they were in harmony. It was only a short drive to *Iguana Joe's,* a waterfront restaurant and bar, splendidly sited between the ferry wharf and the sailing club. Serena happily commented on its architecture, asking if he thought it was inspired by the Sydney Opera House.

'Only insofar as the visual effect is of a boat sitting in the water. The sails of the roof are a different shape and the deep blue facia being shaped like a wave just beneath them, is a masterly touch.'

She pressed for his opinion on other buildings that had changed Sydney's skyline in recent years and this conversation continued until they were settled in the restaurant and given menus to peruse.

Without any hesitation, Serena ordered oysters, to be followed by the char-grilled swordfish with crab risotto and fig compote. She was perfectly at ease in this classy place, and with a classy menu. It raised the tantalising question of what she had done with her life in Sydney.

'How did you and your sister manage when your parents died, Serena?'

Here it comes, she thought, her heart fluttering against the rise of tension that dispelled the far more comfortable sense of floating along in an enjoyable stream of light-hearted fun. But there was no dodging the reality of her life and Serena didn't want to. This was the acid test. If Nic Moretti reacted negatively to her having been a hairdresser, it was best she know now.

She took a deep breath, fiercely telling herself there was no shame in being poor, in having to take what work one could get instead of being in a position where choices could be made. Nic's expression was sympathetic. She watched his eyes, expecting critical assessment to take over from sympathy. A judgment would be made and all her senses were on red alert, acutely aware that this judgment would direct where their relationship would go.

'Michelle and I had no idea how deeply in debt our parents were, the farm mortgaged to the hilt because of years of drought…'

'Where was the farm?'

'Near Mudgee. Dad ran sheep. He bred kelpies, too. Trained them as sheepdogs.' She shook her head, remembering the shock of all she had known in her childhood and teens suddenly ending. 'When everything was cleared, there was no money for us to continue our education. Michelle had been studying law at Sydney University. She dropped out and managed to get into the police force.'

'And you?'

'I had to leave school. Michelle took me to Sydney with her. The only job I could get was as an apprentice hairdresser.'

He frowned.

Serena lifted her chin in defiant pride. 'I was determined to be so good at it they wouldn't think of letting me go. It was a scary time for us, trying to set up a new life together and make ends meet.'

He nodded, the frown clearing, his eyes taking on an appreciative gleam. 'I bet you were the best apprentice hairdresser they ever had.'

'I topped my classes and won competitions for hairstyle and colour. This gave me the qualifications to move myself into a more highly paid position in a trendy city salon.'

'So you kept on in this field until you trekked off overseas?' he prompted, apparently finding this train of events acceptable.

'Yes. In the meantime Michelle had married David and given birth to Erin. They were a very happy family unit.' Not meaning to exclude her from it, Serena knew, yet she had felt like the onlooker, not really belonging. 'I felt free to take off and travel,' she went on, brushing aside the private feelings which could sound too much like envy.

'Your sister was happily settled with her husband and daughter,' Nic murmured, nodding his understanding.

'Yes. So I took myself off. Luckily I managed to get casual work at an upmarket London salon to supplement my savings.' She smiled at the whimsical irony of finding a job advantage in being a foreigner. 'The clients quite liked having *the Australian girl* doing their hair. They used to ask for me.'

'I'm sure you brightened their day,' Nic commented, his smile seeming to approve what she'd done.

'Whatever…it helped. The salon was happy to employ me in between my backpacking trips. I'd been based in London for almost two years when Michelle called me about David's death.'

'Killed in the line of duty, you said,' Nic recalled. 'What duty?'

Serena heaved a sigh to relieve the tightness in her chest before continuing. 'He was a policeman. He'd caught up with a stolen car and the driver had shot him. I flew home straight away, and the next few months were…very hard. Michelle needed me.'

'Another huge upheaval for her,' Nic murmured.

Another load of grief. But how to explain grief to anyone who hadn't experienced it—the vast emptiness of the hole left in one's life at the abrupt and absolute departure of people you've loved and depended upon to be there for you.

'Have you lost anyone close to you in your family, Nic?'

'No, I haven't. Even my grandparents are still alive.'

He'd never had the parameters of his world shaken, Serena thought, couldn't possibly understand the effect it had. He looked so strong, invincible, and maybe that was part of his irresistible attraction for her, the innate confidence that nothing could ever beat him. Did that come from the secure backing of great wealth or was it in his genes? All she really knew was how good it felt to be with him—when she didn't feel torn about their different stations in life.

A waiter arrived with the bottle of wine Nic had ordered. As they were served with it, Serena's gaze drifted out over the water which had turned grey with the twilight. Life had many greys, she decided, and she was treading a very grey area with Nic right now, an area that could turn black.

Nic hesitated over breaking Serena's pensive mood, even though the wine waiter had gone. The guy at the baby grand piano, providing mellow background music for the restaurant, had begun playing and singing *Memories* from Andrew Lloyd Webber's musical, *Cats*. Maybe Serena's memories were very poignant right now and Nic felt he had to respect them, give her time to come back to him.

He reflected on his own relatively smooth path to here and now. No real bumps. No big loads to carry. No huge adjustments to make. All in all, it could be said he'd had a fortunate life. It made him wonder how he would have handled the dark situations Serena and her sister had faced. Impossible to even imagine. He could only admire their strength in emerging from catastrophe and the love and loyalty that bonded them in an unselfish sacrificing of personal ambitions.

Michelle giving up law.

Serena, becoming a hairdresser.

Nic shook his head. A wicked waste of ability. Yet

what choice had they had, given their need to remain together. And who could blame them for that after the tragic loss of their parents?

The guy at the piano raised his voice to deliver the last line of the song—*A new day has begun.*

It must have impinged on Serena's consciousness because her gaze swung back to him, a sad mockery in her eyes. 'At least there was money this time. To begin a new day,' she said.

He nodded, realising she was referring to a compensation settlement for David's death.

'Michelle couldn't bear to stay in Sydney,' she went on. 'I think buying the place at Holgate, working with animals again, was a retreat to what we'd known as kids. To Michelle it was, and is, a safe place.'

'It looks as though she's done well with it,' Nic commented, sincerely impressed by her sister's achievement in establishing an independent business to support herself and her daughter.

'It's been good for her.'

'What about you, Serena?'

She shook her head, a wry little smile tilting her mouth. 'It wasn't good for me. Not then. To me, nothing felt safe. I had this urge to live as much as I could, go after the high life, have the best of everything, forget any planning for a future that might be taken away from me in a split second.'

'I can see how you'd feel that.' He smiled encouragingly. 'So you talked your way into a high-flying job.' This was where practising psychology had come in, Nic reasoned, anticipating her move into some public relations arena.

She laughed, but it wasn't a laugh of happy

achievement. It held a hint of derision, and her eyes were suddenly diamond hard, biting into him. 'Do you need that from me, Nic?' she demanded. 'Something respectably impressive?'

He was instantly aware that the whole atmosphere between them had changed. There was no longer any reaching out for understanding. This was hard-core challenge.

She sat back in her chair, establishing distance, and the air between them bristled with electric needles. The back of his neck felt pricked by them. Even the beating of his heart was suspended, anticipating attack. His mind screamed that the utmost caution was required here, and sweeping in behind this instinctive awareness was the conviction that he didn't care what she'd done. He wanted this woman. Losing her at this point was unacceptable.

He gestured an appeal. 'I'm sorry if I assumed something wrong. Please...I'd really like to know what you did next.'

Scarlet patches burned from her cheeks like twin battle flags. 'I went to what is probably the most fashionable hairdressing salon in Sydney. Have you heard of Ty Anders?'

'No.' He shook his head. 'The name means nothing to me.'

She shrugged off his ignorance. 'Ty is much in demand by socialites, models and movie stars because he can create individual images. My upmarket London experience particularly impressed him. He took me on, though he insisted I be called Rene, not Serena, which he considered downmarket. So I became Rene Fleming.'

She seemed to fling the name at him, as though it should strike some familiar chord, but it didn't. 'I'm not in this kind of fashion loop, Serena,' he offered apologetically, excusing himself by adding, 'I'm a man. When my hair gets too long, I go to a barber.'

'We had many wealthy male clients, believe me,' she said ironically, then paused, perhaps reflecting on his reply. 'The point is…I learnt how the wealthy lived and I spent every cent I earned on going to the *in* places, mixing with the *in* people, wearing designer clothes which I found could be snapped up relatively cheaply from secondhand boutiques where Ty's clients off-loaded stuff they'd only worn once or twice. I was a fun, fashionable person who knew all the hot gossip and all the right moves. Ty had taught me how to flatter, how to cajole, how to press the buttons that opened doors. You could say I was…a brilliant apprentice.'

Her words were laced with bitter cynicism. Being an adept social climber had not brought her joy. 'So what went wrong for you?' Nic asked quietly.

'Oh, I breezed along with all this for years, telling myself I was having a wow of a time, playing the game you beautiful people play, right up until it culminated in a proposal of marriage from a millionaire,' she tossed out flippantly. 'I even thought I was in love with him. I might actually have gone ahead and married him.'

Her alienation from this whole scene was reflected in her eyes…a bleak disillusionment that rejected every aspect of *the high life*.

'Something must have happened to change your mind,' he probed.

She stared at him, her expression flat, unreadable. Finally, she said, '*You* happened, Nic.'

'Me?' It didn't make sense to him. She'd left Sydney behind before they'd ever met.

'I overheard you talking to my erstwhile fiancé at a party.'

He shook his head, still not connecting anything together.

Her eyes mocked his forgetfulness. 'I was left with the very strong impression that you didn't think a *hairdresser* was good enough to be Lyall Duncan's wife. And his reply to you told me I'd been living in a fool's paradise.'

Shock rolled through him, wave after wave of it as recollections hit him; what he'd said to Lyall, what Lyall had said to him, the initial niggle that he'd seen Serena somewhere before, her none too subtle scorn aimed at both him and Justine, the possibly vengeful desire to score off him, her rejection of that first sexual impact, her resistance to any follow-up, the questioning about his association with Lyall...

A waiter arrived at the table with the plates of oysters they'd ordered. Nic was still speechless, totally rocked by the revelations that now coloured his relationship with Serena. She flashed the man a 'Thank you,' and they were left alone again.

With an air of careless disregard for his reaction to her disclosures, she picked up her fork, then flicked Nic a wildly reckless look. 'Bon appetit!'

His stomach cramped.

She jabbed the fork into an oyster.

Payback time, he thought.

And felt sick.

CHAPTER FIFTEEN

SERENA shoved each oyster into her mouth and gulped it down, glad she hadn't ordered something that would need chewing. Even so, it was amazing that her churning stomach didn't reject them. Her whole body was a mass of twanging nerves. She couldn't bear to look at Nic. The shock on his face only added to her torment.

The end, she thought, knowing he had expected her to have taken a different course—a more *intelligent* course—in this latter part of her life, and the bottom line was she now felt ashamed of the choices she had made, hated herself for having spent years pursuing some huge empty mirage that she'd been fooling herself with—the dress-ups, the sophisticated patter, the importance of knowing all the *right* places and things to do. No depth to any of it. No real meaning.

It hurt that she'd wasted so much time on what didn't count at all. She'd been bottling up the hurt, determinedly keeping a lid on it, but it was seeping out now, mingling with the hurt of being found wanting by this man who tugged on every fibre of her being.

She picked up her glass of wine, needing to wash down the lingering taste of oysters, and the bitter taste of loss. Nic had belatedly picked up his fork. She watched the shells on his plate being slowly emptied and sensed he was forcing himself to eat, to see this evening with her through, hiding what he really thought behind a polite facade, which was what polished people did…playing out the game until the whistle was blown and they could go home with honour.

Rebellion stirred in Serena. She was sick of sophisticated pretence, sick of dishonesty, sick of any kind of game-playing. She waited until Nic had consumed his last oyster, then burst into speech.

'I should thank you for instigating the conversation you had with Lyall about me.'

'Thank me?' He looked at her with dazed eyes, uncomprehending.

'It was a humiliating wake-up call to what I was doing with my life, but at least it did make me realise I had to get out of it and find something else.'

Conflicting emotions chased across his face—guilt, anger, pride, shame—all finally coalescing into a burning flash of accusation. 'How could a woman as smart as you even *think* of marrying a pretentious egomaniac like Lyall Duncan?'

It stung. It stung all the more because it portrayed her as a gold-digger who hadn't cared to look past the wealth dangled in front of her, and she had no defence against it, except her own deep-seated need to feel cossetted and secure, and the equally strong need to ensure that the children she wanted to have would always have solid support.

'That's over,' she grated out, shamed by his judgment though also resenting how quickly he'd made it, not pausing to take her circumstances or feelings into account. 'It's all over,' she went on, driven to try to rebalance the scales in his mind. 'I broke my engagement to Lyall. I resigned from my job with Ty Anders. I walked away from all my *fashionable* connections. I was caught up in a stupid fantasy and I woke up.'

He didn't take that into consideration, either. 'But you didn't let it go, Serena,' he shot back at her. 'You've coupled me with Lyall.'

'How could I not? The two of you showed me where I was in your very privileged world. Right on the outer rim,' she argued. 'And you…your intimacy…with Justine Knox certainly reinforced my impression that social status was a higher recommendation to you than any questions of character.'

'I'd made no agreement to *marry* Justine.'

Serena reined in the jealousy that had erupted from her wounded heart. It served no good purpose. As far as she knew, the woman was out of his life so her argument was hopelessly out of line, anyway. She was simply fighting the wretched feeling of being in the wrong because she wasn't really, was she?

Not now.

The mistakes she'd made had been recognised and she was intent on taking a different direction, had already made strides towards doing so. She need not have been so brutally honest about herself with Nic. The desire to be done with false images had driven her into opening up on everything.

The waiter returned to remove their plates, inquiring if everything was to their satisfaction. Nic's curt reply put a swift end to his intrusion. The atmosphere at the table was hardly conducive to genial chat.

Serena sipped some more wine, wanting to anaesthetise the pain. It didn't matter how much she drank.

If this was *the end* with Nic, a taxi could be called to take her home.

'You deceived me from day one, Serena. Deliberately deceived me,' he asserted, his low tone simmering with a violence of feeling which upset her even more.

'I did not!' The fierce denial leapt from her tongue. At least, she could defend this ground! 'You asked if you knew me and you most certainly did not know me. Which I told you.'

'But you knew me,' he countered.

'I didn't *know* you. I simply recognised you as the man who seemed amused that Lyall Duncan should choose to marry a mere hairdresser. Did you expect me to recall your part in a conversation that humiliated me?'

'There was no intention on my part to humiliate you,' he stated vehemently. 'I was just curious. Lyall Duncan is into status symbols in a big way. Marrying a hairdresser didn't fit.'

'Well, we both heard how it did fit, didn't we?'

'The man's a fool! And because I listened to his absurdly feudal idea of marriage, you set out to take me down, didn't you?'

'At the beginning…yes, I did,' she admitted. 'And I honestly felt justified by your initial attitude towards me.'

'What attitude?' he tersely demanded.

She flushed, wondering if she was guilty of misjudging again, yet there had been things that had made her feel…beneath his notice. 'The way you greeted me that first morning. I was so unimportant to you, a nobody whose name you instantly forgot, just someone you could use to alleviate an annoying problem. What I said and did was not so much to take you down, but to score a few points that made me feel better.'

'But once you realised I was strongly attracted...'

'You did all running, Nic.'

'And no doubt you revelled in that fact. Better still if you could bring me to my knees.'

That was so far wrong, Serena refused to dignify it with a reply. 'If you want to believe that, you go right ahead and believe it.'

'That's a cop-out, Serena.'

'For you, yes. Which is what you want, isn't it, now that you know everything about me. I'm sure you feel absolutely righteous about dismissing me as a nasty little schemer.' Riled by his wrong reading of her motives, she flung the snobby prejudice that had been eating at her right in his face. 'That certainly makes me *not good enough* for you.'

His mouth thinned into a grim line. His eyes and silence seethed with a violent challenge to her judgment of him. And maybe it was unfair, Serena thought despairingly. He'd never said it, never implied it, never acted that way. He'd given a reasonable explanation for the way he'd quizzed Lyall. It had nothing to do with *the person she was.*

With those intemperate words, she had given him just cause to believe she'd been playing some vengeful game with him. And in all honesty, she couldn't deny there had, indeed, been a payback element in letting the situation between them run on—a sense of having power over him.

She was so screwed up by *his* wealth and position,

and the fact that he'd been a party to that devastating conversation with Lyall, it was too difficult now to separate all that negative emotional baggage from the attraction Nic exerted. It was mixed up with things she'd wanted to leave behind, except Nic had linked her back to them.

In short, she was a mess again.

Whatever Nic Moretti was or wasn't, she didn't have the right to pass judgment on him or teach him any lessons. Her whole approach to him had been tainted by past events and she should have stayed clear of any personal involvement. Except...

'You weren't the only one who was strongly attracted,' she blurted out, shaking her head in sheer anguish of spirit.

Nic grimaced, shooting her a look of savage mockery. 'You've been neatly skirting around the truth ever since you met me. I don't even know if that's true.'

She heaved a ragged sigh, raising bleakly derisive eyes to his. 'Why do you think I'm here with you?'

'It's part of the pattern of your walking away, then making me work to get you back. That's a power play, Serena.'

A wry laugh gurgled from her throat. 'It's the power *you* have to override every bit of common sense that tells me to stop this...this hopeless relationship. I tried to lay that out to you on Monday.'

'My family has nothing to do with what I felt we could share,' he cut back impatiently.

'What? Some casual sex?' she snapped, completely losing all sense of perspective in the face of his continued assault on her character.

'There was nothing *casual* about it,' he asserted, looking fiercely affronted at the suggestion.

And he had every right to be because that wasn't fair comment, either. She knew the sex between them had been incredibly special, as deeply felt by him as by her. She was handling this badly, plunging straight down a destructive track and unable to pull herself off it. If there'd been any chance of reaching some understanding with Nic, it was long gone now.

'I'm sorry,' she said on a wave of sheer misery. Then in a last-ditch defence, she added, 'Do you think I enjoyed stripping my soul bare for you tonight? Did it sound like a power game to you, Nic?'

His face tightened. The blaze of anger in his eyes was averted, his gaze turned to the water beyond the open deck.

Black water.

Serena wished she could drown in it.

This, too, will pass, she recited with very little conviction. She gathered the shreds of some dignity together, pushed her chair back, and stood up. The action snapped his attention back to her.

'I'm sorry. I didn't set out to play false with you. Nor did I mean to inflict hurt. Things just…got out of hand between us,' she said in a tremulous rush, knowing she was on the verge of tears. 'I'm sorry about dinner, too, but…if you'll excuse me…'

There was no time for Nic to stop her. She was off, making a fast retreat through the restaurant to the reception desk and the exit. Frustration forced him to his feet. This conflict with Serena had not been settled to his satisfaction. She was right. It had got out of hand. Precisely where and how he wasn't sure, but be damned if it was going to be left like this.

He whipped out his wallet as he strode after her, extracting two hundred dollars and handing them to the startled receptionist as he passed her desk. 'To cover what we ordered,' he tossed at her in explanation.

He had no plan. His mind was in total ferment, stewing over everything that had been said and done between him and Serena. Adrenalin was charging his body with an aggressive drive to act first—catch and hold her—because nothing would ever be settled if she got away from him.

Through the glass doors of the foyer, he saw her half running, almost stumbling down the steps to the parking lot. She'd reached the shadow of the palm trees lining the driveway before he caught up with her and forcibly blocked any further attempt at escape by wrapping his arms around her.

'Oh, please...please...' She beat her hands against his chest. Tears were streaming down her cheeks. 'Can't you see this is no good?'

Her distress only served to convince Nic of the rightness in stopping this headlong flight away from him. 'It *was* good!' he fiercely insisted, the words pouring from feelings that would not be denied. 'Earlier tonight. Last Saturday and Sunday morning... It *was* good! And I won't believe anything different.'

Her resistance to his embrace crumpled, the fight draining out of her. She closed her eyes and shook her head dejectedly. 'You make me want to forget...what I should remember. There's too big a gap between us, Nic.'

'No, there isn't.' He gathered her closer, pressing her sagging head onto his shoulder, needing to feel the physical contact that had previously bonded them to a depth of intimacy he had never known before. 'Can you argue a gap now, Serena?'

The soft fullness of her breasts swelled against his chest as she dragged in a deep breath. The release of it in a long shuddering sigh was like a soft waft of her inner life seeping through his shirt and the words that came rawly from her throat opened the gates to understanding.

'I didn't want to want you.'

Pain…torment…

Like a thunderclap, it struck him that he'd delivered another kind of death to her with his careless conversation about a marriage that would have promised her every luxury money could provide. Not that he regretted for one moment that he'd been instrumental in breaking up her engagement to Lyall Duncan. She would have been wasted on a man whose ego demanded she worship the ground he walked on. But he himself had hurt her. Very badly. And unfairly. All on the spurious grounds that she was…a hairdresser.

She'd built herself a bright glittering bubble to banish the dark times and he'd burst it, stripping her of years of effort so she could step into a world he'd been born to. And what merit was there in a set of circumstances that gave him everything with no effort on his part?

None.

She was the one who had worked for it. And he'd unwittingly blighted it for her. Blighted it so comprehensively she'd walked away from all of it. What right did he have to blame her for being tempted to take him down a peg or two, or to show him she was a person to be reckoned with, not a walkover?

Her cry, *I didn't want to want you,* made absolute sense. His course was very clear now. He had to move Serena past that conflict, make her understand where he was coming from, convince her it was okay to want him because the wanting was very, very mutual.

He brushed his cheek over the silky softness of her hair, planted a kiss on it. 'You have nothing to be sorry for, Serena,' he assured her. 'I'm the one who should be apologising for my behaviour. That night at Lyall's party, I was bored. Bored out of my mind with all the big-noting that was going on. And I was niggled by Lyall's pretentious act of owning me. *His* architect. Not *the* architect.'

'It made him look good...you being who you are,' she muttered, a brittle edge to her voice.

'Not me. The Moretti name. He was riding on it. I expected his fiancée to have a name worth dropping, too, so I was surprised...and amused...when he conceded what you actually did for a living. I didn't even think of you as a person. I was irritated with Lyall and I needled him about his choice.'

'Choice!' Her head snapped up. Her whole body stiffened. 'You didn't even pause to find out what that choice entailed—the reputation I'd earned as a topline stylist. You just cast me as some kind of low-life...'

'Okay! I did do that. And I know ignorance is no excuse for what must have sounded like a snobbish criticism of you. I can only say it had to do with the person I knew Lyall to be, not the person he was marrying. And I'm sorry you overheard what was a mean and unkind act on my part. Sorry you were so hurt by it.'

She moved restively in his hold, still uneasy with his explanation. 'It was like…who I was inside didn't matter.'

'It does,' he pressed earnestly, knowing this was the core of her hurt. 'It matters more than anything else. And if I'd met you that night, Serena, those words would never have been spoken.'

She lifted her head and strained against his embrace, looking a pained protest at him when he didn't loosen his hold. 'It's not just me. It's an attitude. And being a victim of that attitude is not a place I want to go. Ever again.'

His gut twisted at the finality he sensed in those words. He had to fight it. He couldn't stomach losing.

'I swear to you it's not an attitude I live by,' he stated vehemently. 'On the whole I take people as I find them. And what I've found in you is what I want, Serena.'

He dropped his embrace to cup her face, to keep her gaze locked to his, desperate now to impart the intensity of his feeling for her. 'You've found something you want in me, too. Or we wouldn't be here now. And it was good. It can still be good. Even better for having all this out in the open.'

'No. It poisons things.'

'I won't let it. Trust me on this.'

'Trust?' Her expression of painful conviction wavered.

'Yes.' He dropped a promising kiss on her forehead. Then he took her hand, gripping it tightly as he pulled her towards the Cherokee, determined on drawing her into his territory and keeping her there.

'Where are you taking me?' It was a fearful cry. Her hand tugged against his.

He stopped to answer her, to use every persuasion he could think of, barely restraining the urge to sweep her off her feet and carry her away with him. Her face held the same wildly vulnerable look he'd seen on it last Sunday morning. It distracted him from his immediate purpose, the compelling need to understand everything about her taking instant priority.

'What was the problem Michelle called you about last Sunday?'

A flood of heat washed into her pale, strained face. 'It was Lyall. He'd come demanding to see me. He…he wanted…'

'To get you back.'

A nod.

'But you wouldn't have him.'

A shake of her head.

'Because of me?'

She took a deep breath, her eyes anxiously searching his, perhaps needing to know how much their connection had meant to him. 'I couldn't go back anyway. What I'd had with Lyall was gone,' she stated with stark simplicity.

'But against the whole tide of those past events, you did choose to stay with me, be with me, even though you didn't want to want me,' he argued, forcefully reminding her of how it had been. 'That says a lot, Serena. You can't want to cut off what we have together any more than I do.'

Helpless turmoil in her eyes.

'It's too good to give up,' he asserted strongly, and led off towards the Cherokee again, pulling her with him.

'It won't work! It can't work!' she wildly insisted. 'Let me go, Nic!'

'I can't undo the past, but be damned if I'll let it wreck the present or the future,' he declared with passionate fervour, ignoring her plea for release.

'But I'll be in the same place with you as I was with Lyall. Worse. *No one's* going to think *I'm* good enough for Nic Moretti.'

'Then I'll tell them why you are. And it sure as hell won't be in the same terms Lyall Duncan used,' he retorted fiercely, whipping out the car keys and pressing the remote control button to unlock the doors.

Before Serena could protest again, he had the passenger door open and took intense satisfaction in picking her up bodily and placing her on the seat where she'd be right beside him on the journey he was determined on their taking together.

'I shouldn't be letting you do this,' she agonised as he fastened the seat belt around her.

'When the going gets rough, the tough get going,' he recited, and stroked her lightly on the cheek. 'You're tough, Serena. You're like that mythical bird, the phoenix. You keep rising from the ashes. Nothing can put you down for long. And I refuse to accept that you'd be happy if you wimped out on us.'

He closed the door on any further argument, strode around the bonnet to the driver's side and climbed into his seat, closing his own door with a sense of triumphant achievement.

'I do have the right to choose,' she threw at him in one last challenge.

He returned a challenge of his own. 'Then make a choice I can respect, Serena. Give us a chance.'

CHAPTER SIXTEEN

THE warm tingling glide of fingertips trailing down the curve of her waist and hip drew Serena out of sleep and put a smile on her lips as she rolled onto her back and opened her eyes.

Nic was propped up on one elbow, a happy glow in his eyes. 'Good morning,' he said with a smile that transmitted he couldn't imagine a better one.

'Hi to you, too,' she replied, loving his unshakable confidence in the rightness of their being together like this.

If it was just the two of them in a world of their own, Serena knew she would have no problem with it, either. Last night Nic had been intent on carrying all before him and she'd been persuaded to let their relationship run on, to *give it a chance*.

It was impossible to regret that decision now. He was a fantastic lover. While sex wasn't the answer to everything, Serena knew she'd passed the point where she might have brought herself to give up this wonderful intimacy with him. Nic was right. It was too good to let go.

'*A new day has begun,*' he sang, then laughed and leaned over to kiss her. 'Our day, Serena,' he murmured against her lips. 'Call Michelle and tell her you're spending it with me.'

'You're getting to be a bossy-boots, Nic Moretti.'

'Oh, I'm sure you'll pull me back into line, Ms. Fleming.'

She wound her arms around his neck and shuffled her body closer to his. 'What about this line?' she teased, loving the feel of him, the scent of him, the taste of him. He was so beautiful, and sexy, and... Serena gave up on thinking as she once again revelled in the sensations Nic aroused.

Much later they let Cleo out of the mud room, Serena called Michelle to let her sister know she wouldn't be coming home today, and Nic set about cooking breakfast. He really was quite domesticated, Serena thought appreciatively, liking that in a man.

It recalled what he'd told her about his family last night. His father was a dyed in the wool empire builder outside his home—a bull of a man—but inside it, his mother ruled the roost, her husband indulging her every wish like a lamb, even to cooking Italian feasts for the family.

She fancied Nic was in the same mould as his father. He certainly had the strength of mind to pursue whatever his heart was set on. She wondered what it might be like to be his wife, then clamped down on that train of thought, wary of wanting too much from him.

She fed Cleo the meaty ring biscuits she liked, making a game of it by tossing each ring on the floor for her to chase and pounce on before chewing it up. Nic laughed at the little terrier's antics, commenting that he'd never thought of making a game of the breakfast food like that.

'You've taught me a lot, Serena,' he warmly added.

'Me?' She gave him a look of quizzical surprise.

He nodded. 'Forced me into reassessing quite a bit of my life. You're the best thing that's happened to me in a long time.'

She flushed with pleasure. 'That's really nice of you to say.'

'It's the truth.'

Nice guy…nice guy… Michelle was right. Serena resolved to keep trusting her instincts with Nic and shut out all the doubts that could spoil her pleasure in him.

He grinned at her, his eyes dancing with wicked mischief. 'You look very fetching in that sarong.'

He'd given her one from a pile kept for the Giffords' house guests. He was wearing nothing but a pair of shorts and she deliberately ran her gaze over his magnificent physique as she replied, 'Best we keep some distance. You're cooking.'

'Mmm…I do have a couple of burning memories.'

They laughed and bantered on over breakfast which they ate at the table on the patio. It was a brilliant summer day. It was easy to relax and browse through the *Saturday Morning Herald,* swapping comments on what they read. Serena pointed out a photo of a model on the social pages.

'I used to do her hair. Whoever's taken over from me is on a personal art trip,' she said in disgust. 'That style doesn't suit her at all.'

'You're right,' Nic agreed, then looked at her seriously. 'Are you sure that walking away from it is right for you, Serena?'

'No question,' she answered without hesitation. 'You've got to be full of hype to keep riding that scene and I'm done with pandering to people, day in, day out.'

'Do you have some other direction planned?'

'Not exactly. I thought I'd do some courses at the local TAFE college while helping out Michelle. Get myself some other qualifications that could help me move forward.'

'There's no particular ambition burning in you?'

'Not at the moment. No.'

'No dream career you want to pursue?'

She shrugged. 'I know it's unfashionable to have this attitude these days, but work has only ever been a means to an end for me. What I want most...'

'Yes?'

She grimaced, realising he could read too much into her dearest dream.

'Please...' he urged, sharp interest in his eyes. 'I'd like to know.'

'Well, don't take this personally,' she warned, frowning at the possibility that he might. 'What I want most is to be...a mother. And have a whole houseful of kids. Somewhere in my future.'

He gave her a wry smile. 'I guess that played a big part in why you agreed to marry Lyall Duncan.'

She returned a rueful look. 'It would have been a bad mistake. A marriage should be about loving each other.'

'That it should,' Nic agreed. He dispelled the awkward moment by going on to tell her about his sister's marriage, how Angelina and Ward couldn't have children but they were still very happy making a life together. 'And Cleo, of course, makes three a delight for them, not a nuisance,' he finished, making Serena laugh again.

They moved down to the pool and were enjoying a lazy and highly sensual swim together when they heard a car zoom up the driveway on the other side of the house. The alien sound intruded harshly on their private intimacy, triggering a nervous flutter in Serena's heart. Up until this moment, Nic had seemed totally absorbed in her, giving her a growing confidence in the relationship being forged. Now he was distracted, his mind dragged elsewhere.

'Are you expecting someone?' she asked anxiously, not wanting what they had been sharing broken by anyone.

'No.' He frowned. 'Guess I'd better go and see who it is.'

Both of them were naked. Serena had loved the physical awareness, the casual caresses that kept excitement simmering, the wonderful sense of being there for each other, freely within reach, no barriers. However, as Nic heaved himself out of the pool and fastened a towel around his waist, the security she'd felt in his company started slipping.

Cleo was racing inside, barking to let them know someone was at the front door, someone who might find her presence highly questionable.

'I'll send them away,' Nic growled, obviously vexed by the situation.

Serena watched him stride across the patio, wondering if he was vexed at the unwelcome interruption or vexed at the thought of being trapped into introducing her to someone he couldn't turn away—a close friend, an important business associate—some-

one who might find his involvement with a local nobody…*amusing*.

Goaded by this spine-chilling possibility, Serena
scrambled out of the pool and raced to the sun-
lounger where they'd dropped beach towels. She
quickly dried herself, fastened the sarong above her
breasts, then wrung the wetness from her wet hair
before raking it back behind her ears, effecting a reasonably tidy appearance. Just in time!

'Well, well, well, who do we have here?' a voice
drawled from behind her.

Nerves screaming, heart clamouring, Serena spun
to find a woman, having apparently chosen to stroll
around the house rather than wait for the front doorbell to be answered.

And not just any woman!

It was Justine Knox, in full battle make-up and full
battle dress, looking as though she'd top the polls at
a photo shoot during Fashion Week.

The message was instantly loud and clear.

Justine had come for Nic Moretti and she still considered him *her man!*

But he wasn't, Serena fiercely told herself, quelling
the sickening rise of panic. Nic had asked her to trust
him. He wouldn't let anyone put her down. Not in his
company. She had to give him the chance to prove
what he'd said and this was undoubtedly a prime opportunity.

Justine came to a halt beside the spa where she had
a commanding view of anyone emerging from the
house, as well as the lower pool level where Serena
had remained, determinedly standing her ground and
refusing to feel intimidated.

On the surface, Justine looked all class. She had a wonderful mane of long tawny hair, falling in rippling waves around her shoulders. Her face would turn heads anywhere, strikingly beautiful. She wore a green silk top with a low cowl neckline above slacks in the same colour, printed with huge pink and gold flowers in an artful splendour that shouted designer wear, probably *Escada*. Gold chains adorned her long graceful neck, gold sandals on her feet, and a pocket-size gold handbag hung from her shoulder.

She looked stunning, and made Serena acutely conscious of her wet straggling hair, bare face, bare everything but for the sarong. On top of that, Justine was tall, statuesque, a much better match in physique to Nic. And, in other people's eyes, a more appropriate match in every way, Serena thought, her heart quailing again at the stark contrast between herself and the other woman.

Justine cocked her head consideringly. 'Do I know you? Your face looks familar but...'

Serena dragged air out of suddenly tight lungs and forced herself to reply, 'We haven't been introduced.'

'I'm Justine Knox, a friend of Nic's,' came the confident announcement, not the slightest hint of uncertainty that she might not be welcomed by him.

'Serena Fleming.' With a sense of doom rushing at her, she added, 'You were here when I picked up Cleo one Monday morning.'

'Good God!' Justine rolled her eyes as memory clicked in. 'The dog-handler!' Her perfect mouth tilted into a smirk. 'So that's why you're here. Nic's had more problems with the wretched little beast.'

Hot angry blood flared into Serena's face at the

patronising assumption. Before she could correct it, Cleo came hurtling out of the house, barking like a maniac at sight of Justine, who drew herself up in haughty contempt at the little terrier's fierce reaction to her presence.

Good dog! Serena silently but heartily approved. At least Cleo wasn't blinded by surface class. She recognised an enemy straight-off. Superficial glamour meant nothing to her.

Nic followed, looking grim-faced, his gaze cutting from Justine to Serena and back again. Clearly he didn't like the situation, but the basis for his ill humour was yet to be determined. Serena couldn't help tensing up. Last night she had believed that snobbery played no part in his character, that he was absolutely genuine in liking and wanting the person she was. She would not change her mind unless he changed it for her.

'Do call this yappy creature off, Nic, or haven't you learnt to control it yet?' Justine said a trifle waspishly, the shrill barking putting a crack in her perfect composure. It was instantly papered over as she switched on a condescending smile, beamed straight at Serena. 'Silly of me. I should have asked you, Serena, since you're the dog expert.'

'Shut up, Cleo!' Nic thundered.

It shocked the little terrier into jumping around to face him, the barking silenced, her little tail frantically wagging as though pleading to know what she'd done wrong. Nic bent and picked up the dog, tucking it protectively in the crook of one arm while using his other hand to calm it down, ruffling the silky hair behind her ears. Cleo responded by eagerly licking every reachable part of Nic's bare skin.

'Well, this is progress,' Justine remarked, trilling an amused laugh.

'I went to the front door, only to find your vacated SAAB parked at the steps,' Nic said tersely.

She shrugged. 'Oh, I thought I'd find you out here. Such a glorious morning!'

'Yes, it is. And I'm wondering why you've come, driving all the way from Sydney without first calling me to…'

'I just dropped in on the off-chance you were home, Nic,' she rolled out, putting on an expression of charming appeal. 'I'm on my way to Terrigal, joining friends for lunch at *The Galley.* You remember the Norths, Sonia and Joel. They're just back from racing their yacht at San Diego. And Liz and Teddy…'

Serena numbly listened to the celebrity status of Justine's *friends,* knowing this was Nic's social circle, too. An A-list luncheon party, without a doubt, and being described to tempt Nic into joining it, as well as spelling out that Serena wouldn't fit, if indeed Justine even saw *the dog-handler* as anyone to be counted.

Nic was frowning, looking impatient with Justine's spiel…or finding himself hooked on the horns of a dilemma. Inconvenient for him that Serena was still here, if he fancied taking up the invitation subtly being offered. Last night Nic had made her feel indispensible to him…or had she been fooling herself, believing in something that had only been generated by the heat of lust?

'So you're off to a luncheon with the people you like mixing with,' Nic drawled mockingly. 'Why drop in here?'

Serena's sluggish heartbeat instantly picked up. It didn't sound as if he cared for the company at all. Nor was he being receptive to having Justine's presence thrust upon him.

'Don't be like that, Nic,' she cajoled, pouting with sexy appeal. 'I'm sorry I left without saying goodbye after my weekend with you.'

'I took goodbye for granted from the manner of your departure,' he answered coldly.

They'd had a fight, Serena swiftly surmised. Was Nic's pride at stake here, or was he truly finished with Justine?

'I'm sorry. Okay? I lost my temper...' She raised her hands in apologetic appeal. 'Put it down to not much sleep because of the dog.' She forced a smile at Cleo. 'Now that you've got her tamed...'

'Thanks to Serena,' Nic slid in and pointedly turned his gaze to her, looking determined that she not be ignored or left out of this conversation any longer.

'Yes. I can see you're very grateful to her. Nice of you to invite her for a swim in the pool,' Justine said dismissively, her eyes glittering green daggers at Serena as she condescendingly added, 'But you're not expecting to stay all day, are you, dear? You won't mind if I carry Nic off to lunch with our friends?'

Nic came in hard and fast. 'I've invited Serena to stay *all* day and I'm not the least bit interested in joining your party, which I would have told you if you'd called instead of coming here uninvited and making unwarranted assumptions,' he stated tersely.

Justine sighed and tried a silky challenge, placing a hand on a provocatively jutting hip. 'Why wouldn't I think I'd be welcome, Nic? We have been lovers for…'

'Just give it up, Justine,' he cut in, the harsh command slightly softened by the follow-up appeal. 'Okay?'

It wasn't okay. It produced a sulky protest. 'I have apologised…'

Angry impatience burst from Nic. 'That currency won't buy you back in. I've moved on.' He flashed Serena a look that commanded her compliance with his next assertion. 'I'm very happy in Serena's company and have no wish to exchange it for anyone else's.'

Serena held her breath. Here it was—the situation punched out in no uncertain terms. Nic's handsome face looked so hard it could have been carved out of granite. Having told Justine where he was at, he wasn't about to excuse his actions, either. This declaration was a straight slap in the face to any hope or expectation of any intimacy with her being resumed. Certainly not today, anyway.

Retaliation was not slow in coming.

'Your bed feeling a bit cold, was it?' Justine mocked, her lip curling up in distaste as she subjected Serena to a contemptuous dismissal. 'And, of course, *you'd* be only too happy to oblige him. Panting for the chance, no doubt, just like a bitch on heat.'

'That's enough!' Nic rasped.

'Oh, for God's sake, Nic!' Her hands scissored total exasperation. 'You can't be serious about taking up with *her!* She might be handy for sex and useful for looking after the dog, but...'

'Serena is a great deal more than that and I am very serious about holding on to her as long as I can,' Nic cut in with such fury in his voice it startled Cleo into barking again.

'This is ridiculous!' Justine glared at the silky terrier, then carried her glare to Nic, returning his fury with all the fury of a woman scorned. 'You're turning *me* down for a common local tart who works with stinky little animals?'

'Serena happens to be the most *un*common woman I've ever met. And be warned about that *tart* crack, Justine. What goes around comes around and if I hear it repeated in public, you'll find yourself tagged with something similarly unpleasant.'

Shock had Justine gaping at him. 'You'd humiliate me...for her?'

'You start it... I'll deliver it back to you in spades. What's more, I wouldn't carry on about stinky little animals if I were you, because you're making a nasty stink yourself right now and I'm finding it extremely *ugly*.'

The *ugly* word was meant to hit hard and it did. Justine visibly recoiled from the offensiveness of it. Serena couldn't help feeling justice had been served, considering the offensiveness the other woman had dished out.

Nevertheless, a haughty recovery was quickly effected. An arrogant pride stamped itself on the beautiful face. The glorious mane of hair was tossed in disdain of everything that had been said as she shook her head and proceeded to adopt a mock-indulgent tone.

'Well, I must admit I'm not enamoured with the dog situation you have here so I'll overlook this temporary aberration of yours, Nic. Call me when you get back to Sydney and we'll pick up from there.'

'It won't happen,' Nick told her with emphatic finality.

Justine chose to ignore him, swinging on her heel and swanning off in catwalk mode, taking her own path around the house again, flaunting *her* message that Justine Knox was not about to be shown the door and she'd still be on call when Nic came to his senses.

It wasn't only Serena watching her go. Nick's gaze was glued to Justine's back until it disappeared from view. Was he wondering if he'd made the right decision? Angry that he'd been caught in a hard place, knowing he'd come off as a real slime if he'd tried to wriggle out of or skate over what had been going on with Serena?

An engine was loudly revved, a decisive signal that Justine was, indeed, on her way out. Nic set Cleo down on the patio, a somewhat premature move since the little terrier went hurtling off around the house to chase the car and bark it off the premises. Nic shrugged and shook his head at the unstoppable action, then started down the steps to the pool level, grimacing his displeasure at having been forced to deal with such a scene.

'Don't take anything Justine said to heart, Serena. That was all just bitchy grandstanding,' he said dismissively.

'You really are finished with her, Nic?'

He looked startled that she could think otherwise. 'No way in the world would I ever get back with Justine Knox.' He frowned at her possible uncertainty. 'You can't believe I would?'

She grimaced. 'I don't want to.'

'Then don't. You're the only woman I want.' A wicked smile broke across his face as he reached out and scooped her into his embrace. 'If you need more convincing...'

The only woman I want... music to her ears, a joyful beat through her heart. She linked her hands around his neck, suddenly yearning to hold on to him forever, though she couldn't help thinking they would be torn asunder sooner or later.

'You know Justine won't be the only one to say such things about me, Nic. You'll be answering to this kind of prejudice for as long as you have me with you. It's about who you are and who I'm not, and nothing you can say or do will really change that.'

'You're wrong, Serena.' His eyes burned with the belief in his own power to beat any criticism of their relationship. 'I promise you, any controversy about our pairing will fade very quickly.'

'You can't dominate people's minds...alter ingrained attitudes.'

He stroked her cheek, smiling with a kind of whimsical indulgence as though she were a child he was instructing. 'You see the power of wealth, Serena, but you don't understand it. Not from the inside as I do. If my family accepts you, believe me, everyone else will be only too happy to acknowledge you and treat you with enormous respect.'

She shook her head, thinking his family's acceptance a highly unlikely eventuality. 'I don't see how that could happen.'

He kissed her doubting eyes closed, kissed the end of her nose, kissed the fear from her mouth, then murmured with passionate confidence, 'Trust me. I have the perfect plan.'

CHAPTER SEVENTEEN

'Wow, little sister!' Michelle exclaimed with a huge sigh of feeling as they finally reached the luxurious bedroom suite assigned to them. 'The Morettis certainly throw everything into celebrating a family wedding. This has been totally, totally overwhelming!'

Serena laughed. Over the past few months, she had gradually become used to the Italian effusiveness in Nic's family, the hugging, the kissing, the generous gift-giving, and she had learnt to gracefully accept the unbelievable extravagance in the planning for this wedding—hers and Nic's. However, she well understood Michelle's reaction to the culmination of all these plans.

Outside, in the grounds of the Moretti compound on the Sydney Harbour shoreline, was a fabulous white marquee, festooned with flowers and thousands of fairy lights, filled with people in dazzling evening wear, the best French champagne flowing from an endless store, gourmet food being constantly offered and served, a variety of live bands providing music for dancing and singing. It was an event, the like of which neither of them had ever experienced before, let alone played star roles in it.

'Did I get through it okay?' Michelle asked a trifle anxiously.

'You were great,' Serena warmly assured her sister. 'The perfect matron of honour.'

Michelle grinned. 'Well, I'd have to say you're the most spectacular bride I've ever seen.'

Serena grinned back. 'I could see Nic's mother adored all this elaborate beading and lace. She just beamed with pleasure when I chose it.'

'It's pure fairy-tale princess stuff. And it's obvious Nic's mum adores you, too.'

'God knows why, but she seemed delighted to welcome me into the family right from the start. Nic's dad, too.'

'Well, they might be filthy rich, but they are nice people,' Michelle declared. 'Now let's get you out of your bridal gear and into your going away outfit.'

This was a frivolous little dress in shell pink silk chiffon, shoe-string shoulder straps, frills around the bodice, frills around the hem of the skirt. After the exquisite, form-fitting formality of the ceremonial bridal gown, it was a relief to simply slide into a dress that skimmed her figure and felt frothy and feminine. Relaxing.

'Don't forget you still have to throw your bouquet,' Michelle reminded her.

'I'll throw it to you,' Serena promised, hoping her older sister would marry Gavin who seemed to share many interests with her. He was here at the wedding with his daughter, who thought it was *excellent* that Erin, her best friend, was the flower girl at the ceremony.

'No need.' Michelle's eyes sparkled above suddenly pink cheeks. 'Gavin proposed to me tonight. I said yes.'

'Oh, that's marvellous!' Serena threw her arms

around her sister and hugged hard. 'I hope you'll both be very happy together.'

Michelle hugged back. 'You, too, with Nic.'

Emotion welled between them.

'Maybe we've reached our journey's end, Michelle.'

'You mean since Mum and Dad died.'

'And David.'

'Do you feel you really belong with Nic, Serena?'

'Yes, I do.'

'Gavin gives me that feeling, too. Like finally filling what's been missing in my life...coming home.'

So much had been missing that Nic had filled, Serena thought as they returned to the marquee. He made her feel protected, provided for, looked after, understood. He was like a rock of absolute and enduring stability, unshakable in bestowing his love and loyalty and support. She'd given him her trust and the reward of that act of faith was still awesome to her. Even his formidable family had welcomed her into their midst without so much as a raised eyebrow.

She smiled as she glanced over at his parents, thinking how lucky she was to have met their son. Beside them were Angelina and Ward, with Cleo on a white satin leash, Nic having insisted the dog be here since the little terrier had been a prime mover in their relationship. And was much beloved by his sister.

They all caught her smile and smiled back. There had not once been any criticism of her from any of these people, no patronising, no hint of condescension. She was sure in her own mind that Nic had made this happen for her. He'd spoken of the power of wealth, and its buying power was all around her, but in her heart, she couldn't believe he could *buy* her this level of genuine approval.

Having completed the last bridal act of throwing her bouquet, she headed straight for him and he left the group of guests he'd been chatting to, moving to meet her, his dark eyes locking onto hers, and what she felt coming from him was the power of love, not wealth.

'One more dance with you in that flirty little dress before we go,' he said with a sexy suggestiveness that had her whole body humming with desire for him as he swept her into his arms and twirled her onto the dance-floor.

He was a superb dancer, fantastic at everything, Serena thought giddily. 'Thank you for loving me, Nic,' she said in a rush of sheer happiness. 'And for bringing me into your wonderful family and making me feel I belong with you.'

'You do belong with me.' He grinned, his whole face lit with triumphant pleasure. 'We're married.'

She laughed at his delight in this achievement. 'So we are. And I love my husband very much.'

'Rightly so. It wouldn't be fair if you didn't since I've applied myself so diligently to winning your love.'

'Now why would you do that when I presented so many problems?' she teased, adoring him for wanting the role of her knight in shining armour.

He heaved a mock sigh. 'I'm a sucker for challenges.'

She arched her eyebrow. 'Don't you think tying yourself to me for life is taking a challenge too far?'

'I'm into bondage with you. Can't help myself. My soul says you're my soul mate, now and forever. If marriage is a challenge, I'm definitely up for it as long as you're my wife.'

He rolled out the words with such relish Serena had to laugh again, but her soul was deeply stirred by his commitment to her and silently echoed it—now and forever. Nic clasped her closer and whirled her around in a burst of exhilaration that left them both simmering with the desire to be by themselves and make wild passionate love together.

'Just tell me one more thing before we take our leave of everyone,' Serena begged.

'I'll grant you one minor delay.'

'Your family seems to think I'm the best thing that's ever happened to you. And I don't know why.'

'That's easy.' His eyes twinkled with devilish delight. 'I had the perfect plan to win their instant approval of our marriage, and to regard you as manna from heaven.'

'Manna from heaven?'

'Serena, the Morettis are of strong Italian blood and the big thing in their lives is family.'

'But I don't have much in the way of family. Only Michelle and…'

'The point is, my darling wife, you're keen to provide one.'

She looked her bewilderment. 'I don't understand.'

'It's a great sorrow to my parents that Angelina and Ward can't have children. So what did I tell them? Apart from the fact that I loved you and couldn't imagine a life without you at my side… I told them what you wanted most was to be the mother of my children and have a houseful of kids.'

'Children,' she repeatedly dazedly. 'Oh, my God! What if I can't have them?'

'Trust me,' Nic said with supreme confidence. 'I'm very potent.'

Trust…that was what it had been about all along…and it worked.

Serena smiled at her all powerful husband. 'You're right, Nic,' she agreed with the same supreme confidence he had shown. 'You *are* very potent.'

Sydney Morning Herald
Personal Columns
Births

Moretti—On the first day of January to very proud parents, Serena and Nic—triplets—a fine son, Lucas Angelo, and two beautiful daughters, Isabella Rose and Katriona Louise—three wonderful grandchildren for Frank and Lucia.

A GROOM WORTH
WAITING FOR

SOPHIE PEMBROKE

For Emma, Helen & Mary.

Sophie Pembroke has been reading and writing romance ever since she read her first Mills & Boon romance at university, so getting to write them for a living is a dream come true! Sophie lives in a little Hertfordshire market town in the UK with her scientist husband and her incredibly imaginative six-year-old daughter. She writes stories about friends, family and falling in love, usually while drinking too much tea and eating homemade cakes. She also keeps a blog at www.sophiepembroke.com.

CHAPTER ONE

'WHAT DO YOU MEAN, he's coming here?' Thea Morrison clasped her arms around her body, as if the action could somehow hide the fact that she was wearing a ridiculously expensive, pearl-encrusted, embroidered ivory wedding dress, complete with six-foot train. 'He can't!'

Her sister rolled her big blue eyes. 'Oh, calm down. He just told me to tell you that you're late to meet with the wedding planner and if you aren't there in five minutes he'll come and get you,' Helena said.

'Well, stop him!'

No, that wouldn't work. Nothing stopped Flynn Ashton when he really wanted something. He was always polite, but utterly tenacious. That was why his father had appointed him his right-hand man at Morrison-Ashton media. And why she was marrying him in the first place.

'Get me out of this dress before he gets here!'

'I don't know why you care so much,' Helena said, fumbling with the zip at the back of the dress. 'It's not like this is a real wedding anyway.'

'In two days there'll be a priest, a cake, some flowers, and a legally binding pre-nup saying otherwise.' Thea wriggled to try and get the strapless dress down over her hips. 'And everyone knows it's bad luck for the groom to see the bride in the wedding dress before the big day.'

It was more than a superstition, it was a rule. Standard Operating Procedure for weddings. Flynn was not seeing this dress a single moment before she walked down the aisle of the tiny Tuscan church at the bottom of the hill from the villa. Not one second.

'Which is why he sent me instead.'

Thea froze, her blood suddenly solid in her veins. She knew that voice. It might have been eight years since she'd heard it, but she hadn't forgotten. Any of it.

The owner of that voice really shouldn't be seeing her in nothing but her wedding lingerie. Especially since she was marrying his brother in two days.

Yanking the dress back up over her ivory corset, Thea held it tight against her chest and stared at him. 'I thought you weren't coming.' But there he was. Large as life and twice as… Hell, she couldn't even lie in her brain and finish that with *ugly*. He looked…grown up. Not twenty-one and angry at everything any more. More relaxed, more in control.

And every inch as gorgeous as he'd always been. Curse him.

Helena laughed. 'Eight years and that's all you have to say to him?' Skipping across the room, blonde hair bouncing, she wrapped her arms around him and pressed a kiss against his cheek. 'It's good to see you, Zeke.'

'Little Helena, all grown up.' Zeke returned the hug, but his gaze never left Thea's. 'It's good to see you too. And rather more of your sister than I'd bargained on.'

There was a mocking edge in his voice. As if she'd planned for him to walk in on her in her underwear. He wasn't even supposed to be in the country! Flynn had told her he wouldn't come and she'd been flooded with relief— even if she could never explain why to her husband-to-be.

But now here Zeke was, staring at her, and Thea had never felt so exposed.

She clutched the dress tighter—a barrier between them. 'Well, I was expecting your brother.'

'Your fiancé,' Zeke said. 'Of course. Sorry. Seems he thought I should get started with my best man duties a few days early.'

Thea blinked. '*You're* Flynn's best man?'

'Who else would he choose?' He said it as if he hadn't been gone for eight years. As if he'd never taunted Flynn about not being a real Ashton, only an adopted one, a fall-back plan. As if he hadn't sworn that he was never coming back.

'Anyone in the world.' Quite literally. Flynn could have appointed the Russian Prime Minister as his best man and Thea would have been less surprised.

'He chose his brother,' Helena said, giving Thea her usual *are you crazy?* look. She'd perfected it at fifteen and had been employing it with alarming regularity ever since. 'What's so weird about that?'

Helena hadn't been there. She'd been—what? Sixteen? Too young or too self-absorbed to get involved in the situation, or to realise what was going on. Thea had wanted to keep it from her—from everybody—even then. Of course with hindsight even at sixteen Helena had probably had a better idea about men than Thea had at eighteen. Or now, at twenty-six. But Helena had been dealing with her own issues then.

'So, you're here for the wedding?' Thea said.

Zeke raised his eyebrows. 'What else could I possibly be here for?'

She knew what he wanted her to say, or at least to think. That he'd come back for her. To tell her she'd made the wrong decision eight years ago and she was making a worse one now. To stop her making the biggest mistake of her life.

Except Thea knew full well she'd already made that. And it had nothing to do with Zeke Ashton.

No, she had her suspicions about Zeke's return, but she didn't think he was there for her. If he'd come back to the family fold there had to be something much bigger at stake than a teenage rebellion of a relationship that had been dead for almost a decade.

'I need to get changed.'

Keeping the dress clasped tight to her body, Thea stepped off the platform and slipped behind the screen to change back into her sundress from earlier. She could hear Helena and Zeke chatting lightly outside, making out his amused tone more than the words he spoke. That was one thing that hadn't changed. The world was still a joke to him—her family most of all.

Hanging the beautiful wedding dress up carefully on its padded hanger, Thea stepped back and stared at it. Her fairytale dress, all sparkle and shine. The moment she put it on she became a different person. A wife, perhaps. That dress, whatever it had cost, was worth every penny if it made her into that person, made her *fit*.

This time, this dress, this wedding…it had to be the one that stuck. That bought her the place in the world she needed. Nothing else she'd tried had worked.

Shaking her head, Thea tugged the straps of her sundress up over her shoulders, thankful for a moment or two to regroup. To remind herself that this didn't change anything. So Zeke was there, lurking around their Tuscan villa. So what? He wasn't there for *her*. She was still marrying Flynn. She belonged with Flynn. She had the dress; she had the plan. She had Helena at her side to make sure she said, wore and did the right thing at the right time. This was it. This villa, this wedding. This was where she was supposed to be. Everything was in its right place—apart from Zeke Ashton.

Well, he could just stay out of her perfect picture, thank you very much. Besides, the villa was big enough she probably wouldn't even notice he was in residence most of the time. Not a problem.

Sandals on, Thea smoothed down her hair and stepped back out. 'Now, if you'll excuse me, I have a meeting with the wedding planner to attend.'

'Of course,' Zeke said, with that infuriating mocking smile still in place. 'We wouldn't dream of delaying the blushing bride.'

Thea nodded sharply. She was *not* blushing.

She'd made a promise to herself eight years ago. A decision. And part of that decision meant that Zeke Ashton would never be able to make her blush again.

That part of her life was dead and buried.

Just two days until the wedding. Two more days—that was all. Two days until Thea Morrison got her happily-ever-after.

'In fact,' Zeke said, 'why don't I walk you there? We can catch up.'

Thea's jaw clenched. 'That would be lovely,' she lied.

Two days and this miserable week would be over. Thea couldn't wait.

She barely looked like Thea. With her dark hair straightened and pinned back, her slender arms and legs bronzed to the perfect shade of tan…she looked like someone else. Zeke studied her as she walked ahead of him, long strides clearly designed to get her away from his company as soon as physically possible.

Did she even remember the time when that had been

the last thing she'd wanted? When she'd smile and perform her hostess duties at her father's dinner parties and company barbecues, then sneak off to hide out somewhere private, often dark and cosy, with him...? Whoever she'd pretended to be for their parents—the good girl, the dutiful daughter—when they were alone Zeke had seen the real Thea. Seen glimpses of the woman he'd always believed she'd become.

Zeke shook his head. Apparently he'd been wrong. Those times were gone. And as he watched Thea—all high-heeled sandals, sundress and God only knew what underneath, rather than jeans, sneakers and hot pink knickers—he knew the girl he'd loved was gone, too. The Thea he'd fallen in love with would never have agreed to marry his brother, whatever their respective fathers' arguments for why it was a good idea. She'd wanted love—true love. And for a few brief months he'd thought she'd found it.

He'd been wrong again, though.

Lengthening his own stride, he caught up to her easily. She might have long legs, but his were longer. 'So,' he asked casually, 'how many people are coming to this shindig, anyway?'

'Shindig?' Thea stopped walking. 'Did you just call my wedding a *shindig*?'

Zeke shrugged. Nice to know he could still get under her skin so easily. It might make the next couple of days a little more fun. Something had to. 'Sorry. I meant to say your fairytale-worthy perfect day, when thou shalt join your body in heavenly communion with the deepest love of your heart and soul. How many people are coming to *that*?'

Colour rose in her cheeks, filling him with a strange sense of satisfaction. It was childish, maybe. But he wasn't going to let her get away with pretending that this was a real, true love-match. It was business, just like everything else the Morrisons and the Ashtons held dear.

Including him, these days. Even if his business wasn't the family one any more.

'Two hundred and sixty-eight,' Thea said, her tone crisp. 'At the last count.'

'Small and intimate, then?' Zeke said. 'Just how my father likes things. Where are you putting them all up? I mean, I get that this place is enormous, but still…I can't imagine *your* guests doubling up on camp beds on the veranda.'

'We've booked out the hotel down the road. There'll be executive coaches and cabs running back and forth on the day.'

A small line had formed between her eyebrows, highlighting her irritation. That was new, too.

'Why do you care, anyway?'

'I'm the best man,' he reminded her. 'It's my job to know these things.'

That, apparently, was the line that did it. Spinning round to face him straight on, Thea planted her hands on her hips and scowled at him. 'Why are you here, Zeke? And don't give me some line about brotherly duties. I know full well what you think about Flynn.'

Did she? Maybe she could enlighten *him*, then. Zeke had long since given up trying to make sense of his relationship with his adopted brother. After he'd left home he'd spent months lying awake thinking about it. Wondering if he could have changed things if he'd realised sooner, before that last conversation with his father that had driven him away for good… But in the end the past was the past. He'd had to move on. Besides, this wasn't about him and Flynn. It was about Flynn and Thea.

'Well, if you're not going to buy brotherly affection,

I doubt you'll go for family loyalty either.' He shrugged. 'I'm far more interested in what our fathers said to get you to agree to marry the Great Pretender.'

'Don't call him that,' Thea snapped. 'It wasn't funny when we were kids, and it's not funny now. And is it so hard to believe that I might actually *want* to marry Flynn?'

'Yes,' Zeke said automatically. And not just because she wasn't marrying *him*, whatever his business partner, Deb, said.

'Well, I do.' Thea stared at him mulishly, as if she were barely resisting the urge to add, *So there!*

Zeke leant back against the sunny yellow stone of the hallway, staring down through the arches towards the terrace beyond and the green vines snaking up the trellis. Clearly they were no longer in a hurry to get to the meeting, which gave him a chance to find out what had been going on around here lately.

'Really?' he said, folding his arms across his chest. 'So you're saying that the fact that your marriage will merge both sides of the business for all time, and give your heirs total control, hasn't even crossed your mind?'

Thea pulled a face. 'Of course it has.'

'And if it hadn't I'm sure your father would have made it very clear.' Thomas Morrison was always very good about making his daughter understand the implications of her actions, as Zeke remembered it. Especially when they could benefit him—or threatened to inconvenience him.

'But that doesn't mean it wasn't my decision,' Thea said.

And suddenly all Zeke could think about was the last decision Thea had made, right before he'd skipped out on the family, the business and the rest of his life.

'Of course not,' he said, with a sharp, bitter taste in his mouth at the words. 'I know you like to weigh your decisions very carefully. Make sure you're choosing the most beneficial option.'

Thea's jaw dropped slightly. What? Had she expected him not to notice exactly how mercenary her behaviour was? Maybe eight years ago she might have fooled him, but he knew better now. He knew exactly what mattered to her—and it wasn't him.

'What, exactly, are you trying to say?' She bit the words out, as if she were barely holding back a tirade of insulted pride. 'And I'd think very carefully before answering.'

Zeke gave her his most blinding smile. 'Exactly what you think I'm trying to say. That suddenly it makes an awful lot of sense why you chose to stay here instead of coming away with me eight years ago. What was the point once you knew I wasn't the heir any more?' He shrugged, nonchalantly, knowing it would irritate her even more. 'Gotta say, though…I'm surprised it took you this long to bag Flynn.'

She was going to explode. Literally just pop with rage and frustration, spilling bitterness and anger all over the expensively rustic scrubbed walls of this beautiful villa.

Except that would probably make Zeke Ashton smirk even more. So, instead, Thea took a deep breath and prepared to lie.

'As hard as it may be for you to believe, I am in love with your brother.' Her voice came out calm and cool, and Thea felt a small bubble of pride swelling up amongst all the fury. There'd been a time when any words Zeke had spoken to her had provoked an extreme reaction. When they were kids it had usually been annoyance, or anger. Then, when they were teenagers, that annoyance had suddenly become attraction, and then anger, arousal… By the time he'd left… all sorts of other complicated reactions had come into play.

But not any more. Now she was an adult, in control of

her own life and making her own decisions. Zeke Ashton's barbs and comments had no power over her any longer. It felt incredibly freeing.

'Love?' Zeke raised an eyebrow. 'You know, I'm starting to think you've got your definition of that word wrong.'

'Trust me, I know *exactly* what it means.' Love meant the incredible pain of loss when it was gone. Or the uncertainty of never knowing if it was returned. It baffled Thea why so many people thought love was a good thing.

'Really? Well, I'm sure I'm just thrilled that you've finally found true love. Guess I was just a practice run.'

Thea's stomach rolled at the reminder. It wasn't that she'd thought he'd forgotten their teenage fling, or even forgiven her for the way it had ended—he'd made it very clear in the half-hour he'd been in the villa that neither had happened. But she hadn't expected him to want to actually *talk* about it. Weren't men supposed to be strong and silent on matters of the heart? Suffering in silence, and all that?

Except Zeke had always loved the sound of his own voice. Apparently that hadn't changed, even if nearly everything else had.

'That was a long time ago, Zeke. We were kids.' Too far in the past to bring up now, surely? Even for Zeke, with his ridiculous need to *talk* about everything. 'We've both moved on. We're different people now.'

'Want to throw in a few more clichés with that?' Zeke shook his head. 'Look, you can rewrite history any way you like. And, trust me, I'm not here to try and win you back—even to get one over on Flynn. But you're not going to convince me that this is anything but a business deal with rings.'

'You're wrong,' Thea lied. 'And you'll see that. But...'

'But?' Zeke asked, one eyebrow raised again in that mocking expression that drove her crazy. 'But what?'

'Even if it was a business deal…what would be wrong with that? As long as we both know what we're getting into…' She shrugged. 'There are worse reasons to get married.'

'Maybe.' Zeke gave her a slow smile—the one that used to make her insides melt. 'But there are so many better reasons, too.'

'Like love,' Thea said, apparently still determined to stick to her story.

Zeke didn't buy it, and knew he wouldn't, no matter how hard she tried to convince him. He knew what Thea in love looked like, and this wasn't it.

At least not his Thea. The old Thea. He shook his head. He couldn't let doubt in now. The only thing in his life that had never let him down was gut instinct. He had to trust himself, especially since he couldn't trust anyone else. Not even Thea.

'Love's the big one,' Zeke agreed. 'But it's not the only thing that counts. Trust. Respect. Common values—'

'We have those too,' Thea broke in.

'Sexual compatibility,' Zeke finished, smirking when her mouth snapped shut. 'That's always important for long-term happiness, I find.'

Her gaze hardened. 'Really? And how's that working out for you? I can't help but notice you've come to my wedding alone, after all.'

He had a comeback for that somewhere, he was sure. But since Flynn arrived at that moment—cool, collected, and always an inch and a half taller than Zeke—he didn't have to search for it.

'Zeke! You made it.' Flynn stepped up and held out a hand, but before Zeke could even take it Thea had latched on to her fiancé's other arm, smiling up at him in a sickeningly adoring manner.

Keeping the handshake as perfunctory as possible, Zeke moved out of their circle of love and into his own space of scepticism. 'How could I resist the opportunity to be the best man for once? Might be the only chance I get.'

Flynn's smile stiffened a little at that, but he soldiered on regardless. Always so keen to play up the family loyalty—to be a part of the family he'd never really thought he belonged in. Zeke would have thought that their father choosing Flynn over him would have gone a long way to convincing his brother that there was only one golden boy in the family, and that blood didn't matter at all.

'I wouldn't want anyone but my brother beside me on such an important day,' Flynn said.

He didn't even sound as if he was lying, which Zeke thought was quite an accomplishment.

'Really? Because I have to admit I was kind of surprised to be asked.' Zeke glanced at Thea, who gave him an *I knew it!* look. 'Not as surprised as Thea was to see me here, of course,' he added, just because he could. She glared at him, and snuggled closer against Flynn's arm. There was absolutely no chemistry between them at all. And not a chance in hell they'd ever slept together. What on earth was Thea doing with him?

'You said he wasn't coming,' Thea pointed out—rather accusingly, Zeke thought.

'I wasn't sure he would,' Flynn admitted, glancing down at Thea with an apologetic smile.

Zeke wasn't sure he liked the idea of them talking about him in his absence. What had she said? How much had she told him?

'But, Zeke, you were the one who left us, remember? Not the other way round. Of course I asked you. You're my brother.'

'And that's the only reason?' Zeke asked. An uncomfortable feeling wriggled in his chest at the reminder of his disappearance, but he pushed it aside. He hadn't had a choice. His father had made his position very clear, and that position had taken any other options Zeke might have had off the table. He'd only hung around long enough to waste his time talking to Thea that same night, then he'd been gone. And nobody looking at Zeke now, at how far he'd come and how much he'd achieved, could say that he'd made a mistake by leaving.

Flynn didn't answer his question. With a sigh, he said, 'Dad's got a dinner planned for tonight, by the way. To welcome you home.'

Zeke appreciated the warning too much to point out that a luxury Tuscan villa belonging to some client or another wasn't actually 'home', no matter how many swimming pools it had. 'A prodigal son type thing? Hope he's found a suitably fatted calf.'

'I'm sure there was some poor animal just *begging* to be sacrificed on your behalf,' Thea said. 'But before then don't we have a meeting with the wedding planner to get to, darling?'

The endearment sounded unnatural on her tongue, and Flynn actually looked uncomfortable as she said it. Nobody would ever believe these two actually loved each other or wanted to see each other naked. Watching them, Zeke couldn't even see that they'd ever met before, let alone been childhood friends. He could imagine them on their wedding night—all unnatural politeness and a wall of pillows down the middle of the bed. If it wasn't Thea doing the marrying, it would be hilarious.

'She had to leave,' Flynn said. 'But I think we sorted out all the last-minute details. I said you'd call her later if there was anything you were concerned about.'

'I'm sure it's all fine,' Thea said, smiling serenely.

Even that seemed false. Shouldn't a woman getting married in two days be a little bit more involved in the details?

A door opened somewhere, slamming shut again as Hurricane Helena came blowing through.

'Are you guys still here?' she asked, waves of blonde hair bobbing past her shoulders. 'Shouldn't you all be getting ready for dinner? Thea, I had the maid press your dress for tonight. It's hanging in your room. Can I borrow your bronze shoes, though?'

'Of course,' Thea said, just as she always had to Helena, ever since their mother had died.

Zeke wondered if she even realised she did it.

'Come on, I'll find them for you now.'

As the women made their way down the corridor Helena spun round, walking backwards for a moment. 'Hope you brought your dinner jacket, Zeke. Apparently this welcome home bash is a formal affair.'

So his father had been sure he'd come, even if no one else had. Why else would he have set up a formal dinner for his arrival?

Helena turned back, slipping a hand through her sister's arm and giggling. Thea, Zeke couldn't help but notice, didn't look back at all.

Beside him, Flynn gave him an awkward smile. He'd always hated having to wear a bow tie, Zeke remembered suddenly. At least someone else would be miserable that evening.

'I'll see you at dinner,' Flynn said, setting off down another corridor.

'Can't wait.' Zeke's words echoed in the empty hallway. 'Gonna be a blast.'

CHAPTER TWO

THEA SHOULD HAVE known this wasn't just about shoes.

'So…Zeke coming home. Bit of a shock, huh?' Helena said, lounging back on Thea's ridiculously oversized bed.

'Yep.' Thea stuck her head in the closet and tried to find her bronze heels. Had she even packed them?

'Even though old Ezekiel Senior has planned a welcome home dinner?'

'I told you—Flynn didn't think he'd come,' Thea explained. 'So neither did I.'

'So Flynn was just as shocked?' Helena asked, too innocently.

'Probably,' Thea said. 'He just hides it better.'

'He hides *everything* better,' Helena muttered. 'But, to be honest, he didn't seem all that surprised when I told him Zeke had arrived.'

Thea bashed her head on the wardrobe door. Rubbing her hand over the bump, she backed out into the room again. 'Then maybe he just had more faith that his brother would do the right thing than I did. I really don't think I brought those bronze shoes.'

'No? What a shame. I'll just have to wear my pewter ones.' Helena sat up, folding her legs under her. 'Why don't you trust Zeke? I thought you two were pretty close before he left.'

Thea stared at her sister. She'd known all along she didn't have the stupid shoes, hadn't she? She'd just wanted an excuse to quiz her about Zeke. Typical.

'We were friends,' she allowed. 'We all were. Hard not to be when they were over at our house all the time.'

'Or we were there,' Helena agreed. 'Especially after Mum…'

'Yeah.'

Isabella Ashton had quickly taken pity on the poor, motherless Morrison girls. She'd been more than happy to educate fourteen-year-old Thea in the correct way to run her father's household and play the perfect hostess. At least until Thea had proved she wasn't up to the task and Isabella had taken over all together. Thea would have been relived, if she hadn't had to bear the brunt of her father's disappointment ever since.

And been made to feel like an outsider in my own home.

Thea swallowed and batted the thought away. Helena probably didn't remember that part of it. As far as she was concerned Isabella had just made sure they were supplied with any motherly advice they needed. Whether they wanted it or not.

Thea moved over to the dressing table, looking for the necklace Isabella had given her for her eighteenth birthday. The night Zeke had left. She'd wear it tonight, along with her own mother's ring. Isabella always appreciated gestures like that.

'And you've really not spoken to Zeke at all since he left?' Helena asked.

Thea wondered how much her sister suspected about her relationship with Flynn's brother. Too much, it seemed.

'Not once,' she said firmly, picking up Isabella's necklace. 'Not once in eight years.'

'Strange.' Helena slipped off the bed and came up behind her, taking the ends of the chain from her to fasten it behind her neck. 'Do you think that's why he's come back now? Because you're getting married?'

'Well, he was invited, so I'm thinking that was probably the reason.'

'No,' Helena said, and something about her sister's quiet, firm voice made Thea look up and meet her eyes in the mirror. 'I meant because *you're* getting married.'

Thea swallowed. 'He didn't come and visit the last time I almost got married.'

'Or the time before that,' Helena said, cheerfully confirming her view of Thea as a serial fiancée. 'But then, those times you weren't marrying his brother.' The words *And you didn't go through with it...* went unsaid.

Thea dropped down onto the dressing table stool. Wouldn't that be just like Zeke—not to care that she might marry someone else as long as it wasn't a personal slight to him? But did he even know about the others? If he did, she predicted she'd be subjected to any number of comments and jibes on the subject. *Perfect.* Because she hadn't had enough of that at work, or from her friends, or even in the gossip pages.

Only Helena had never said anything about it. Her father had just torn up the pre-nups, asked his secretary to cancel the arrangements, and said, 'Next time, perhaps?' After the last one even Thea had had to admit to herself that she was better off sticking to business than romance.

It was just that each time she'd thought she'd found a place she could belong. Someone to belong to. Until it had turned out that she wasn't what they really wanted after all. She was never quite right—never quite good enough in the end.

Except for Flynn. Flynn knew exactly what he was getting, and why. He'd chosen it, debated it, drawn up a contract detailing exactly what the deal entailed. And that was exactly what Thea needed. No confused expectations, no unspoken agreements—this was love done business-style. It suited her perfectly.

Zeke would think it was ridiculous if he knew. But she was pretty sure that Zeke had a better reason for returning than just mocking her love life.

'That's not why he's back.'

'Are you sure?' Helena asked. 'Maybe this is just the first time he thought you might actually go through with it.'

'You make me sound like a complete flake.' Which was fair, probably. Except she'd always been so sure... until it had become clear that the men she was supposed to marry weren't.

Helena sighed and picked up a hairbrush from the dressing table, running it through her soft golden waves. Thea had given up wishing she had hair like that years ago. Boring brown worked fine for her.

'Not a flake,' Helena said, teasing out a slight tangle. 'Just...uncertain.'

'"Decisionally challenged", Dad says.'

Helena laughed. 'That's not true. You had a perfectly good reason not to marry those guys.'

'Because it turned out one was an idiot who wanted my money and the other was cheating on me?' And she hadn't seen it, either time, until it had been almost too late. Hadn't realised until it had been right in front of her that she couldn't be enough of a lover or a woman for one of them, or human enough to be worth more than hard cash to the other. Never valuable enough in her own right just to be loved.

'Because you didn't love them.' Helena put down the

brush. 'Which makes me wonder again why exactly you're marrying Flynn.'

Thea looked away from the mirror. 'We'll be good together. He's steady, sensible, gentle. He'll make a great husband and father. Our families will finally be one, just like everyone always wanted them to be. It's good for the business, good for our parents, and good for us. This time I know exactly what I'm signing up for. That's how I know that I've made the right decision.'

This time. This one time. After a lifetime of bad ones, Thea knew that this decision had to stick. This was the one that would give her a proper family again, and a place within it. Flynn needed her—needed the legitimacy she gave him. Thea was well aware of the irony: he needed her Morrison bloodline to cement his chances of inheriting the company, while she needed him, the adopted Ashton son, to earn back her place in her own family.

It was messed up, yes. But at least they'd get to be messed up together.

Helena didn't say anything for a long moment. Was she thinking about all the other times Thea had got it wrong? Not just with men, but with everything...with Helena. That one bad decision that Helena still had to live with the memory of every day?

But when she glanced back at her sister's reflection Helena gave her a bright smile and said, 'You'd better get downstairs for cocktails. And I'd better go and find my pewter shoes. I'll meet you down there, okay?'

Thea nodded, and Helena paused in the doorway.

'Thea? Maybe he just wanted to see you again. Get some closure—that sort of thing.'

As the door swung shut behind her sister Thea wished she was right. That Zeke was ready to move on, at last, from all the slights and the bitterness that had driven him away and kept him gone for so long. Maybe things would never be as they were when they were kids, but perhaps they could find a new family dynamic—one that suited them all.

And it all started with her wedding.

Taking a deep breath, Thea headed down to face her family, old and new, and welcome the prodigal son home again. Whether he liked it or not.

It was far too hot to be wearing a dinner jacket. Whose stupid idea was this, anyway? Oh, that was right. His father's.

Figured.

Zeke made his way down the stairs towards the front lounge and, hopefully, alcohol, torn between the impulse to rush and get it over with, or hold back and put it off for as long as possible. What exactly was his father hoping to prove by this dinner?

Zeke couldn't shake the feeling that Flynn's sudden burst of brotherly love might not be the only reason he'd been invited back to the fold for the occasion. Perhaps he'd better stick to just the one cocktail. If his father had an ulterior motive for wanting him there, Zeke needed to be sober when he found out what it was. Then he could merrily thwart whatever plan his dad had cooked up, stand up beside Flynn at this ridiculously fake wedding, and head off into the sunset again. Easy.

He hadn't rushed, but Zeke was still only the second person to make it to the cocktail cabinet. The first, perhaps unsurprisingly, was Thomas Morrison. The old man had always liked a martini before dinner, but as his gaze rose to study Zeke his mouth tightened and Zeke got the odd impression that Thea's dad had been waiting for him.

'Zeke.' Thomas held out a filled cocktail glass. 'So you made it, then.'

Wary, Zeke took the drink. 'You sound disappointed by that, sir.'

'I can't be the only person surprised to see you back.'

Zeke thought of Thea, standing in nothing but the underwear she'd bought for his brother, staring at him as if he'd returned from the dead. Was that really how she thought of him? In the back of his mind he supposed he'd always thought he *would* come back. When he was ready. When he'd proved himself. When he was *enough*. The wedding had just forced his hand a bit.

'I like to think I'm a pleasant surprise,' Zeke said.

Thomas sipped his martini and Zeke felt obliged to follow suit. He wished he hadn't; Thomas clearly liked his drinks a certain way—paint-stripper-strong. He put the glass down on the cocktail bar.

'Well, I think that depends,' Thomas said. 'On whether you plan to break your mother's heart again.'

Zeke blinked. 'She didn't seem that heartbroken to me.' In fact when she'd greeted him on his arrival she'd seemed positively unflustered. As if he was just one more guest she had to play the perfect hostess to.

'You never did know your mother.' Thomas shook his head.

'But *you* did.' It wasn't a new thought. The two families had always been a touch too close, lived a little too much in each other's pockets. And after his wife's death…well, it hadn't been just Thomas's daughters that Zeke's mother had seemed to want to look after.

'We're old friends, boy. Just like your father and I.'

Was that all? If it was a lie, it was one they'd all been telling themselves for so long now it almost seemed true.

'And I was there for both of them when you abandoned them. I don't think any of us want to go through that again.'

Maybe eight years had warped the old man's memory.

No way had his father been in the least bit bothered by his disappearing act—hell, it was probably what he'd wanted. Why else would he have picked Flynn over him to take on the role of his right-hand man at Morrison-Ashton? Except Zeke knew why—even if he didn't understand it. He had heard his father's twisted reasoning from the man's own lips. That was why he'd left.

But he couldn't help but wonder if Zeke leaving hadn't been Ezekiel Senior's plan all along. If he'd *wanted* him to go out in the world and make something of himself. If so, that was exactly what Zeke had done.

But not for his father. For himself.

'So, you think I should stick around this time?' Zeke asked, even though he had no intention of doing so. Once he knew what his father was up to he'd be gone again. Back to his own life and his own achievements. Once he'd proved his point.

'I think that if you plan to leave again you don't want to get too close while you're here.'

The old man's steely gaze locked on to Zeke's, and suddenly Zeke knew this wasn't about his father, or even his mother.

This was about Thea.

Right on cue they heard footsteps on the stairs, and Zeke turned to see Thea in the doorway, beautiful in a peacock-blue gown that left her shoulders bare, with her dark hair pinned back from her face and her bright eyes sharp.

Thomas clapped him on the shoulder and said, 'Welcome home, Zeke.' But the look he shot at Thea left Zeke in no doubt of the words he left unsaid. *Just don't stay too long.*

The air in the lounge felt too heavy, too tightly pressed around the stilted conversation between the three of them—until Helena breezed in wearing the beautiful pewter shoes that had been a perfect match for her dress all along. She fixed drinks, chatting and smiling all the way, and as she pressed another martini into their father's hand some of the tension seemed to drop and Thea found she could breathe properly again.

At least until she let her eyes settle on Zeke. Maybe that was the problem. If she could just keep her eyes closed and not see the boy she remembered loving, or the man he'd turned into, she'd be just fine. But the way he stood there, utterly relaxed and unconcerned, his suit outlining a body that had grown up along with the boy, she wanted to know him. Wanted to explore the differences. To find out exactly who he was now, just for this moment in time, before he left again.

Stop it. Engaged to his brother, remember?

Flynn arrived moments later, his mother clutching his arm, and suddenly things felt almost easy. Flynn and Helena both had that way about them; they could step into a room and make it better. They knew how to settle people, how to make them relax and smile even when there were a million things to be fretting about.

Flynn had always been that way, Thea remembered. Always the calm centre of the family, offset by Zeke's spinning wild brilliance—and frustration. For Helena it had come later.

Through their whole childhood Thea had been the responsible eldest child, the sensible one, at least when people were looking. And all the while Helena had thrown tantrums and caused chaos. Until Thea had messed up and resigned her role. Somehow Helena had seemed to grow to fill it, even as Isabella had taken over the job of mother, wife and hostess that Thea had been deemed unsuitable for. If it hadn't been for her role at the company,

Thea wondered sometimes if they'd have bothered keeping her around at all. They certainly hadn't seemed to need her. At least not until Flynn needed a bride with an appropriate bloodline.

'Are we ready to go through for dinner?' Isabella asked the room at large. 'My husband will be joining us shortly. He just has a little business to finish up.'

What business was more important than this? Hadn't Ezekiel insisted on this huge welcome home feast for his prodigal son? The least he could do was show up and be part of it. Thea wanted nothing more than for Zeke to disappear back to wherever he'd been for eight years, and *she* was still there.

Thea glanced up at Zeke and found him already watching her, eyebrows raised and expression amused. He slid in alongside her as they walked through to dinner.

'Offended on my behalf by my father's tardiness?' he asked. 'It's sweet, but quite unnecessary. The whole evening might be a lot more pleasant if he *doesn't* join us.'

'I wasn't…it just seemed a little rude, that's all.'

'Rude. Of course.'

He offered his arm for her to hold, but Thea ignored it. The last thing she needed was to actually touch Zeke in that suit.

'That's why your face was doing that righteously indignant thing.'

Thea stared at him. '"Righteously indignant thing"?'

'Yeah. Where you frown and your nose wrinkles up and your mouth goes all stern and disapproving.'

'I…I didn't know I did that.'

Zeke laughed, and up ahead Helena turned back to look at them. 'You've always done it,' he said. 'Usually when someone's being mean about me. Or Flynn, or Helena. It's cute. But like I said, in this case unnecessary.'

Thea scowled, then tried to make her face look as neutral as possible. Never mind her traitorous thoughts—apparently now she had to worry about unconscious overprotective facial expressions, too.

There were only six of them for dinner—seven if Ezekiel managed to join them—and they clustered around one end of the monstrously large dining table. Her father took the head, with Isabella at his side and Flynn next to her. Which left Thea sandwiched between Zeke and her father, with Helena on Zeke's other side, opposite Flynn. Thea couldn't help but think place cards might have been a good idea. Maybe she could have set hers in the kitchen, away from everybody...

They'd already made it through the starter before Ezekiel finally arrived. Thea bit her lip as he entered. Would he follow the unspoken boy-girl rule and sit next to Helena? But, no, he moved straight to Flynn's side and, with barely an acknowledgement of Zeke's presence in the room, started talking business with his eldest son.

Thea snuck a glance at Zeke, who continued to play with his soup as if he hadn't noticed his father's entrance.

'Did he already welcome you back?' Thea asked. But she knew Ezekiel Senior had been locked in his temporary office all day, so the chances were slim.

Zeke gave her a lopsided smile. 'You know my father. Work first.'

Why was she surprised? Ezekiel Ashton had always been the same.

'Well, if he's not going to ask you, I will.' Shifting in her seat to face him a little, Thea put on her best interested face. 'So, Zeke... What have you been up to the last eight years?'

'You don't know?' Zeke asked, eyebrows raised. 'Aren't you supposed to be in charge of PR and marketing for the company? I'd have thought it was your business to keep on top of what your competitors are up to.'

Too late Thea realised the trap she'd walked straight into. 'Oh, I know about your *business* life,' she said airily. 'Who doesn't? You set up a company purposely to rival the family business—presumably out of spite. It's the kind of thing the media loves to talk about. But, really, compared to Morrison-Ashton This Minute is hardly considered a serious competitor. More a tiny fish.'

'Beside your shark?' Zeke reached for his wine glass. 'I can see that. But This Minute wasn't ever intended to be a massive media conglomerate. Big companies can't move fast enough for me.'

That made sense. Zeke had never been one for sitting in meetings and waiting for approval on things he wanted to get done. But according to industry gossip even his instant response news website and app This Minute wasn't enough to hold his attention any more.

'I heard you were getting ready to sell.'

'Did you, now?' Zeke turned his attention across the table, to where his father and Flynn were still deep in conversation. 'That explains a lot.'

'Like?'

'Like why my father added his own personal request that I attend to my wedding invitation. He wants to talk about This Minute.'

So *that* was why he was back. Nothing to do with her, or Flynn, or the wedding. Not that she'd really thought it was, but still the knowledge sat heavily in her chest. 'You think he wants to buy it?'

'He's *your* CEO. What do you think?'

It would make sense, Thea had to admit. Their own twenty-four-hour news channels couldn't keep up with the fast response times of internet sites. Buying up This

Minute would be cheaper in the long run than developing their own version. And it would bring Zeke back into the family fold…

'Yes, I think he does.'

'Guess we'll find out,' Zeke said. 'If he ever deigns to speak to me.'

'What would you do?' Thea asked as the maid cleared their plates and topped up their wine glasses. 'Would you stay with This Minute?' It was hard to imagine Zeke coming back to work for Morrison-Ashton, even on his own terms. And if he did he'd be there, in her building, every day…

'No.' Zeke's response was firm. 'I'm ready to do something new.' He grinned. 'In fact, I want to do it all over again.'

'Start a new business? Why? Why not just enjoy your success for a while?'

'Like your father?' Zeke nodded at the head of the table, where Thomas was laughing at something Isabella had said.

Thea shook her head. 'My dad was never a businessman—you know that. He provided the money, sat on the board…'

'And left the actual work to my father.' He held up a hand before Thea could object. 'I know, I know. Neither one of them could have done it without the other. Hasn't that always been the legend? They each brought something vital to the table.'

'It worked,' Thea pointed out.

'And now you and Flynn are ready to take it into the next generation. Bring the families together. Spawn the one true heir.'

Thea looked away. 'You need to stop talking about my wedding like this.'

'Why? It's business, isn't it?'

'It's also my future. The rest of my life—and my children's.' That shut him up for a moment, unexpectedly. Thea took advantage of the brief silence to bring the conversation back round to the question he'd so neatly avoided. 'So, you didn't tell me. Why start up another new business?'

Zeke settled back in his chair, the thin stem of his wine glass resting between his fingers. 'I guess it's the challenge. The chance to take something that doesn't even exist yet, build it up and make it fantastic. Make it mine.'

It sounded exciting. Fresh and fun and everything else Zeke seemed to think it would be. But it also sounded to Thea as if Zeke was reaching for something more than just a successful business venture. Something he might never be able to touch, however hard he tried.

'You want to be a success,' she said slowly. 'But, Zeke, you've already succeeded. And you still want more. How will you know when you've done enough?'

Zeke turned to look at her, his dark eyes more serious than she'd ever seen them. 'I'll know it when I get there.'

But Thea was very afraid that he wouldn't.

CHAPTER THREE

SO NOW HE KNEW. Had Thea told his dad about the rumours, Zeke wondered, or had the old goat had his own spies on the lookout? Either way, his presence in Italy that week suddenly made a lot more sense. Ezekiel Senior wanted This Minute.

And Zeke had absolutely no intention of giving it to him.

As the rest of the guests enjoyed their dessert Zeke left his spoon on the tablecloth and studied his father across the table. How would he couch it? Would he make it sound as if he was doing Zeke a favour? Or would he—heaven forbid—actually admit that Zeke had achieved something pretty great without the backing of Morrison-Ashton? He'd have to wait to find out.

After dinner, Zeke decided. That would be when his father would finally acknowledge the presence of his youngest son. Probably he'd be summoned to the study. But this time he'd get to go on his own terms. For once Ezekiel wanted something he, Zeke, possessed, rather than the other way round.

That, on its own, made it worth travelling to Flynn and Thea's wedding.

Zeke only realised he was smiling when Flynn suddenly looked up and caught his eye. Zeke widened his grin, raising an eyebrow at his brother. So, had dear old dad just broken the news to the golden boy? And did that mean Thea *hadn't* told her beloved about the rumours she'd heard?

Flynn glanced away again, and Zeke reached for his spoon. 'You didn't tell Flynn, then?'

Thea's dropped her spoon against the edge of her bowl with a clatter. 'Tell Flynn what?' she asked, eyes wide.

Interesting. 'Well, I meant about the This Minute sale,' he said. 'But now I'm wondering what else you've been keeping from your fiancé.'

Thea rolled her eyes, but it was too late. He'd already seen her instinctive reaction. She was keeping things from Flynn. Zeke had absolutely no doubt at all.

'I didn't tell Flynn about the sale because it doesn't directly affect him and it's still only a rumour. If your father decides to make a bid for the company I'm sure he'll fill Flynn in at the appropriate time.' Thea looked up at him through her lashes. 'Besides, we don't talk about you.'

'At all?' That hit him somewhere in the middle of his gut and hit hard. Not that he'd been imagining them sitting around the dining table reminiscing about the good old days when Zeke had been there, or anything. But still, despite his initial misgivings over them talking about him in his absence, he thought this might be worse. They didn't talk about him *at all*?

'Apart from Flynn telling me you weren't coming to the wedding? No.' Thea shrugged. 'What would we say? You left.'

And she'd forgotten all about him. Point made. With a sharp jab to the heart.

But of course if they didn't talk about him… 'So you never told Flynn about us, either?'

She didn't look up from her dessert as she answered. 'Why would I? The past is very firmly in the past. And I had no reason to think you would ever come back at all.'

'And now?'

Raising her head, she met his gaze head-on. 'And now there's simply nothing to say.'

'Zeke.'

The voice sounded a little creakier, but no less familiar. Tearing his gaze away from Thea's face, Zeke turned to see his father standing, waiting for him.

'I'd like a word with you in my office, if you would. After eight years…we have a lot to discuss.'

They had one thing to discuss, as far as Zeke was concerned. But he went anyway. How else would he have the pleasure of turning the old man down?

Ezekiel had chosen a large room at the front of the villa for his office—one Zeke imagined was more usually used for drinks and canapés than for business. The oversized desk in the centre had to have been brought in from elsewhere in the house, because it looked utterly out of place.

Zeke considered the obvious visitor's chair, placed across from it, and settled himself into a leather armchair by the empty fireplace instead. He wasn't a naughty child any more, and that meant he didn't have to stare at his father over a forbidding desk, waiting for judgement to be handed down, ever again.

'Sit,' Ezekiel said, long after Zeke had already done so. 'Whisky or brandy?'

'I'd rather get straight down to business,' Zeke said.

'As you wish.' Ezekiel moved towards the drinks cabinet and poured himself a whisky anyway. Zeke resisted the urge to grind his teeth.

Finally, his father came and settled himself into the armchair opposite, placing his glass on the table between them. 'So. You're selling your business.'

'So the rumour mill tells me,' Zeke replied, leaning back in his chair and resting his ankle on his opposite knee.

'I heard more than rumour,' Ezekiel said. 'I heard you were in negotiations with Glasshouse.'

Zeke's shoulders stiffened. Nobody knew that, except Deb and him at the office, the CEO at Glasshouse and his key team. Which meant one or other of them had a leak. Just what he *didn't* need.

'It's true, then.' Ezekiel shook his head. 'Our biggest competitors, Zeke. Why didn't you just come to me directly? Or is this just another way of trying to get my attention?'

Zeke will never stop trying to best his brother. The words, eight years old, still echoed through Zeke's head, however hard he tried to move past them. But he didn't have time for the memory now.

'I haven't needed your attention for the last eight years, Father. I don't need it now.'

'Really?' Ezekiel reached for his whisky glass. 'Are you sure? Because you could have gone anywhere, done anything. Yet you stayed in the country and set up a company that directly competed with the family business.'

'I stuck to what I knew,' Zeke countered. Because, okay, annoying his father might have been part of his motivation. But only part.

Ezekiel gave him a long, steady look, and when Zeke didn't flinch said, 'Hmm…'

Zeke waited. *Time to make the offer, old man.*

'I'm sure that you understand that to have my son working with Glasshouse is…unacceptable. But we can fix this. Come work with us. We'll pay whatever Glasshouse is paying and you can run your little company under the

Morrison-Ashton umbrella. In fact, you could lead our whole digital division.'

Somewhere in there, under the 'let me fix your mistakes' vibe, was an actual job offer. A good one. Head of Digital… There was a lot Zeke could do there to bring Morrison-Ashton into the twenty-first century. It would give him enough clout in the company in order not to feel as if Flynn was his boss. And he would be working with Thea every day…

'No, thanks.' Zeke stood up. He didn't need this any more. He'd grown up now. He didn't need his father's approval, or a place at the table, or even to be better than Flynn. He was his own man at last. 'I appreciate the offer, but I'm done with This Minute. Once I sell to Glasshouse I'm on to something new. Something exciting.'

Something completely unconnected to his family. Or Thea's.

'Really?'

Ezekiel looked up at him and Zeke recognised the disappointment in his eyes. It wasn't as if he hadn't seen that peculiar mix of being let down and proved right at the same time before.

'And if I appeal to your sense of family loyalty?'

Zeke barked a laugh. 'Why would you? You never showed *me* any. You gave Flynn all the chances, the job, the trust and the confidence. You wanted me to find my own road.' He crossed to the door, yanking it open. 'Well, Dad, I found it. And it doesn't lead to Morrison-Ashton.'

'Well,' Flynn said, dropping to sit beside her on the cushioned swing seat. 'That was a day.'

'Yes. Yes, it was.' Thea took the mug he offered her and breathed in the heavy smell of the coffee. 'Is this—?'

'Decaf,' Flynn assured her. 'You think I don't know what my wife-to-be likes?'

'Less "likes",' Thea said, taking a cautious sip. Everyone knew that on a normal day she'd be on her third double espresso well before lunch. 'More that I don't need anything else keeping me awake at night right now.'

'Hmm…' Flynn settled against the back of the seat and, careful of her coffee cup, wrapped an arm around Thea's shoulders, pulling her against him. 'Want to tell me what's keeping you awake?'

Thea tucked her legs up underneath her, letting Flynn rock the swing seat forward and back, the motion helping to relax the tension in her body.

They didn't share a room yet; it hadn't really seemed necessary, given the agreement between them. So he didn't have to know exactly how many hours she spent staring at the ceiling every night, just waiting for this wedding to be over, for the papers to be signed and for her future to be set and certain. But on the other hand she was marrying the man. He'd be her companion through life from here on in, and she wanted that companionship badly. Which meant telling him at least part of the truth.

'I guess I'm just nervous about the wedding,' she admitted.

'About marrying me?' Flynn asked. 'Or getting through the day itself?'

'Mostly the latter.' Thea rested her head against his comfortable shoulder and sighed. 'I just want it to be done. For everyone else to leave and for us to enjoy our honeymoon here in peace. You know?'

'I really, really do.'

Thea smiled at the heartfelt tone in his voice. This was why a marriage between them would work far better than any of the other relationships she'd fallen into, been passionate about, then had end horribly. They were a fit—a pair. If they actually loved each other it would be a classically perfect match.

But then, love—passion, emotion, pain—would be what drove them apart, too. No, far better this friendship and understanding. It made for a far more peaceful life.

Or it would. Once they got through the wedding.

'Feeling the strain, huh?' Thea patted Flynn's thigh sympathetically. 'Be grateful. At least my sister didn't walk in on you in your wedding lingerie this morning.'

'I don't have any wedding lingerie,' Flynn pointed out. 'I have the same boring black style I wear every day. Hang on. Did Zeke…?'

'Yep. He said you sent him to fetch me to meet with the wedding planner. So you wouldn't see me in my dress before the big day.'

'Sorry,' Flynn said, even though it obviously wasn't really his fault. 'I just know how important the traditions are to you. I didn't want to upset you.'

Thea waved a hand to brush away his apology, and Flynn reached over to take her empty coffee cup and place it safely on the table beside him. 'It's not your fault. Just something else to make this day difficult.'

'That does explain why he was in such an odd mood this afternoon, though,' Flynn mused. 'All those defensive jokes. He always did have a bit of a crush on you, I think. Even when we were kids.'

A bit of a crush. Thea ducked her head against Flynn's chest to hide her reaction. Had there ever been such an understatement? She'd assumed at first that Flynn had known something of her relationship with his brother— despite their attempts at secrecy it seemed that plenty of others had. But it had quickly become clear he'd no idea.

And they'd never talked about him, so she'd been perfectly happy to consign it to the realms of vague memory.

'I don't think that's why,' she said. 'I'm sure it's just being here, seeing everyone again after so long. It must be strange.'

'It was his choice.' Flynn's voice was firm, unforgiving. 'He could have come home at any time.'

'Perhaps.' What had *really* brought Zeke back now? *Was* it his father's summons? Not to satisfy the old man, of course, but to show him how much Zeke no longer needed him. To deny him whatever it was he wanted just out of spite?

The Zeke she'd seen today hadn't seemed spiteful, though. He was no longer the angry boy, lashing out, wanting revenge against his family, his life. Her. So why was he here?

Thea didn't let herself believe Helena's theory for a moment. If Zeke had really wanted to see her he'd had eight years. Even if he hadn't wanted to see his family again he could have found her—made contact somehow. But he hadn't. And by the time Thea had known where he was again any lingering regret or wish to see him had long faded. Or at least become too painful to consider. That wound was healed. No point pulling it open again.

Except now he was here, for her wedding, and she didn't have a choice.

Flynn shifted on the seat, switching legs to keep them swinging. 'Anyway… Talking about my prodigal brother isn't going to help you feel any more relaxed about the wedding. Let's talk about more pleasant things.'

'Like?'

'Our honeymoon,' Flynn said decisively, then faltered. The swing stopped moving and his shoulder grew tense under her cheek. 'I mean… I don't mean…'

Thea smiled against his shirt. He was so *proper*. 'I know what you mean.'

'I was thinking about the day trips we might take—that sort of thing,' Flynn explained unnecessarily. 'There are some very fine vineyards in the region, I believe. I don't want you to think that I'm expecting…well, *anything*. I know that wasn't our agreement.'

Thea pushed herself up to see his face. The agreement. It had been written, signed, notarised months ago—long before the wedding planning had even begun. They both knew what they wanted from this marriage—the business convenience, the companionship, fidelity. The document had addressed the possibility of heirs—and therefore sex—as something to be negotiated in three years' time. That had been Thea's decision. Marriage was one thing. Children were something else altogether. She needed to be sure of her role as a wife first.

But now she wondered if that had been a mistake.

'Maybe we should… I mean, we can talk again about the agreement, if you like?'

Flynn's body stilled further. Then he started the swing moving again, faster than before. 'You've changed your mind?'

'I just…I want our marriage to be solid. I want the companionship, and everything else we discussed, but more than anything I want us to be partners. I don't want doomed passion, or anger and jealousy. I want true friendship and respect, and I know you can give me that.'

'And children?' Flynn asked, and Thea remembered just how important that was to him. How much he needed a family of his own—she suspected not just to make sure there was a legitimate Morrison-Ashton heir for the business.

'In time,' she said, 'yes, I think so. But I'd still like a

little time for us to get to know each other better first. You know…as husband and wife.'

Was that enough? Would he get the hint?

'You want us to sleep together?' Flynn said. 'Sorry to be blunt, but I think it's important we both know what we're saying here.'

Another reason he'd make a good husband. Clarity. She'd never had that with Zeke. Not at all. 'You're right. And, yes, I do.'

'Okay.'

Not exactly the resounding endorsement she'd hoped for. 'Are you all right with that?'

Flynn flashed a smile at her. 'Thea, you're a very beautiful woman and I'm proud that you're going to be my wife. Of course I'm okay with that.'

'You weren't sounding particularly enthusiastic.'

'I am. Really.' He pulled her close again and kissed the top of her head. 'Who knows? Maybe we'll even grow to love each other as more than friends.'

'Perhaps we will,' Thea said. After all, how could she tell her husband-to-be that the last thing she wanted was for either of them to fall in love with each other. Sex, marriage, kids—that was fine. But not love.

Hadn't it been proved, too many times already, that her love wasn't worth enough?

The corridors of the villa were quieter now. Zeke presumed that everyone was lingering over after-dinner drinks in the front parlour or had gone to bed. Either way, he didn't particularly want to join in.

Instead, he made his way to the terrace doors. A little fresh air, a gulp of freedom away from the oppression of family expectation, might do him some good.

Except the terrace was already occupied.

He stood in the doorway for a long moment, watching the couple on the swing. Whatever he'd seen and thought earlier, here—now—they looked like a real couple. Flynn's arm wrapped around Thea's slender shoulders... the kiss he pressed against her head. She had her legs tucked up under her, the way she'd always sat as a teenager, back when they'd spent parties like this hiding out together. The memories were strong: Thea skipping out on her hostessing duties, sipping stolen champagne and talking about the world, confiding in him, telling him her hopes, plans, dreams.

It hurt more than he liked, seeing her share a moment like that with someone else. And for that someone else to be his brother...that burned.

It shouldn't, Zeke knew. He'd moved past the pain of her rejection years ago, and it wasn't as if he hadn't found plenty of solace in other arms. She'd made her choice eight years ago and he'd lived by it. He hadn't called, hadn't visited. Hadn't given her a chance to change her mind, because he didn't want her to.

She'd chosen their families and he'd chosen himself. Different sides. Love had flared into anger, rejection, even hate. But even hate faded over the years, didn't it? He didn't hate her now. He didn't know what he felt. Not love, for certain. Maybe...regret? A faint, lingering thought that things might have been different.

But they weren't, and Zeke wasn't one for living in the past. Especially not now, when he'd finally made the last cut between himself and his father. He'd turned down the one thing he'd have given anything for as a boy—his father's acceptance and approval. He knew now how little that was worth. He was free, at last.

Except for that small thin thread that kept him tied to the woman on the swing before him. And by the end of the week even that would be gone, when she'd tied herself to another.

His new life would start the moment he left this place. And suddenly he wanted to savour the last few moments of the old one.

Zeke stepped out onto the terrace, a small smile on his lips as his brother looked up and spotted him.

'Zeke,' Flynn said, eyes wary, and Thea's head jerked up from his shoulder.

'I wondered where you two had got to,' Zeke lied. He hadn't given it a moment's thought, because he hadn't imagined they could be like this. *Together.* 'Dinner over, then?'

Thea nodded, sitting up and shifting closer to Flynn to make room for Zeke to sit beside them. 'How did things go? With your father?'

'Pretty much as expected.' Zeke eyed the small space on the swing, then perched on the edge of the low table in front of them instead.

'Which was…?' Flynn sounded a little impatient. 'I don't even know what he wanted to talk to you about. Business, I assume?'

'You didn't tell him?' Zeke asked Thea, eyebrow raised.

'We were talking about more important things,' Thea said, which made Flynn smile softly and kiss her hair again.

Zeke's jaw tightened at the sight. He suspected he didn't want to know what those 'more important things' were. 'Your father wanted to try and buy my business,' he told Flynn.

'He's your father too,' Flynn pointed out.

Zeke laughed. 'Possibly not, after tonight.'

'You told him no, then?' Thea guessed. 'Why? To spite him? You've already admitted you want to sell.'

'He wanted me to come and work for Morrison-Ashton.'

'And that would be the worst thing *ever*, of course.' Sarcasm dripped from her voice. 'Are you really still so angry with him?'

Tilting his head back, Zeke stared up through the slats of the terrace roof at the stars twinkling through. 'No,' he answered honestly. 'This isn't… It's not like it was any more, Thea. I'm not trying to spite him, or hurt him, or pay him back for anything. I just want to move on. Sever all ties and start a whole new life. Maybe a new company, a new field. A new me.'

'So we won't be seeing you again after the wedding, then?' Flynn said, and Zeke realised he'd almost forgotten his brother was even there for a moment. He'd spoken to Thea the same way he'd always talked to Thea—with far more honesty than he'd give anyone else. A bad habit to fall back into.

'Maybe you two would be worth a visit,' he said, forcing a smile. 'After all, I'll need to come and be favourite Uncle Zeke to your kids, right?'

At his words Flynn's expression softened, and he gave his fiancée a meaningful look. Thea, for her part, glanced down at her hands, but Zeke thought he saw a matching shy smile on her face.

Realisation slammed into him, hitting him hard in the chest until he almost gasped for breath. *That* was what they'd been talking about—their 'more important things'. Children. He'd been so sure that this marriage was a sham, that there was nothing between them. But he hadn't imagined kids. Even when he'd made the comment he'd expected an evasion, a convenient practised answer. Another sign that this wasn't real.

Not *this*. Not the image in his head of Thea's belly swollen with his brother's child. Not the thought of how much

better parents Flynn and Thea would be than his own father. Of a little girl with Thea's dark hair curling around
a perfect face.

'Well, you know you'll always be welcome in our home,'
Flynn said.

The words were too formal for brothers, too distant
for anything he'd ever shared with Thea. And Zeke knew
without a doubt that he'd never, ever be taking them up
on the offer. Maybe he didn't love Thea any more, but that
tightly stitched line of regret inside him still pulled when
she tugged on the thread between them.

He couldn't give Thea what she wanted—never had
been able to. She'd made that very clear. And in two days
she'd be married, that thread would be cut, and he'd never
see her again.

'I should get to bed,' Thea said, unfolding her legs from
under her. 'Another long day tomorrow.'

Flynn smiled up at her as she stood. 'I'll see you in the
morning?'

Thea nodded, then with a quick glance at Zeke bent and
kissed Flynn on the lips. It looked soft, but sure, and Zeke
got the message—*loud and clear, thanks*. She'd made her
choice—again—and she was sticking with it.

Fine. It was her choice to make, after all. But Zeke knew
that the scar of regret would never leave him if he wasn't
sure she was happy with the choice she was making. If he
wanted the freedom of that cut thread, he had to be able
to leave her behind entirely. He had to be sure she knew
what she was doing.

Zeke got to his feet. 'I'll walk you to your room.'

CHAPTER FOUR

THIS WAS EXACTLY what she didn't want. Which, in fairness, was probably why Zeke was doing it.

It had been too strange, sitting there with the two brothers, talking about her future as if Zeke might be part of it—in a role she'd simply never expected him to take. Hard enough to transition from fiancée to wife to mother with Flynn, without adding in her ex as her brother-in-law. It had all been so much easier when she'd imagined he was out of her life for good. That she'd never have to see him again. She'd got over the hurt of that loss years before.

The villa was in darkness, and their footsteps echoed off the tiled floors and painted stone walls. The place might be luxurious, but in the moonlight Thea couldn't help but find it creepy. From the hanging tapestries to the stone arches looming overhead, the shadows seemed oppressive. And it felt eerily empty; everyone else must have gone to bed hours before.

She'd expected Zeke to talk, to keep up the banter and the cutting comments and the jokes, but to her surprise they walked in a companionable silence. She could feel him beside her, the warmth of his presence a constant reminder of how close he was. If she stretched out a finger she could reach his hand.

But she wouldn't.

As they climbed the stairs, Zeke only ever one step behind her, his hand next to hers on the banister, she catalogued all the questions she wanted to ask.

Why are you back?

Why didn't you call?

Are you really going to stay?

What do you want from me now?

There had to be a rhyme and reason to it all somewhere, but Thea couldn't quite put her finger on it. Maybe he didn't know the answers, either. Maybe that was why he seemed always on the edge of asking a question he wasn't sure he wanted her to answer.

'I'm just down here,' she whispered as they reached the top of the stairs. 'You're over that way, right?'

Zeke nodded, but made no effort to head to his own room. After a moment Thea moved towards her door, very aware of him still behind her.

Hand on the door handle, she stopped again. 'What do you want, Zeke?' she asked, looking at the door in front of her.

She felt his sigh, a warm breath against her neck. 'I want to be sure.'

'Sure of what?'

'Sure that you're...happy. That this is really what you want. Before I leave.'

'You're not going to come and visit again, are you?' She'd known that even as he'd talked about being Uncle Zeke. She'd known the truth of it all along. She already knew the answers to all her questions in her heart.

Zeke was here to say goodbye.

'No.'

She turned at the word, and found herself trapped between Zeke's body and the door. He had one arm braced against the wood above her head, the other at his side, fist clenched.

'Why?' More of a breath than a question.

'I need…I need to move on. Away from my family, from yours. For good.'

'Eight years wasn't long enough for you to stop hating us, then?'

'I didn't—'

He stopped short of the lie, which Thea appreciated even as his meaning stabbed her heart. She'd known he hated her. She couldn't let herself be surprised by the confirmation.

'It's not about that any more,' Zeke said instead. He gave a low chuckle. 'I've spent so long caught up in it, in proving myself to my father even as I hated him. So long living my life because of my past, even if I didn't realise I was doing it. And it's time to stop now. Time to build a life for myself, I guess.'

Without us, Thea finished for him in her head.

'So what I need to know is—*are* you happy? Is this really what you want? Or is it just what you think you're supposed to do?'

Zeke's gaze caught hers as he asked his questions, and Thea knew she couldn't look away from those dark eyes even if she'd wanted to.

Was this what she wanted? She thought about Flynn. About how easy it was with him compared to in her previous disastrous attempts at relationships. About everything she could have with him. This wasn't just for their fathers, this time, or even for Helena. This was for her. To give her security, the safety of knowing her place in the world. Knowing where she belonged.

She blinked, and told Zeke, 'This is what I want.'

Time stretched out between them as he stared into her

eyes as if scanning for truths. Finally his eyelids fluttered down, and Thea snapped her gaze away.

'Okay…' Zeke spoke softly, and she was sure she heard relief in the word. 'Okay.'

When she looked back he lowered his lips and kissed her, soft and sweet, before stepping away.

'I hope to God you're not lying to me this time, Thea,' he said, and he turned and walked away to his room.

Thea stood and watched him go, the wood of the door at her back and her grip on the door handle the only things holding her up.

'So do I,' she whispered when his door had closed behind him.

Loosening his tie, Zeke threw himself onto the bed and pulled out his phone. He'd promised Deb an update when he arrived, but between Thea in her underwear and thwarting his father he hadn't had much of a chance.

He checked his watch; London was behind them anyway. She'd still be up.

'So?' Deb said when she answered. Her usual greetings and pleasantries were apparently not deemed necessary for him. 'How's it going?'

'My father wants to buy This Minute.'

'He heard we were selling to Glasshouse?' Deb asked, but there didn't seem to be much of a question in her words. More of a sense of inevitability.

Suspicion flared up. 'Yeah. Any idea how that might have happened?'

'Not a clue,' she replied easily. 'But it's kind of handy, don't you think?'

'No.' Had she leaked it? Why? He should be mad, he supposed, but he trusted Deb. She always had a perfectly logical reason for her actions, and he was kind of curious to find out what it was this time.

'I do,' she said. 'I mean, with two interested parties the price will go up, for starters. And, more than that, this gives you a chance to decide what you really want.'

'Other than to get out of here?'

'That's one option,' Deb said. 'The other is to return to the family fold.'

Zeke remembered the look on his father's face when he'd turned him down. That had felt good. 'I think I already burnt that bridge tonight.'

'That works too.' Deb sounded philosophical about the whole thing. 'At least it was your choice to make this time.'

Sometimes Zeke really regretted the occasional late-night drinking sessions with his business partner. His tongue got loose after alcohol, and she knew him far too well as a result.

'Anyway, it's done,' he said, steamrollering past any analysis of his relationship with his father that she had planned. 'Now I just need to get through the wedding and then I can get back to my real life again.'

'Ah, yes. "The Wedding".' Her tone made it very clear that it had capital letters.

'That is what I came here for.'

'And how was it? Seeing Thea again?'

A vision of her standing there, wedding dress around her waist, flooded his mind. But Deb really didn't need to know about that. 'Fine.'

'You think she really wants to marry your brother?'

'I do.' He was just unsure about her motives.

'Then do you really have to stay?'

'I'm the best man, Deb. Kinda necessary to the proceedings.'

'Zeke…' Her voice was serious now, and he knew it was time to stop joking.

'It's fine. It's just a couple of days and I can put it all behind me.'

'You don't have to put yourself through this, you know. If you're satisfied that she's not being coerced into this by your father—'

'Oh, I'm pretty sure she is.'

'But you said—'

'Which doesn't mean she doesn't want to go through with it.' He sighed. Explaining the peculiarities of the Morrison and Ashton families to outsiders was never easy. 'Look, I need to stay. I need to see this through. It's the only way I'm ever going to…I don't know.'

'Have closure?' Deb said, knowing his own thoughts better than himself as usual. That was always disturbing. 'Fine. But if you need me to manufacture a work emergency to get you out of there…'

'I know where you are. Thanks, Deb.'

'Any time.' She paused, and he got the impression she wasn't quite done with him yet. 'Just…don't stay just to punish yourself, okay?'

'Punish myself for what?'

'Leaving her in the first place.'

The phone went dead in his hand. Apparently goodbyes were no longer necessary, either. He tossed it onto the bedside table and flopped back onto the bed.

This time Deb didn't know what she was talking about. Zeke had absolutely nothing to feel sorry for.

He just hoped Thea knew that, too.

Thea didn't sleep.

She dotted concealer under her eyes the next morning, knowing that Helena would spot the dark shadows anyway.

She'd just have to tell her that it was pre-wedding nerves. Which would no doubt lead to another rousing rendition of the *'It's not too late to back out'* chorus. Still, that had to be better than telling her sister the truth.

The truth about the past, that was. Thea wasn't even sure if *she* understood the truth of her and Zeke in the present.

Helena had laid out her chosen outfit for Thea to wear the day before her wedding and Thea slipped into the pale linen dress without question. One of the advantages of having a younger sister with an eye for style, colour and fashion was never having to worry if she'd chosen the right outfit for an occasion. This week, more than ever, she needed the boost to her confidence of knowing she looked good.

She appreciated it even more when, as she reached the bottom of the stairs, she was accosted by Ezekiel Ashton, Senior.

'Thea! Excellent. I just need a little word with you, if you wouldn't mind.'

Whether she minded or not, Ezekiel ushered Thea into his temporary office—away from the tempting smells of hot coffee and pastries.

Ezekiel's desk was covered in papers and files, his laptop pushed away to the corner, precariously balanced on a stack of books. Thea cleared a ream of paper covered in numbers from the visitor's chair and sat down. His office at the company headquarters was usually neat to the point of anal. Had he been up all night working after his meeting with Zeke? Or was he just missing his terrifyingly efficient PA Dorothy? And, either way, what exactly did he think he needed Thea for?

What if this wasn't business? What if this was some sort of *'welcome to the family, don't hurt my son'* talk? And, if so, how could she be sure which son? Because he was a little late for one of them...

Laughter bubbled up in her chest and Thea swallowed it down as Ezekiel creakily lowered himself into his chair. This was Ezekiel Ashton. Of course it was going to be about business.

'Now, Thea. I appreciate that work might not be your highest priority today, given your imminent nuptials. But this wedding has given us a unique opportunity. One I need you to take full advantage of.'

He gave her a meaningful look across the desk, and Thea's heart sank. This was business, yes, but it was personal, too. This was about Zeke.

'What are you hoping I'll be able to do?' Thea crossed her legs and stared back at her father-in-law-to-be. She couldn't promise anything when it came to Zeke. She'd burnt that bridge long ago. But how to explain that to Ezekiel without telling the whole miserable story?

Ezekiel leant back in his chair, studying her. 'Zeke has always been...fond of you.'

He waited, as if for confirmation, and Thea forced a nod.

'We were friends. When we were younger.'

'I'm hoping you might be able to utilise that friendship.'

No sugarcoating it, then. Not that she'd really expected any such thing from Ezekiel.

'We haven't seen each other in eight years,' Thea pointed out. 'And we didn't...we weren't on the best of terms when he left.'

A slightly raised eyebrow was the only hint that this came as a surprise to Zeke's father. 'Still. After all this time I'm sure you can both forgive and forget.'

Forgive? Thea thought she'd managed that years ago, until Zeke had shown up and reminded her of all the reasons she had to be angry with him. Almost as many as he had to be angry with her.

Forget? Never.

Thea took a breath. Time to refocus the conversation. 'This is about This Minute, right?'

Ezekiel gave a sharp nod. 'I'm sure you can understand the value to Morrison-Ashton of bringing Zeke's little business under the company umbrella.'

'I'd hardly call it a "little business",' Thea said. Its turnover figures for last year had been astronomical. Far higher than their own digital news arm. 'And I think the detrimental effect of *not* buying This Minute is of far higher importance to you.'

'True.'

His gaze held a hint of grudging appreciation. *Good.* In her five years working her way up to running the PR department of Morrison-Ashton Ezekiel had never given her a single sign that he appreciated the work she did, or believed it really added value to the company. It was about time he realised she brought more than a name and some money to the table. She wasn't her father, after all.

'Which is why I need you to persuade him to sell This Minute to us,' Ezekiel finished.

Any satisfaction Thea had felt flew away. *Why did he have to choose this day to suddenly have faith in my abilities?*

'I was under the impression that Zeke had already declined your offer.' And he would continue to do so. She might not have seen him in eight years, but she knew Zeke. He'd never give his father what he wanted without a fight.

'Of course he has,' Ezekiel said, impatiently. 'Otherwise why would I need you? Zeke's letting his pride get in the way, as usual. He knows that the best thing for him and This Minute is to become part of Morrison-Ashton, and for him to take up his rightful role here.'

The role you refused to give him eight years ago. 'He seems very set on moving on to something new.'

'And selling This Minute to Glasshouse.'

'Glasshouse?'

That would be a disaster. For Morrison-Ashton, at least. This Minute would give their main competitor a huge advantage in the digital arena, and the PR fallout from Zeke Ashton defecting to Glasshouse would run and run. It would certainly eclipse any positive coverage her wedding to Flynn was likely to garner.

'Precisely,' Ezekiel said, as if he'd heard every one of her thoughts. 'We need Zeke to sell to Morrison-Ashton. For the family as much as the business. So, you'll do it?'

Could she? Would Zeke listen to her? Would he care? Or would he go out of his way to do the opposite of anything she asked, just as he did with his father? If she could make him see reason…if she could win this for them… This wouldn't just be a business victory. This would assure her place in the Ashton family more than marrying Flynn could achieve.

But even if he did listen…could she ask this of him? Could she choose the business and the family over Zeke all over again, knowing it would hurt him?

Only one way to find out.

'I'll do it.'

Zeke had never given very much thought to weddings beyond showing up in an appropriate suit and whether or not there'd be a free bar. But sitting at a small wrought-iron table at the edge of the villa's huge entrance hall, taking his time over coffee, he had to conclude that, really, weddings were a whole lot of palaver.

The villa had been humming with activity since dawn, as far as he could tell. Before he'd even made it downstairs garlands of flowers and vines had been twisted round the banisters of the staircase, the floors had been polished, and potted trees with ribbons tied around their trunks had been placed at the base of each arch that spanned the hall.

He had no doubt that every other room in the villa would be receiving similar treatment over the next twenty-four hours, but they'd started with the area most likely to be seen by the greatest number of people that day.

And, boy, were there a lot of people. Guests had started arriving very early that morning, flying in from all over the world. From his chosen seat he had a great view of the front door, through a large arch that opened onto the hall-way. Clearly not everyone was staying at the hotel down the road, as several couples and families with suitcases had pitched up already and been shown to their rooms. Family, Zeke supposed. He recognised some and recognised the looks he received even better. First the double-take, checking that it really was him. Then the raised eyebrows. Then a whisper to a companion and the whole thing started over again.

Zeke had seriously considered, more than once, taking a pen to the linen napkin he'd been given and fashioning some sort of sign.

Yes, it would say, *it really is me. Zeke Ashton Junior, black sheep, passed-over heir, broke his mother's heart and had the cheek to come back for his brother's wedding. And, no, I'm not selling my father my company, either. Shocking, isn't it?*

The only thing that stopped him was that, even if he managed to fit all that on a napkin, no one would be able to read it from the sort of distance they were keeping. So instead he smiled politely, raised his coffee cup, and refused point-blank to leave his table. People wanted to stare? Let them.

As the hour became more reasonable other people started to stop by, ostensibly to drop off presents but probably to gawp at the villa and try and catch a glimpse of the bride. Zeke wished them luck; he hadn't seen hide nor hair of her since he'd said goodnight the evening before.

That, Zeke thought ruefully, had been a mistake. Swilling the dregs of his coffee around at the bottom of his cup, he tried not to remember the way Thea had smelled, so close in the darkness, and failed. Just as he'd failed to forget every moment of that last night he'd spent with her before he left.

The way she'd smiled at him before the party. The way she'd kissed him and sworn that it didn't matter when he told her about Flynn taking his job. The way she'd supported him when he'd decided to go and face his father, tell him what he really thought of him.

How his rage had bubbled to the surface as he'd approached his father's office. How unprepared he'd been for what he'd heard there.

Mostly he remembered the moment he'd known he had to leave. Right then—that night. He remembered climbing up to Thea's window to ask her to come with him, and her tears as she told him she couldn't. Wouldn't. The way his heart had stung as he'd realised she really meant it.

Eight years and he couldn't shake that memory.

Couldn't shake the hurt, either.

Catching the eye of the maid, Zeke gave her his most charming smile. She frowned, but headed off to fetch the coffee carafe anyway. Zeke supposed she had other things she was supposed to be doing today, and he was stopping her. But no one had told *him* what to do. He might be the best man, but it seemed the title was wholly ceremonial.

Flynn had disappeared out earlier with one of their cousins, apparently not even spotting Zeke at his table. Whatever tasks there were to be performed today, Flynn seemed to have plenty of help.

Which left him here, drinking too much coffee, and overthinking things. Not ideal.

Across the wide hallway he heard heels clicking on stone and looked up, already knowing somehow who it was.

Thea looked tired, Zeke thought. Was that his fault? Had she been kept awake thinking about exactly where everything had gone wrong between them as he had? He motioned to the maid for a second coffee cup and waited for Thea to cross the hall and sit down at his table. Even if she wanted to avoid him he knew the lure of coffee would be too strong for her.

It took her a while, because another crowd of people had arrived with gifts wrapped in silver paper and too much ribbon and she'd got caught up playing hostess. Zeke watched her smiling and welcoming and thanking and thought she looked even less like the girl he remembered than she had in her wedding dress. The Thea he'd known had hated this—all the fake smiles and pretending to be delighted by the third set of champagne flutes to arrive in the last half-hour. She'd played the part well enough after her mother died, at her father's insistence, the same way she'd acted as a mother to Helena and run the Morrison household for the three of them. But she'd always escaped away upstairs at Morrison-Ashton company parties, as soon as it was at all polite. These days it seemed she relished playing the part.

Eventually Isabella arrived, her smiles and gestures even bigger than Thea's. As his mother took over the meet-and-greet, Thea stepped back from her guests, a slightly disappointed frown settling onto her forehead, looking suddenly out of place. After a moment she moved across the hallway towards him. And the coffee. Zeke had no doubt that the caffeine was more appealing to her than his presence.

'Good morning, Zeke.' Thea swept her skirt under her as she sat, and smiled her thanks at the maid as she poured the coffee. 'Did you sleep well?'

'Like a baby,' Zeke lied. 'And yourself?'

'Fine, thank you.'

'Up early on wedding business?' he asked, waving his coffee cup in the direction of the new arrivals.

'Actually, I was just catching up on a few work things before tomorrow.' Thea picked up her cup and blew across the surface. 'I'll be off for almost a month for the honeymoon, so I'm trying to make sure everything is properly handed over.'

'I'd have thought you'd have more important things to do today than work. Wedding things,' he added when she looked confused.

Thea glanced down at her coffee cup again. 'To be honest, I've been able to leave most of that to the wedding planner. And Helena and Flynn.'

'Most brides *want* to be involved in their wedding plans, you know.' At least, the ones who wanted to get married. Who were marrying a man they loved. And Zeke was beginning to think that Thea didn't fall into *either* of those categories, whatever she said.

'I didn't say I haven't been involved,' Thea said, her voice sharp. 'But at this point it's all the last-minute details and fiddly bits, and Helena is much better at making things look good than I am.'

'So, what *are* you doing today, then?' Zeke asked.

'Actually, I do have one very important wedding-related task to do,' Thea said. 'And I could really use your help.'

Zeke raised his eyebrows. 'Oh?'

Thea nodded. 'I need to buy Flynn a groom's gift. I thought you might be able to help me find something he'd like.'

He hadn't seen his brother in eight years, and he'd had precious little clue what the man liked before then. But if this was the excuse Thea needed to talk to him about whatever was really on her mind, he'd play along. It might even be fun.

'Okay,' he said, draining his coffee. 'I'll bring my car round while you get ready to go.'

But Thea shook her head. 'Oh, no. *I'm* driving.'

CHAPTER FIVE

THE MORE SHE thought about it, the more Thea was convinced that this was a brilliant idea. She could use the shopping trip to sound Zeke out on his plans for This Minute before she approached the more difficult task of convincing him to sell it to Morrison-Ashton. And at the same time she could prove exactly how happy she was to be marrying Flynn by choosing her husband-to-be the perfect wedding gift.

Plus, it got her out of the villa—*and* she got to drive. That was almost enough to assuage the twinges of guilt that still plagued her about her mission that morning.

'Why am I not surprised?' Zeke asked as she pulled up outside the front door in her little red convertible.

'I like to drive.' Thea shrugged, her hands never leaving the wheel as Zeke opened the passenger door and lowered himself into the seat. 'It was an engagement present from Flynn.'

Well, he'd given it to her anyway. She rather suspected that Helena had helped him choose it. Flynn's idea of appropriate gifts tended to be more along the line of whatever the jeweller recommended.

'Of course it was.' Zeke buckled up his seat belt and rested his arm along the side of the door.

He looked casual enough, but Thea knew he was gripping the seat with his other hand. He'd complained regularly about her driving in the eleven months between her passing her test and him leaving.

'So, where are we going?'

'There's a small town just twenty minutes' drive or so away.' Smoothly, Thea pulled away from the villa and headed down the driveway, picking up speed as they passed another load of guests coming up. She'd just have to pretend she hadn't seen them later. 'It has some nice little shops, and there's a wonderful trattoria where we can stop for lunch.'

'Sounds nice. And I'm honoured that you're choosing to spend your last day of single life with me. Really.'

Thea rolled her eyes and ignored him. There was plenty of time to deal with Zeke and his terrible sense of what counted as funny once they reached the town. For now, she just wanted to enjoy the drive.

Zeke fiddled with the car stereo as Thea turned off onto the main road, and soon they were flying through the gentle hills and green and yellow fields of the Tuscan countryside to the sound of the classic rock music he'd always insisted on.

'I *know* I don't own this CD,' Thea said—not that she cared. Somehow it sounded right. As if they'd fallen back in time to the day she'd passed her driving test, just a few weeks after her seventeenth birthday, and Zeke had let her drive his car for the first time.

Zeke held up his phone, connected to the stereo by a lead she hadn't known existed. 'You know me. I never travel without a proper soundtrack.'

The summer sun beamed down on them as they drove along the winding road, past farms and other villas and the occasional vineyard. She'd have two weeks to explore this land with Flynn, Thea thought. Two whole weeks to get used to the idea of being his wife, to get to know him as her husband, before they headed back to London to set up their new home together. It would be perfect.

The heat on her shoulders relaxed her muscles and she realised that Zeke was blissfully silent beside her, not even commenting on her speed, as any other passenger might have done. Maybe he was remembering that first trip out, too. Maybe he was remembering what had happened afterwards, when they'd found a ruined barn on the edge of a nearby farm and he'd spread his jacket out over the hay as he laid her down and kissed her…

Thea glanced at the speedometer and relaxed her foot off the accelerator just a touch.

Time to think of calmer things. Like Flynn, and their honeymoon.

Eventually she slowed down to something approaching the speed limit as they passed rows of stone houses on the outskirts and joined the other traffic heading over the bridge into the town. Thea pulled into the same parking space she'd used the last time she'd visited, just outside the main *piazza*. She grabbed her handbag, waiting for Zeke to get out before she locked the car.

'So,' he asked, pushing his sunglasses up onto his head as he stepped into the shade of the nearest building, 'where first?'

Thea stared down the street, through its red stone arches and paving, and realised she hadn't a clue. What *did* you buy your future husband as a wedding gift, anyway? Especially one who, even after decades of friendship, you didn't actually know all that well?

Glinting glass caught her eye, and she remembered the jeweller's and watch shop she and Helena had found down a winding side street off the *piazza*. Surely there'd be something there?

'This way,' she said, striding in what she hoped was the right direction through the crowds gathered to watch a street entertainer in the *piazza*.

'Where you lead…' Zeke said easily, letting her pass before falling into step with her.

Thea's stride faltered just for a moment. He didn't mean anything by it, she was sure—probably didn't even remember the song. But at his words a half-forgotten melody lodged in her head, playing over and over. A promise to always follow, no matter what.

Her mum had sung it often, before she died. And Thea remembered singing along. The tune was as much a part of her childhood as bickering with Helena over hairbands and party shoes. But more than that she remembered singing it to Zeke, late at night, after half a bottle of champagne smuggled upstairs from the party below. Remembered believing, for a time, that it was true. That she'd follow him anywhere.

Until he'd actually asked her to leave with him.

Shaking her head to try and dislodge the memory, she realised they were there and pushed open the shop door. There was no time for dwelling on ancient history now. She was getting married tomorrow.

And she still needed to find her groom the perfect gift.

'Right,' she said. 'Let's see what this place has that screams *Flynn*.'

The answer, Zeke decided pretty quickly, was not much.

While Thea examined racks of expensive watches and too flashy cufflinks he trailed his fingers over the glass cases and looked around at the other stuff. Flynn wasn't a flashy cufflinks kind of guy, as far as he remembered. But maybe Thea knew better these days.

He glanced over and she held up a gold watch, its oversized face flashing in the bright overhead lights. 'What about this?'

'Flynn has a watch,' Zeke pointed out.

'Yeah, but maybe he'd like a new one. From his wife.'

'Wife-to-be. And I doubt it. The one he wears was Grandad's.' He'd spotted it on his brother's wrist the night before, at dinner, and stamped down on the memory of the day their father had given it to him.

'Oh.' Thea handed the watch back to the assistant. 'Maybe we'll look at the cufflinks instead, then.'

With a sigh, Zeke turned back to the other cases, filled with precious gems and metals. Maybe he should get something for his mother. Something sparkly would probably be enough to make up for any of the apparent pain Thomas had said she'd felt at his departure. Not that Zeke had seen any actual evidence of that pain.

Maybe she was just too caught up in the wedding festivities to remember that she'd missed him. It wouldn't be the first time that other people, other events, had taken precedence over her own sons.

A necklace caught Zeke's eye: pale gold with a bright blue sapphire at the centre. The same colour as Thea's dress the night before. He could almost imagine himself fastening it around her neck as they stood outside her room—a sign that he still...what? Cared? Remembered what they'd had? Regretted how things had ended? Wanted her to be happy? Knew that even though they'd both moved on they'd always be part of each other's past?

That was the hardest thing, he decided. Not even knowing what he wanted to tell Thea, what he needed her to understand. It wasn't as simple as hating her—it never could be, with Thea. But it wasn't as if he'd shown up here this weekend to tell her not to marry Flynn, to run away with him at last instead. As they should have done eight years ago.

No, what he felt for Thea was infinitely more complicated. And if there was a single piece of jewellery that could convey it to her, without him having to find the words, he'd buy it for her in a heartbeat—no matter the cost. But there wasn't.

With a sigh, Zeke dragged his gaze to the next case, only to find tray after tray of sparkling diamond solitaires glinting up at him.

Engagement rings. *Not helpful, universe. And why choose now to get a sense of humour, huh?*

Besides, she already had one of those. He'd glimpsed it flashing in the candlelight at dinner, recognising it as his grandmother's, and had barely even managed to muster any surprise about it. What else would the favoured Ashton heir give to his fiancé-cum-business partner? They were building an empire together, based on their joint family history.

A history Zeke had all but been written out of eight years ago.

'I'm going to have to think about it,' Thea told the shop assistant apologetically, and Zeke, realising he was still staring at the engagement rings, spun round to face her.

'We're leaving?'

'For now,' Thea said.

Zeke followed her out of the shop, letting the door swing shut behind him. 'Nothing that screamed *Flynn*, huh?'

'Not really. He's not really a flashy cufflinks kind of guy, is he?'

Something tightened in Zeke's chest, hearing her echo his thoughts, but he couldn't say if it was because she knew Flynn better than he'd thought or because her thought processes still so closely resembled his.

'So, where next?' he asked, trying to ignore the feeling.

'Um, there's a leather shop down here somewhere.' She waved her hand into an arcade of small, dark but probably insanely expensive shops, hidden under the arched stone roof. She hadn't even let Helena explore them properly last time. 'Do you think Flynn needs a new briefcase?'

'I think Flynn will love whatever you buy him, because it's from you.'

Thea gave him a look. One that suggested she was trying to evaluate if he might have been taken over by aliens recently. 'Seriously?'

'Okay, I think he'll pretend to love it, whatever it is, because that's the appropriate thing to do.'

'And Flynn *does* like appropriate.' She sighed and headed towards the leather shop anyway. 'Do you remember the hideous tie you bought him that last summer?'

'He wore it for his first day at work,' Zeke said, relishing the thought all over again. It had been the most truly horrendous tie he'd been able to find anywhere. Expensive, of course, so that his mother couldn't object. But hugely inappropriate for the serious workplace with its neon tartan. The perfect graduation gift for the perfect brother. Zeke had known Flynn would wear it just so as not to offend him. And that Flynn would never realise it was a joke gift.

'He changed it on the train before going into the office,' Thea told him, thus ruining a perfect memory.

'Seriously? That's a shame. I did love thinking of him sitting in meetings with the board wearing that tie,' Zeke said wistfully.

'He's probably still got it somewhere,' Thea said. 'He might not be stupid enough to wear it for work, but he's definitely sentimental enough that he won't have thrown it away. After all, it was the last thing you gave him before...'

'Before I left,' Zeke finished for her. 'Yeah, I don't think he was as bothered by that as you think.' Seemed like no-body had been.

She gave him a small sad smile. 'Then maybe I do know your brother better than you, after all.'

Did she? She should—she was marrying the guy. But the very fact she'd admitted she wasn't sure that she did... The contradictions buzzed around Zeke's brain, and at the heart of them was the disturbing thought that maybe Flynn *had* cared after all.

And another question. Had Thea?

The problem, Thea decided, wasn't that she didn't *know* what sort of things Flynn liked. It was just that he knew them better and had, in pretty much every case, provided them for himself. He already had the perfect briefcase, his grandfather's watch and a reliable pair of cufflinks. Whatever the item, he'd have researched it, chosen the best-quality one he required, and been satisfied with his purchase. Whatever she bought would be used a few times, to show his appreciation, then shoved to the back of a cupboard like that hideous neon tartan joke tie.

This whole trip had been a mistake. She'd wanted to show Zeke that she knew her fiancé, that they were in tune as a couple. Instead all she seemed to be proving was that whatever she brought to the marriage wasn't really required.

No. This wasn't about briefcases and watches. She brought a lot more to the table than material goods. She wasn't her father, just providing the money and then sitting back to watch the tide of success come rolling in. She was part of the company, part of Flynn's life, and part of their future together.

Which was great as a pep talk, but rubbish at helping her find a wedding present for her husband-to-be.

'What about this one?' Zeke held up a tan leather hand-bag. 'It's a man bag!'

'I'm pretty sure it's not,' Thea said. 'It has flowers decorating the strap.'

'Flynn's secure enough in his masculinity to carry it off,' Zeke argued, slinging the bag over his shoulder and pouting like a male model.

'I am *not* buying him the wedding present equivalent of a neon tartan tie, Zeke.' Thea turned back to the brief-cases and heard him sigh behind her.

'Then what *are* you going to buy him?' Zeke picked up a black briefcase and flipped the latch open. 'Hasn't he already got one of these?'

'Yes.'

'So does he need a new one?'

'No.'

'Then can we go for lunch?'

Thea sighed. He did have a point, and she *was* hungry. She'd missed breakfast, thanks to Ezekiel Senior and his request.

She tensed at the memory. Never mind the perfect wedding gift, she had another job to do today. And lunch would be the perfect time to broach the subject. Preferably after Zeke had enjoyed a glass or two of wine. Or three. Three might be the magic number.

'Come on, then,' she said, opening the door and preparing to leave the cool shadows of the shopping arcade behind and step back out into the piazza. She waved a hand in the direction of a familiar-looking dark alleyway. 'The little trattoria I was talking about is down here somewhere.'

It wasn't fancy, but Zeke had never been one for the expensive restaurants and big-name places. He'd used to prefer hidden gems and secret spots that were just their own. She was always surprised, even after so long, when she caught a magazine photo of him at some celebrity chef's opening night at a new restaurant, or on the red carpet with some actress or another. That wasn't the Zeke she remembered. And now, spending time with him again, she wondered if it was even the Zeke he'd become. Was it just that being seen was the only way he had to let his father know that he was a success now, in his own right?

Maybe she'd ask him. After the wedding. And after she'd persuaded him to sell This Minute to his father.

So probably never, then.

Thea pushed open the heavy painted wood door under a sign that just read 'Trattoria' and let Zeke in first. He smiled at the nearest waitress and she found them a table next to the window without hesitation; only a few other tables were occupied. Thea couldn't help but think this was probably a good thing. If Zeke threw pasta all over her when she tried to talk to him about his father at least there wouldn't be too many witnesses. Helena would be cross about the dress, though…

'Can I get you some drinks?' the waitress asked, her English clearly far better than Thea's Italian had ever been. She let Zeke order a local beer before she asked for a soft drink. Alcohol really wasn't going to help the conversation they needed to have.

'So, you've been here before?' Zeke asked, looking around him at the faded pictures on the stone walls and the bare wooden tables.

The small windows had all been thrown open to let in air, but the heat of the day and the lack of breeze meant that not much coolness was moving around, save from the lazy spin of the lone ceiling fan. Thea's dress had started to stick to her back already, and she longed for that soft drink.

'I came here with Helena last week,' she said. 'Just

after we arrived. I can recommend the *pappardelle* with wild boar sauce.'

'With Helena? Not Flynn?' Zeke pressed.

Thea wondered why he cared anyway. He'd left, and had every intention of leaving again, without even the faint hope that he might return this time. What did he care if she married Flynn or not? Besides not letting his brother win, of course.

Maybe that was what this came down to. All Zeke wanted was to prove a point and then he'd move on. In which case she had pretty much no chance of talking him into selling them This Minute.

But she still had to try.

'No, not with Flynn. He didn't fly in until a couple of days ago. They needed him in the office.'

'But they didn't need you?'

Dammit. Why did Zeke always know exactly what niggled at her? And why did he always have to push at that point?

'My planning for the wedding kind of *is* part of my job at the moment.' Thea toyed with the menu in her hand so she didn't have to see his reaction to that.

'Of course,' Zeke said. 'The final union of the two biggest families in media. It's quite the PR stunt.'

'It's also my life,' Thea snapped back.

'Yeah, but after the last twenty-four hours I still can't tell which of those is more important to you.'

Thea looked up, searching for a response to that one, and gave an inward sigh of relief when she saw the waitress coming over with their drinks.

'Are you ready to order?' she asked, placing the glasses on the table.

Zeke smiled at her—that charming, happy-go-lucky

smile he never gave Thea any more. 'I'll have the wild boar *pappardelle*, please. I hear it's excellent.'

'The same, please,' Thea said. But she wasn't thinking about food. She was thinking about how she'd let her work become her life, and let her life drift away entirely.

Zeke sipped his beer and watched Thea, lost in thought across the table. He'd thought it would be fun, needling her about how her wedding was actually work. He'd had a run of honeymoon jokes lined up in his head—ones he knew she'd hate. But now…well, the humour had gone.

'I'm sorry,' he said, even though he wasn't sure he was, really. He'd only told the truth, after all. Something that happened far too little in their families.

'You're *sorry*?' Thea asked disbelievingly.

Zeke shrugged. 'Not really the done thing, is it? Upsetting the bride the day before her wedding.'

'I'm not upset.'

'Are you sure? Because you look a little…blotchy.' The way she always had moments before she started crying.

But Thea shook her head, reaching for her glass with a steady hand. 'I'm fine. Like you say, you've been back less than twenty-four hours. I don't expect you to understand the relationship and the agreement that Flynn and I have developed and nurtured over the past two years.'

'Two years? You've been with him that long?'

'Yes. You don't think marriage is something I'd rush into, do you?'

Actually, he'd assumed that the idea had come up in a board meeting, that their respective fathers had put forward a proposal document to each of them and they'd weighed up the pros and cons before booking the church. But Zeke didn't think she'd appreciate *that* analysis.

'You did last time,' he said instead. 'With What's-his-name.'

'Cameron,' she supplied. 'And how did you know about him?'

'I wasn't thinking about him.' How many guys *had* she almost married since he'd left? 'I meant the Canadian.'

'Scott.'

'Yeah. I read about him on our Canadian news site. Hockey player, right?'

'Right.'

'Whirlwind engagement, I heard.'

'And he was equally quick with the cheating, as it turned out.'

'Ah.' He hadn't known that. All that had been reported was that the wedding had been called off with hours to spare. So like Thea to protect the guy's reputation even as he was hurting her. 'So who was this Cameron guy, then?'

'A business associate. Turned out he loved my business, and my money, a lot more than he loved me.'

'Never mix business with pleasure, huh?' Zeke said, before remembering that that was exactly what she was doing with Flynn. 'I mean...'

Thea sighed. 'Don't worry. I am well aware of the disastrous reputation of my love-life. You can't say anything I haven't heard before.'

He hated seeing her like this. So certain she would make a mistake. Was that why she was marrying Flynn? The safest bet in a world full of potential mistakes?

Sometimes a woman has to choose the safest road, Zeke. We can't all afford to hike the harder trails if we want to arrive safely.' The words were his mother's, eight years old now, but he could see their truth in Thea's face. For the first time he wondered who Thea would have become if her own mother had lived. Or if Thomas Morrison had never met Ezekiel Ashton. Would she be happier? Probably, he decided.

'You weren't always rubbish at love,' Zeke said, the words coming out soft and low.

Her gaze flashed up to meet him, as if she was looking for a hidden jibe or more mockery. He tried to keep his expression clear, to show her that all he meant was the words he'd said.

Clearly he failed. 'Yeah, right. Funny man. Of course you know *exactly* how early my failure at love started.'

'I didn't mean—' he started, but she cut him off.

'My first love—you—climbed out of a window to escape from me on my eighteenth birthday, Zeke. I think we can all see where the pattern started.' Bitterness oozed out of her voice, but all Zeke could hear was her saying, *'No, Zeke. I can't.'* Eight years and the sound had never left him.

Hang on. 'Wait. Are you blaming *me* for your unlucky love-life?' Because as far as he was concerned he was the one who should be assigning blame here.

'No. Yes. Maybe.' She twisted her napkin in her hands, wrapping it round her fingers then letting it go again.

'I feel much better for that clarification.'

'I don't want to talk about this any more.'

She might not, but after eight years Zeke had some things he wanted to say. And she was bloody well going to listen. 'And, in the name of accuracy, I wasn't trying to escape you. In fact you might recall me begging you to come with me.' Standing on that stupid wobbly trellis, wrecking whatever that purple flower had been, clinging onto the windowsill. She'd looked out at him, all dark hair and big eyes, and broken his heart.

'I wouldn't call it begging,' Thea said, but even she didn't sound convinced.

'You said no. You chose to stay. You can't blame me for

that.' That moment—that one moment—had changed his entire life. Made him the person he was today. She could at least *try* to remember it right.

'You chose to leave me. So why can't I blame you? You're still blaming me. Isn't that why you're here? To make my life miserable because I made the right decision eight years ago and you hate that I was right for once?'

No. That wasn't it. That wasn't what he was doing. He was here to draw a line under everything there had ever been between them, under his bitter resentment of his family that had ruled his life for too long. Zeke was moving on.

But sometimes moving on required looking backwards. Closure—that was what this was.

'The right decision,' she'd said. 'You never once imagined what life might have been like if you'd left with me that night?' Because he had driven himself crazy with it even when he'd known it was pointless. Self-destructive, even. Had she been spared that?

Apparently not. 'Of course I did, Zeke! Endlessly, and a thousand different ways. But it doesn't change the fact that I was needed at home. That I was right to stay.'

And suddenly Zeke knew what it was he needed to move on. What it would take to get the closure he craved.

So he looked up at her and asked the question.

'Why?'

CHAPTER SIX

WHY?

As if that wasn't a question she'd asked herself a million times over the past eight years.

She knew the answer, of course. Helena. She'd needed a big sister right then, more than ever. Thea couldn't have left her, and she didn't regret staying for her for one moment.

But if she was honest that wasn't the only answer. And it wasn't the one she wanted to give Zeke. It wasn't her secret to tell, apart from anything else.

'Because we were too young. Too stupid. Zeke, I was barely eighteen, and you were asking me to leave my whole life behind. My family, my future, my plans and dreams. My place in the world. Everything.'

'I'd have been your family. Your place. Your future.'

Zeke stared at her, his face open and honest. For the first time since he'd come back Thea thought she might be seeing the boy she'd known behind the man he'd become.

'You know I'd have moved mountains to give you anything you wanted. To make every dream you had come true.'

The worst part was she did know that. Had known it even then. But she hadn't been able to take the risk.

'Perhaps. But, successful as you are now, I bet it wasn't like that to start with. You'd have had to struggle, work every hour there was, take risks with your money, your reputation.' She could see from his face it was true. 'And what did you think I'd be doing while you were doing that? I wanted to go to university, Zeke. I had my place—all ready and waiting. I didn't want to give that up to keep house for you while you chased your dream.'

'I wouldn't… It wouldn't have been like that.'

'Wouldn't it?'

'No.' He sounded firmer this time. 'Look, I can't change the past, and I can't say what would have happened. But, Thea, you know me. *Knew* me, at least. And you have to know I would never have asked you to give up your dreams for mine.'

'Sorry…' the waitress said, lowering their plates to the table. 'I didn't mean to… Enjoy!'

She scampered off towards the kitchen and Thea wondered how much she'd heard. How much she was now re-telling to the restaurant staff.

Zeke hadn't even looked at his lunch. 'Tell me you know that, Thea. I wouldn't have done that.'

Thea loaded pasta onto her fork. 'Maybe you wouldn't. Not intentionally. But it happens.' She'd seen it happen to too many friends, after they got married or when they started a family. At eighteen, she didn't think she'd have had the self-awareness to fight it.

'What about now, then?' Zeke asked, still looking a little shaken. 'Do you really think it will be different with Flynn?'

'Yes,' Thea said, without hesitation. She knew about business—knew what she needed to do there. Her marriage with Flynn would only enhance that. She wouldn't give it up just to be someone's wife. 'We've talked about it. About our future. We both know what we're getting into.'

Had it all written down in legalese, ready to be signed along with the marriage register.

Their conversation on the terrace the night before came back to her and she felt a jangle of nerves and excitement when she thought about what she'd agreed to now. Maybe that—a family—would be what she needed to make the whole thing feel real. She knew it was what Flynn wanted, after all. She frowned. But they hadn't spoken yet about what would happen then. Would he expect her to stay at home and look after the kids? If so, they had a problem.

Mentally, she added the topic to the list of honeymoon discussions to have. They had time. They hadn't even had sex yet, for heaven's sake.

The thought was almost amusing—especially sitting here with her fiancé's brother, a guy she had actually slept with. Lost her virginity to, in fact. *Along with my heart.*

Was that why none of the others had stuck? She had wondered sometimes, usually late at night, if Zeke had broken something inside her. If, when he'd left, he'd taken something with him she could never get back. But now he was here and she'd decided she was better off without whatever it was he'd taken. Better off choosing a sensible, planned sort of relationship. Maybe it didn't burn with the same intensity, but she stood a better chance of making it out without injury.

She might not have been able to fulfil the role her father had hoped she would, after her mother's death. Maybe she hadn't been a great hostess or housekeeper, or able to help Helena in the way a mother would have. But those were never supposed to be her roles, anyway. Not in her father's household. This time she'd found her own role. Her own place in her own new family. And she wasn't giving that up.

She couldn't. Not when she risked returning to that

empty, yawning loneliness that had followed Zeke's departure. With Zeke gone, Helena sent away for months, her father locked in his study and Isabella taking over everything Thea had thought was her responsibility…the isolation had been unbearable. As if the world had shifted in the wake of that horrible night and when it had settled there'd been no room for Thea any more. Nowhere she felt comfortable, at home.

And she'd been looking for it ever since. University hadn't provided it, and the holidays at home, with Helena floating around the huge house like a ghost, certainly hadn't. Working her way up at Morrison-Ashton, proving she wasn't just there because of her father, that had helped. But a corner office wasn't a home, however hard she worked.

Flynn…their marriage, their family…he could be. And Thea couldn't let Zeke, or anyone, make her question that.

She watched Zeke, digging into his *pappardelle* and wondered why it was he'd really come back. Not for her—he'd made that much clear. So what was he trying to achieve?

'Zeke?'

He looked up from his bowl, eyes still unhappy. 'Yeah?'

'Why did you come back? Really? I mean, I know it wasn't just for my wedding. So why now?'

With a sigh, Zeke dropped his fork into his bowl and sat back. 'Because…because it was time. Because I'm done trying to win against my father. I'm done caring what he thinks or expects or wants. I'm ready to move on from everything that happened eight years ago.'

'Including me?'

'Including you.'

Thea took a breath, held it, and let it out. After this week they'd be done with each other for good. She'd be married, and the past wouldn't matter any more. It felt…strange. Like an ache in a phantom limb. But she felt lighter, too, at the idea that everything could be put behind them at last.

Except, of course, she had one more thing to do before she could let him go.

Her gaze dropped down to her bowl as guilt pinged in her middle. This might be the one thing she could do to make sure Zeke never came back. But it was also one more step towards earning her place as an Ashton. And that meant it was worth it.

The way Thea's body relaxed visibly at his words left Zeke tenser than ever. Was she that relieved to be finally rid of even the memory of him? Or, like him, was she just so tired of lugging it all around every day? Was she happy to have the path clear for her happy-ever-after with Flynn? Or just settling for the safety of a sensible business marriage?

He'd ask…except those kind of questions—and caring about the answers—didn't exactly sound like leaving her behind.

One more day. He'd make sure she got down the aisle, said 'I do', and rode off into the sunset. Then his new life, whatever it turned out to be, could begin.

'Before you leave us all behind completely, though…' Thea said.

Zeke's jaw clenched. There was always one more thing with Thea.

'I need to talk to you about something.'

A hollow opened up inside him. This was it. Whatever reason Thea had for dragging him out to buy a stupid gift for his brother, he was about to find it out. And suddenly he didn't want to know. If he had to leave her behind for ever he wanted to have this last day. Wanted to leave believing that she'd honestly wanted to spend time with him before he went. For the sake of everything they'd had once and knew they could never have again. Was that so much to ask?

Apparently so.

'I spoke to your father this morning,' Thea said, and Zeke's happy bubble of obliviousness popped.

'Did you, now?' He should have known that. Should have guessed, at least. He'd let himself get side-tracked by the experience of being with Thea again, and now he was about to get blindsided. Another reason why being around Thea Morrison was bad for his wellbeing.

'He wanted me to talk to you about—'

'About me selling This Minute to Morrison-Ashton,' Zeke finished for her. It wasn't as if his father had any other thoughts in relation to him.

'Yes.'

One simple word and the hollow inside him collapsed in on itself, like a punch to the gut folding him over.

'No,' he said, and let the anger start to fill him out again.

How could she ask? After everything they'd been to each other, everything they'd once had…how did she even dare?

His skin felt too hot and his head pounded with the betrayal. He knew exactly why she was doing it. To make sure he left. To make sure her perfect world went back to the way she thought it should be. To buy her place in his family, at his brother's side.

Because Morrison-Ashton and their families had always mattered more to her than he had. And he should have remembered that.

Thea pulled the face she'd always used to pull when he'd been annoying her by being deliberately difficult. He'd missed that face until now. Now it just reminded him how little his feelings mattered to her.

'Zeke—'

'I'm not selling you my company, Thea.' He bit the words out, holding in the ones he really wanted to say. He wasn't that boy any more—the one who lost control from just being near her. This was business, not love. Not any more.

'Your father is willing to match whatever Glasshouse are offering...'

'I don't care.' *Just business*, he reminded himself.

'And even if you don't want to take up a position within Morrison-Ashton we could still look at share options.'

'I said no.' The rage built again, and he flexed his hand against his thigh to keep it from shaking.

'Our digital media team are putting together a—'

'Dammit, Thea!' Plates rattled as Zeke slammed his fist down on the table and the restaurant fell silent. 'Will you just listen to me for once?'

'Don't shout, Zeke,' Thea said, suddenly pale. 'People are looking.'

'Let them look.' He didn't care. Why should he? He'd be out of here tomorrow. 'Because I'm going to shout until you start listening to me.'

Thea's face turned stony. Dropping her fork into her bowl, she pulled out her purse and left several notes on the table. Then she stood, picked up her bag, and walked out of the restaurant.

The rage faded the moment she was out of his sight and he was Zeke Ashton the adult again. The man he'd worked so hard to become, only to lose him the moment she prodded at a sore spot.

Picking up his bottle of beer, Zeke considered his options. Then he drained the beer, dropped another couple of notes onto the stack and followed her, as he'd always known he would.

So had she known, it seemed, which irritated him more than it should have. Thea stood leaning against the wall of the restaurant, waiting for him.

'I left a very decent tip,' he said, watching her, waiting to see which way she'd jump. 'It seemed only fair since we walked out without finishing our meals.'

'Yelling suppresses the appetite.' Thea pushed away from the wall.

'It seemed the only way to get you to listen to me.'

Turning to face him, she smiled with obviously feigned interest. 'I'm listening.'

Suddenly his words felt petty, unnecessary. But he said them anyway. 'I will not sell This Minute to Morrison-Ashton.'

She gave a sharp nod. 'So you've mentioned. Now, if that's all, I want to go back to the villa.'

'What about Flynn's present?' Zeke asked, matching her stride as she headed for the car at speed.

'It can wait.'

'The wedding's tomorrow. I think you're pretty much out of time on this one.'

Thea opened the car door and slid into her seat. 'So I'll give him a spectacular honeymoon present instead.'

Zeke didn't want to think about what she might come up with for that. Except he already had a pretty good idea.

'Like the present you gave me for my twenty-first?' he asked, and watched Thea flush the same bright red as her car as she started the engine.

'You have to stop that,' she said, pulling away from the kerb.

'Stop what?' he asked, just to make her say it.

She glared at him. 'Look. I'm getting married tomorrow. So all this reminiscing about the good old days is getting kind of inappropriate, don't you think?'

'Oh, I don't know.' Zeke watched her as she drove, hands firm on the wheel, shoulders far more tense than they had been on the drive in. He was getting to her. And for some reason he really didn't want to stop. 'I think the question is whether Flynn thinks it's inappropriate.'

'Flynn doesn't know.'

'You mean you're not going to tell him about our shopping trip?'

'I mean he doesn't know about us at all. That we were ever…anything to each other.'

Thea took the last turning out of the town and suddenly their speed rocketed. Plastered back against his seat, Zeke tried to process the new reality she'd just confronted him with. She'd said they didn't talk about him, but he hadn't realised it extended this far. She'd written him out of their history completely, and the pain of that cut through his simmering anger for a moment.

'But…how?' How could anyone who knew them, who had seen them together back then, not known what they were to each other? They had been seventeen and twenty-one. *Subtle* hadn't really been in their vocabulary, despite Thea's requests to keep things secret. He hadn't cared who knew. Certainly their parents had known. How could Flynn have missed it?

'He was away at university, remember?' Thea said. 'And not just round the corner, like you. He was all the way up in Scotland. I guess he just…he was living his own life. I didn't realise at first, when we…started this. But it became clear pretty quickly. He just…didn't know.'

'And you didn't think it was important enough to tell him about?' Didn't think *he* was important enough. Suddenly Zeke wanted nothing more than to remind her just how important he'd been to her once.

'Why would I? You were gone. You were never com-

ing back as far as I was concerned. And even if you did…
even now you have…'

'Even now I have, what?'

'It doesn't change anything. You and I are ancient history, remember? What difference does it make now what
we might have had eight years ago?'

But it did make a difference. Zeke couldn't say how, but
it did. And suddenly he wanted her to admit that.

Thea tried to focus on the road, but her gaze kept slipping to the side, watching Zeke's reactions. It wasn't a
test, wasn't as if she'd said anything untrue, but he wasn't
reacting quite the way she'd expected.

She knew Zeke—had always known Zeke, it seemed.
She knew that for him to come back now, into this situation…whatever his reasons…he wouldn't pass up the opportunity to drag up the past. He'd want his brother to feel
uncomfortable, to know that he'd had her first. Punishment, she supposed. Partly for her, for not leaving with
him, for breaking their deal. And partly for Flynn, for taking everything Zeke had always assumed was his.

Not telling Flynn… It had seemed like the best idea at
the time. And when Zeke had returned she'd been so relieved that she hadn't. One less thing to drive her crazy
this week. Her relationship with Flynn might not be the
most conventional, but their marriage agreement did have
a fidelity clause, and she really didn't want to have an ex-
cruciatingly awkward conversation with her fiancé and
probably their lawyers, maybe even their fathers, about
whether Zeke's return would have any effect on that.

Of course it didn't. They'd both moved on. But Flynn
liked to be thorough about these things.

'It makes a difference,' Zeke said suddenly, and Thea

tried to tune herself back into the conversation, 'because you're lying to your fiancé. My brother.'

Thea gave a harsh laugh. 'Seriously? You're going to try and play the loving brother card? Now? It's a little late, Zeke.'

'I'm the best man at your wedding, Thea. Someone tomorrow is going to ask me if I know of any reason why you shouldn't get married.'

'You don't! Me sleeping with you eight years ago is not a reason for me not to get married tomorrow.'

Zeke raised an eyebrow. 'No? Then how about you lying to your fiancé? Or the fact you left your last two fiancés practically at the altar?'

'Why were you reading up on my love-life anyway?' She hadn't thought to ask when he mentioned Scott before. She'd been more concerned with getting the conversation away from her past romantic disasters. 'I don't believe for a second you just happened to stumble across that information on your site.'

'Did you think I hadn't kept up with you? Kept track of what was going on in your life?'

'Yes,' Thea said. 'That's exactly what I thought. I thought you left and forgot all about the people you left behind.'

'I didn't leave you behind.'

The countryside sped past faster than ever, but Thea couldn't bring herself to slow down. 'Zeke, you left and you didn't look back.'

'I asked you to come with me.' His mulish expression told her that even eight years couldn't change the fact that she'd said no. Too late now, anyway.

'And I told you I couldn't.'

Zeke shook his head. 'Not couldn't. Wouldn't.'

'It was eight years ago, Zeke! Does it really matter which now?'

'Yes!'

'For the love of God, why?'

'Because I've spent eight years obsessing about it and I need closure now, dammit! Preferably before you marry my brother and send me away again.'

Thea's head buzzed with the enormity of the idea. Eight years of obsession, and now he wanted closure. Fine. She'd give him his closure.

Slamming on the brakes, Thea pulled over to the side of the road, half into a field of sunflowers, and stopped the engine. Opening the door, she stepped out onto the dusty verge at the edge of the road, waiting for Zeke to follow. He did, after a moment, walking slowly around to where she leant against the car. She waited until he stopped, his body next to hers against the warm metal.

'You want closure?' she said.

'Yes.'

He wasn't looking at her—was choosing to stare out at the bright flowers swaying in the breeze instead. Somehow that made it all a little easier.

'Fine. What do you need to know to move on?'

Now he turned, his smile too knowing. 'I need to know that *you've* moved on. That you're not still making the same bad choices you made then for the same bad reasons.'

'I made the right choice,' Thea said, quietly. 'I chose to stay for a reason.'

'For Helena. For your father.'

'Yes.'

'You were living your life for other people to avoid upsetting your family, just like you are now.'

'No. I'm living my life for me.' And making the right

decisions for the future she wanted. She had to hang on to that.

'Really? Whose idea was it for you to marry Flynn?'

'What difference does it make? I'm the one who chose to do it.'

'It makes a difference,' Zeke pressed.

Did the man not know how to just let go of something? Just once in his intense life? Was it too much to ask?

'Fine. It was your father's idea,' Thea said, bracing herself for the inevitable smugness. Lord, Zeke did love being right.

'Of course it was.' But he didn't sound smug. Didn't sound vindicated. If anything, he sounded a little sad.

Thea turned to look at him. 'Why did you ask if you already knew?'

'Because I need you to see it. I need you to see what you're doing.'

His words were intense, but his eyes were worse. They pressed her, demanded that she look the truth in the face, that she open herself up to every single possibility and weigh them all.

Thea looked away, letting her hair fall in front of her face. 'I know what I'm doing.'

Zeke shook his head. 'No, Thea. I don't think you do. So, tell me. Why did you stay when I left?'

'Why do you think? We were too young, Zeke. And besides, my family needed me. Helena needed me.' More than ever right then.

'Why?'

'Oh, I don't know, Zeke. Why do you think? Why would a motherless teenage girl *possibly* need her big sister around to look out for her?' That wasn't the whole reason, of course, but the rest of it was Helena's secret to tell.

'She had your father. And my mother.'

A bitter laugh bubbled up in her throat. 'As much as she might pretend otherwise, your mother is not actually *our* mother.'

'Just as well, really,' Zeke said, his voice low, and she knew without asking that he wasn't thinking about her marrying Flynn. He was thinking about all the things they'd done in dark corners at parties, about his twenty-first birthday, about every single time his skin had been pressed against hers.

And, curse him, so was she.

'I had to stay, Zeke,' she said.

'Give me one true reason.'

Thea clenched her hand against her thigh. Did the man simply not listen? Or just not hear anything he didn't like? 'I've given you plenty.'

'Those weren't reasons—they were excuses.'

'Excuses? My family, my future—they're excuses?' Thea glared at him. 'Nice to know you hold my existence in such high esteem.'

'That's not what this is about.'

'Then what *is* it about, Zeke?' Thea asked, exasperated. 'If you don't believe me—fine. Tell me why *you* think I stayed.'

'Because you were scared,' he said, without missing a beat.

'Ha!'

'You stayed because other people told you it was the right thing to do. Because you knew it was what your father would want and you've always, *always* done what he wanted. Because you've never been able to say no to Helena ever since your mother died.' He took a breath. 'But mostly you stayed because you were too scared to trust your own desires. To trust what was between us. To trust *me*.'

The air whooshed out of Thea's lungs. 'That's what you believe?'

'That's what I know.'

When had he got so close? The warm metal of the car at her back had nothing on the heat of his body beside her.

'You're wrong,' she said, shifting slightly away from him.

He raised an eyebrow. 'Am I?' Angling his body towards her, Zeke placed one hand on her hip, bringing him closer than they'd been in eight long years. 'Prove it.'

'How?' Thea asked, mentally chastising her body for reacting to him. This was over!

'Tell me you don't still think about us. Miss us being together. Tell me you don't still want this.'

Thea started to shake her head, to try and deny it, but Zeke lowered his mouth to hers and suddenly all she could feel was the tide of relief swelling inside her. His kiss, still so familiar after so long, consumed her, and she wondered how she'd even pretended she didn't remember how it felt to be the centre of Zeke Ashton's world.

Except she wasn't any more. This wasn't about her—not really. This was Zeke proving a point, showing himself *and* her that he could still have her if he wanted. And he'd made it very clear that he didn't—not for anything more than showing his father and his brother who had the power here. She was just another way for him to get one over on the family business.

And she had a little bit more self-respect than that, thank you.

'Thea,' Zeke murmured between kisses, his arm slipping further around her waist to haul her closer.

'No.' The word came out muffled against his mouth, so she put her hands against his chest and pushed. Hard.

Zeke stumbled back against the car, his hands abandoning her body to stop himself falling. 'What—?' He stopped, gave her one of those ironic, mocking looks she hated.

'I said no.' Thea sucked in a breath and lied. 'I *don't* still think about us. I *don't* miss what we had. It was a childish relationship that ran its course. I was ready for my own life, not just to hang on to the edges of yours. That's why I didn't come with you.' She swallowed. 'And I certainly don't want *that*. Especially not when I'm marrying your brother tomorrow.'

For once in his life Zeke was blessedly silent. Thea took advantage of the miracle by turning and getting back into the car. She focussed on her breathing…in and out, even and slow. Strapped herself in, started the engine. Familiar, easy, well-known actions.

And then she said, 'Goodbye, Zeke,' and gave him three seconds to clear the car before she screeched off back to the villa.

CHAPTER SEVEN

ZEKE STARED AFTER the cherry-red sports car kicking up dust as it sped away from him. Thea's dark hair blew behind her in the breeze, and he could still smell her shampoo, still feel her body in his arms.

He was an idiot. An idiot who was now stranded in the middle of nowhere.

Pushing his fingers through his hair, Zeke started the long trudge up the path towards the villa. At least Thea had driven him most of the way home before kicking him out.

Not that he could really blame her. He knew better than to ambush her like that. He'd just been so desperate to hear her admit it, to hear her say that she'd made a mistake not going with him that night.

That she still thought about him sometimes.

But clearly she didn't. She stood by her decision. And he had to live with that. At least for the next couple of days. Then he'd be gone, ready to start his own life for once, without the memories and the baggage of trying to prove his family wrong.

He'd told Thea he wanted closure, and she'd given it to him. In spades.

It was a long, hot, depressing walk back to the villa. By the time he got there, dusty and sweaty, the only thing he wanted in the world was a shower. It was nice, in a way, to have his desires pared down to the basics. Simpler, anyway.

Of course just because he only wanted one thing, it didn't mean he was going to get it. Really, he should have known that by now.

'Zeke!' Helena jumped up from her seat in the entrance hall, blonde waves bouncing. 'You're back! Great. I wanted to— What happened to you?'

'Your sister,' Zeke said, not slowing his stride as he headed straight for the stairs. 'She's trying to destroy my life, I think.'

'Oh,' Helena said, closer than he'd thought. Was she going to follow him all the way to his room?

'Don't worry,' Zeke told her. 'I know how to thwart her.' All he had to do was not sell his company to Morrison-Ashton—which he had no intention of doing regardless— and let her marry Flynn—which he appeared to have no choice in anyway.

Even if both things still made him want to punch some poor defenceless wall.

'Right…'

Helena sounded confused, but she was still following him. Clearly he needed to address whatever her problem was if he were to have any hope of getting his shower before the rehearsal dinner.

Sighing, Zeke stopped at the top of the stairs and leant against the cool, stone wall for a moment. 'You wanted to…?'

Helena blinked. 'Sorry?'

'You said you wanted to…'

'Talk to you!' Helena flashed him a smile. 'Yes. I did. I mean, I do.'

'Can it wait until after I've had a shower?'

She glanced down at the elegant gold watch on her slender wrist. 'Um…no. Not really.'

'Then I hope you can talk louder than the water pressure in this place.' Zeke pushed off the wall and continued towards his room. 'So, what's up, kid?'

'I'm hardly a kid any more, Zeke,' Helena said.

'I suppose not.' She had been when he'd left. Barely sixteen, and all big blue eyes and blonde curls. Actually, she was still the last two, but there was something in those big eyes. Little Helena had grown up, and he wondered how much he'd missed while he'd been gone. What had growing up in this family, this business, done to her? Because he already knew what it had done to Thea, and he wouldn't wish that on anyone.

'In fact I'm the maid of honour tomorrow. And you're the best man.'

Zeke froze outside his bedroom door. What on earth was she suggesting?

Helena's tinkling laugh echoed off the painted stone of the hallway. 'Zeke, you should see your face! Don't worry—I'm not propositioning you or anything.'

Letting his breath out slowly, so she wouldn't suspect he'd been holding it, Zeke turned the door handle. 'Never thought you were.'

'Yes, you did,' Helena said, brimming with confidence. It was nice to see, in a way. At least that hadn't been drummed out of her, the way it had Thea.

'So, what are you saying?' Zeke kicked his shoes to the corner of the room, where they landed in a puff of road dust.

'We have responsibilities. We should co-ordinate them.' Letting the door swing shut behind her, Helena dropped down to sit on the edge of his bed, folding her legs up under her.

'As far as I can tell, other than an amusing yet inoffensive speech, I'm mostly superfluous to the proceedings.' Not that he cared. He knew his role here—show up and prove a point on behalf of the family that he was still a part of Morrison-Ashton. And he'd give them that for Flynn and Thea's wedding day. Not least because he knew it would be the last thing he ever had to give them. After tomorrow he'd be free.

'You're the best man, Zeke. It takes a little more than that.'

'Like dancing with you at the reception?' Stripping off his socks, Zeke padded barefoot into the bathroom to set the shower running. It took time to warm up, and maybe Helena would take the hint by the time it was at the right temperature.

'Like making sure the groom shows up.'

Zeke stopped. 'Why wouldn't he?' Did Helena know something he didn't? That *Thea* didn't?

'Because… Well…' Helena gave a dramatic sigh and fell back to lean against the headboard. 'Oh, I don't know. Because this isn't exactly a normal wedding, is it?'

That's what he'd been saying. Not that anyone—or at least not Thea—was listening. 'I'm given to understand that this is something they both want,' he said, as neutrally as he could.

Helena gave him a lopsided smile. 'She's been giving you the same line, huh? I thought maybe she'd admit the truth to *you*, at least.'

'The truth?' Zeke asked, when really what he wanted to say was, *Why me, 'at least'?*

'I know she thinks this is what she should do,' Helena said slowly. 'That it's the right thing for the company and our families. She wouldn't want to let anyone down—least of all Isabella or Dad.'

'But…?'

Tipping her head back against the headboard, Helena was silent for a long moment. Then she said, 'But…I think she's hoping this wedding will give her something it can't. And I don't think it's the right thing for her, even if she won't admit it.'

A warm burst of vindication bloomed in Zeke's chest. It wasn't just him. Her own sister, the one she'd stayed for eight years ago, could see the mistake Thea was making. But his triumph was short-lived. There was still nothing he could do to change her decision.

Zeke sank down onto the edge of the bed. 'If you want to ask me to talk to her about it…you're about two hours too late. And, as you can see, it didn't go particularly well.' He waved a hand up and down to indicate the state of him after his long, hot, cross walk home.

Helena winced. 'What did she do? Leave you on the side of the road somewhere?'

'Pretty much.'

'Dammit. I really thought…'

'What?' Suddenly, and maybe for the first time ever, he really wanted to know what Helena thought. Just in case there was a sliver of a chance of it making a difference to how tomorrow went.

Helena gave a little one-shouldered shrug. 'I don't know. I guess I thought that maybe she'd talk to you. Open up. There was always something between you two, wasn't there? I mean, she never talked about it, but it was kind of obvious. So I thought…well, I hoped… But she's so scared of giving Dad and Isabella something else to use against her, to push her out…'

'That's what I told her,' Zeke said, but then something in Helena's words registered. 'What do you mean, push her out? And what was the first thing they used against her?'

She stared at him as if it wasn't possible he didn't already know. But then she blinked. 'Of course,' she murmured. 'It was the night you left. I told her... I told her right before her eighteenth birthday party—talk about insensitive. But I guess she never told you...'

Zeke was losing patience now. He felt as if there was a bell clanging in his head, telling him to pay attention, that this was important, but Helena kept prattling on and he *needed to know*.

'What, Helena? What did you tell her?' And, for the love of God, could this finally be the explanation he'd waited eight years for, only to have Thea deny him?

Helena gave him a long look. 'I'll tell you,' she said, her tongue darting out to moisten her lips. 'But it's kind of a long story. A long, painful story. So you go and have that shower, and I'll go and fetch some wine to make it slightly more bearable. I'll meet you back here in a little bit, yeah?'

Zeke wanted to argue—wanted to demand that she just *tell* him, already—but Helena had already slipped off the bed towards the door, and it looked as if once again he wasn't being given an option by a Morrison woman.

'Fine,' he said with a sigh, and headed for the shower.

At least he wouldn't stink of sweat and sun and roads when he finally got his closure.

She had her wedding rehearsal dinner in two hours. She should be soaking in the bath with a glass of something bubbly, mentally preparing herself for the next thirty-six hours or so. She needed to touch up a chip in her manicure, straighten her hair, check that her dress for the evening had been pressed. There were wedding presents to open, lists of thank-you notes to make, a fiancé to check in with, since she hadn't seen him all day... And at some point she should probably check with Housekeeping that

Zeke had made it home alive—if only so she could slap him again later, or something.

But Thea wasn't doing any of those things. Instead she sat in Ezekiel Ashton's office, waiting for him to get off the phone with London. Just as she had been for the last forty minutes.

'Well, that's one way of looking at it, I suppose,' Ezekiel said into the receiver, and Thea barely contained her frustrated sigh.

Dragging a folder out of her bag she flipped through the contents, wishing she could pretend even to herself that they were in any way urgent or important. At least then she wouldn't feel as if she was wasting her time so utterly.

'The thing is, Quentin…'

Thea closed the folder. He could have asked her to come back later. He could have cut short his call. He could have looked in some way apologetic. But all Ezekiel had done was wave her into the visitor's chair and cover the receiver long enough to tell her he'd be with her shortly. Which had been a blatant lie.

She'd leave, just to prove a point, except he was almost her father-in-law and he already wasn't going to like the news she was bringing.

She sighed again, not bothering to hide it this time, and realised she was tapping her pen against the side of the folder. Glancing up at the desk, she saw Ezekiel raising his eyebrows at her.

Oops. Busted.

'I think I'm going to have to get back to you on that, Quentin,' he said, in his usual calm, smooth voice. The one that let everyone else know that as far as he was concerned he was the only person in the room that mattered. Zeke had always called it his father's 'Zeus the All-Powerful' voice. 'It seems that something urgent has come up at this end.'

Like the existence of his PR Director and soon-to-be daughter-in-law. Or perhaps the possibility of buying This Minute. Thea didn't kid herself about which of those was more important to the man across the desk.

'So, Thea.' Ezekiel hung up the phone. It was a proper old-fashioned one, with a handset attached by a cord and everything. 'Dare I hope that you're here with good news about my youngest son?'

Thea winced. 'Not…exactly.'

'Ah.' Leaning back in his seat, the old man steepled his fingers over his chest. 'So Zeke is still refusing to consider selling This Minute to Morrison Ashton?'

'I'm afraid so,' Thea said. 'He…he seems quite set on his decision, I'm afraid. And he says he's ready to move on from This Minute, so even offering him positions within the company didn't seem to help. He's looking for a new challenge.'

Ezekiel shook his head. 'That boy is always looking for an impossible challenge.'

He was wrong, Thea thought. Apart from anything else, Zeke was certainly no longer a boy. He'd grown up, and even if he'd always be twenty-one and reckless in the eyes of his family, *she* could see it. Had felt it in the way he'd kissed her, held her. Had known it when he'd told her the real reasons she hadn't left with him. He saw the truth even if she didn't want to face it. She *had* been scared. Even if in the end the choice had been taken away from her, and she'd had to stay for Helena, she knew deep down she'd never really thought she'd go. Hadn't been able to imagine a future in which she climbed out of that window and followed him.

Which was strange, because it was growing easier by the hour for her to imagine running out on this wedding and chasing after him. Not that she would, of course.

And not that he'd asked.

He'd wanted her to admit her mistake, had wanted to prove a point. But, kiss aside, there'd been no real thought or mention of wanting *her*.

Maybe Ezekiel was right. Maybe she was just his latest impossible challenge.

'Well, I can't say I'm not disappointed,' Ezekiel said, straightening in his chair. 'Still, I'm glad that you tried to convince him. That tells me a lot.'

Thea blinked at him. 'Tells you what, exactly?'

'It speaks to your commitment to the company—and to Flynn, of course. And it tells me that both you and Zeke have moved past your…youthful indiscretion.'

Heat flared in Thea's cheeks at his words. *Youthful indiscretion.* As if her history with Zeke was something to be swept under the carpet and forgotten about.

But wasn't that what she was doing by not telling Flynn about it?

Thea shook her head. 'I don't think that the childhood friendship Zeke and I shared would influence either of us in the matter of a business decision,' she said, as calmly and flatly as she could manage.

'Thea,' Ezekiel said, his tone mildly chastising. 'My son was in love with you once. He would have done anything for you. That he's said no to you on this matter tells me that he has moved on, that he no longer feels that way about you. And the fact that you asked him in the first place, knowing his…*feelings* for the family business—well, as I say, it's good to know where your loyalties lie.'

Nausea crept up Thea's throat as she listened to the old man talk. She knew he was right. She chosen work and business over a man she'd once thought hung the moon. Over someone who, whatever she might say to his face, still *mattered* to her. All because the old man across the desk had asked her to.

Worst of all was the sudden and certain knowledge that he'd known exactly what he was doing. This was the only reason Ezekiel had asked her to talk to Zeke about This Minute in the first place. It had been a test. Just like suggesting that she marry Flynn. Just like Zeke asking her for one true reason why she'd stayed. Just like her father, eight years ago, when she'd broken the news to him about Helena. Just like her first two engagements.

It was all a test—a way to find out if she was worthy of being a Morrison or an Ashton. Pushing her and prodding her to see how she'd react, how she'd cope, what decision she'd make, how she'd mess up this time. Her whole life was nothing more than a series of tests.

And the worst thing was she knew she was only ever one wrong answer away from failing. Just as she'd failed Helena.

Slowly, her head still spinning with angry thoughts, Thea got to her feet. 'I'm glad that you're satisfied, sir,' she said. 'Now, if you'll excuse me, I need to go and prepare for the rehearsal dinner.'

'Of course…of course.' Ezekiel waved a hand towards the door. 'After all, your most important role in this company is still to come tomorrow, isn't it?'

Thea barely managed a stiff nod before walking too fast out of the office, racing up the stairs, and throwing up in her bathroom.

When Zeke stepped out of the bathroom, a towel tightly tied around his waist, Helena was already sitting on his bed, halfway through a large glass of wine.

'Hang on.' Grabbing his suit hanger from the front of the wardrobe, he stepped back into the steam-filled bathroom and dressed quickly. At least he'd be ready for the rehearsal dinner early, and he'd feel better having whatever conversation this was fully dressed.

Helena handed him a glass of wine and he sat on the desk chair across the room, watching her, waiting for her to start.

She bit her lip, took another sip of wine, then said, 'Okay, so this isn't a story many people know.'

'Okay...'

'But I think it's important that you know it. It... Well, it might explain a bit about how Thea became...Thea.'

Anything that did that—that could explain how the free and loving girl he'd known had become the woman who'd left him at the side of the road today—had to be some story. 'So tell it.'

Helena's whole upper body rose and fell as she sucked in a breath. 'Right. So, it was a month or so before Thea's birthday. Before you left. I was sixteen. And stupid. That part's quite important.' She dipped her head, gazing down at her hands. 'Thea was babysitting for me one night. Dad was off at some business dinner, I guess. And even though I'd told him a million times that sixteen-year-olds don't need babysitters he was very clear. Thea was in charge. What she said went, and she was responsible for anything that happened while he was out.'

'Sounds like your dad,' Zeke murmured, wondering where this was going. 'I guess something happened that night?'

'I...I wanted to go out. I asked Thea, and she said no, so I nagged and whined until she gave in. I had a date with this guy a couple of years ahead of me in school. I knew Thea didn't like him, so I kinda left that part out when I told her I was going.'

Zeke had a very bad feeling about this story all of a sudden. 'What happened?' he asked, the words coming out raw and hoarse.

'He took me to his friend's house. There was beer, and

some other stuff. And the next thing I knew...' Helena scrubbed a hand across her eyes. 'Anyway... They told me it was my own fault—that I'd said yes and I just couldn't remember. I was so ashamed that I didn't tell anyone. Not even Thea. Not until six weeks later.'

'The night of her party?' Zeke guessed. She'd been crying, he remembered, when he'd climbed in her window to tell her he was going and ask if she'd decided to come or not. He'd thought it had been because she'd decided to stay.

'Yeah. I wouldn't have, but...I was pregnant.'

The air rushed out of Zeke's lungs. 'Oh, Helena...'

'I know. So I told Thea, and she told Dad for me, and then I got sent away for the summer until the baby was born.'

Helena's voice broke at last. Zeke thought most people would have given in to tears long before. Happy-go-lucky Helena hid a core of steel.

'She was adopted, and I never saw her again.'

Zeke crossed the room in a second, wrapping an arm around her as she cried. 'I should have been here.' Helena had been a little sister to him in a way Thea never had been. They'd been more. But Helena... Helena had been important to him too, and he hadn't even said goodbye. Hadn't dreamt of what she might be going through.

Helena gave a watery chuckle. 'What could you have done? Besides, I had Thea.'

This was what she'd meant. Why she'd had to stay. He'd always thought—believed deep down—that her words about Helena and her family were excuses. But they weren't. Helena really *had* needed her. Of course she'd stayed. But why hadn't she told him?

'But there's a reason I've told you this,' Helena said, snapping him back to the present. 'You have to understand, Zeke. Things changed after that night, and you weren't there to see it. You remember how it was—how

Dad pushed her into taking over Mum's role after she died? He expected her to be able to do everything. School, the house, playing hostess for his clients, looking after me…'

'I remember,' Zeke said, bitterness leaking into his voice. She'd hated it so much. 'It was wrong. Hell, she was—what? Fourteen? Nobody should have that kind of responsibility at that age.'

'Well, she thought it *was* her responsibility. And so did he. So when all this happened…' Helena swallowed so hard Zeke could see it. 'He blamed her. Said that if she'd paid more attention it never would have happened. He took it all away from her. And that was when Isabella stepped in.'

'My mum?'

Helena nodded. 'She took over. She ran our house as well as yours. She became part of the family more than ever. She looked after me, played hostess for Dad…'

'She pushed Thea out,' Zeke finished for her. How had he not noticed that? Not noticed how little a place Thea seemed to have, even in her own wedding.

'Yeah. I wasn't here to start with, so I don't really know the whole of it. But ever since it's been like Thea's been trying to find her way back in. Find a place where she belongs.'

'And you think that's why she's marrying Flynn?'

Helena tilted her head to the side. 'I don't know. That's what I… I worry, that's all.'

And she was right to. Of *course* that was what Thea was doing. She'd practically admitted as much to him, even if he hadn't understood her reasoning.

'And the thing is, Zeke,' Helena went on, 'despite everything Thea blames herself for what happened to me and what happened next. She always has. Even though it isn't her fault—of course it isn't. But she was responsible for me that night. That's what Dad told her. And she thinks that if she hadn't let me go out that night everything would have been different.'

'*Her* fault?' Zeke echoed, baffled. 'How can she possibly…?'

'She calls it the biggest mistake she ever made.'

Suddenly Zeke was glad that Helena didn't know what Thea had given up to stay with her. He couldn't blame either of them any more. But could he make Thea see that one mistake didn't mean she had to keep making the same safe decisions her whole life?

'Thank you for telling me this, Helena.'

Helena gave a little shrug. 'Did it help?'

'Yeah. I think so.'

Pulling away, Helena watched his face as she asked, 'So, do you think you can talk Thea out of this wedding?'

'I thought I was supposed to be making sure the groom showed up on time?'

'If she decides to go through with it, yeah. But I want to be very sure that she's doing this for the right reasons. Not just because she's scared of being pushed out again for not doing what the family wants.'

Zeke grinned. 'Looks like we're on the same side, then.'

'Good.' Standing up, Helena smoothed down her dress and wiped her eyes. 'About time I had some help around here. Now, come on, best man. We've got a rehearsal dinner to get to.'

'And a wedding to get called off,' Zeke agreed, following her to the door.

He had his closure now, but he had far more, too. He had the truth. The whole story. And that was what would make all the difference when he confronted Thea this time

CHAPTER EIGHT

THEA SCANNED THE dining room through the crack of the door, then glanced down at her deep red sheath dress, wondering why she felt as if she was walking into a business dinner. Of all the people she'd recognised in the room, waiting for them to walk in, only three had been family. Everyone else was someone she'd met across a conference table. This time tomorrow she'd be married, and her whole new life would start. But she was very afraid, all of a sudden, that her new life might be a little too much like her old one.

'Ready?' Flynn asked, offering her his arm.

He looked handsome in his suit, Thea thought. All clean-shaven and broad shoulders. Safe. Reliable. Predictable. Exactly what she'd decided she wanted in life.

'Or do you want to sneak into Dad's study for a shot of the good brandy before we face the gathered hordes?'

Thea smiled. 'Tempting, but probably not advisable. Besides, your Dad's almost certainly still working in there.'

'There is that.' Flynn sighed. 'I had hoped he'd see this as more of a family celebration than a networking opportunity.'

Nice to know she wasn't the only one who had noticed that. 'I guess he doesn't see any reason why it can't be both. I mean, he knows our reasons for getting married. He helped put together the contract, for heaven's sake.'

'Yeah, I know,' Flynn said, sounding wistful. 'It's business. I just… It would be nice if we could pretend, just for a couple of days, that there's something that matters more to us.'

Thea stared at him. She was going to marry this man tomorrow, and she'd never once heard him speak so honestly about their life or their relationship.

'Flynn? Are you…?' *Are you what? Getting cold feet? Unhappy with me? Not the time for that conversation, Thea.* 'Did you want to wait? To get married, I mean? To someone you're actually in love with?'

Because it was one thing to marry a man you didn't love because that was the deal. Another to do it when he was secretly holding out for more. She thought back to their conversation on the porch, about kids and the future. How happy he'd been at the idea of a family.

But Flynn shook his head, giving her a self-deprecating smile. 'Don't listen to me,' he said. 'We're doing the right thing here. For us and for the business. And, yeah, the fairytale would be nice, I guess. But it's not all there is. And who knows? Maybe you and I will fall in love one day.'

But they wouldn't, Thea knew, with the kind of sudden, shocking certainty that couldn't be shifted. As much as she liked, respected and was fond of Flynn, and as much as she enjoyed his company, she wasn't ever going to be in love with him. She knew how that felt, and it wasn't anything like this.

Thea tried to smile back, but it felt forced. 'Are you ready to go in?' she asked, wishing she'd just said yes when he'd asked her the same question. The knowledge she'd gained in the last two minutes seemed too much for her body—as if she could barely keep it inside on top of every other thought she'd had and fact she'd learned since Zeke came home.

'As I'll ever be,' Flynn said, flashing her a smile. 'Let's go.'

He pushed the door open and the volume level of conversation in the room dipped, then dropped, then stalled. Everyone stood, beaming at them, waiting for them to walk in and take their seats as if they were some kind of royalty. And all Thea could see was Zeke and Helena, standing together near the head of the huge table, leaning into each other. Helena murmured something Thea couldn't hear, and Zeke's lips quirked up in a mocking grin. Talking about her? Thea didn't care. All she knew was that she wanted to be over there, chatting with them, and not welcoming the fifty-odd other people who had somehow got themselves invited to her rehearsal dinner.

She let Flynn take the lead. His easy way with people meant that all she had to do was smile and nod, shake the occasional hand. She let him lead her to their seats, smiled sweetly at everyone around them as she sat down.

Her father nodded to Flynn, and Isabella said, 'Oh, Thea, you look so beautiful tonight. And those pearls are a perfect match! I'm so glad.'

Thea's hand unconsciously went to the necklace Isabella had given her. The perfectly round pearls were hard and cold under her fingers. You were supposed to wear pearls often, weren't you? To keep them warm and stop them cracking or drying, perhaps?

'Aren't pearls supposed to be bad luck?' Helena asked, topping up her glass of wine from the bottle on the table.

'Oh, I don't think so,' Isabella said, laughing lightly. 'And, besides, who believes those old superstitions, anyway?'

'"Pearls mean tears",' Helena quoted, her voice firm and certain. 'And you're the one who insisted on Thea having all the old, new, borrowed and blue stuff.'

'I like pearls,' Thea said, glancing in surprise at her sis-

ter. It wasn't like Helena to antagonise Isabella. For a moment it was almost as if the old teenage Helena was sitting
beside her. 'I don't think they mean anything.'

There was silence for a moment, before the door
opened and a fleet of waiters entered, ready to serve the
starters. They waited until every bowl was ready and in
position, then lowered them all to the table at the same
time, before disappearing again as silently as they'd come.

'Saved by the soup,' Zeke murmured from two seats
down as he reached for the butter.

Thea studied him as he buttered his roll, and kept
watching as Helena topped up his wine, too. He must
have walked home, she supposed. His forehead was ever
so slightly pink from the sun. But he didn't seem angry
or tense as he had earlier. He seemed calm, relaxed. Even
happy.

Maybe he'd got the closure he needed. Maybe he was
thinking ahead to leaving the day after tomorrow. To selling This Minute to Glasshouse and moving on to his new
life. Thea could see how that might be appealing. Not that
she had that option. She didn't want out of this family—
she wanted in.

Besides, Zeke had been gone eight years already and
still not really moved on. What reason was there to believe he'd be able to put it all behind him for real this time?

Isabella and Flynn kept up the small talk across the table
through all three courses. Thea drank her wine too quickly
and tried to pretend her head wasn't spinning. And then
as the waiters came round to pour the coffee, her father
stood up and clinked his fork against his glass.

'Oh, no,' Thea whispered. 'What's he doing?'

Flynn patted her hand reassuringly, somehow managing to make her even more nervous.

'I know tonight isn't the night for big speeches,' Thomas

Morrison said. 'And, trust me, I'll have the traditional light, adoring and entertaining father of the bride speech for you all tomorrow. But I wanted to say a few words to-night for those of you who've been so close to our family all these years. Who've seen us through our dark times as well as our triumphs.'

'Which explains why almost everyone here is a busi-ness associate,' Helena muttered, leaning across towards Thea. 'We've barely seen any family since Mum died.'

'Shh…' Isabella said, without moving her lips or letting her attentive smile slip.

'You all know that getting here, to this happy event, hasn't always been a smooth path. And let me say can-didly that I am both delighted and relieved that Thea has finally made a decision in her personal life that's as good as the ones she makes at work!'

The laughter that followed buzzed in Thea's ears, but she barely heard it. Her body felt frozen, stiff and cold and brittle. And she knew, suddenly, that even marrying Flynn wouldn't be enough. To her father she'd still always be a liability. A mistake just waiting to happen.

'And I want to say thank you to the person who has made all this possible,' Thomas went on, waving his arm expansively to include the food, the villa, and presumably, the wedding itself.

Thea held her breath, bracing herself for the blow she instinctively knew was coming next.

'My dear, dear friend, Isabella Ashton.'

More applause—the reverent sort this time. People were nodding their heads along with her father's words, and Is-abella was blushing prettily, her smile polite but pleased.

Thea thought she might actually be sick.

'So, let us all raise our glasses to the mother of the

groom and the woman who has been as a mother to the bride for the last twelve years.'

Chairs were scraped back as people stood, and the sound grated in her ears. Wasn't it enough that she'd given them all what they wanted? She was marrying the families together, securing their future, their lineage, and the future of their business. And even today, the night before her wedding, she wasn't worthy of her father's approval, or love.

Thea staggered to her feet, clutching the edge of the table, as the guests lifted their glasses and chanted, 'Isabella!' Even Flynn, next to her, had his wine in the air and was smiling at his mother, utterly unaware of how his fiancée's heart had just been slashed with glass.

It was almost as if she wasn't there at all.

Zeke watched Thea's face grow paler as Thomas wound up his ridiculous speech. Who said something like that about his own daughter the day before her wedding? Especially when that daughter was Thea. He *had* to know how sensitive she was about her perceived mistakes, surely? And then to toast Isabella instead… That had been just cruel and callous.

Maybe he truly didn't care. Not if he could get in a good joke, amuse his business associates… Zeke ground his teeth as he waited for his coffee to cool. He'd never been Thomas Morrison's biggest fan, but right then he loathed the man more than he'd ever thought possible.

Thomas sat down to a round of applause and more laughter, and Zeke saw Thea visibly flinch. Flynn, however, was shaking his father-in-law-to-be's hand and smiling as if nothing had happened. As if he couldn't see how miserable Thea was. He was going to marry her tomorrow and he couldn't even see when her heart was breaking.

Zeke gulped down his rage at his brother along with

is coffee. All that mattered was getting Thea the hell out of there.

Helena appeared over his left shoulder suddenly, pushing something cold and bottle-shaped into his hand. 'Go on,' she said, nodding towards Thea. 'I'll cover for you both here.'

'Thanks,' Zeke murmured, keeping the bottle of champagne below table level as he stood. Catching Thea's eye, he raised his eyebrows and headed for the door, not waiting to see if she followed. Helena would make sure that she did.

Outside on the terrace the air held just a little bite—a contrast to the blazing sun he'd walked back in earlier. Dropping onto the swing seat, Zeke held up the bottle and read the label. The good stuff, of course. Old Thomas wouldn't serve anything less while he was insulting his daughter in front of everyone she'd ever met. Shame Helena hadn't thought to provide glasses... Although, actually, swigging expensive champagne from the bottle with Thea brought back its own collection of memories.

The door to the hallway opened and Thea appeared, her face too pale against her dark hair and blood-red dress. Her skin seemed almost translucent in the moonlight, and suddenly Zeke wanted to touch it so badly he ached.

'Have a seat,' he said, waving the bottle over the empty cushion beside him. 'I think your sister thought you might need this.'

'She was right.' Thea dropped onto the seat next to him, sending the whole frame swinging back and forth. 'Although why she decided I also needed you is beyond me.'

'Ouch.' Unwrapping the wire holding it in place, Zeke eased the cork out of the neck of the bottle. He didn't want the pop, the fizz, the explosion. Just the quiet opening and sharing of champagne with Thea. To show her that *he* knew tonight was about her, even if no one else seemed to.

'Oh, you know what I mean,' Thea said, reaching over to take the bottle from him. 'We're not having the best day, apart from anything else.'

'I don't know what you're complaining about,' Zeke said. 'You weren't the one left in the middle of nowhere in the blazing heat.'

Thea winced, and handed him the bottle back. 'Sorry about that.'

'No, you're not.' Zeke lifted the bottle to his mouth and took a long, sweet drink. The bubbles popped against his throat and he started to relax for the first time that day.

'Well, maybe just a little bit. You deserved it, though.'

'For telling the truth?'

'For kissing me.'

'Ah. That.'

'Yeah, *that*.'

Zeke passed the bottle back and they sat in silence for a long moment, the only sound the occasional wave of laughter from inside or the squeaking of the hinges on the swing.

'I'm not actually all that sorry about that, either,' Zeke said finally.

Thea sighed. 'Yeah. Me neither. Maybe we needed it. You know—for closure, or whatever you were going on about.'

'Actually, your sister helped me with that more than you did.'

Thea swung round to stare at him, eyes wide. 'Tell me you have *not* been kissing my sister this afternoon.'

'Or what?'

'Or I'll drink the rest of this champagne myself.' She took a long swig to prove her point.

Zeke laughed. 'Okay, fine. I have not been kissing Helena. This afternoon or any other.'

'Good.'

'Not that it would be any of your business if I had.'

'She's my sister,' Thea said, handing back the champagne at last. 'She'll always be my business.'

'But not your responsibility,' Zeke said. 'She's an adult now, Thea. She can take care of herself.'

'Perhaps.' Thea studied him carefully. 'When you said that Helena had helped you find closure...what did you mean?'

Zeke tipped his head back against the swing cushion. 'She told me some of what happened. Things I didn't know. About what really happened the night of your eighteenth birthday. Why you didn't come with me. And about what happened next.'

He heard the breath leave Thea's lungs in a rush. 'She told you? About the...?'

'About what happened to her. And about the baby.' He rolled his head to the left to watch her as he added, 'And how it really wasn't your fault.'

Thea looked away. 'That's up for debate.'

'No. It isn't.' No response. 'Thea. Look at me.'

She didn't. 'Why?'

'Because I'm about to say something that matters and want to be sure that you're listening to me.'

Slowly she lifted her head and her gaze met his. Zeke felt it like a jolt to the heart—the connection he'd thought they'd lost was suddenly *right there*. Part of him again after all these years.

'Whatever mistakes you think you've made in your life, Thea, that wasn't one of them. You cannot make yourself responsible for what those boys did to her.'

'My father did,' Thea whispered. 'I was in charge. I was responsible. And I let her go out.'

'No.' He had to make her understand. Wrapping his arm around her shoulder, he pulled her closer, still keeping them face to face, until she was pressed up against his chest. 'Listen to me, Thea. It wasn't your fault. And you can't live your whole life as if it was.'

Thea stared up into his eyes for a long moment. They were filled with such sincerity, such certainty. Why could she never feel that way about her life? That unshakeable conviction that whatever choice she made was the right one. That fearlessness in the face of mistakes.

Of course in Zeke it also led to occasional unbearable smugness, so maybe she was better off without.

Swallowing, Thea pulled away, and Zeke let her go. 'Is that what you think I'm doing?'

'I know it,' Zeke said, unbearable smugness firmly in place.

'You're wrong, you know,' she said conversationally, looking down at her hands.

Part of her still couldn't believe that Helena had really told him everything. She'd barely discussed it with Thea ever since it happened. As far as she knew Helena had never willingly told anyone else about it—something their father and Isabella had been in full support of. After all, why make a scandal when you can hide one? And coming so soon after Zeke running away... Well, no one wanted to make headlines again. Thea assumed that Ezekiel Senior knew, but maybe not. Isabella had taken care of everything. Maybe she'd never seen the need to brief him on the shocking events.

'Am I? As far as I can see you stayed eight years ago for Helena, and because you were scared. And now—'

'I made the right decision eight years ago,' Thea interrupted. Because if he had to know everything at least he could admit that much. 'And I don't regret it for a moment.'

'Fair enough,' Zeke said, more amicably than she'd ex

pected. 'And we'll never know how things might have worked out if Helena hadn't gone out that night, or if she'd waited one more day to tell you about it. But the point is Helena's all grown up now. She doesn't need you to protect her any more. And yet you're still staying.'

She shook her head. 'My whole life is here. My place is here.'

'Is it?' He gripped her arm, tightly enough that she had to pay attention. 'They pushed you out, Thea.'

The coldness that settled over her was familiar. The same chill she'd felt that whole summer after Zeke had left. 'You don't...you don't know what it was like.'

'Helena told me. She told me everything.'

But that wasn't enough. A description, a few words—it couldn't explain how it felt to have your whole existence peeled away from you. She wasn't sure if even she could explain it to him. But she knew she had to try...had to make him understand somehow.

'It was as if I'd stopped even existing,' she whispered in the end. 'I couldn't be what Dad needed, so there was no place for me any more. I wasn't good enough for him.'

Zeke's grip loosened, but just enough to pull her against his body. She could feel his heart, thumping away in his chest, and the memory of how his arms had always felt like home cut deeper now.

'Then why are you trying so hard to get back in? Surely you can see you're better off without him. Without all of them.'

'You think I should run away, like you?' She pulled back enough to give him a half-smile. 'This is my place. Besides, where else would I go, Zeke?'

'Anywhere! Anywhere you can be yourself. Live your own life. Not make decisions about your personal happiness based on what is best for the family business, or what

our fathers want you to do. Anywhere in the world, Thea.'
He paused, just for a moment, then added, 'You could even
come with me, if you wanted.'

Thea's heart stopped dead in her chest. She couldn't
breathe. She couldn't think. Couldn't process what he was
saying…

'I'm marrying Flynn tomorrow.' The words came out
without her permission, and she watched Zeke's eyes turn
hard as she spoke.

'Why?' he asked. 'Seriously, Thea. Tell me why. I don't
understand.'

'I love him.'

'No, you don't.'

'I might!'

Zeke laughed, but there was no humour in the sound.
'Thea, I'm sure you do love him—in a way. But don't try
and tell me you're in love with him, or vice versa. He didn't
even notice how distressed you were tonight.'

'*You* did.' She could hear the anger in his voice as he
talked about Flynn. Was that for her?

He gave a slight nod. 'Me and Helena. We're your team.'

'And you're leaving me tomorrow.' How could he offer
her a place in the world when he didn't even know where
he'd be tomorrow? Didn't he understand? She needed more
than that. Somewhere she could never be pushed out or
left behind. Somewhere she was enough.

'Yeah.'

'Great teamwork, there.'

Thea stared out into the darkness of the Tuscan hills
beyond. She hadn't answered Zeke's question—something
she knew he was bound to call her on before too long. But
what could she say? Whatever it was, he wouldn't agree or
approve. Should that matter? She didn't want Zeke to leave
hating her. But why not? She would never see him again

once she was married. He'd made that perfectly clear. If all she was protecting was the memory of something already eight years dead, what was the point?

'So?' Zeke asked eventually. 'The truth this time. Why are you so set on marrying Flynn tomorrow?'

'Maybe I think it'll make me happy,' Thea said.

Zeke shifted, turning his body in towards hers, one knee bent to let his leg rest on the seat. 'Do you? Think you'll be happy?'

She considered lying, but there didn't seem much point. Zeke never believed her anyway. 'I think I'll be safe. Secure. I'll have someone to help me make the right decisions. I think I'll have the agreement of all my friends and family that I'm not making a mistake.'

'Not all of them,' Zeke muttered.

'I think I'll have a place here again. A place I've earned…a place I belong. One that's mine by blood and marriage and can never be taken away from me. I'll be content,' Thea finished, ignoring him.

'Content? And is that enough for you?'

Thea shrugged. 'What else is there?' she asked, even though she knew the answer.

'Love. Passion. Happiness. Pleasure.'

'Yeah, you see, that's where I start to make mistakes. I know business. I know sensible, well thought out business plans. I know agreements, contracts, promised deliverables. Pleasure is an unknown quantity.'

Zeke shifted again and he was closer now, his breath warm against her cheek. Thea's skin tingled at the contact.

'You used to know about pleasure,' he said, his voice low.

'That was a long time ago,' Thea replied, the words coming out huskily.

'I remember, though. You used to crave pleasure. And

the freedom to seek it. To do what felt right and good, not what someone said you were supposed to do.'

His words were hypnotising. Thea could feel her body swaying into his as he spoke, but she couldn't do anything to stop the motion. The swing beneath them rocked forwards and back, and with every movement she seemed to fall closer and closer into Zeke. As if gravity was drawing her in. As if nothing she could say or do or think could stop it.

'Don't you miss it?' he whispered, his mouth so close to hers she could feel the words on her own lips.

'Yes,' she murmured, and he kissed her.

CHAPTER NINE

SHE TASTED JUST as Zeke remembered—as if it had been mere moments since his mouth had last touched hers. This wasn't the angry kiss of earlier that day, a kiss that had been more punishment than pleasure. This…this was something more.

Pleasure and pain mingled together. The years fell away and he was twenty-one again, kissing her goodbye even as he hoped against hope that she might leave with him.

Maybe this time it would end differently. Maybe this time he could persuade her. After all, he'd learnt a lot in eight years.

Slipping a hand around her back, he held her close, revelling in the feel of her body against his, back where she belonged. How had he let himself believe, even for a moment, that he could watch her marry someone else and then walk away?

Flynn… The thought of his brother stalled him for a moment, until he remembered him shaking Thomas's hand after that godforsaken speech. He didn't know Thea—didn't know what she needed, let alone what she wanted. He didn't love her any more than Thea loved him. Zeke knew that for sure.

Maybe he'd even understand. And even if he didn't… Zeke was close to the edge of not caring. Flynn didn't deserve her—he'd proved that tonight. And Zeke needed this. Needed her more than ever before.

Zeke ran his palms up Thea's back, deepening the kiss, and felt his heartbeat quicken at the little noises she made. Half moans, half squeaks, they let him know exactly how much more she wanted. And how much he planned to give her...

'Zeke,' Thea murmured, pulling back just a little. 'What about—?'

'Shh...' Zeke trailed his fingers over her neck, feeling her shiver against him. 'Just pleasure, remember?'

Thea gave a little nod, as if she couldn't help but agree, and Zeke took that as permission to kiss her again. First her lips, deep and wanting. Then her jaw, her neck, her collarbone, down into the deep V of her dress and the lacy bra beyond.

'Oh, Zeke.' Thea shuddered again as his hand crept up her thigh, under her skirt, and he smiled against her skin. He remembered this, too. Remembered how natural it felt to have her in his arms, how she responded to his every touch, every kiss. How she arched up against him, her body begging for more. How could she pretend that she wanted anything other than this, than *him*, when her whole body told him otherwise?

He wanted to get her upstairs. Wanted her in his bed, her naked skin against his. But he knew that he had only this moment to convince her, to change her mind, and he couldn't risk the pause being enough to break her out of pleasure's spell. No, he knew Thea. With cold air between them, and a whole staircase to climb to find a bed, she'd start doubting herself. He didn't have time for her to have second thoughts. She was supposed to get married tomorrow, and he couldn't let that happen.

So it would have to be here. He'd seduce her right here

on the terrace. Then she'd see she couldn't marry Flynn. And Flynn would understand that. Wouldn't he?

Tightening his hold on her, Zeke pulled Thea up from the swing across onto his lap, so her knees fell neatly either side of his thighs, all without breaking their kiss. Her body seemed to know exactly what he had planned, moving with his without hesitation. As if it had done it before... Which, of course, it had. Zeke smiled at the memory.

'This remind you of anything?' he murmured, kissing his way back up her throat.

Thea murmured in agreement. 'Your twenty-first birthday party.'

'Out on the balcony...'

'With the party going on right underneath us.'

'That was all *you*, you know.'

Thea pressed against him and he couldn't help but gasp. 'I seem to remember you being there, too.'

'Yeah, but you're the one who dragged me up there.' He could see it now, in his memories. The bright blue dress she'd worn, the naughty look in her eye, the way she'd bitten her lip as she raised her eyebrows and waited for him to follow her into the house...

'I didn't hear you complaining,' Thea said, her hands pushing his shirt up to get to his skin.

Zeke sucked in a breath at the feel of her fingers on his chest. 'I really wasn't.'

She stilled for a moment, and Zeke's hands tightened instinctively on her thighs, keeping her close. 'What is it?' he asked.

'I just... I've never felt that again. What I felt that night, with you...'

The words were a whisper, an ashamed admission, but Zeke's eyelids fluttered closed in relief at the sound of them. 'Me neither. It's never been like it was with you. Not with anyone.' Never felt so much like coming home.

She kissed him then, her hands on his face, deep and loving, and he knew for the first time in eight years that things were going to be okay again.

'Make love to me, Zeke,' Thea whispered, and Zeke looked up into her eyes and smiled.

'Always.'

Thea blinked in the darkness and wondered how it was possible that she'd forgotten this feeling. The sense that her whole body had relaxed into the place where it belonged. That moment of sheer bliss and an empty mind.

Maybe she hadn't forgotten. Maybe, as great as her memories were, it had never been like this for them before. Because, seriously, surely she'd remember something that good.

She breathed in one last breath of satisfaction…pleasure and *home*.

Then she sat up and faced the real world again.

Her senses and thoughts crashed in immediately—a whole parade of them, ranging from her complete idiocy to her goosebumps. It was cold on the terrace…colder than Thea had thought Tuscany could be in the summer. Of course it would probably be warmer if she was still wearing her dress… Beside her Zeke lay on the swing seat, his shirt unbuttoned to reveal a broad expanse of tanned chest.

Somehow this seemed far more dignified for men.

Reaching for her dress and slipping it over her shoulders, Thea tried to stop her mind spinning with the idea of what she'd just done. She'd cheated on her fiancé. She'd become *that* woman—the one who made a stupid mistake that might cost her everything. The night before her own wedding. At her rehearsal dinner! All because Zeke had started talking about pleasure and making her remember how good things had used to be... And hadn't she just finished telling him that wasn't what she wanted any more?

But she couldn't blame Zeke, however manipulated she felt. She'd wanted it. Asked for it, even. All he'd done was give her what she'd craved. What she'd spent eight years trying to forget.

Thea sighed and Zeke stirred at the sound, snaking an arm around her waist to pull her closer. She sank into him as if, having given in once, all her will power had gone.

This was the hardest part. If it was just great sex with Zeke she was giving up it would be easy. Well, maybe not easy, but certainly doable. But that wasn't all it was.

'You're thinking too loudly,' Zeke murmured against her ear, and she sighed again.

It wasn't the sex. It was the way her body felt in tune with his...the way he could anticipate what she needed before she knew she needed it. The way she felt right in his arms. The way she fitted—*they* fitted together. Not just physically, either.

It just felt so natural with Zeke, in a way she knew it never would with Flynn.

But was that enough?

Zeke might know what she needed, but there was no guarantee that he'd give it to her. As much as she'd loved him when they were younger, she knew him, too. Knew what mattered most to him. And while he might have proclaimed from the rafters that the only thing that mattered to him was her, in the end he'd still left her behind when she wouldn't fit in with his plans. Hadn't even listened when she'd tried to explain why she couldn't go.

Sometimes she wondered if it really had been love. It had felt like it, then. But they'd been kids. What had they known?

And even now Zeke didn't understand about doing the careful thing, the *right* thing. About not taking the risk of making things worse. For him, the risk was half the fun—always had been. He'd liked the thought of getting caught at his twenty-first birthday party. And she knew, from watching This Minute grow and develop through the business pages, that half the fun for Zeke was knowing that he was only ever one step, one chance, one risk away from it all coming down. He'd been lucky—brilliant too, of course—but it could have gone either way.

And Thea didn't have room for any more mistakes in her life. Couldn't risk being left with nothing, no place, again.

'Seriously,' Zeke said, shifting to sit up properly, his shirt flapping closed over his chest.

That might make it easier for her to think clearly, at least.

'What's going on in that head of yours?'

Thea sat up. 'I have to go. I need to… My guests are inside.'

Zeke's expression hardened. Reaching over, he picked up her bra and held it out to her, dangling from his fingers. 'You might need this.'

Thea snatched it from him. 'What did you think I was going to do next, Zeke? I'm supposed to be getting married tomorrow, and I'm out here with the best man! That's never a good decision.'

He shook his head ruefully. 'I should have known. You think I'm a mistake.'

'I didn't say that, Zeke.' She never would, knowing how much of his childhood he'd spent thinking that. That his parents would have been happier with just Flynn, their planned and chosen child, rather than the biological one who had come along at exactly the wrong moment. 'I just…

I need to tell Flynn.' That much was a given, surely? 'I need to sort all this out.'

Zeke blew out a breath and settled back against the swing. 'Yeah, okay. I guess disappearing in the middle of the night at some party never was your style, was it?'

'No, that was all you.' Thea gave him a sad smile, remembering that night eight years ago and knowing with absolute certainty, for the first time, that she could never have gone with him even if Helena hadn't needed her. She wasn't built for Zeke's kind of life.

She just hoped he realised that, too.

Zeke watched Thea walk back inside, her hair no longer so groomed and her make-up long gone. Would she go and fix herself up first? What was the point, if she was just going to tell Flynn that she couldn't marry him? Sure, Flynn would know exactly what they'd been doing, but was that such a bad thing? It gave a point-of-no-return sort of feel to things.

Settling back against the swing seat, Zeke pushed aside the guilt that flooded him at the thought of his brother. It wasn't a love match; he knew that. And this wasn't like when they were kids. He wasn't taking Thea just so that Flynn couldn't have her. She belonged with him—always had. Surely Flynn would understand that?

He hoped so. With conscious effort Zeke relaxed his muscles, feeling the happy thrumming that buzzed through his blood, the reminder of everything the evening had brought him. Who would have thought, when she'd dumped him on the roadside that afternoon, that the day would end here?

He should have known that appealing to her reasonable side wouldn't work. Thea wasn't like other people.

She needed to see the truth, *feel* it, not just be told it. Why hadn't he remembered that?

It didn't matter now. He'd shown her they belonged together. Even her most conservative, analytical, risk-averse side couldn't deny that now. She wanted a place to belong? He could give her that. He could give her everything she needed if she let him. Finally they'd get the life they'd been denied eight years ago, and he was going to make it so good for her. Make her loosen up a bit, reveal the Thea he knew was hiding in there somewhere.

Once the sale of This Minute went through to Glasshouse they could go anywhere, do anything. Maybe they'd just travel for a bit, see the world, get to know one another again as adults. He'd have to take things slowly, so as not to scare her. He knew Thea: even after the jump forward their relationship had taken this evening she was bound to scuttle a few paces back. But Zeke didn't care how slowly it went, how much he had to gentle her along. He'd have Thea in his arms every night, just as he'd always wanted. This time *he* was her choice. Not Flynn, not Helena, not the business, not her father or his. *Him*. Zeke. And he could live with everything in their past as long as he was her last choice.

Zeke smiled to himself as he listened to the sounds of the dinner finishing up and people starting to leave inside. He'd go back in soon, find Thea when she was ready for him.

Sure, there was a lot to figure out first—starting with calling off the wedding tomorrow. But once that was done there was a whole new future out there for them.

He was sure of it.

The sounds of the rehearsal dinner were fading. How many people must have left already without even seeing her? She should have been there, playing hostess, saying goodbye to people, looking excited about tomorrow. If Isabella would let her, of course. She had to start reclaiming that role if she was going to be Flynn's wife. People needed to see that she belonged there, at the head of table, running things.

Image was everything; she was the PR face of Morrison-Ashton and, however much this should have been a private event, it wasn't. These were clients, associates, investors, and she should have been there, working the room. Putting on a show.

And instead she'd been outside on the terrace, sleeping with the best man in the open air.

A shudder ran through her. What had she been thinking? Anyone could have walked out and seen them, and then everything would have been destroyed.

Of course, she reminded herself, it might still be once she told Flynn.

'Thea?' Helena clattered into the hall on her high heels. 'Are you okay? I kept everyone else off the terrace and they're all starting to leave now. Do you want to say goodbye? If not I can cover for you if you want to just go to bed?'

Thea gave her sister a half-smile. 'You take such good care of me.'

Helena shook her head and stepped forward to wrap her arms around Thea's waist. 'Not nearly as good as you take of me.'

Was that true? Thea wasn't sure. She'd stayed, yes, when Helena had needed her, and she'd done the best she could to help her. But she'd never pressed her sister to talk about what had happened, never pushed her to get counselling or other help. Whereas ever since she'd come back, thinner and paler, with her stomach still slightly rounded and hidden under baggy jumpers, Helena had made looking out for Thea a priority. She'd been there when her engagements had gone bad, she'd helped Isabella look after the house and Dad while Thea got on with climbing the corporate ladder, she'd smoothed out every difficult conversation, every awkward dinner party between the Morrisons and the Ashtons.

And tonight she'd protected Thea's privacy while she made another huge mistake.

'I need to talk to Flynn.'

Helena pulled back, frowning. 'Are you sure? Now?'

'Yes. Before I lose my nerve.'

'What are you going to tell him?' Helena asked.

Thea wondered how much her sister knew about her and Zeke. What Zeke had told her. What she imagined had happened out on the terrace.

Thea took a breath. 'Everything.'

Helena studied her for a long moment, then nodded. 'Okay, then. I'll fetch him. You go and wait in the library, yeah?'

'Okay.'

The library was shaded and dark, the tiny haloes of light around the table lamps barely enough to illuminate the chairs beside them, let alone the bookcases. Thea trailed her fingers across the shelves, waiting for Flynn, trying not to listen to the sounds of the guests leaving.

Helena's tinkling laugh caught her attention, though. 'She's been up since dawn! She's so excited about tomorrow. I think she's just crashed! I sent her to bed when she couldn't stop yawning. Can't have the bride looking anything but well rested on her wedding day, can we?'

Murmurs of amused agreement from the departing guests made Thea wince. How many lies had Helena told for her tonight?

The library door cracked open, and Thea spun away from the bookshelf.

'Thea?' Flynn asked, his voice as calm and even as it always was. 'Are you in here?'

Stepping into the light, Thea tried to smile. 'I'm here.'

Flynn closed the door carefully behind him with a click, then turned to her. 'Are you okay? Helena said you wanted to talk to me. I'd have come sooner, but our guests...'

Thea winced again. 'Yeah, sorry. I should have been there to talk with them. To say goodbye, at least.'

'Where were you?' Flynn asked. 'Helena's telling everyone you went to bed, but to be honest you don't look that tired. You look... I don't know...'

But Thea did. Her jaw tightened as she imagined what she must look like. Her hair would be rumpled, her dress creased, her make-up faded. She wished the library had a mirror for her to assess the damage. And maybe, a small part of her insisted, to see if she had that same glow, same radiance, that truly great sex with Zeke had always given her.

She kind of hoped not. She couldn't imagine that was something any man would want to see on his fiancée's face if he hadn't put it there. Even someone as affable and not in love with her as Flynn.

'I was on the terrace,' Thea said. 'With Zeke.'

'But Helena said...' Flynn's face hardened. 'Helena lied. What's going on, Thea?'

'I...I need to tell you some things.' Pacing over to the reading area, Thea placed her hands on the back of one leather wingback chair, her fingernails pressing into the leather. 'Perhaps you should sit.'

'You too, then,' Flynn said, motioning at her chair. When she hesitated, he added, 'Come on, Thea, you look like you're about to fall over.'

Thea slipped around and sat down, instantly regretting it as the stupid table lamp that gave only a glow to the rest of the room illuminated her completely. She could feel the light on her face and see the lamp opposite doing the same to Flynn's as he took his seat. It felt as if she was sitting in an interrogation room, which really didn't give her a good feeling about how the rest of this conversation was going to go.

'So…' Flynn said. 'Talk.'

She should have asked for a drink. Should have stolen the rest of the champagne she'd left outside with Zeke. Should have stayed at her rehearsal dinner if she was going to rewrite the evening.

Instead she took a breath and searched her mind for where to begin.

'Eight years ago,' she said—because wasn't that when everything had started?—'when Zeke left…he asked me to go with him.'

'Why?'

'Because we were in love.' Facts, even painful ones, were the only way to do this. The only way to make Flynn understand what had happened tonight.

Flynn shifted in his chair. 'I should have brought whisky.'

'Yeah. Sorry.'

'So. You didn't go with him. Why?'

'Because…' Could she tell him? It was Helena's secret. She'd told Zeke, but that had been her choice. Flynn deserved the truth… In the end she plumped for the simplified version. 'Helena needed me. She was sixteen, and she had a lot of stuff going on in her life. Our mother had died…she needed me. I couldn't leave her.'

'But if it hadn't been for Helena?'

The million-dollar question. 'I don't know.' Except she

id—in her heart. 'Zeke and I…we're very different peo-
le. Especially these days.'

'Okay. So what does this all have to do with tonight?'

Heat flooded Thea's cheeks as the shame of her actions
it home. 'I slept with Zeke tonight.'

'On the terrace? Where anyone could see?' Flynn's eye-
rows shot up. 'That…doesn't sound very like you.'

Thea blinked at him. '*That's* your concern?'

Flynn sighed. 'Thea, I'm not an idiot. I knew the mo-
1ent Zeke came back that there was unfinished business
etween you. I guess I was away at university when he
:ft, so maybe I didn't know the ins and outs of it then.
ut seeing the two of you together this week, seeing how
ou act around me when he's there…neither of you are
xactly subtle, Thea.'

'Oh. Okay.' Thea swallowed around the lump that had
rmed in her throat. 'Do you…do you hate me?'

Flynn's smile was gentle, far gentler than she deserved,
nd tears stung at Thea's eyes. 'Of course I don't hate you,
hea…' He sighed. 'Look. We know this isn't a love match.
Ve're not married yet, so the fidelity clause isn't in effect.'

She'd forgotten all about that clause. One moment of
eke's hands on her skin and she'd lost all reason.

'Quite honestly, if you have doubts like this and things
ou need to resolve, I'd far rather them happen now than
a year's time.'

'So…what happens now?'

'Well, that's up to you.' Flynn sat back in his chair and
udied her. 'You need to decide what you want, Thea. If
ou think you could be truly happy with Zeke, that he can
ive you everything you need, then we'll go and talk to
ur parents and call the wedding off right now. But if you
ant the life we have planned—the business, the family

support, kids, everything—if you still want that, then ye
need to forget about Zeke and marry me tomorrow.'

Thea stared at him, waiting for something more—som
thing to make the choice for her, to make sure she mad
the right one. To tell her the right answer to this test.

But Flynn didn't offer advice. Didn't counsel...didn
help her reason it out. He just sat there and watched he
How could he be so impassive? But then, she'd wante
businesslike, detached, practical. She hadn't wanted Flyr
to love her. He was giving her exactly what she'd alwa
said she needed. And, against all the odds, she was st
enough for him. She could still give him what he wante
too, even knowing how much she'd messed up.

'It has to be your choice, Thea,' he said.

And, worst of all, she knew he was right.

CHAPTER TEN

'ARE YOU OKAY out here?'

Zeke turned at the sound of Helena's voice and saw
the concerned crumple of her forehead as she stood in the
door, watching him.

'I'm fine.' He patted the swing seat beside him. 'Wanna sit?
Your sister has left us a little of the champagne.' He thought
it wise not to mention exactly how Thea had been distracted
from the champagne, right there on that very swing.

But Helena didn't sit anyway. Instead she leant against
the railing opposite and reached out a hand for the bottle.
Her high heels had been discarded, Zeke realised, and she
seemed far smaller than the loss of a few inches should
achieve.

'Everything okay in there?' he asked as Helena lifted
the bottle to her lips. Of course what he really wanted to
ask was, *Where's Thea? How did Flynn take it? When is
he coming back?*

'Fine,' Helena said, passing the bottle back. 'The guests
have all gone, or retired to their rooms. Thea and Flynn are
in the library, talking. Your dad's in the study, and Isabella
and Dad are sipping brandy in the back parlour, I think.'

That strange split again, Zeke thought. Everyone with
the wrong person. Mum with Thomas, Thea with Flynn,
and him out here with Helena.

'Do you know what they're talking about?' he asked.

Helena raised her eyebrows. 'Dad and Isabella? I drea
to think.'

'I meant Thea and Flynn.' Zeke paused. 'And why drea
to think?'

'Who knows what those two find to talk about?' He
ena shrugged, but the look in her eyes told him there wa
more to it than a weird choice of phrase.

'Helena. What am I missing here?'

She tilted her head to look at him. '*Are* you missing i
though? Or just pretending you don't see it, like Thea?'

'I've been gone for eight years, Helena. I might hav
missed some stuff.' But he suspected. Always had. An
the horrible certainty was already rising up in his gut.

'I knew when I was fourteen,' she replied.

How much more of life had Helena seen before sh
was an adult? What else had she been doing while Flyn
had been at university and he and Thea had been sneak
ing around thinking that they were being so clever that n
one knew about them?

'Knew what?' Zeke asked, even though he was sure h
didn't want to know the answer.

'That my father and your mother were having an affair

Zeke grabbed the champagne bottle and drank deeply
'Knew or suspected?' he asked, after wiping his mouth
Because *he'd* suspected, even when he hadn't wanted to
And he'd been very careful not to look any closer just i
case he was proved right.

'Knew.'

Helena looked him straight in the eye, as if she wante
to prove the truth of her words.

'I saw them once. And once I'd seen…it was so obviou
I saw the proof of it in every single thing they did. It was

lief, in a way. At least I understood at last why Isabella
as so determined to try and be my mother.'

'Yeah.' It explained a lot, even while Zeke wished that
didn't. What a mess. Tipping his head back against the
all behind the swing, he let his mind rerun the memories
f twenty-one years of watching them but not seeing. Hel-
1a was right. Once you knew it was impossible not to see.

Was that how people had been with him and Thea?

The thought made him sit bolt-upright. 'Why are you
lling me this now? I mean, there's no chance that I'm...'
[e couldn't even finish the sentence.

Helena's eyes widened. 'Our half-brother? God, no!
hat's...' She shuddered. 'No. Mum was still alive then,
nd I'm pretty sure it didn't start until after her death. Be-
des, Zeke, you look exactly like Ezekiel Senior. I don't
iink there's ever been any doubt about who your father is.'

'True.' Zeke's muscles relaxed just a little. 'Funny. For
ears I hated how much of him I saw when I looked in the
iirror. Now...I'm profoundly grateful.'

'Hell, yes.'

'So why tell me now?'

Helena paused, her lower lip caught between her teeth.
uddenly she looked like the naughty schoolgirl he remem-
ered, not the poised, sophisticated woman he'd found when
e returned. Where had she gone, that Helena? Had all her
)ugh edges and inappropriate comments been smoothed
ut by the things that had happened to her? By all the se-
rets she'd had to keep buried? He'd seen a glimpse of her
t dinner, though, winding his mother up about the pearls.
Iaybe she wasn't gone for ever. He hoped not.

'Did you ever wonder why Isabella stayed with your
ad?'

Zeke blinked. He hadn't, he realised. But he should
ave. 'I guess the money. The family. The business.'

'But if she'd left him for *my* dad...'

'They'd have had all of that, to some degree.' And Zek
would have grown up with Thomas Morrison as his step
father. He really couldn't be sure if that would have bee
an improvement, or not.

'Yeah.'

'So why?'

Helena shrugged. 'I don't know. I never asked. Bu
maybe somebody should.'

'Why?' What did it matter now, anyway? He'd be gor
tomorrow—leaving all this behind for his future wit
Thea.

'Because...' Helena took a deep breath. 'Because I thin
Thea is about to make the same mistake.'

Zeke's world froze. 'No. She's not. She's in there rig
now, telling Flynn she can't marry him.'

Helena's gaze was sad and sympathetic. 'Are you sure'

'Yes,' Zeke lied. 'I'm absolutely sure.'

Isabella was waiting for her outside the library when The
finally left Flynn alone with the books and headed for be
It wouldn't do for the bride to look tired and distraught c
her wedding day, after all. Just as Helena had said.

'Oh, my dear,' Isabella said, clasping her hands togeth
at the sight of her. 'Come on. We'll go and have some tea

'Really, Isabella, I'm fine.' The last thing she wante
after the surrealism of her evening so far was to sit an
sip tea with her future mother-in-law. 'I just need to g
some sleep. It's been a long day.'

But Isabella wasn't taking no for an answer. 'You'
never sleep like this. Come on. Tea.'

Dutifully Thea trailed behind her, wondering how muc
longer this day could feasibly get. It had to be past mi
night already. Even if the wedding wasn't until tomorro

fternoon she couldn't imagine she'd actually get a lie-in,
hatever happened. Apart from anything else she still had
 talk to Zeke. Flynn had insisted she did, before making
ny final decisions.

The kitchens were in darkness, the last of the staff hav-
ng gone home at last. The dishwashers were still run-
ing, though, so Thea suspected it had been a late night
or all concerned. Isabella found the light switch without
ifficulty and flicked it on, before heading unerringly for
 cupboard which, when opened, revealed a stock of dif-
erent varieties of tea.

'Camomile?' she asked, glancing back at Thea. Then
he frowned. 'Or maybe peppermint. Good for soothing
he stomach.'

'My stomach is fine,' Thea replied. It was just her mind
hat was spinning and her heart that was breaking.

'As you say.' Isabella selected a tin then, opening an-
ther cupboard, pulled out a small silver teapot and two
ragile-looking cups and saucers. 'I always make it my
irst priority to locate the teapot, wherever I'm staying. I
ust can't sleep without a soothing cup of something be-
ore bed.'

'I didn't know that.' Thea watched Isabella as she pot-
ered over to the sink to fill the kettle then, while it was
oiling, selected a couple of teaspoons and a tea strainer
nd stand from another drawer.

'Now, Thea…' Isabella placed the tea tray, complete
ith lace cloth, onto the kitchen table and took a chair op-
osite her. 'I want to talk to you about Zeke.'

'About Zeke?' Thea's fingers slipped on the handle of
he teapot and she pulled back. She should let Isabella
our, anyway.

'Yes. I know you've always been…close to my son.'

'Your husband already asked me to talk to him about

This Minute,' Thea interjected, wishing she didn't soun
as if she was babbling so much. 'And I tried—I did—bu
no dice. I think tomorrow he plans to leave and sell t
Glasshouse, regardless of what we offer.'

'That's interesting,' Isabella said. 'But not what I wante
to talk about.'

'Then…what? Did you want to know where he's beer
Because I have a pretty good idea, I think. Or what h'
plans are now? Because you'd really have to ask him, ex
cept…'

Except he was probably still waiting for her on the te
race. Did he know what she'd planned to tell Flynn? C
did he hope…? No. She couldn't think about it.

'I wanted to talk about your relationship with him. An
my relationship with your father.'

Thea blinked. 'I don't understand.'

'Then you haven't been paying very close attention
Isabella reached for the teapot and, placing the straine
over Thea's cup, started to pour. 'This should be brewe
by now.'

'What exactly *is* your relationship with my father'
Thea asked, even though she suspected she already kne'
the answer. Should have known it for years.

'What exactly is *your* relationship with my younge
son?' Isabella didn't even look up from pouring the te
into her own cup as she turned the question round on The

'I haven't seen him in eight years,' Thea said. 'I thin
that any relationship we did have will have been legall
declared dead by now.'

'Except he was the one who came after you when yo
were upset tonight. And I suspect he's the one who's le
you looking like your whole world is upside down.'

'Tell me about you and Dad.'

Placing the pot back on the tray, Isabella picked up h

eacup and saucer and sat back, surveying Thea over the im of her steaming cup. 'I think, in some ways, our situation is very similar, you know.'

'I *don't* know,' Thea said. 'I don't know what you're alking about.'

'After your mother died your father was a wreck. I tried o help out where I could. And then, after that nastiness vith Helena...'

'You saw your chance and pushed me out,' Thea said, er hackles rising. But Isabella merely raised her eyebrows a few millimetres as she sipped her tea.

'I did what was needed to keep things...settled.'

Sending Helena away and taking over Thea's home. moothing over the rough edges of the actual truth and roviding a glossy finish. Thea shook her head. 'I don't ee how this applies to me and Zeke.'

'Wait,' Isabella said. 'Drink your tea and listen. Over ime, your father and I grew close. We talked a lot. We istened a lot. That was something we both needed. You might not have noticed, but my husband is not one of the vorld's great listeners and his only subject of conversation s the company. It was...different with Thomas.'

Thea's hands tightened around the warmth of her teaup. 'You fell in love.'

'We did. Very deeply.'

No wonder her father had chosen Isabella over her. For ne first time Thea saw her past through new eyes. No, she adn't been up to the job her father had thrown her into. But maybe that had been because it was a role that was ever meant to be hers. Maybe he'd wanted Isabella there t his side all along.

Except he'd never got all of her, had he?

'You never left Ezekiel.'

'I never even considered it,' Isabella said without paus 'And your father never asked me to.'

'Why?'

Isabella sighed. 'Because I was old enough and wis enough, by the time I fell in love for real, to know that lov isn't everything. Thea, we all need different things in th life. Yes, we need someone to listen to us, to laugh with to love. But we need other things, too.'

'Like money,' Thea guessed, not hiding the bitternes in her voice. How different might her life have been wit Isabella as a real stepmother rather than someone wh had to help out because Thea couldn't manage things o her own? 'Dad could have given you that, too, you know

'Not just money. Yes, Thomas could have given m that—and stability, and lots of other things. But what abou the business? What about our social standing? My plac in the world? What about Ezekiel and the vows I made?

'You mean, what about the scandal?' Thea shook he head. 'Is that what it's always about with you? Was th just Helena all over again?'

'All I am saying is there are many aspects of a woman life for which she has needs. You need to look at your re quirements over the course of a lifetime when you're mak ing a decision about whom to marry.'

'And Ezekiel gave you what you needed over the cours of your lifetime? Because, if so, why did you feel the nee to have an affair with my father?'

Isabella sipped at her tea delicately before responding 'That's what I'm saying. Did it ever occur to you that per haps it is unreasonable to expect one person to fulfil you every need?'

'No.' The response was instinctive, automatic. Even i she were willing to contemplate such a thing, neither Zek nor Flynn was the sort of man who liked to share.

Isabella gave her a sad smile. 'You're young. You're
ill holding out for the dream. So, which of my sons do
ou think can give you that?'

Thea had no answer to that at all.

'If that's the way you feel you have only two options,'
abella said. 'One: you marry Flynn as planned. Every-
ne is happy and no one needs to be any the wiser about
ur...indiscretion. You go about your life and probably
ver see Zeke again.'

'What's option two?' Thea asked, her mouth dry.

'You call off the wedding and leave with Zeke. You
ave behind your career, your family and reputation, your
ance at a stable and loving future, for a man who has al-
ady left you behind once. In an effort to put a good face
the company my husband will probably marry Flynn off
someone else pretty quickly. Helena, I imagine, would
the best candidate.'

'No.' The very idea chilled Thea's core. 'She wouldn't.'

'She would,' Isabella replied, with certainty in her
ice. 'She couldn't bear to let everyone down *again*. Be-
les, surely you've noticed the way she looks at him.'

'No.'

Was Isabella just saying that to convince her to marry
ynn? Didn't she know that if she'd thought Helena
anted him she'd step aside in an instant? Probably not.
abella had spent so many years watching Ezekiel drive
wedge between her sons she probably believed everyone
anted what their sibling had.

'I'd look closer, then.'

Thea shook her head. 'You're imagining things, Isa-
lla. And it doesn't matter anyway.'

'Oh? Have you found a magical third path, then? Other
an my original suggestion?'

'No.' Thea stared down into her teacup. If she was hon-

est, she'd known all along what she really had to do. F
her future and for her family. 'I'll marry Flynn, just
we've always planned.'

Isabella watched her for a long moment, then nodde
'Good. Now, more tea?'

'No. Thank you.' Thea pushed her chair away from t
table and stood. 'I need to go to bed. Lots to do tomorro

Starting with explaining her decision to the one pers
in the world who would never, ever understand it.

Zeke woke early the next morning. He'd waited up f
Thea on the terrace until he'd realised all the lights insi
had been turned off. Helena had kept vigil with him f
a while, before patting him on the shoulder and biddi
him goodnight. When he'd finally given up and gone
bed he'd lingered outside Thea's door for long momen
contemplating knocking and going in. But Thea had
make this decision for herself—even he knew that muc

In the end he'd headed to bed alone, for a night of re
less dreams and uncertainty. And now it was the mor
ing of Thea and Flynn's wedding, and he still didn't kno
her decision.

From the moment he woke he felt panic surge throu
him at the realisation that he was alone again. Why had
she come? He'd been so sure… Flynn must have said som
thing. Threatened her, perhaps… Except that wasn't h
style. No, he'd have baffled her with logic. Probably ha
spreadsheet of reasons they should get married as planne

Just what Thea didn't need.

Sitting up in bed, Zeke stamped down on the fear cree
ing across his brain and contemplated his next move. I
could still fix this, still win, if he played the right han
Did he wait for Thea to come to him, or did he seek h
out? There was always the chance that she might not cor

all. If she'd made her decision—the wrong decision—
what would be the point? But Zeke knew he couldn't live
with the not knowing.

So what other choice did he have? He could just cut his
losses now. He could go and say goodbye to Thea, give her
one last chance to go with him, then leave if she said no.

In the end the choice wasn't his or Thea's. As he exited
his bedroom, freshly showered and casually dressed—no
way was he getting stuck in a tux this early in the day, even
if the wedding went ahead and he actually attended—he
saw Flynn, marching towards him.

'You and I need to talk,' his adopted brother said, face
solemn. 'And then you need to talk to Thea.'

'Okay.' Zeke fell into step with Flynn, his heart rising
lightly in his chest. Maybe he wouldn't need to convince
Thea again after all. If Flynn wanted him to talk to her
surely that meant he didn't approve of her decision. Well,
he was damned if he thought Zeke would try to persuade
her otherwise. 'What exactly do we need to talk about?'

Flynn gave him an exasperated look. 'Thea, of course.'

'Right.'

Zeke waited until Flynn had yanked open the door to
the library and impatiently motioned him in before asking
any more questions. Settling down into a wingback chair,
he suddenly remembered Helena's words from the night
before. This was where Flynn and Thea had talked after
the interlude on the terrace. How he wished he could have
heard what they'd said...

Maybe Flynn would tell him. If he asked right.

'So,' Zeke said, folding one leg up to rest his ankle on
the opposite knee. 'What's up? Last-minute nerves?'

Flynn glared at him. 'In precisely six hours I'm supposed to marry Thea. If you have any interest at all in that
event, however twisted, you need to stop playing *now*. I

need you to be my brother, for once, and I need you to b
honest with me.'

Zeke flinched under his brother's gaze. How had h
become the kid brother again, the screw-up, the one wh
couldn't be serious about anything that mattered? Espe
cially when he'd worked so hard to get away from tha
Away from the bitter rivalry for something that had turne
out not to matter at all—their father's approval.

'Fine. Then talk.'

'Thea told me that she slept with you last night.'

'She said she was going to.' Zeke looked Flynn right i
the eye as he talked. He wasn't ashamed, even if he shoul
be. Thea belonged with *him*, not in some soulless, lovele
marriage of convenience. Getting her out of that was n
a sin. Trapping her was.

'I still plan to marry her.'

'For the love of God, *why*?' Zeke grabbed the arms
the chair and sat forward. What else did he have to *do
'You don't love her—I know you don't. You couldn't b
this calm right now if you did. And she doesn't love you

'Do you think she's still in love with you?'

'I know she is. And I know she deserves a lot bett
than what you have to offer.'

'And what, exactly, are *you* offering?' Flynn asked, sta
ing at Zeke. 'The chance to say *screw you* to our father

'That's not...' Zeke sank back down into his chai
'That's not why.'

'Are you sure?' Flynn tilted his head as he conside
his brother. 'It's been eight years, Zeke. Why come bac
now, if not to prove a point?'

'Oh, I don't know—maybe to stop Thea making a hu
mistake.'

'And you think you're the best judge of Thea's mi
takes?'

'Better than her, at least,' Zeke said, thinking about Helena and all the guilt Thea carried on her behalf.

Flynn shook his head. 'You're wrong. But I told Thea last night she had to decide for herself what to do. I told her to think about it overnight, then talk to us both this morning. She'll be here any minute.'

And just like that the decision about how to approach Thea was taken away from him.

'Good,' Zeke said, hoping his surprise didn't show on his face.

He didn't want to have this conversation in front of his brother. Flynn made him a different person even now, after all these years. He needed it to be just him and Thea, so they could just be themselves, the people he remembered so well. But apparently his love life was now in the public domain. And before he could even object the library door opened and Thea was standing there, looking pale and lovely—and determined.

Zeke stood up. Time to win this.

CHAPTER ELEVEN

THEA SUCKED IN a breath as she opened the library do
and saw Zeke and Flynn waiting for her. This was it. Th
moment that decided the rest of her life. Whatever she
told Isabella, whatever she'd told herself in the dark of th
night, her decision couldn't be final until she'd told the tw
men in this room. This might be the biggest choice ar
possibly the biggest mistake she'd ever made as an adu
So of course it involved Zeke Ashton.

'Thea, you're here. Good.'

Flynn gave her a gentle smile that made Thea's insid
tie up in knots. She didn't want to be there *so much.*

But she was, and she was out of other options, so sl
moved to the centre of the room and took the chair Flyr
indicated. This was his condition: he'd marry her today
she talked things through with both of them and still d
cided it was the best option. Since she'd slept with som
one else the night before their wedding, Thea had to adm
that this was more than fair. That was the thing abo
Flynn. He was always scrupulously fair. Even when sl
wanted him to just yell, or walk out, or make a decisic
for her.

'Okay, so here's what I'm thinking.' Flynn settled in
his own chair, looking for all the world as if this was an e
eryday meeting or discussion. As if they weren't debatin

whether or not to get *married* that afternoon. 'We all know the situation. And we all agree that Thea has to be the one to make a decision about what happens next—correct?'

He glanced between them, focussing first on Zeke, who eventually nodded in a way that made it very clear he was doing so under duress, and then at Thea, who whispered, 'Yes,' even though she didn't want to.

'So... I think the best way to proceed is—'

'Oh, for God's sake!' Zeke interrupted. 'This isn't a board meeting, Flynn.'

'No,' Flynn replied, his voice calm and even. 'It's a meeting about my future. And since you're the one who's put that into the realm of uncertainty, I think you should just let me deal with it my own way, don't you?'

Zeke settled back into his chair at that, and Thea risked a glance over at him. His eyes were dark and angry, and she could see the tension in his hands, in the way they gripped the arms of the chair, even if his posture was relaxed. How he must hate this—must hate waiting to see if Flynn was going to beat him again. Because of course that was how Zeke would see it, even if it wasn't true. This wasn't about either of them, really, even if only Flynn seemed to realise that.

It was about Thea. About her making the right decision for once. Whatever that might be.

'So, here's what I propose,' Flynn said, and Thea tried to concentrate on listening to him instead of watching the way Zeke's jaw tightened with every word. 'Zeke and I will both lay out our arguments for why we feel you should choose our proposed course of action. You can listen, ask questions, and then we'll leave you alone to make your decision. The only thing I ask is that you decide quickly; once guests start arriving it will be a lot harder to cancel this thing, if you choose to.'

Thea nodded, and stopped looking at Zeke altogether.

'Okay. Shall I go first?' Flynn asked, and when no one answered he continued, 'Right. Thea, obviously I want to marry you today. I understand what happened last night and I think, after talking with you yesterday, I can see why. But I don't believe that one impulsive action has to change the course of your whole life. We agreed to a contract— marriage between us based on very sound reasoning and mutual desires. Everything we discussed and decided still stands. I can give you the security, the business, the future that you want. And marriage is only a small part of our lives; we have to consider the other people we love— what *they* want. I think we both know that everyone in this villa except Zeke wants a future with us as a couple in it. We can do so much together, Thea. And, quite honestly, I'd worry about your future if you left with Zeke today.'

He got up from the chair and came to stand by her side, gently taking her hand in his.

'Because, Thea, I care about you. Maybe we don't have that grand passion. But we have more. Mutual respect, caring, common interests and values. They matter too. And I suggest to you, right here, that they matter more for what we want to achieve in life.'

He wasn't just thinking about the business, Thea realised. He was talking about kids. Flynn would be a great father—calm and fair. And she was pretty sure he wouldn't ever sleep with his best friend's wife. Unlike her own father. Unlike Zeke, she thought, stealing a glance at him. Hell, he'd slept with her the night before her wedding. Morality had never been a strong motivation for him.

Or for her this week, it seemed.

Flynn seemed to be waiting for an answer, so Thea nodded and said, 'That all makes a lot of sense,' even

ough her poor muddled brain could barely remember
hat he'd said.

Maybe it didn't matter, she realised. Maybe, whatever
ey each had to say, it all meant nothing in the end. She
uldn't weigh up the pros and cons of two people, could
e?

Except she had to. And not just of the two men in front
her but of the whole lives they represented. She could
e two futures for herself, branching off from this mo-
ent, and she simply didn't know which one was more
rrifying.

But she still had to decide.

Flynn gave a sharp nod, then moved away to his own
air, yielding the floor to his brother. 'Zeke. Your turn.'

Zeke looked up slowly, his dark gaze finally meeting
rs. 'I don't know what you want me to say.'

'Neither do I,' Thea admitted. Did she want him to
lk her out of marrying Flynn—really? Or did she want
m to say something so awful that she stopped feeling
ilty about marrying Zeke's brother in the first place?
e wasn't sure.

He blew out a long breath. 'Okay. I don't want you to
arry Flynn. I think it's a mistake.'

Thea flinched at the word, even though she tried not to.
's mine to make, though.'

'It is,' Zeke conceded. 'I just... I really don't want to
this with him in the room.'

'He's your brother. And he's right—he does have kind
a big stake in this conversation.'

'I know.' Zeke took another breath. 'Okay, fine. I know
u think you're doing this for the family, to prove your-
lf to them somehow. And I know you believe that ev-
yone will be happy if you just go along with their plans.
t you're wrong.'

'And our happiness is suddenly of such importance
you? Zeke, you haven't cared about us for the last eig
years. I find it hard to believe that we suddenly matt
that much to you.'

'Of course I've cared!' Zeke yelled, and Flynn's ga
shot to the door, as if he was worrying about who mig
be listening. It was a fear that seemed all the more reaso
able when Zeke's words were followed by a knock on t
library door a moment later.

'Ah, here you all are,' Isabella said, giving them all h
best hostess smile. 'Thea, darling, there's a small questi
about the table settings that we could use your input on,
you have a moment.'

Isabella's eyes were knowing, but Thea refused to me
them.

'I'll deal with it,' Flynn said, getting to his feet. 'Th
and Zeke are just reminiscing about old times, Moth
Something they won't have much of a chance to do on
we're married.'

She had to know it was a lie, but Isabella let it go non
theless. 'Come on, then. And once this is sorted, perha
you can help me with the question of the gift table.'

Flynn shut the door firmly behind them, and Thea f
as if he'd taken all the air in the room with him. Now
was just her and Zeke and every moment of their histor
weighing down on them like the books on the shelves.

'That's better,' Zeke said. 'Now we can do this properl

How could she look so poised and calm, when he felt
if his insides were about to combust? For Thea this mig
as well be just another business meeting. Maybe she w
a perfect match for Flynn after all.

No. If this was his last chance to try and uncover t
Thea he'd known and loved, the one he'd glimpsed again

e'd made love to her on the terrace last night, then he was
rasping it with both hands. He had to make her see sense.

'Maybe we should wait until Flynn gets back,' Thea
aid, as if she truly believed that any part of this discus-
on really did involve his brother.

'This isn't about Flynn,' Zeke said. 'He could be any-
ne. Any poor bloke you'd roped in to try and make your
fe safe and predictable. Just like the last two. No, this is
bout you and me, and it always has been.'

Thea's gaze shot up to meet his, dark and heated. 'You
ean it's all about *you*. You proving a point to your father.
ist like it always is.'

'Last night wasn't just about me,' Zeke replied, enjoying
e flush of red that ran up her neck to her cheeks. 'In fact I
istinctly remember it being all about you more than once.'

'This isn't about sex, Zeke,' Thea snapped. 'This is my
ature you're playing with.'

'Who said I'm playing?' Because he wasn't—not one
it. He knew exactly how important this moment was.
ut with Thea sometimes you had to get her mad to see
e truth. To let her true self break out from all the rules
id restrictions she'd tucked herself in with like a safety
anket.

Thea gave a bitter laugh. 'It's always been a game to
ou—all of it. You've always cared more about beating
ur father and Flynn than anything else. If you'd paid
iy attention at all you'd know that Flynn isn't even com-
eting. He's just getting on with his life, like an ordinary,
ood man.'

'And that's what you want, is it? Ordinary?' If she
ought it was, she was wrong. Thea deserved much, much
ore than ordinary.

'I want to not be a trophy! I want to not be one more

thing you can use against your family for some misguide
slight almost a decade ago!'

The words hit him hard in the chest. 'That's not wh.
I'm doing.'

'Isn't it? Are you sure? Because it seems to me tha
coming back here—right when you're about to sell yo
company to our competitor, just when I'm about to get c
and make a success of my life—is far more about you ar
your need to win than anything else.'

'You're wrong.'

'Prove it.'

'How?'

'I don't know, Zeke! But if you really want me to thro
over all my plans for the future, to upset both our familie
probably damage the company's reputation...you need
offer me a little more than a cheap victory over your f
ther and one night on a terrace.'

One night. Was that what it was to her? Was that a
he'd ever been? A bit of fun, but never the one you cho
for the long haul. No wonder she'd stayed eight years ag

'Helena must have been a real handy excuse that nigh
he said, letting the bitterness creep into his voice.

Thea blinked. 'What?'

'Tell me honestly. If it hadn't been for Helena wou
you have come with me when I asked, that night of yo
birthday party?'

The colour faded from Thea's cheeks and he knew tl
answer before she even spoke the word.

'No.'

Zeke tightened his muscles against the pain, stiffe
ing into strength and resolve. With a sharp nod, he sai
'That's what I thought.'

'I just... I wanted...'

'You don't need to justify yourself to me.' A stran

calm had settled over him now. At last he knew, and to his surprise the truth made all the difference. 'I understand.'

'No! You don't,' Thea said, but Zeke just shook his head.

'Sure I do. You want a safe and predictable life, even if it makes you miserable.' How had he thought for so many years that Thea was different from the rest of them? He should have known that they were all the same at heart. More concerned with the appearance of the thing than the substance. Better that he realised that now, however belatedly, than go on believing she was something more than she was.

'That's not... It's not just that,' Thea said unconvincingly.

'Yeah, Thea, it is. Deny it all you want, but I know what's going on here. You're doing exactly what Daddy wants, as usual. You're going to marry Flynn to buy yourself the place you think you deserve.'

She looked away, but Zeke wasn't looking for shame in her expression. It was too late for that now, anyway. She'd made her choice and he knew his future now. But that didn't mean he couldn't open her eyes to a few home truths before he left.

'You realise you could be pregnant with my child already?' They hadn't used protection last night. Had been too caught up in the moment even to think of it.

'I know.'

'Does Flynn?'

'Yes.' A whisper...barely even a word.

'And he's happy to marry you anyway?' Of course he was. In fact he probably hoped that she was. 'Because that would give him the one thing he's never had, wouldn't it? Legitimacy. Raising a true Ashton blood heir with the Morrison heiress. Perfect.'

Thea sprang to her feet to defend her fiancé. 'You don't

have a clue what you're talking about! And anyway Flynn *is* the Ashton heir, remember? You gave it all up to run away and seek revenge.'

'Because my father chose him over me!' Zeke couldn't keep the anger from his voice this time. However far he moved past the pain, the sting of unfairness still caught him unawares sometimes.

'Your father made a business choice, not a personal one.'

Zeke flinched at her words. 'You're wrong there,' he said.

'Am I?'

He knew she was, but couldn't bring himself to explain, to argue. To revisit in glorious Technicolor the night he' left. The things he'd heard his father say. What had really driven him away. Why he'd had to go even when Thea wouldn't leave with him. Why her rejection had been just one more slam to the heart.

What was wrong with him? He'd moved past this years ago. Wasn't that one of the reasons he'd come back in the first place? To prove that he'd moved on, that he had his own life now, that he didn't need his family or the business? So why was he letting her arguments get to him?

Was it the idea of a possible baby? The thought that *his child* might be brought up in the Morrison-Ashton clan, living its whole life waiting to see if it would be deemed *worthy enough* to inherit everything that Zeke had walked away from…? It made him sick to his stomach. No child— no person—deserved to go through that. But what were the honest chances that Thea was pregnant? Slim, he'd imagine. And she'd tell him, he knew. Thea might not be everything he'd thought she was, but she was honest. She told Flynn about sleeping with him, hadn't she? She'd tell Zeke if he were a father.

And then he'd be tied into this accursed family for ever.
rfect.

What had he been thinking, sleeping with her last night?
ke wanted to beat himself up for it, except he knew
actly what he'd been thinking—that he might be able to
ve Thea from herself this time.

But Thea didn't want to be saved. She'd rejected him
ain, and this time it cut even deeper. She'd chosen Flynn.
e wanted Flynn.

Fine. She could have him. But Zeke was making sure
e knew exactly what she was letting herself in for first.

CHAPTER TWELVE

THEA THOUGHT SHE could bear anything except sitting o
moment longer under Zeke's too knowing gaze. Who w
he to judge her, to condemn her? To think he knew I
better than she knew herself?

Except he just might.

No. She couldn't let herself believe that. After a slee
less night, spent with Flynn and Isabella's words resour
ing in her brain while her memories ran one long, sens
video of her evening with Zeke, she knew only one th
for certain: she was done with doing what other peo
said she should. Everyone in the whole villa thought th
knew what was best for her, and Zeke was just the lat
in a long line.

Well, she was done with it.

'You realise that you're choosing what other people
pect of you over what you really want, right?' Zeke sa
and she glared at him.

'How would you know what I want? And if you ma
one single innuendo or reference to last night after tl
comment I'm walking out right now.'

The smirk on his face told her that was exactly w
Zeke had been about to do, but instead he said, 'Beca
I've seen you do it before, far too many times. You a
mitted you wouldn't have come with me even if Hele

dn't needed you. But why? I can tell you, even if you
n't know yourself.'

Thea rolled her eyes. 'Enlighten me, oh, wise one,' she
id, as sarcastically as she could manage.

'Because you're scared. Because you've spent your
hole life doing what other people think is best for you
d you don't even know how to stop. You can't make
ace with your own desires because you think they might
set someone.'

'They upset *me*!' Thea yelled. 'Zeke! Do you think I
ant to be this person? The sort of woman who sleeps with
e best man the night before her wedding? I hate myself
ght now! The best thing I can do is try and get back to
y regularly scheduled life, without the chaos you bring
to it. Is that so bad?'

'Not if the regularly scheduled life is what you really
ant.'

Zeke moved closer, and Thea's body started to hum at
s nearness.

'But I don't think it is. I think that you want more. You
ant a life that makes your heart sing. You want it all.'

He swayed closer again, and before she knew it his hand
as at her waist, pulling her towards him, and his lips were
pping towards hers...

She wanted this so badly. Wanted his mouth on hers,
s body against her. But she couldn't have it. Not if she
anted all the other things she'd promised herself—her
mily, security, her work. This was her last chance to get
ings right—and she had to take it. However tempted she
as to give in to desire over sense.

'No, Zeke.' She pushed him away, not letting her palms
ger on his chest for a moment longer than necessary.
m marrying Flynn.'

'Then you're a fool.'

Zeke stepped away, turning his back on her, but not be
fore she saw the flash in his eyes of—what? Anger? Frus
tration? She couldn't be sure.

'I'm making the sensible decision,' Thea said, eve
though it felt as if her heart might force its way out
her sensible ribcage at any moment to fight its own cas

'You're making a mistake.'

'Am I?' Thea shook her head. This was going to hur
And this was going to make him angry. But she neede
to say it. Hell, she'd been waiting eight years to tell hi
this. It was past due. 'What about you? You say I'
relying on other people to tell me how to live, but how a
you any better?'

'I live my life exactly the way I want.' Zeke ran his ha
through his messy hair as he turned back towards her. 'I
my own judgement. No archaic family loyalty rules or du
to manipulative men.'

'Really? Seems to me that everything you've done sin
you left—hell, even leaving in the first place—has all be
more about your father than you.'

Zeke shook his head. 'You don't know what you're talk
ing about.'

'I do,' Thea said firmly. 'Because I know you, Zek
You said you wanted to leave Morrison-Ashton and ever
thing it represented behind when you left. But what did y
do? You went and worked for another media conglomer:
and then set up your own rival company, for heaven's sak

'Stick with what you know, and all that,' Zeke said w
a shrug, but Thea wasn't listening.

'And now you're here, still trying to prove to everyo
that you don't need them. You're still so bitter about yo
father giving Flynn the job you wanted—'

'It's not just that!'

'You're so bitter,' Thea carried on, 'that you can't mo

. I bet even when you were away you were still check-
g up on your family. People keep saying that you walked
t and left us, but you didn't. You've carried us with you
ery step of the way and, Zeke, that chip on your shoul-
r is only getting bigger and heavier. And until you let it
 you're never going to be happy. Not even if I left with
u right now.'

ou're wrong,' Zeke said, but even as he spoke he could
el the truth of her words resonating through his body.
m done with the lot of you for good this time.'

Her smile was sad, but it enraged him. Who was she
tell him the mistakes he was making in his life? Thea
orrison—the queen of bad decisions. And, even if she
dn't know it yet, this was the worst one. Well, she'd have
long, miserable marriage during which to regret it.

Zeke might have been willing to take a lot from Thea
orrison, but this was the last. The last rejection he'd ever
ce from anyone with the surname Morrison or Ashton.
He was done.

His chest ached as he realised this might be the last time
ever saw her. That he was walking away again and she
ouldn't be coming with him this time, either. He choked
ck a laugh as he realised the awful truth. She'd been
ght all along. She'd been right not to leave with him eight
ars ago. They *had* been kids. And he knew now that he
dn't even understood what love was then.

He couldn't have loved Thea at eighteen—not really.
 hadn't known her the way he did now, for a start. But
ostly he knew it had to be true because, however much
'd thought it had hurt to leave her last time, it didn't come
ose to the pain searing through his body at the thought
leaving her now..

He loved Thea Morrison, the woman she'd grown up

to be, more than he'd ever believed possible. And it did▉
make a bit of difference.

None of it mattered now. Not their past, not this horri▉
week in Tuscany, and certainly not their impossible futu▉
When he left this time he wouldn't be coming back. A▉
he knew just how to make sure that every atom of his ▉
lationship with these people was left behind too.

'Maybe you don't know it yet,' he said, keeping h▉
voice calm and even, 'but you're going to make yourse▉
my brother, and everyone else around you desperately u▉
happy if you go through with this wedding. I love you. A▉
I would have done anything to make you happy. Anythi▉
except stay here and live this safe life you think you wa▉
But it will end up driving you mad. One day you're goi▉
to wake up and realise all that, and know what a mista▉
you've made. But, like you say, it's your mistake to mak▉

He didn't look back as he walked to the door. He did▉
want to see her standing there, beautiful, sad and resolve▉
She loved him—he knew it. But she wasn't going to ▉
herself have the one thing that could make her happy.

Fine. It was her mistake, as she'd said.

But she couldn't make him watch.

'Goodbye, Thea,' he said as he walked out through t▉
door.

The door shut behind him with a click, although it felt li▉
an earth-shattering slam to Thea. She'd done it. She'd ▉
ally done it. She'd sent him away, made the right decisi▉
for once. Avoided the oh, so tempting mistake she'd ma▉
so many times before. She'd won.

So why did she feel so broken?

Sinking into the chair, Thea sat very still and wait▉
for whatever would happen next. The stylist would be h▉
soon, she vaguely remembered, to do her hair and mak▉

. Helena would come and find her when it was time,
uldn't she? And in the meantime…she'd just wait for
meone to tell her what she was supposed to do.

The irony of her thoughts surprised a laugh from her,
d she buried her face in her hands before her laughter
rned to tears. The decision was made and Zeke would
ve now. She could get back to that regularly scheduled
e she'd been hankering after for the past three days.

It was over at last.

Hearing a click, she looked up again in time to see the
or open. For one fleeting moment her heart jumped at
 thought that it might be Zeke, coming back to try and
n her one last time. But, really, what else was there to
y? They'd both said everything they needed to, every-
ng they'd been holding in for the last eight years. That
oment had passed. *Their* moment.

Flynn stuck his head around the door and, seeing she
s alone, came in, shutting it behind him.

'Everything okay?' he asked, hovering nervously at a
stance.

Poor Flynn. The things she'd put him through this
ek… He was such a good man. He didn't deserve it.

So she tried very hard to smile as she looked up at him,
make him feel wanted and loved. To feel like the win-
r he'd turned out to be. Her man, her choice, her future.
w and always.

'Fine,' she said, her cheeks aching. 'But I'm afraid
u're going to need a new best man.'

The look of relief on his face was almost reward enough.
hink I can arrange that.'

He moved towards her, settling on the arm of her chair,
 hand at her shoulder in a comforting fatherly gesture.
'd be a brilliant dad, Thea thought again. It was impor-
t to focus on all the excellent reasons she had for mar-

rying him, rather than the one uncertain and confusi
reason not to.

'Are you okay?' Flynn asked, and Thea nodded.

'I'm fine. It was…a little difficult, that's all.'

'And you're sure you want to go through with t
today? I mean, I appreciate you choosing me, Thea, I
ally do. And I think it's the right decision. We're going
have a great future together, I know. But it doesn't have
start today—not if you don't want. We could postpone-

'No,' Thea interrupted. 'I've made my choice. I wa
to do this.'

Before she changed her mind.

Zeke didn't knock on his father's office door. He did
need permission or approval from his father for what w
going to happen next. In fact he didn't need anything fr
him. That was sort of the point.

Ezekiel Ashton looked up as Zeke walked in, and l
eyebrows rose in amused interest. 'Zeke. Shouldn't you
off practising your best man's speech somewhere?'

'I believe that by now Flynn will have chosen a bet
man.' Zeke dropped into the visitor's chair, slouching
sually. 'I'll be leaving as soon as I'm packed.'

Guests would start arriving soon, he was sure, for
pre-wedding drinks reception that Isabella had insisted
when she'd discovered that Thea planned a late afternc
wedding. He could probably grab one of the taxis bring
people up from the hotel to get him to the airport. He'd
his assistant while he packed and get her to book a flig

This time tomorrow he'd be in another country. A
other life.

'You're not staying, then.' Ezekiel shook his head sa
and turned his attention back to his paperwork. 'I dc
know why I'm surprised.'

He doesn't matter. Nothing he thinks or does matters me any more.

'I have one piece of business to conclude with you be-re I go,' Zeke said, watching in amusement as he became f interest to his father again.

'Oh, yes? I was under the impression that the very idea f doing business with your own father was distasteful you.'

'It is,' Zeke said bluntly. 'But it has come to my atten-on that it may be the only way to sever my ties with you r good.'

'You make it sound so violent,' Ezekiel said. 'When re-ly all you're doing is running away from your respon-bilities. And, Zeke, we all know that you'll come back gain eventually. We're family. That's what you do for mily.'

Zeke shook his head. 'Not this one. Do you know why eft eight years ago?'

'Because you felt slighted that I'd given a position you nsidered rightfully yours to your brother.'

'No.' Zeke thought back to that horrible day and for e first time felt a strange detachment from the events. ecause I finally understood why you'd done it. I heard u that day, talking to Thomas about us. I'd come to talk you about you giving Flynn my job—the one I'd al-ys been promised. I had all these arguments ready...' shook his head at the memory of his righteous younger f. 'I heard you laugh and say that you realised now that rhaps it wasn't such a misfortune that Mum had fallen egnant twenty-one years ago, just as Flynn's adoption s confirmed. That while you hadn't planned for two ildren perhaps it had all been for the best after all.'

He'd stood frozen outside his father's office door, Zeke membered, his hand half raised to knock. And he'd lis-

tened as his father had ruined his relationship with h
brother for good.

'This way,' Ezekiel had said, 'they have built-in comp
tition. In some ways it's better, having two sons. Flynn h
always felt he has to earn his place, so he fights for it—
fights to belong every day. And as long as I let Zeke fe
that he's the disappointment, the second son, he'll kee
fighting to best his brother. It's a perfect set-up.'

'"I've told Zeke I've given Flynn the position as n
right-hand man,"' you said.' Zeke watched the memor
dawning in his father's eyes. '"Of course Zeke will g
the company one day. But I want him to fight his broth
for it, first."'

The words still echoed in Zeke's skull—the mome
his whole life had made horrifying, unbelievable sens
and everything he'd ever thought he wanted had ceased
matter. He'd had to leave—had to get away. And so he
run straight to Thea and asked her to go with him, only
have his world, his expectations, damned again. That or
night had changed his whole life.

'Do you remember saying that, *Dad*?'

Ezekiel nodded. 'Of course I do. And what of it? Healt
competition is good for the soul.'

'That wasn't healthy. Nothing you did to us was *health*

Zeke leant forward in his chair, gripping the armres
tightly to stop himself standing and pacing. He wanted
look his father in the eye as he told him this.

'What you did to us was unfair at best, cruel at wor
You pitted two people who should have been friends, bro
ers, against each other. You drove a wedge between
from the moment we were born. You made me feel
jected, inadequate. And you made Flynn believe that
had to fight for every scrap from the table. You dro
your wife into the arms of your best friend, you drove

the other end of the country, and you drove Flynn and
Thea to believe that marrying each other is the only way
serve the family business, to earn their place in the fam-
y. You are a manipulative, cold, uncaring man and *I am
one with you.*'

Ezekiel was silent at his words, but Zeke didn't bother
oking for remorse in his expression. He wouldn't find it,
d even if by some miracle he did it didn't matter now.

'I am here today to undertake my final act of business
ith you, old man,' Zeke said, relaxing back in the chair.
am going to sell you This Minute, for twice what Glass-
use were offering.' He scribbled down the figure and
shed the scrap of paper across the table.

Ezekiel read it and nodded. 'I knew you'd see sense
out this in the end.'

'I'm not done,' Zeke said. 'That's just the financial cost.
want something more.'

'A position at the company?' Ezekiel guessed. 'Would
rector of Digital Media suffice for now?'

'I don't want a job. I never wanted to work for you in
e first place. I want you to give Thea that role. I want you
make sure she has the freedom to run it her way, and
make her own mistakes. You cannot interfere one iota.'

Ezekiel gave a slow nod. 'That should be possible. As
r father always says, her business decisions are far more
edible than her personal ones. And she's due a promo-
n once the wedding is over.'

Zeke knew this game. By the time he left Ezekiel would
ve convinced himself that Thea's new job had been all
s idea in the first place.

He'd have a harder time doing that with his second de-
nd, Zeke wagered.

'One more thing,' Zeke said, and waited until he had
father's full attention before he continued. 'I want you

to step down and appoint Flynn as the CEO of Morriso
Ashton. You can take a year for the handover,' he sai
talking over his father's objections. 'But no more. By h
first wedding anniversary Flynn will be in charge.'

'The company is supposed to come to you,' Ezekiel sai

Zeke shook his head. 'I don't want it. Flynn does. He
your son, as much as I am, and he's earned it a lot mo
than I have. It's his.'

Ezekiel watched him for a long moment, obvious
weighing up how much he wanted This Minute again
how much he hated his son right then. Zeke waited. I
knew that his father's pride wouldn't allow him to let Th
Minute go to his main rival. Plus he probably thought he
be able to get out of stepping down somehow.

He wouldn't. Zeke's lawyers were very, very good
what they did, and they would make sure the contract w
watertight. But he'd let the old man hope for now.

'Fine,' Ezekiel said eventually.

Zeke jumped to his feet. 'I'll have my team draw up t
papers. They'll be with you by next week.'

'And what about you? What are you going to do?'

Zeke paused in the doorway and smiled at his fath
'I'm going to go and live my own life at last.'

CHAPTER THIRTEEN

ISABELLA WAS WAITING for her in the hallway with the stylist when Thea finally pulled herself together for long enough to make it out of the library. Flynn still hovered nervously at her shoulder, but she tried to give him reassuring smiles when she could, in the hope that he might leave her alone for a few minutes.

'Thea! We're running behind schedule already, you know. And you look dreadful!'

'Thanks,' Thea said, even though she knew her mother-in-law-to-be was probably completely correct.

'Sorry. But…well, you do. Now, come with me and Sheila, here, will get you sorted out. Flynn, I think your father is looking for you. I saw Zeke come out of his office a few moments ago, so God only knows what that is about. Why don't you go and find out?'

Was Isabella just trying to get rid of Flynn for a moment? Thea wondered. Or did Ezekiel really want him? And, if so, why? Had Zeke finally agreed to sell This Minute to them?

And why did she still care?

It was business, that was all, Thea told herself. It was all business from here on in.

'Will you be okay?' Flynn asked.

'Oh, Flynn, don't be ridiculous. Of course she will! It's her wedding day.'

But Flynn was still looking at Thea, and ignoring hi
mother, so she nodded. 'I'll be fine. Go.'

Flynn gave her an uncertain smile. 'Okay. I'll see yo
at the church.'

'At the church,' Thea agreed weakly.

Sheila had set up in Thea's bedroom, so she followe
the stylist and Isabella up the stairs, trying to focus o
what happened next. One foot in front of the other—tha
was the way. One small step at a time until she was mar
ried and safe. Easy.

'So, what are we doing with your hair, then?' Sheil
asked. 'Did you decide? I think all the styles we trie
looked good on you, so really it's up to you.'

Thea tried and failed to remember what any of the prac
tice styles had looked like. It had been days ago, befor
Zeke arrived. And everything before then was rapidly fad
ing into a blur.

'I liked the curls,' Isabella said. 'With the front pinne
up and the veil over the ringlets. It looked so dramatic wit
your dark hair. Don't you think, Thea?'

'Uh, sure. Sounds good.'

'Great!' Sheila said brightly, obviously used to bride
almost comatose on their wedding day. Did everyone fee
like this? Shell-shocked? Even if they hadn't been throug
the sort of drama Thea had in the last few days, did ever
bride have this moment of disbelief? This suspended reality

Maybe it was just her.

Sheila started fussing with her hair and Thea sat bac
and let it happen, focussing on the feel of the strands a
they were pinned, the warmth of the straighteners as th
stylist used them to form ringlets. There was a strang
calm in the room as Isabella flicked through a magazin
and Sheila got to work, but still Thea had the feeling tha
she was being watched by her jailer as she was restraine

Crazy. She'd shake her head to dispel the notion, but heila might burn her with the straighteners.

'Thea!'

The door burst open at the same time as Helena's shout ame, and Sheila wisely stepped back before Thea spun ound.

'What's happened?' Thea asked. Even Isabella closed er magazine for the moment.

'Zeke's leaving!'

Oh. That. 'I know.'

'He's supposed to be the best man!'

'Daniel's going to stand in, I think.'

'Right.' Helena leant back against the door. 'And… ou're okay with this?'

'Helena,' Isabella said, putting her magazine aside and etting to her feet. 'Why don't we let your sister finish etting ready? Go and check on the centrepieces and the ouquets. Then you can come and have your hair done ext. Okay?'

'Right. Sure.' Helena's brow crinkled as she looked at hea. 'Unless you need me for…anything?'

Thea gave her a faint smile. 'I'm fine,' she lied. 'You'll ome and help me get into my dress later, though, yeah?'

'Of course,' Helena promised as Isabella ushered her ut of the door—presumably in case her little sister gave er the chance to reconsider her decision to marry Flynn.

Thea settled back into her chair, feeling comfortably umb and barely noticing that Isabella had left with Hel-na. It was almost time, and Zeke was almost gone.

There was nothing to reconsider.

eke had almost expected the knock at his door. Placing roughly folded shirt on top of the clothes already in his ase, he turned and called, 'Come in.'

His mother looked older, somehow, than she had sinc
his return. Maybe it was just that she'd let the perma-smil
drop for a moment.

'You're leaving me again, then?'

'Not just you,' Zeke pointed out, turning back to h
wardrobe to retrieve the last of his shirts.

'I don't imagine you were planning on saying goodby
this time, either.'

Isabella moved to sit on the bed, to one side of his sui
case. The one place in the room he couldn't hope to i
nore her.

'I wasn't sure you'd miss me any more this time tha
last,' he said, dropping another shirt into the case. 'Wh.
with the wedding to focus on. And I'm sure you have pla
for marrying Helena off to someone convenient next.'

Picking up the shirt, Isabella smoothed out the creas
as she folded it perfectly. 'I suppose I should be gratef
that you're not staying to ruin Thea's wedding.'

Zeke stopped, turned, and stared. 'Thea's wedding? N
Flynn's?' He shook his head. 'You know, for years I nev
understood why you cared so much more about someor
else's children than your own. I guess I thought it mu
be because they were girls, or because you felt sorry f
them after their mother died. I can't believe it took m
until now to realise it was because you thought they shou
have been yours.'

'I don't know what you're talking about,' Isabelle sai
her gaze firmly fixed on the shirt. 'I loved all four of yc
equally. Even Flynn.'

'Ha! *That*, right there, shows me what a lie that is
Grabbing the shirt from her, he shoved it into the cas
making her look up at him. 'Why didn't you just leav
Mum? And marry Thomas? It can't have been for ou
sakes. We'd have been downright grateful!'

'My place is at my husband's side.' She folded her hands in her lap and met his eyes at last. 'Whatever else, I am is wife first and foremost.'

Zeke stared at her in amazement. 'You're wrong. You're *yourself* first.'

She gave him a sad smile. 'No, Zeke. That's just you.'

Zeke grabbed his case, tugging the zip roughly round . He'd probably forgotten something, but he could live without it. He had his passport and his wallet. Everything else was replaceable. *Except Thea.*

'Do you even know how you made us feel all those years?' He wasn't coming back again. He could afford to tell her the truth. 'You let our father pit us against each other like it was a sport, and you ran off to another man's family whenever we weren't enough for you. For years I felt like an unwanted accident, every bit as much as Flynn felt like the outsider.'

'That's not...that's not how it was.'

'It's how it felt,' Zeke told her, pressing the truth home. 'And when I left... Thomas says that you missed me. That I broke your heart. But, Mum, how would I even know?'

'Of course I missed you. You're my son.'

'But you never thought to contact me. I wasn't hiding, Mum. I was right there if you needed me.'

'You made your feelings about our family very clear when you left.'

She still sounded so stiff, so unyielding. Zeke shook his head. Maybe her pride would always be too much for her to get over. Maybe his had been too, until now. But he'd already cut all ties with his father—could he really afford to do the same with his mother?

'I'm going now, Mum. And to be honest I'm not going to be coming back in a hurry. Maybe not ever. But if you

mean it—about missing me—call me some time.' He lifte
his carry-on bag onto his shoulder. 'Goodbye, Mum.'

But she was already looking away.

Outside his room, the corridors were cool and empt
He supposed most people would be in their rooms, ge
ting ready for the wedding. A few were probably alread
down at the church, making sure they got a good seat fo
the wedding of the year. If he was quick he could grab or
of the taxis milling about and be on his way to the airpo
before anyone even said 'I do'.

'Dad says that you're leaving.'

Zeke stopped at the top of the stairs at the sound of h
brother's voice ahead of him. So close. And now he'd hav
to deal with all three family members in the space of a
hour. At least it was the last time.

'Well, yeah,' he said, turning slowly and leaning h
case against the wall. 'Not a lot of reason to stay now.'

'Is that truly the only reason you came back? For Thea
Flynn asked. 'To try and win her back, I mean.'

'No. I thought…' With a sigh, Zeke jogged down a fe
steps to meet his brother in the middle of the staircase.
thought I'd moved on. From her, from the family, fro
everything. I came back to prove that to myself, I guess

'Did it work?'

Zeke smiled ruefully. 'Not entirely as planned, n
Turns out I was a little more tied in to things here than
thought.'

'And now?'

'Now I'm done,' Zeke said firmly. 'Ask our father.'

'I did.' Hitching his trousers, Flynn sat on the step, rig
in the middle of the stairs.

After a moment Zeke followed suit. 'I feel about fiv
sitting on the stairs,' he said.

Flynn laughed. 'We used to—do you remember? Whe

Mum and Dad had parties, when we were really little, we'd sneak out of bed and sit on the stairs, watching and listening.'

'I remember,' Zeke said. He must have been no more than four or five then. Had he known, or sensed, even then that he and Flynn were different? Or rather that their father believed they were?

'Dad told me your terms for selling This Minute to Morrison-Ashton.'

Zeke glanced up at his brother. 'All of them?'

Flynn ticked them off on his fingers. 'No role for you, Director of Digital Media for Thea, and...' Flynn caught Zeke's gaze and held it. 'CEO for me.'

'That's right.' Zeke dipped his head to avoid his brother's eyes.

'It was yours, you know,' Flynn said. 'I always knew that in the end Dad would give it to you. You're Ashton blood, after all.'

'I don't want it,' Zeke said. 'And you deserve it.'

'I'll do a better job at it, too.'

Zeke laughed. 'You will. I want to build things, then move on. You want to make things run smoothly. You're the best choice for it.'

'Was that the only reason?'

Zeke stared out over the hallway of the villa, all decked out in greenery and white flowers, with satin ribbons tied in bows to everything that stayed still long enough for the wedding planner to attack. 'No. I wanted to show Dad that his plan hadn't worked.'

'His plan? You mean, the way he always pitted us against each other?'

'Yeah. I wanted him to know that despite everything, all his best efforts, you were still my brother. Blood or not.'

Flynn stretched his legs out down the stairs and leant

back on his elbows. 'You know, that would sound a whole lot more sincere and meaningful if you hadn't slept with my fiancée last night.'

Zeke winced. 'Yeah, I guess so. Look, I'm...' He trailed off. He wasn't sorry—not really. He hadn't done it to hurt his brother, but he couldn't regret having one more night with Thea. 'That wasn't about you. It was about Thea and I saying goodbye to each other.'

'That's not what you wanted it to be, though, is it?'

'Maybe not.' Zeke shrugged. 'But it's the way it is. She wants a different life to the one I'm offering. And I need to live my life away from the bitterness this family brings out in me.'

'She told you that, huh?'

'Yeah.'

'So I guess I have her to thank for my promotion, really?'

'Hey! I played my part, too.'

'Let's just agree to call it quits, then, yeah?'

'Sounds like a plan.' Although Zeke had to think that all Flynn had got out of that deal was a company. He'd got to sleep with Thea. Clearly he was winning.

Except after today Flynn would get to sleep with Thea whenever he wanted. And Zeke would be alone.

Maybe Flynn was winning after all, even if he *did* have to deal with their parents and Morrison-Ashton for the rest of time.

'But, Zeke, after today... She's off-limits, yeah?'

'I know.' Zeke grabbed hold of the banister and pulled himself up. 'It's not going to be a problem. As soon as I'm packed I'll grab a cab to the airport and leave you guys to get on with your happy-ever-after.'

'You're not coming back?' Flynn asked.

Zeke shook his head. 'Not for a good while, at least.

eed to…I need to find something else to make my life
bout, you know?'

'Not really,' Flynn said with a half-smile. 'I've spent
ny whole life trying to get in to this family, while you've
pent it trying to get out.'

'I guess so.' Zeke wondered how it would feel to finally
et the one thing you'd always wanted. Maybe he'd never
now. 'Something you and Thea have in common.'

Flynn tilted his head as he stared up at him. 'You really
ve her, don't you?'

Zeke shrugged, and stepped past his brother to climb the
airs to retrieve his suitcase. 'Love doesn't matter now.'

CHAPTER FOURTEEN

'Wow,' HELENA SAID as Thea stepped out from behind th
screen. 'Maybe you should just walk down the aisle lik
that. I'm sure Flynn wouldn't complain. Or any of th
male guests.'

Thea pulled a face at her sister in the mirror. She wasn
even sure she looked like herself. From the ringlets an
veil, to the excess layers of make-up Sheila had assure
her were necessary to 'last through the day'—despite th
fact the wedding was at four in the afternoon—she looke
like someone else. A bride, she supposed.

She let her gaze drop lower in the mirror, just lon
enough to take in the white satin basque that pushed he
breasts up into realms they'd never seen before and th
sheer white stockings that clipped onto the suspende
dangling from the basque. She looked like a stripper brid
She hoped Flynn would appreciate it.

Zeke would have.

Not thinking about that.

'Help me into the dress?' Thea said, turning away fro
the mirror. 'We're late already, and I think the weddir
planner is about to have a heart attack. She's been ca
ing from the church every five minutes to check whe
we are.'

Helena reached up to take the heavy ivory silk co

ction from its hanger, then paused, biting her lip as she
oked back at Thea.

'Don't, Helena,' Thea said, forestalling whatever ob-
ction her sister was about to raise. 'Just pass me the
ress, yeah?'

Helena unhooked the dress and held it up for Thea to
ep into. Then, as Thea wriggled it over her hips, pulling
up over the basque, Helena said, 'Are you sure about
is? I mean, really, *really* sure?'

Thea sighed. 'Trust me, Helena. You are not the only
erson to ask me that today. But I've made my decision.
m marrying Flynn.'

'I'm glad to hear it.'

Thea spun around at the words, to see Flynn leaning
gainst the doorframe.

'What are you *doing here*?' The last couple of words
ame out as a shriek, but Thea didn't care.

'I need to tell you something,' Flynn said, perfectly rea-
onably. 'It's important.'

'Not *now*!'

'You look beautiful, by the way,' Flynn added, as if
at meant anything. The groom wasn't allowed to see
e bride in her wedding dress before the wedding! It was
rrible, *terrible* luck!

'Flynn, why don't you tell her what you came to tell her
o she can stop freaking out?' Helena suggested. 'Plus, you
ould be down at the church already.'

Flynn nodded his agreement. 'Zeke has agreed to sell
his Minute to Morrison-Ashton.'

Thea stopped trying to cover up her dress with her arms
d stared at him. 'Seriously? *Why*?'

'Probably because someone convinced him he had to
ave everything here behind and find his own path in life.'

'Ah,' Helena said, eyes wide. 'Thea, what—?'

'It doesn't matter.' Thea cut her off. 'Does that mea
he's not taking the director job?'

'No. He insisted that Dad give that to you.'

Thea started to shake. Just a tremor in her hands ar
arms to start with, but she could feel it spreading.

'And he's made Dad agree to step down within the ne
year and pass the company to me,' Flynn finished. Eve
he looked a little shell shocked at that bit.

Thea dropped into the nearest chair as the tremors l
her knees. 'Why? Why would he do that?'

But she already knew. He'd given in. He'd given his f
ther exactly what he wanted so he could walk away cle
and free. Just as she'd told him he'd never be able to do

'I think he wanted to make things right,' Flynn sai
and Thea felt the first tear hit her cheek.

Zeke was free of them all at last. Even her. And sl
was being left behind again, still trying to prove she w
good enough to belong. After today she'd be tied in fo
ever, never able to walk away.

Was she *jealous*?

'Thea? Are you okay?' Helena asked.

'*No!*' Thea sobbed, the word a violent burst of soun
'I'm a mess. I'm a mistake.'

'That's not true,' Helena said soothingly, and Thea cou
see her giving Flynn looks of wide-eyed concern. 'Wh
would make you think that?'

Thea gave a watery chuckle. 'Oh, I don't know. Mayl
sleeping with the best man the night before my weddin₃
Perhaps having to have an intervention with my almos
mother-in-law about how it was better to have an affa
than marry an inappropriate guy?'

Flynn swore at that, Thea was pleased to note.

'Or maybe sending away the guy I love so I can mar₃
the guy I'm supposed to? And now, on top of everythin

e, Flynn's seen me in my wedding dress. That's not just
e pearls! Everyone knows that's *absolute* bad luck! It's
inst all the rules!'

With another glance back at Flynn—who, Thea was
strated to note, was still standing perfectly calmly in
doorway, with just a slight look of discomfort on his
e—Helena knelt down beside her.

'Thea. I don't think this is about rules any more.'

'No. It's about me messing up again. I was so close to
ng happy here! And now I'm making a mess of every-
ng.'

Helena shook her head. 'No, you're not. And today's not
out family, or business, or any of the other things you
m to think this wedding should be about.'

Thea looked up at her sister. 'Then what *is* it about?'

'It's about love,' Helena said. 'It's about trusting your
irt to know the right thing to do. And, since you're sit-
g here sobbing in a designer wedding dress, I think your
irt is trying to tell you something.'

It couldn't, Thea wanted to say, because it had stopped.
r heart had stopped still in her chest the moment Zeke
d walked out of the library that morning, so it couldn't
l her anything.

But her head could. And it was screaming at her right
w that she was an idiot. She'd spent so long trying to
d her place in the world, trying to force her way into
ole that had never been right for her, she'd ignored the
e place she truly belonged all along.

She looked up at Flynn, still so calm and serene and
rfect—but not perfect for her.

'Go,' he said, a faint smile playing on his lips. 'You
ght still catch him.'

'But...but what about the wedding? Everyone's here,
d our parents are waiting, and—'

'We'll take care of it,' Helena promised, glancing o
at Flynn.

Was there something in that look? Had Isabella be
right? Thea couldn't be sure.

'Won't we?'

'We will,' Flynn agreed. 'All you have to do now is ru

Somewhere in the villa a door slammed, and Thea kn
it had to be Zeke, leaving her again. But this time she w
going with him.

Shoving the heavy wedding dress back down over I
hips, Thea stepped out of it and dashed for the door, pa
ing only for a second to kiss Flynn lightly on the che
'Thanks,' she said.

And then she ran.

Zeke shut the front door to the villa behind him and walk
out into the late-afternoon Tuscan sun. Everyone must ha
already headed down to the little chapel at the bottom
the hill, ready for the wedding. His talk with Flynn h
delayed him, and now there were no taxis hanging arou
He might be able to find one down at the church, but
didn't want to get that close to the main event. Not w
Thea due to make her grand entrance any time now. T
wedding planner's schedule had her down there alrea
he remembered, unless they were running late.

No, he'd call for a cab and sit out here in the sunsh
while he waited. One last glimpse of his old life before
started his new one.

Phone call made, he settled onto the terrace, sitting
the edge of the warm stone steps rather than the swi
seat round at the side. Too many memories. Besides,
wouldn't see the cab arrive.

He heard a car in the distance and stood, hefting I
carry-on bag onto his shoulder and tugging up the p

ong handle of his case. No car appeared, though, and he
started to think it must have been another guest heading
for the chapel. But he made his way down the driveway
anyway, just in case.

'Zeke!'

Behind him the door to the villa flew open, and by the
time he could turn Thea was halfway down the stairs and
racing down the drive towards him.

He blinked in disbelief as she got closer, sunlight glowing behind her, making the white of her outfit shine.

White. But not her wedding dress.

'Isn't this where I came in?' he asked, waving a hand
towards her to indicate the rather skimpy lingerie that was
doing wonderful things for her heaving cleavage as she
tried to get her breath back.

'Don't,' she said, scowling.

'Don't what?' Zeke asked. 'You're the one chasing me
in your underwear. Five more minutes and my cab would
have been here and I'd have been out of your life, just as
you wanted.'

'Don't joke. Don't mock. I need you to…' She took a
deep breath. 'I need you to stop being…you know…*you* for
a moment. Because I need to tell you something.'

'What?' Zeke dropped his bag to the ground again. Apparently this was going to take a while.

'I don't want you out of my life.'

Zeke's breath caught in his chest—until he realised what
she was *actually* saying. 'Thea, I can't. I can't just stick
around and be Uncle Zeke for Christmas and birthdays.
You were right; I need a fresh start. A clean break. Besides…' *I can't watch you live happily ever after with my
brother when I'm totally in love with you myself.*

But Thea was shaking her head. 'That's not what I mean.'

'Then *what*, Thea?' Zeke asked, exasperated. He'd so

nearly been done. So nearly broken free for good. And he he was, having this ridiculous conversation with Thea her underwear, when she was supposed to be getting ma ried *right now*.

Unless…

'I've spent all day listening to people tell me wha should do. What's best for me. Where my place is. A I'm done. You were right—but don't let it go to your hea I need to make my own decisions. So I'm making o right now. I'm choosing my home, my place in the wor And it's the only choice that's going to matter ever agai

She stepped closer, and Zeke's hands itched to take ho of her, to pull her close. But this was her decision, and s had to make it all on her own. And he had to let her.

'I'm choosing you,' she whispered, so close that could feel the words against his lips. 'For better or wors for mistake or for happily-ever-after, for ever and ever.

Zeke stared into her soft blue eyes and saw no dou hiding there. No uncertainty, no fear. She meant this.

'You're sure,' he said, but it wasn't a question. He kne

'I'm certain. I love you. More than anything.'

Thea's hands wrapped around him to run up his bac and the feel of her through his shirt made him warmer

'I should have known it sooner. *You're* my place. *You* where I belong.'

'I can't stay here, Thea,' he said. 'Maybe we can co back, but I need some time away. I'm done obsessing abo the past. It's time to start my own life.'

'I know.' Thea smiled. 'I'm the one who told you th remember?'

'I remember.' Unable to resist any longer, Zeke dipp his head and kissed her, long and sweet and perfect. 'I lo you. I thought when I came back that I was looking for girl I'd known—the one I loved as a boy. But I could

ve imagined the woman you'd become, Thea. Or how
ach more I'd love you now.'

Thea buried her laugh in his chest. 'I'm the same. I
ought it would kill me, saying goodbye to you last time.
at the thought of living the rest of my life without you…'
e shook her head and reached up to kiss him again.

'Unacceptable.' Zeke finished the thought for her. And
en he asked the question that had echoed through his
nd for eight long years, hoping he'd get a different an-
er this time. 'Will you come with me?'

Thea smiled up at him and said, 'Always.'

And Zeke knew, at last, that it didn't matter where they
ent, or who led and who followed. They'd always be to-
ther, and that was all he needed.

* * * * *

Join Britain's BIGGES
Romance Book Club

50% OFF your first parcel

- **EXCLUSIVE offe** every month

- **FREE delivery d** to your door

- **NEVER MISS a t**

- **EARN Bonus Bo** points

Call Customer Services
0844 844 1358*

or visit
millsandboon.co.uk/subscripti

BKCB3